Sacrilege

what good are sheep among wolves?

T. N. Vitus

979-8-9868415-0-2 (paperback)
979-8-9868415-1-9 (ebook)

Cover art and design by: Sarah Lee
Printed in the United States of America

Trigger Warnings

This story contains several sensitive topics, which I've done my best to handle with care. If you would like to go into this book fully informed, the trigger warnings are as follows:

—Disordered eating habits
—Emotional and physical abuse
—Violence
—Catholic trauma
—Mild Gore
—Body horror
—Gender dysphoria

For those whose voices are too loud and ask too many questions. With too many dreams to chase, who are hungry for so much more. For those with too sharp teeth—the better to devour with, my dear.

"The woods are lovely, dark, and deep,
But I have promises to keep,
And miles to go before I sleep."
-Robert Frost

CHAPTER ONE

The whispers started with the first snowfall. The elders told us to never go near the woods, especially not once the green was covered with an impenetrable white. As a child, my mother would clutch me to her side, fist balled up in the back of my coat so tight—almost like she thought I would be dragged away if she didn't. Taken, as if by force, as if the wind between the trees didn't whisper to me, calling me by name. I didn't understand then what fear was, only curiosity.

I think I understand now.

I snap back to the present, back to the steaming bowl of oatmeal in front of me. I scowl, picking at it with my spoon. My gaze keeps drifting to the window, frosted over enough that it blurs the view but not enough that I can't see the edge of the tree line. By now the woods have been overtaken by the furious cold, and though the village carries many ridiculous superstitions, it only means that my already small world will grow ever smaller. An angry winter means paranoid village elders, which likely means curfew and quiet nights spent indoors, reading books or tailoring clothes.

Mother is the seamstress, the only one in this house worth any coin with a needle in her hand. I did not inherit the skill, but she insists I help her regardless. Whatever money I make is mine, though it keeps me humble that I rarely make enough coin to purchase the barest necessities at the market. I'll grow into it, she says. I do not believe her.

Her encouragement cannot cover the crooked stitching and dissatisfied customers. If Mother wasn't the only qualified seamstress in the village, it's likely I would have driven them all away. Though it's not as if they have much choice, what with how few of us there are left.

The oatmeal burns my tongue as I force it down, its taste bland and texture disappointing, but I cannot risk losing even a pound in this weather. Even if it weren't for the snow, the stitching on my clothing is on its last limb, having been taken out several times to accommodate what is being called my "woman's body." I despise the term almost as much as I despise the fact that we cannot afford new clothes. It's not embarrassing, I am not the only burgeoning adult wearing the same dresses I've had since adolescence, but I find it hard to not yearn for new things as I enter my adulthood.

"Are you finished?" Mother asks, bursting into the room in a whirlwind of noise. She is a force, one I do not like to confront. "I have work for you."

"Finished," I mutter, the half-eaten oatmeal being plucked away from me before I am even finished swallowing. The day begins whether I am ready or not.

Mother sits me down in the front room, a pile of fabric and needles at my feet. We usually set aside the entire day to finish such a feat, but she shoves a bundle into my hands and ushers me to hurry, that we have to be finished before sundown. She shushes me when I try to question, stating simply that we cannot work at night. A new superstition, likely. Though there hasn't been a wolf attack in recent history, the elders are haunted by tragedies long since passed, and those of us too poor to move out of Kliransk must atone for whatever sin they believe brought that fate upon our ancestors.

I am not a believer in such things. I am not a believer in anything, truly.

"You must take care to do good, Emelie," she says from her seat across from me. "The neighbors will be angry if your stitches are crooked again."

"I am trying my best," I mutter. "My hands are not built for this."

2

"They are built for women's work, and so that is what you will do." No room for arguments. Her word is law. She cannot fathom that I might want a life outside of the one she has envisioned for me. No one in this village can; they all long ago resigned to the roles designated for them. The baker's son, Calder, has been rolling dough since he was five. The banker's daughter, Magda, can count coin faster than she can form a sentence. I am, at least outwardly, the only outlier.

Well. Not the *only* one.

The needle pricks my finger, drawing me once again back to the present. I can see the scolding Mother is holding back, but my wince lets her know I am aware of my fault. I stick my finger in my mouth before the blood can pool. It's bitter and metallic and I fight the urge to scowl, not wanting to give her another reason to chide me.

We work in discomfiting silence, our eyes only meeting between garments as we decide who takes which piece of cloth. She offers the small mercy of taking the ones that require the most work, a more skilled hand. Sunlight moves through the house, coming in through different windows as it travels across the sky. By the time we break for supper, the sun is nearly down, and all but a handful of garments are finished. Though we have more than enough hours left to finish, Mother refuses to continue working. She ushers me back into the kitchen, shoving vegetables at me to chop, and begins preparing our meal.

I hear my father come in the front door, praying to himself rather than greeting us. Mother doesn't try to speak to him, allowing him to finish his prayers as he settles into a seat at the table. At last, he crosses himself and deigns to speak.

"We should be expecting more business in the coming months." His voice is gruff from disuse, he is a man of few words.

Father is in the business of wood, the village's head carpenter. A few of the local men assist him, but he is the brains of the operation. Given the oncoming winter, families will be scrambling for firewood, for reinforced doorways and windows, and he will be the one to do it, or the one to assign someone else to. He and his team are the only ones that dare to go within spitting distance of the woods, and the village treats them like heroes for that.

Even crossing the tree line is considered dangerous.

They believe themselves to be staring danger in the face, to walk alongside Death itself. And yet my father has never failed to come home every evening. Mother calls it a blessing. I call it another day.

He and Mother recount their days to each other, with me chiming in here and there. I chop the vegetables. I help my mother plate our dinner. I serve my father. It is nothing earth-shattering, and yet I feel something inside me begin to roar.

But then the roaring fills the room, the house, and I realize it is not me, and it is not a roaring, but the shrill cry of the town warning bell. There are certain chimes for various emergencies: unsavory weather, a missing child, bears. But this is one I have only heard in practice drills in my lessons as a child. This is an alarm I have never heard rung for its true purpose.

This is the alarm for when they believe someone has been killed by a wolf.

My father springs into motion immediately. The procedure is simple: the windows and doors are to be boarded up, the lanterns turned out, and then we are to sit waiting in a huddle on my parents' bed. Despite not needing to prepare for such a situation in decades, he works quickly, almost mechanically. I try to ask questions, but my mother hushes me, urging me to wait for my father's guidance.

Once the house is secure, he comes into the room, his face drawn as he checks on Mother and I in turn. Though he never looks particularly happy, the hard lines around his mouth are more pronounced than usual.

"It may just be a warning. A priest should be by before full dark to tell us the news. Until then, we wait." He drops onto the bed beside my mother, sighing heavily.

I open my mouth, try to speak. "Do you think—"

"Emelie." My mother's voice is cold water to a sleeping body. "Your father has had a long day. He has protected our family. Please, cease with your questions."

And so the silence drags out, prayers being muttered under breaths the only interruption. I can feel Mother stealing glances at me out of the corner of my eye, watching my lips to see if I am praying. I do not have the energy to fake it.

The evening continues to fall and I can see the exhaustion bearing down on my parents' faces. The house feels darker than it should be and I can no longer tell the time. The more minutes tick by, the stronger the inclination I have grows; the priest will not be coming. I am far from tired, but all I want is to crawl into my bed and pretend to sleep, if only to avoid the hum of prayer that is slowly driving nails into my skin.

It is through no fault of my parents that I have lost my faith; I see how this village, these people, judge one another, how they judge me. I ask too many questions and my curiosity is a threat to their way of life. I like to think that if we lived anywhere else, if my parents had decided to move when they had the chance, my curiosity would have been nourished instead of smothered.

My head is spinning with questions I will not get the answers to. The most pressing is when I may be free to go to bed, but my gut tells me it won't be soon. When I try to lay back on my parents' bed, Mother sits me up, fussing over my hair as she insists I cannot look indecent in front of the priest. The priest who is likely not coming.

After another half hour, Father sighs at last. "We will seek out guidance once the sun rises again. For now, let us rest. Emelie, barricade the door to your bedroom before you fall asleep."

It is as much a dismissal as anything. I kiss each of their cheeks and hurry to my bedroom. The wood blocking my window sinks my stomach. While it doesn't look out onto much of a view, I cherish it nonetheless. I ponder the consequences of taking down the wood, but know my father's wrath is worse than that of a wolf.

The worst part is that it covers the blooms of daffodils that pop up beneath my window. A patch of them lingers along the grassy yard that borders my room, and though their petals catch the falling snowflakes, they bloom shamelessly as if it were already spring. Despite the frost that has taken over the ground, they won't seem to die. I tend

5

to them when I remember to, but even after days of my neglectful mind they continue to bloom.

I feel anything but tired. Surprisingly, fear has not come to me yet. The likelihood that a killer wolf is on the prowl after generations of peace feels...wrong. My gut tells me it is some other animal, or the consequence of a harsh winter on an unprepared body.

I search through my books until I find the one I am looking for: *Creatura*. My prized possession, and the largest book I have stolen from the library. We are not supposed to study monsters, we are supposed to fear them and hope they leave us alone. We are supposed to pray them away, yet I cannot help but be utterly fascinated by the idea of them.

I turn to the chapter about wolves. There is a brief summary of common wolves, the kind that would be in any wood. I skim this until I get to the section about shifter wolves. The wolves of our wood. They are indistinguishable from common wolves in most ways. Their size does not vary, they are as large as any wolf would be; they are not much faster or stronger, but their true strength lies in their intelligence. The older folklore might have said that shifters lost their humanity once they turned into beasts, and maybe that is not wholly untrue, but they still possess every bit of a human brain inside of that inhuman form. This makes them cunning, smarter than the average animal. It makes them dangerous.

On the following pages there are a few accounts of ages-old attacks. Cases of villagers wandering too close to the tree line in view of a hungry shifter wolf. Haughty young men who thought they could best a beast. All of the accounts are decades past, before even my parents' time. Back when Kliransk was larger. Before the exodus. I have to wonder if things were better then, if even despite the occasional death, they were happier.

A detailed illustration covers the lower half of the page. Blinking back at me is a shifter, teeth bared in a hungry snarl. Its fur is raised in all directions, making it look even larger. Written below the image in a scrawling script is a paragraph of the church's stance on shifter wolves. They believe them to be demons sent to pick off our townspeople until there is no one left to worship. No mention of the lives lost, rather the horror of an empty church. I scoff, shutting the book.

I lie back on the bed, gaze fixed to the ceiling. From my readings, I have learned of predatory animals native to various territories. I can't imagine that the rest of the world lives like this, in fear of what lurks in the shadows. It certainly doesn't seem that way in books I have read, but perhaps they are only a fiction.

I cannot escape the church even in the comfort of my bedroom, even in a book that's full of things they'd deem impious. Their presence seeps across everything in the village, oppressive and heavy. I lost the will to carry the weight several years ago and yet have not worked up the courage to be honest about it. I mouth the prayers and half-heartedly cross myself when judgmental eyes are watching.

In my childhood I tried to be good. I memorized the prayers until I could recite them forward, backward, in my sleep. I believed in the God they told me to, I worshiped him on Sundays and tried to avoid sin during the week. I was pious and devoted and reverent. And yet I felt nothing; I never felt the presence of holiness wash over me as they said it would. I spoke to God and was met with silence.

My father has not picked up on my lack of faith yet, though something as drastic as my death would have to happen for him to take notice of me. My mother is a crow, waiting for me to slip enough to be punished with cause.

She knows when I'm faking. I can see it now in the way she glares at me out of the corner of her eye, in the way that she won't look at me unless it has to do with prayer or work. I know she is judging me and yet she cannot even bring herself to chide me out loud. Her sharpest weapon is her silence and she wields it expertly. With her, I can always tell when she believes me to be in the wrong. I cannot find it in me to be what she wants.

I told myself throughout adolescence I would get away someday. I would run far, far away from this claustrophobic village and make something of myself. I would hone my skills, once I figured out what they were, and make enough money to live in a big house all by myself. But now that I've entered my twenty-first year with no prospects on the horizon, I am quickly losing hope of that dream ever coming true. It was a murky dream to begin with, and now I fear it will never become clear to me.

Dreams are better meant for sleep, yet I cannot even relish in them before the sound of a hammer against nails pulls me from a sleep I hadn't even realized I'd settled into. My eyes take a moment to adjust against the still dark of the room as I rouse myself. The previous night comes back to me in all its urgency and forces me out of bed. I don my favorite dress. It is a plain green thing and Mother despises how it hides my figure, but that is why I love it.

In the front room, Father works to persuade the nails out of the wooden boards barring the front door. He does not look at me as I pass but I bid him good morning all the same. Mother gives me a once-over as I enter the kitchen, her lips pursing in dissatisfaction but she says nothing, instead she hands me a bowl of oatmeal. I sit and stare at it as I do every day. The windows are still boarded and the presence of a lit lantern this early in the morning is offensive to my eyes. I keep my eyes on my breakfast, unappetizing as it may be.

"Get your coat as soon as you finish your breakfast." Mother's words are clipped, and if I didn't know better, I would think she was annoyed. But the crease in her brow tells me that is not the case. In fact, she's nervous. I want to reassure her, but shove the spoon in my mouth instead.

It does not take me long to finish my meal and it would be a stretch to say I am full. By the time I am done, Father has gotten the boards off of the entryway and the cold morning air seeps through gaps in the threshold. His work occupies so much of his time that he cannot be bothered to come home and do even more work. I don't blame him, but it would be nice to have a room without a draft. I shove my arms into a coat and my feet into boots. Mother fusses over me, putting a wool hat over my hair and a scarf around my neck.

The walk into town is not a lengthy one; no walk in this village is. One could cross the entire expanse in well under an hour. Villagers fall into step with us as we walk, keeping pace and making conversations amongst themselves. I offer small greetings to the people I might call friends under different circumstances. In truth, they are people my age and nothing more.

Everyone files toward the town square to seek guidance. We have had town meetings regularly throughout my life, sometimes even on the topic of shifter wolves. How to protect ourselves, how to avoid them. But we have never reached this stage of action beyond playacting. In the wake of real tragedy, all of our preparation feels pointless. I wonder if the elders have prepared for as much. I yearn to ask questions, the curiosity pushing out of me, but I know I will be met with a hushing. So I hold my tongue once more.

We arrive at the town square and my parents push through the small crowd towards the front where the village elders stand. It's rare to see the three of them separated. Father, Son, and Holy Ghost. Who is who, I have yet to determine. They wear their liturgical vestments and carry bibles in hand. One holds a bucket of holy water. I cringe, thinking of how cold it must be, how frigid it will feel to have them sprinkle it over us.

The scattered murmurs throughout the crowd are silenced by the priests crossing themselves. One of them, Father Levi, leads us in prayer. I mutter the empty words as I watch my breath cloud in front of me. The snow is not deep yet, but the tops of my boots are dusted in a light layer of flakes.

Father Dasco clears his throat. "Last night, my brothers and I came upon a grave disturbance. As you all know, we avoid setting off the alarms unless it is an emergency. Unfortunately, that time is upon us. A body was found at the woods' edge— "

He has to pause as cries break out through the startled villagers. This was to be expected—given how out of place the alarm sounded— but the confirmation that someone has died still sends shock coursing through everyone present. Voices rise up, demanding details out of the elders.

The priests look between one another. "We have reason to believe a wolf is at fault. The snowfall covered any tracks, so we must assume the creature is on the hunt. We are imposing a curfew once the sun begins its descent. Do not come out of your homes once the sun sets, it is only safe while the sun is up."

I can feel the stares turning towards us, towards my father. People will want their houses barricaded. I wonder what this will mean for his work; his livelihood is in the woods, among the trees. It would be wise to charge more coin for his stock, but knowing my father he will practically give it away in exchange for favors.

Marie, the baker's wife, raises a hand looking stricken. "How do you know it is a wolf?"

Father Dasco pulls on his collar, and I can see his jaw tense up. "The wounds are consistent with our records of past wolf attacks."

Another hand raises. "Will there be a funeral, Father?"

Father Patrick nods. "We will begin making preparations as soon as this meeting concludes. The funeral will take place on Sunday during mass."

"Who was it, Father?"

A chorus of voices takes up once again, everyone demanding to know the details. Their hesitation tells me the priests do not want to tell us who, but given that the entire village is in attendance, it would only take someone with a perceptive headcount to figure out who is dead.

Father Dasco calls for silence. His mouth is set in a straight line, not quite sorrowful but sorry nonetheless. "The body belonged to Abel."

Someone screams. Clusters of people begin to weep. Though Abel didn't have any living blood relatives, the rest of the village will take this as a loss of one of their own, as if he was each of their sons and brothers and nephews and cousins. He wasn't much older than I; I'm almost certain we attended lessons together. Father had taken him on as one of his apprentices not two years ago, and by the look on his face I can see he will grieve this loss. He does not react beyond his face falling, but my mother clings to him and rubs soothing strokes up and down his arm.

"We will grieve as a community, and we will pray and come out on the other side strengthened by our faith." Father Patrick's voice booms above the shock and sobbing. "You are safe to go about your days while the sun is high. Please, do not let your fears keep you shut inside. You are all protected by the Lord—"

His well-wishes are drowned out by the crowd, now mingling and consoling one another. A few of my old classmates come up to me and hug me, covering my cheeks in kisses. I suppose they assume I should be upset, given that he worked for my father and was close to my age. I take their condolences and they sit heavy like rocks in my pocket. It's not that I don't feel the weight of what's happened. But selfishly, I am consumed by how his death will affect my life in the village.

My father gathers with the remainder of his men. He turns to Mother and I only once, signaling that he will be a while. Mother goes to cry with the rest of the village women. My classmates and kin stand around me in distressed huddles. I make eye contact with someone— Magda—and we give each other the same look of discomfort. Neither of us wants to be here. I consider going to her so we can at least appear to be grieving.

And then I see him, standing at the edge of the town square. He is much taller than he was when I last saw him, and he is bundled up in layers of dark fabric that nearly obscure his face. But I know those eyes and that nose. I know that stance.

Halvar.

A number of questions run through my mind: why is he here, when did he arrive back in town?

But right now I don't care for answers. I push through sobbing acquaintances and glaring adults before breaking from the crowd and I run to him. My boots skid on the frosted cobblestones but I catch myself. When I arrive in front of him, his eyes flash with immediate recognition. He pulls down his scarf and I see that mouth that I remember.

"Emelie," he breathes.

I launch myself into his arms, burying my face into his chest as my arms wrap around his neck. He stiffens, and for a moment I think he will deny me. But then he relaxes into my touch and hugs me back fiercely.

"It's good to see you, too," he chuckles.

I pull away and take him in. I have remembered a boy only to be met with a man. He looks so changed that I almost feel ashamed to stand before him so stagnated. It's easy to ignore that, though, as more emotions swirl in me. A hot upset rises in my throat. I want to be angry with him for leaving me here, alone, without so much as a goodbye. I swallow tears, swallow my indignation to make room for the lighter feelings. He is in front of me, in the flesh, and that is enough for now.

"Where have you *been*?"

"It doesn't matter now." His face momentarily darkens before he shakes the thought away. It evidently *does* matter. "You're looking well yourself."

"You haven't seen me in six years and that's all you have to say?" I scoff to disguise the hurt in my tone. "We certainly have a lot more catching up to do than that, Halvar."

He shivers when I say his name and I tell myself it is because of the cold. I can see his lips quirking in the beginning of a smile, but he forces it down. His gaze is fixed over my shoulder, turning grim. I follow and am met with the entire town watching us.

A flush blooms across my face at the attention. I didn't expect my greeting to be something of note. And yet everyone glares at us with fear in their eyes. I can't find my parents in the crowd, but imagine they must be happy to see him; he was in our home so often throughout our childhood they should be as over the moon as I am. Certainly these looks of fear are only because of some misunderstanding, some fear of the unknown that will become known once they remember who Halvar is.

The elders push through the crowd to stride toward us. I can see in their postures that they are not as happy as I am. The rest of the crowd hangs back but cast nosy looks our way without shame.

Father Levi stops in front of Halvar, and though he is several inches shorter he still manages to look down his nose at him. "What business do you have here?"

Halvar raises a brow, nonplussed. "Do you not recognize me?"

"Oh, I remember you, Halvar. Where is that troublesome father of yours, is he with you?"

Halvar frowns. "He passed away. He was unwell for some time."

My heart lurches. Though his father was a harsh man, he was still Halvar's sole caretaker, and I feel sorry that he lost his only family. I grip his arm in silent apology. He tenses beneath my touch, but I ignore it the same way I ignore the elders' eyes as they take note of the gesture.

"My condolences," Father Levi says, though he sounds anything but sorry. "Why have you returned after all this time?"

"Is it so inconceivable for a man to return to his hometown?"

"Don't play coy, child," Father Patrick warns.

Halvar returns his cold tone. "I am no more a child than you are, Father."

I watch this play out in front of me, confused by their icy reactions upon seeing Halvar. As did all of the children here, he grew up in the church. They know him, albeit a much younger version of him. They should remember the playful, curious child who sat in their pews. I cannot conceive of a reason for their scowls and scorning now.

Halvar raises his hands in acquiescence. "I heard the alarms last night from my cabin and thought I would come see what was wrong."

"You know the reputation your father had, Halvar," Father Dasco starts. Halvar glowers, but the priest continues. "It may be in our village's best interest if you leave—"

He can't leave. He just got here. I look between the priests and him, confusion flooding me. He hasn't done anything wrong.

"I am not staying in the village," Halvar says, and something in me sinks. "I am staying on the outskirts. I am not here to cause trouble, just wanted to see what the alarm was about."

The outskirts. He means the woods. I watch the creases form on the elders' faces as their eyebrows go up in shock, as their frowns deepen.

"The woods aren't safe, even for your kind, boy," Father

13

Patrick says.

Your kind.

Halvar narrows his eyes. "I am not my father."

"You are of his bloodline, and for that we won't have you."

"He's done nothing wrong," I bark out, surprising both the elders and Halvar. "You would deprive him of the information that would protect him from the same beast that stalks both our houses?"

The priests lock eyes with each other, having some strange silent conversation that only they understand.

To Halvar, Father Levi says, "Your father was not the kind of man we wanted in our village." Halvar opens his mouth to object, but the priest continues. "You arrive here on thin ice. Should you prove to us that you are indeed your father's son, you won't be welcome here, either."

Halvar says nothing. I don't know what he *could* say to that.

To me, Father Dasco says, "I would not keep company with this one, Emelie."

Satisfied with their conviction, the priests disperse among the crowd once again. Halvar and I wait for them to be out of earshot before saying anything.

He lowers his eyes to the snow-covered ground. "I understand if you want to do as they say."

I'm not sure if it's his polite tone that grates at me, or the fact that he means what he's said. "Do you truly believe I would do that?"

He allows himself a long look at me before saying, "You of all people know how they feel about outsiders here."

The truth of it settles in my stomach. He and I were always a pair in our youth, hardly ever apart if we could help it. If one of us was seen as odd, so was the other. We never minded as long as we had each other. When he left, the burden of being the black sheep fell solely on me.

I swallow the thought and push my shoulders back, feigning a confidence I don't really have. "I don't care what they think."

His gaze is over my shoulder, cautious. "You should probably pretend to," is all he says before nodding a greeting to someone approaching us.

My parents come to stand on either side of me. Their eyes are on Halvar, and my heart sinks when I see the fear in my mother's eyes, and the protective wariness in my father's.

"Halvar," is all my father says, a greeting and dismissal. "Emelie, we're going home." It is not up for debate; my mother grips my arm and pulls me away.

I give one fleeting look to Halvar and mouth, *I'm sorry*. He only shrugs.

As we walk away, she chides me right in my ear. "You are not to associate with that boy. He's nothing but trouble."

I frown. "But what did he *do*? Don't you remember him? He was at our home all the time."

"Yes, well, childhood is over. He is not like us, Emelie."

"In what way?" Her vagueness strikes my nerves, and I find myself growing more annoyed with how little everyone tells me.

"In all of the ways that matter. Stop dragging your feet, you'll scuff your only good boots."

I feel stuck, full of questions and empty of answers. I want to blame myself for getting so excited to see Halvar and drawing attention to him, but I cannot find it in me to regret hugging him. After so many years without him, it was all I wanted to do. Maybe I needed it. Maybe he did, too.

Perhaps it is the weight of today that bears down on me, or maybe I was already a dam pressure-set to burst. But I can only be denied so many times. And on this I will not compromise, not when it comes to Halvar. Despite what the elders and my parents have said, I must see him again.

CHAPTER TWO

Despite my best efforts, I end up where I started. In an armchair with a needle in my hand. I fixate on the stitching, how poor my work is even after several years of practice. I spoke true when I said I was not meant for this.

I wonder where my talents lie, what I could have been if given the opportunity to explore them. None of my practical skills are advanced enough to make a living off of, and I am too old to be taken on as an apprentice for anything that I am half-decent at. In my bones, I know my mother tolerates my shoddy work because I am her daughter, not because she believes in some untapped potential lying beneath my skin waiting to be pricked by the needle.

"You have such a faraway look in your eye," Mother says, drawing me back in.

"I'm focusing," I say, not looking up.

"No, you're not. I can tell when you are focused and right now you are anything but."

"I am just thinking." Thread. Pull.

"About."

"The town meeting." Not quite a lie, not the full truth either.

"You are thinking about that boy," she says, her voice unnervingly smooth and her hands so steady as she continues her work. She has completed one garment in the time it has taken me to thread my needle.

"His name is Halvar," I mutter. "Although I'm not surprised you don't remember him. It's not as if he was at our house every day, eating our food and playing with me. It's not as though he was my best friend."

"Watch how you speak to me. And do not speak such things about him now. I told you, he's not like us."

I set down my sewing. "And who are *we*, Mother? What is so different about us?"

This makes her set down her work as well. "Don't play at stupidity, Emelie. You accomplish it well enough on purpose. You would do well to focus on your prayers and be well with God, not running around with some outsider."

"Outside of *what*? Everyone is treating me like a child, not telling me anything."

"Maybe if you acted like an adult," she says, taking up her needle again, "we would be able to."

This puts a crack in my armor. I drop the clothes and my needle on the chair and stalk off to my room. I realize this only furthers her point, but I refuse to sit and be insulted. In the privacy of my room, at least I can scowl and not have that be turned into a lecture.

I know my mother's persistent pushing of the faith is only mostly due to the saving of my immortal soul, yet another large portion of it is her fear of being ostracized by the elders for having a heathen daughter. What would the neighbors think? Never mind judging lest ye be judged—the scorning eyes of the elders are judge, jury, and executioner.

It seems they have already sentenced Halvar and his late father. I have to assume that is why they moved out of the village. He may have brushed my questions aside, but his tone and visual discomfort were enough to tell me that *something* had happened.

The harsh words of the elders swim through my brain. I want to call myself heartbroken over it, but I haven't had enough time to be happy about Halvar's return to be crushed once again by their dismissal. Six years gone, and they were ready to send him away within minutes. My jaw clenches at the thought of him having to prove himself to these pompous people. Not just the elders, but the whole village. They are sheep in the worst sense of the word, following whatever inane message is broadcast to them. If one of the Fathers proclaimed that the sky was actually red, they would believe it.

Belief is a funny thing in that it is so moldable. The church prides itself on being the voice of God, but the mistranslation of something consecrated into something so profane astounds me, and yet I feel as though I am the only one who notices. The priests operate on a model of fear, and though it is the most effective way to make people listen, it twists my stomach into knots to watch them distort a prophet's teachings into a means of control. And the people are afraid. I see it in the way my mother clutches her hands against her heart, the way my father tenses when the sounds of the house settling are too loud.

I have to admit that Halvar returning the day after a supposed murder is not a good look. Emerging from the woods like a demon out of hell is reason enough for them to be suspicious. Yet I cannot wrap my head around the fact that they should *know* him, they should remember who he was when he lived here, and not condemn him for some perceived sins. Though I suppose that alone is too much to ask of them. I have to blame myself, too, for drawing attention to him in the first place; if I hadn't run to him, the elders might have never noticed his presence.

He was just so...overwhelming. Were it any other man, I might not have known him. But I looked into those eyes nearly every day for the first fifteen years of my life. I had committed them to memory as much as my own reflection. After six years of silence, of feeling abandoned, I almost felt like a fool for throwing myself at him until he returned my embrace. I would be lying to myself if I said I hadn't missed him.

I think of us as children. The way it felt to wake up and have my first thought be of him and the endless possibilities open to us.

Most mornings started the same way: he would walk through the front door as though this was his home too, and my mother would ruffle his hair and feed him breakfast. She was softer back then, her exterior not yet hardened by the austerity we've come to know. After, Halvar and I would race each other to lessons on school days, or play in the vast expanse of farmland in our free time.

Things changed as we started to get older. Adult conversations surrounding our friendship were held in hushed tones; it simply did not *do* for a growing boy and girl to be so close. Along with that, our catechism shifted towards talk of vocation, of what we would all become once we came of age. For the girls, they wanted wives and mothers. That path never appealed to me, I couldn't see myself fulfilling the role it required. By then womanhood had already started to feel like one of my old coats, it fit well enough if a little too snug. But if it was the path I was to walk, I wanted to walk it with Halvar. I didn't want to be a wife, but I could be content being *his* wife.

There were moments I thought he might feel the same. There were the lingering glances that he wouldn't shy away from when I caught him staring. Fingertips brushing against mine beneath tables, a hand wrapping around my arm in the crowd. The tenderness it took to sweep a lock of hair behind my ear. Then there were the deeper things that felt too difficult to put into words. The quiet comfort in being understood, the assurance that came from knowing we could tell each other anything.

The things I wanted, however, quickly became irrelevant. I couldn't marry a man who wasn't there. I can still feel the way my world shifted when I woke up, same as any other morning, and couldn't find him. I can hear the sound of my shoulder banging against his front door when he wouldn't answer. I can feel the rawness of my throat from crying my heart out. I thought I had done something wrong. That I must have hurt his feelings and so he went away. I begged for an explanation from anyone: my mother, his neighbors, the elders. I was met with dismissal and a plea to move on.

I think the entire village felt my grief after that.

Lessons continued for several years and I pushed through

them, alone and lonely. Were I a different person, I could have made new friends. I could have said yes to the groups of girls who asked me to play with them, entertained the boys who wanted to court me. But none of them were him, so I didn't want them.

I might've been content with being alone forever, with only my parents as distant company. I wouldn't be happy, but that loneliness was already known to me. That contentment feels further away, though, now that he is known to me once more.

My face warms when I think of how he held me, and so I shove the thought away. Instead, my thoughts turn once again to anxiety, to the thought of being sent away as Halvar and his father were. If I were to confirm my mother's suspicions that I had indeed lost my faith, perhaps I would be sent away as well. I don't know that that would be such a bad thing, but I certainly wouldn't be able to live in the forest as Halvar does. I am not strong like him.

Once, being sent away for my differences would seem extreme, and surely out of the question. Back when the village was larger, flourishing the way any small collective would. The elders were still the de facto leaders, but the hand they held on the neck of Kliransk was the gentle hand of a spiritual guide. I remember little from this time, as the church was already tightening its grip by the time I came of age.

Now, two-thirds of our population have fled, having seen and felt the corruption that had been brewing beneath the surface for decades. The ones who left were the lucky ones, with coins to spare and a desire for greater things. Kliransk is not in any position of power in relation to other villages. We are at the mercy of the elements and the wildlife, and only the right amount of coin would be enough to escape the knotting noose.

Even then, however, the amount of experienced travelers who pass through becomes fewer every year. Not many are willing to brace further south, into the vast expanse of mountains. To the west lies the sea, where sailors refuse to take on any more passengers than they already carry. Then there is the north. Most of our people fled through the woods in hopes of making it to the villages on the other side of the trees. None ever sent word back, so we can only guess what happened to them. The options are grim. And even if a traveler were willing to take some of us through safe passage, we've been conditioned to see them as a threat. As trespassers. As an *other*.

Once our population shrank, that was when the elders took the opportunity to seize control. Where they were once only spiritual guides, now they control the everyday trajectory of every remaining villager.

A smaller population is an easier pet to keep, easier to control.

I feel for those who got away, just as I feel for my parents who could not afford to do such a thing. In truth, I don't think they wanted to leave badly enough to try, and so our fates were sealed. We might have become these people anyway, distant from one another and on opposite sides of faith, but maybe it wouldn't have felt this isolating had we made it to a different village.

I spend the remainder of my afternoon buried in a book, reemerging only to help my mother with supper. She glares at me but says nothing about my outburst. That is half of the problem, her saying nothing. I almost wish she would yell at me just so I could yell back. I feel like I could start screaming and she would stay silent, and that only infuriates me more.

We eat in silence. The grief is palpable on my father, and I wish I could find it in me to comfort him. I wish my mother would help beyond praying for his strength.

Once we've all finished eating, Father gestures for us to retire to the living room. He takes up his rosary and the look on his face is clear: *join me*. My mother takes up a seat beside him without hesitation, drawing beads from her apron pocket. It has been some time since they've asked—demanded—I pray the rosary with them, and it takes me a minute to dig out a string of beads from my room. Father leads, Mother and I follow. I can recite the prayers from memory, but my fingers keep losing track of the beads, and I watch my mother's fingers for guidance.

The prayers do not take long and after we sign the final cross, I move to stand, eager to return to my brooding and reading. My mother stops me with a hand on my knee as her mouth continues to move in prayer. I frown, confused. I know I didn't forget any of the prayers. My father's hands are raised as his voice rises above my confused thoughts, and it takes me a moment to realize they are praying *for* me. My skin crawls and I feel the walls begin to cave in around me.

I hated when they'd do this as a child; it was always to beg for intercession on my character—my perceived moral failings—and though they won't come out and say it, I have the stark inclination that now they are praying for me to avoid Halvar, to listen to their demands and the demands of the elders. They want me to assimilate into their blind prejudice and fear. I want to vomit.

My mother sees the look on my face. "We only want what is best for you, Emelie. What God wants for you."

"How can you expect me to understand what that means when you never tell me anything? I have to make assumptions on my own, and even then I have no idea what's going on half the time."

"You don't need to know—"

"I think I deserve to know why the entire village was staring at Halvar and I this morning. What did he do? Why do you all scorn him?"

She sighs and looks at my father. He gives her a small nod. I assume this is permission for her to speak. "You know his father was not a believer. He wasn't raising his boy right, he could have passed down his heathen ideals."

"But Halvar kept going to Sunday school, he was active in the church!"

"Even so. His father was a violent, angry man from a line of other violent and angry men. They weren't right, *he* wasn't right. He was almost...*feral*. He was a danger to the town and so they asked him to leave."

"Why should Halvar pay for his father's sins?" I look between my parents, but my father won't even look at me.

My mother speaks on his behalf. "Because he was raised in that mindset, and we cannot afford that sort of trouble right now."

I scoff. "Do you realize how ridiculous you sound? Are the elders feeding you these ideas? Because they sound contrived at best."

"Do not speak ill of the elders," my father warns.

"Why are we so prejudiced towards outsiders? Are people who leave and come back not still a part of this village? He was raised among us, he is one of us." I shove away from my mother's touch and stand up from my seat. "You are just afraid of what you don't understand. I see the way you look at me when you think I don't notice, and I won't stand for it. The elders said Halvar has to prove himself, and when he shows himself to be nothing less than a good man, I will laugh at your prejudice."

"Sit down, Emelie," my father says.

"I hope you get to have that laugh." My mother's voice is cold in a way I have never heard. "I hope that he is nothing like his father, and that we don't have our suspicions proven correct."

"You knew I missed him," I say, my voice not far above a whisper. "You watched me cry for weeks over his departure, and yet you did nothing to comfort me, but you also did nothing to try and make me hate him. Why not poison my perception of him while I was still vulnerable?"

The words feel traitorous as they leave my mouth; even back then I was beginning to question my beliefs, and my parents' words may not have been enough to turn my opinion of Halvar.

"As your mother said," my father says, "it was not for you to know. Your job is to listen, and you fail at that as much as we fail at guiding you."

My mother settles herself, slipping back into the mask of the godly wife rather than the angry parent. "If the elders have given him a chance to prove himself, then we will allow that. But we must follow their directions. If they say he is dangerous, we must obey."

I scoff, though I regret it almost immediately upon seeing the way both of their eyebrows furrow. "Neither of you have any idea of true danger."

"A man is *dead*, Emelie, and you think to question us—"

"If there were real dangers to living here, then we would have moved out during the exodus when I was a child. You all think you're so brave, when really you face no challenge greater than following simple directions."

When my mother slaps me across the face, it is surprising only because I didn't notice that she had stood and raised her hand to me. It stings. She hasn't hit me in years. I touch my cheek reflexively, and even the featherlight brush of my fingers is too much. I don't dare argue when they send me to my room.

When I barricade my door, it is not the wolf I fear.

I strike a match to try and light the lantern beside my bed, but the flame won't catch. I try and try again, but it's as if the wick is immune to the flame. Frustrated, I shove the matches back down on my night table. I have no desire to go out and face my parents again, so my room is awash in darkness. It is suffocating. I look to the windows, still covered in wooden boards. Would it be so bad if I took down just one?

There is a hammer lying on my desk from when Father secured my room. I grip it and feel its weight in my hands. I will have to be quiet if I want them to remain unawares. I take the back end, press it to a nail, and pull. It gives way with a few tugs, and part of me thinks that these mere planks of wood would do nothing against an angry shifter.

I get the rest of the nails loose and the board on top comes free, allowing moonlight to flood into the room. I shove the board beneath my bed, telling myself I will fix it tomorrow.

Digging a nightgown out of a drawer, I climb into bed with the book I had almost finished earlier. I start to drift off as I reach the final pages. The near-silence of the room is unnerving, but I am pulled towards sleep by the sound of the wind whispering outside. If I weren't half-conscious, I would think those whispers sounded like someone was calling my name. If I were more awake, the sound of the tree branches hitting the roof would sound like footsteps.

The days leading up to Abel's funeral pass without much event, dragging and rushing by in turn. My parents ignore my existence when I'm not needed, and tolerate me when I am. There are no apologies on either end and though the tension hasn't fully dissipated, it isn't as suffocating as that awful night.

There never are apologies, though.

When not shackled to an armchair repairing garments, I read in my bedroom or gaze through the slim opening at my window. I hadn't bothered to put the board back up, not yet at least.

The villagers have continued to fall further and further into their paranoia. I can see it in their eyes when I walk through the market. I can see it in the way people shut their doors while I do my chores in the yard. It's not just Halvar they're suspicious of anymore, they're afraid of each other now, too. Most of the people wear mourning black, some of the women even donning veils to cover their faces. Grief washes over the whole village like a sobering rainstorm.

Halvar doesn't come into town, or if he does, I don't see him. But I certainly hear his name passed around in whispers between market stalls. Whispers about how it was likely him who caused the death. Ridiculous, all of it.

Dinners with my family remain pin-drop quiet, our silverware scraping against dishes and mumbled requests for seconds the only sounds. Though my curiosity only grows with each passing day, I have no desire to pester my parents with questions. The memory of my stinging cheek is answer enough.

The night before the funeral, I lay staring at my ceiling, turning it all over in my head. Their vitriol towards Halvar, the timing of finding Abel's body, my parents' incessant prayer. I hadn't been through much hardship in my life beyond the general stress of life in a poor village, and even that wasn't much to complain about.

We have a roof over our heads, I have an income—however small—and we have edged away from the brink of starvation. In a greater sense, it doesn't matter that I've been wearing the same clothes since adolescence, or that I have no passions or useful skills. The stress of the past few days has been more than I have experienced in a lifetime, and while I am eager for this, too, to pass, the growing knot in my stomach tells me it won't be that easy.

I think I hear the snow falling, or maybe it's the small sounds of the house settling. But the sounds turn consistent, too rhythmic to be natural. It sounds like a gentle *tap, tap, tap* coming from outside. I can't keep pretending that it is in my head.

When I look up at the window I nearly jump out of my skin upon seeing Halvar's face on the other side of the glass. I half-leap out of bed and edge towards the glass, whispering furiously, "What are you doing here?"

He gestures to the latch that is still covered by wooden boards. I rummage for the hammer still lying on my desk. Father was a fool to leave it with me. Quietly as possible, I try to take out all of the nails. It is an agonizing process, not helped by Halvar's face on the other side, patient as he waits for me. Hook, yank, wiggle, release. One by one the nails come free and the boards follow. Finally, enough come free that I can pry the window open. I only crack it enough for us to hear each other properly.

"What are you doing here?" I hiss.

His face gives nothing away. "I need to talk to you."

I look to my unprotected door, then back to him. "Let me barricade the door."

I shove my dresser in front of the door, not bothering to be quiet about that. I am only following my parents' instructions in that sense. Once I am certain the door cannot be flung open without warning, I rush back to the window and push it all the way open for Halvar to come in. It is an awkward fit since he is much larger than the last time we did this. He trips once he is inside, and I make an attempt to catch him, which only pushes us both onto my bed. His elbows catch him so his weight does not bear down on me completely.

We both freeze, eyes unblinking as we watch each other. The moment breaks as he pushes up onto his hands to give me room. I blush, rolling out from under him and moving to close the window.

"You do realize you're out past curfew," I say. My voice is a ghost of what it normally is, I am afraid to raise it above a whisper.

"I don't care." He sits up on my bed. His voice has deepened over the years and sounds almost silly when dropped to a whisper. It crunches over his words and gives them a sharpness, an edge that wasn't there before. "I had to see you."

In the lantern glow of my bedroom I can see his features better than the bright morning glare from the other day. When he pulls his scarf down I notice something I didn't in the town square; deep scars mar his left cheek, reaching up towards his eye. Facial hair partially obscures the scars, but they are too angry pink to not be noticed. They're clearly not fresh, and have long since healed, and I am shocked by how deep-set they are in his face. I gasp, which makes him not meet my gaze. He doesn't want me to address it.

I cross my arms over my chest. "Talk to me, then." I feel defensive and I cannot pin down why. It's not his fault his father moved them out of the village, but perhaps I am jealous. Perhaps I am confusing my missing him with anger. Or maybe I am angry.

"I want to firstly apologize for my briefness with you in the town square. I didn't exactly expect a warm welcome from the elders, but I wasn't expecting...that...either. But I wanted to thank you for the kindness you showed me, and I also apologize for any trouble that's brought you."

His language is painfully formal, and though I can tell he means every word of it, it saddens me that we've lost the casual familiarity that was once second nature to us. Though I suppose Mother was right in that sense; childhood is over.

I clear my throat. "No apology necessary. Could this not wait until daylight? I wouldn't want you to get in trouble."

"Screw the elders and their inane rules," he says, cutting me off. "I did my waiting, six years of it."

"What if there is a wolf?"

He scoffs, the first almost-smile I've seen on him. "I fear no wolf nor man, Emelie."

"I've gathered that. Did you only come to apologize?"

27

For a moment, I think he looks hurt. Then he blinks and the look is gone. "Do I need more of a reason?"

I cannot help the annoyance that flares up in me. "I missed you, Halvar. You left without warning, and now you're back and no one will tell me why they're treating you like filth. I don't need you to be short with me, too."

He stands, but keeps his distance. It is then that I realize how much taller than me he really is; I have to look up to see his face. "I missed you too, Emelie. Every day. God, I would have told you if my father had let me, but he didn't. You know I wouldn't have just left without saying anything unless I had to."

"Why *did* you leave?"

His face darkens. He does that look a lot, I can tell by the crease in his brow. "My father kept things from me, too. I know little besides the fact that he got into an argument with the elders, which they found unforgivable. It was the last straw for them."

"And so you had to leave town in the middle of the night."

"They didn't send us away in the middle of the night, my father insisted we leave before first light."

"Fear of wolves doesn't run in the family, it seems." I cannot decide if I mean my voice to sound playful or harsh. I find that I don't mind either one. "I suppose we've both been left in the dark, then."

"I can't say I'm afraid of the dark," he murmurs.

"I don't fear it," I say. "I am annoyed that no one will tell me anything."

"Well," he says, striding to my desk. He turns my chair around and sits in it backward, his chest pressed to the back. It creaks against his weight. "What do you want to know?"

"I want to know why everyone is treating you like a monster, and not a child of this village."

"Because my father was one, and they think he raised me to be like him." His words are a truth bared before me, and I am almost sorry he believes it.

I raise an eyebrow. "Your father was cruel, but isn't it a stretch

28

to call him a monster?"

His next words crack something inside of me. "I couldn't tell you everything he did to me, Emelie."

"What does it matter now that he's dead?"

"I don't want to."

Fair enough. His half-confession tampers down my annoyance, but I still feel it sitting inside my gut. I am not necessarily annoyed *at* him, but rather the situation. I take a breath, not wanting to lash out at him. He doesn't deserve to be punished with my pent-up anger at this village, at my parents, at myself.

"What changed, while you were gone?" It is a question I am dying to know the answer to, but am not eager to answer myself.

"I grew up. I took up a trade. I cannot think of anything more."

"You're colder," I add. "You're not as quick to smile. In fact, I don't believe I've seen you smile once since returning."

"It's not often that I have much to smile about," he says, scratching at his scarred cheek.

"I apologize," I say, my voice almost overrun by the roaring of wind outside. I shiver as the draft makes its way in, but try to ignore the cold. "I shouldn't be so harsh to you."

He completely sheds his scarf then, tossing it to me. I catch it in one hand and wordlessly wrap it around myself as a shawl. If nothing else, we at least still have a lack of pretense between one another.

"I would be angry, too," he says then. "If you left without a word, I would be angry, too."

"You were my best friend," I say, fighting to keep the waver out of my voice. I refuse to cry in front of him. "I thought I had done something wrong."

His knuckles whiten as he clenches the back of the chair. "You did nothing wrong."

I sniffle, but force humor back into my voice. "I should have known. I never do anything wrong."

That, at last, gets a laugh out of him. A real one that he has to stifle by shoving his face into his sleeve. It feels like the dam breaks and we are able to shift back into something similar to how we used to be, allowing us to catch each other up on what we missed over the past six years. On who we have become in the meantime.

He tells me little more than I already knew; his father was cruel and unjust, but kept him fed and educated and alive once they moved away. He was already falling away from the church during his last few years in Kliransk, and being exiled was the final push he needed. He still has his guard up, I can tell, but it is a step further than I ever thought we would get again.

Though I feel wholly uninteresting telling him about my life, he listens intently, his eyes never leaving me. I tell him about losing my faith, about the oppressive weight my mother places on me, how abandoned I feel by my father. He interjects with a comment here and there, but for the most part he just listens. It's been a long time since someone has let me talk.

It's not until I voice it out loud to someone else that I realize how many complaints I have collected over the years. Halvar's expression grows more frustrated the more I describe my life with my parents, though I can't imagine it's anything comparable to what he went through with his father.

Our talk leads us long into the night, our bodies drifting closer as we fight to keep our voices below a whisper. When I get him to smile, I feel like I can breathe again.

I don't remember falling asleep, but I wake while the sky is in the murky state between evening and dawn. The window is shut, and for a moment I wonder if I dreamt it all, but the feel of Halvar's scarf still wrapped around my shoulders grounds me back in reality. I drift back to sleep with the scent of cedar and sage enveloping me.

CHAPTER THREE

The sound of my mother knocking on my door rattles the dresser in front of it. The racket draws me up slowly, and I blink back the grogginess and the sleep that threatens to pull me under again.

"Emelie? Are you awake? You need to get dressed for the funeral. We're leaving soon."

I groan something akin to affirmation and drag myself out of bed. Reluctantly, I unwrap Halvar's scarf from around me and shove it beneath my pillow. My best dress is laid across my desk chair, taunting me. It is the best only in the sense that it is well made and not covered in reworked stitching. It is far from flattering; in fact, it's a plain cream thing that hangs like a sack.

Once dressed, I fix my hair into something presentable and shove the dresser away from my door. It only takes me a few minutes to freshen up in the washroom, but even those precious few minutes are haunted by my mother's hovering presence urging me to hurry.

There is no time to eat. Tradition says we are supposed to fast before attending mass, but I find it difficult to ignore my rumbling stomach. My father pries the blockade off of the front door, letting a rush of cold air in. My parents are dressed in what is our version of finery: modest plain things that won't draw attention to us and our lack of funds. We are a fine picture of grief.

We walk in silence, heads bowed and hands folded as we fall in line with the rest of the villagers. Some are crying, some stare stone-faced at the path. I lower my gaze if anyone meets my eye, lest I be caught without the waves of grief that are so palpable on everyone else. It is a sorry situation, for certain, but it would be a disservice to Abel for me to pretend to feel more sadness than I do.

The church looms ahead, dark against the severe morning light. It sits domineeringly in the center of Kliransk, just behind the town square. There is a line of people down the front steps, everyone stopping to talk with the priest out front. The wait is brief, a pause rather than a full stop. No one wants to be outside longer than they have to, be it because of the dropping temperature or the faceless threat stalking just out of sight.

Father Patrick greets us at the threshold, shaking my father's hand and nodding to my mother and I. He looks tired and won't quite meet our eyes. I can't help the low note of sympathy that roils in my gut. He's always been the kindest of the three, and in my opinion the most Christlike. He is the only one I believe when he offers well-wishes.

The lights are low inside but my gaze immediately latches onto Halvar, sitting with his head bowed in the furthest back pew. He shares the pew with no one. Several rows in front of him sit empty as well. Our eyes meet as I pass him, and I duck my head like a schoolgirl, fighting off the blush that wants to warm its way across my face.

"Stand up straight, Emelie," my mother scolds.

Instinct has me do as she says, but a wave of rebellion moves me to excuse myself from her side. Mother mutters a warning under her breath but I know she won't make a scene in front of the rest of the village. Using this leverage, I start towards Halvar's pew. He lifts his gaze to mine, but before we can speak, someone blocks my path.

I haven't spoken to Magda since we were in lessons together. We're roughly the same age, though I think I am a few months her senior. Her round eyes look downturned, making her normally cherub-like face look aged and sad. She stands before me, wringing her hands and looking like she wants to crawl out of her own skin. Her eyes dart around, noting everyone around us.

"Isn't this madness?" She says, no greeting to soften her introduction.

I shrug one shoulder, already peering around her towards Halvar. "Something like that."

She lowers her voice, speaking conspiratorially as though we are both in on some secret. "The elders certainly had a lot to say yesterday."

A lot of horse-shit, I think. I don't dare say it aloud, though. Talking to Magda feels like a test. Though I can't keep the derision out of my voice as I say, "The answer to everyone's prayers, I'm certain."

She snorts. "My prayers rarely center on such fanatical hysteria."

I almost wonder if she agrees with my unspoken insults, but I don't have time to analyze her tone before the doors to the church are pulled shut. The blare of an organ fills the room, and that is our cue to find our seats. I give Magda a dismissive nod and hurry to find my parents.

They've settled a few pews from the front. I slip in on one end, brushing off their side-eyed glares. It's an undertaking to appear attentive; my eyes drift around the room as I fidget with my hands in my lap. Perhaps I look sad to others. Devastated, even. I knew Abel as much as I knew everyone in this village, that is to say on a surface level. I knew his face, his routine, which hymns were his favorite to sing. I knew he was loud and brash and did not sit well in lessons. The elders were constantly on him, trying to tame his burgeoning rakish ways.

Part of me still doesn't believe he was truly killed by a wolf, and that doubt pushes away the feelings that could've mutated into grief. Death does not sadden me, death is a constant. If anything I am only saddened that this has shrunk my already-small bubble. Guilt wracks through me at that, but it is no match for the feelings that have already been festering inside.

The service begins and I work my way through the motions of

mass. Mass is long, funerals are longer. Longer still when the ceremony grinds to a halt every time someone is overcome by their grief. The cries of the villagers rise above the prayers, and even Father Dasco stops to clear his throat of tears a few times.

It is a stop-and-go process, but we arrive at the part of the mass where Abel's loved ones are invited to the podium to speak. A line of people wait to be heard, and I wonder how many of them are actually grieving, and how many just want to be seen grieving.

One of my former classmates is babbling her way through a speech about how nice Abel was to her in our school years. I am trying to remember if she ever actually spoke to him when the door bursts open, partially from force but harshened by the wind. Father Patrick runs in, and though his nose is pink from waiting out in the cold, his face is pale and his eyes are wide. I assume he had been waiting for stragglers, made watchdog by his brothers. He runs up the aisle between the pews, nearly tripping over his robes. Heads turn to look at him, incredulous.

"What is the meaning of this?" Father Dasco demands.

Father Patrick takes a few breaths to collect himself, trying and failing to regain a sense of authority. At last, he gives in to the clear fear on his face and yells in his breathy voice, "There has been another body. Someone else has been killed by the wolf."

Screams of the villagers fill the church and the elders can do little to soothe after the awful truth Father Patrick just bequeathed to us. As people burst from their seats, Father Patrick and Father Levi bar the door, yelling for everyone to be still. My mother grips my arm, her nails digging into my skin. I want to tell her I'm not going to run anywhere.

I can hear Father Levi over the crowd, his voice shrill and hiding any of the fear that is so clearly written across his face. "We cannot let anyone in or out of this church. It is your only claim to innocence. Please sit down!"

The elders herd the people so that everyone is perched back in a pew, though more thoroughly unsettled than before. Death at a funeral is the twist of the knife. Everyone glances around at their friends, neighbors, even their family members with looks nothing short of accusation. No one here is safe.

What good are sheep among wolves?

Someone cries out, "What do we do, Father?"

The elders look amongst each other, formulating some confounded plan on the spot. Father Patrick is still clearly shaken, and he moves to sit down behind the altar. Father Levi looks out at the crowd, catching my father's eye and waving him forward. He rises to the call, to the dismay of my mother. She grips his arm, but he gently pushes her away with some murmur of comfort. A few other village men, mostly my father's men, rise to crowd in the aisle.

Father Dasco turns to us. "Father Levi and our men are going to take a headcount of who did not attend mass. In the meantime, please, we must continue to pray for the souls of the deceased."

I feel sorry for Abel, that he was upstaged even at his own funeral. Father Dasco ushers us back into prayer as the men leave to take account of who is not here. I am too shocked to do anything besides what I am told, and so I pray. I could doubt the existence of a wolf when there was just one body, but now with this fresh kill, I am less certain. But why now, after all this time of relative peace? I resist the urge to turn around to check on Halvar, but I can see in my peripheral vision that people are doing just that. I hate to think that they are already assuming the worst of him.

As the minutes tick by, prayers become jumbled into the low murmur of gossip spreading around us. Some are fully turned around in their seats, eyes fixed on the back of the church. I want to believe they're watching the door in anticipation of the village men's return, but my gut sinks knowing that they're staring at Halvar. When I try to crane my neck, my mother hisses at me to pay attention. I catch the look in her eye, fear for my father. It is not like the everyday worry like when he goes to work. This is something new. This is founded fear.

Voices drift into silence until a cluster of people in another pew speak up, begging for Father Patrick to tell what he knows. Still pallid and shaken, he spouts off a story of wandering the village on his way to pray over those unable to attend mass, when he spotted a bloody pile in the distance, right on the tree line. He did not get close enough to see who it was, fear of the woods overtaking him.

"What if the person is still alive?" I whisper to my mother. She shushes me, not entertaining what I have to say. "I mean it, Mother. What if the person is bleeding out right now?"

"Hold your tongue," she snaps. Her eyes are fierce, and her mouth is set in a straight line. I am not winning this battle.

This whole situation feels wrong. Not just the deaths, but the air of circumstance around them. Were I a braver person, I would run into the snow to see if the body is just a body, if they're still alive, what caused the wound. But I am a coward.

It does not take long for the men to return, grouped in one fixed unit. They are shielding a few who are carrying something—no, *someone.*

The body.

Some stare in morbid curiosity, but I turn my eyes towards the front of the church. Towards the crucifix where another corpse hangs. We cannot escape death here.

Father Levi directs them through the back of the church where the mortuary waits. The eyes of the people follow, captured by their own worst fears. I can't make myself look, can't make it real. Crying fills the church once more, grief now usurped by painstaking fear. Maybe a little disgust, too. We were prepared for this exact scenario while growing up, having been told that this would someday happen. The drills are nothing compared to the real thing. The drills never included a bloody body being paraded through the church.

The men file back into the pews, now thoroughly shaken. Father Dasco demands an update from Father Levi, who reports that only the elderly, the sick, and a few children are not in attendance. No one capable of killing another person. That leaves them with little to go off of.

The funeral is completely forgotten at this point. All three of the priests come to stand in the middle of the aisle so they are in the center of the room, in the center of everyone's view. I twist to watch them. Father Patrick still looks pale, and while I cannot blame him—it must be difficult to come across a dead or dying body—I feel resentment over the fact that he did not bother to check to see if they were still breathing. Or who the body belonged to. That he made the rest of the village men check for him. He is a coward like I am. Like we all are, evidently.

"Our faith is being tested by God," Father Dasco says, drawing the attention back in. "We have not experienced an attack in decades, and now there have been two in less than a week. We must pray over what God is trying to teach us, and we must heed His word."

"Father, are you not worried?" Marie asks. Tears stream freely down her face. I know her son, Calder, was friends with Abel.

"I only worry that we will fail to understand what God is trying to tell us. We are protected by Him, as long as we remain faithful."

Though I know he means this to be comforting, it has the opposite effect. Voices break out, arguing over one another. People rise from their pews and to my surprise, several of them crowd the elders as they demand answers.

"Do you know whose body we had to carry from the border?" One of my father's men bellows. "My nephew, Nathaniel. All because you and your *brothers* have failed to keep us safe. Is that not what you promised when the rest of our people fled?"

Father Levi's eyes flash, daring him to continue. "And we have kept our promise. Don't you find it odd that there were two attacks in such a short time? Look around!" He throws open his arms, making a circle about the aisle. "Is it not suspicious that after an outsider enters our borders two of our own are dead?"

This further splinters the fragile composure the villagers hold. They turn their ire away from the elders and instead make their way towards Halvar's pew. Even if no one else does, I see the sick light this brings to Father Levi's eye.

Halvar stays seated, not looking at anyone, but I can see his hands gripping each other tightly. I did not spend years by his side to not know his tells, even after all this time, and right now his body is practically screaming with what can only be rage. Rage at being accused, rage at his dying innocence, rage at the unfairness of it all.

The priests follow, shoving their way towards the front of the mob. They point accusatory fingers in his face and ask him questions for the whole crowd to hear and pass judgment on.

"Do you think we like playing these games, child?"

"Would you like to tell us where you were this morning? And last night for that matter."

"Did you lead the wolf into our village?"

More cries chime in with accusations—baseless, ridiculous claims that make me want to pull my hair out.

"He's one of them! He is a shifter!"

The walls of the sanctuary feel smaller than they were. The air is too warm for the winter morning. We are in hell. I cannot take this. I rise out of my pew, my legs working before my brain processes what I am doing.

"Emelie, be seated," my mother hisses.

She tries to pull me back into the pew but I shake her off with little resistance, walking towards Halvar almost as if in a trance. A few of the adults cast scornful eyes on me as I pass. I hear them muttering, I hear them tell each other that they always knew I was odd. One of the village grandmothers *tsks* as I pass her, calling me a magnet for trouble. I arrive at Halvar's pew, shoving past the reaching bodies thirsty for his blood, wanting justice no matter if it is true.

I stand between him and the crowd, one hand on his shoulder and one on the pew to keep me upright as people shove at me. My parents have followed, but are stuck behind a few villagers. Or perhaps they are keeping their distance, not wanting to be associated with me.

"Halvar is innocent. Please, listen! You all know him, he is one of our own. You raised him as you raised me!"

"Emelie, please," he mutters, but I don't relent.

"None of my children were raised to be sinners," an elder woman says. It stings, because she knows me. She *should* know me by now. She helped me fix my dresses when my mother fell ill. I sat in her kitchen, eating her food as I played with her grandchildren.

38

I feel Halvar grip the back of my dress, the tension palpable in that mere touch, but I won't be swayed. Even as I see new eyes watching me. All of these people I have grown up around, been raised by in turn just as much as my own parents, now glaring at me as though I am an outsider. An other. The exact type we were raised to abhor.

"You know nothing of his innocence, Emelie." Father Dasco tries to pull me away, tries to shove me towards my parents. "Please, stop this."

"But he has done nothing!" I cry. "If someone has been killed, it was not by Halvar's hand!" Tears of frustration, not sadness, start to spill over. Halvar's grip on me tightens, and I can feel that he is shaking. I silently beg him to keep quiet, because I fear that even the sound of his voice would be the crowd's undoing. And also my own.

"How can you be so certain of this?" Father Levi asks, turning his suspicious eye on me.

The crowd quiets some, then. I feel the weight of everyone's gaze. I feel their grief, their anger. They want someone to crucify if only to say that they tried to absolve themselves of any sin. That they tried to do what they thought was best. I cannot bear it, and yet I must.

"I know that it wasn't Halvar." I look at my mother and father in turn, one last time. My mother is mouthing for me to return to their side, to stop this. My father ever so slightly shakes his head, but I can see the anger there, the embarrassment. There is no going back from what I am about to do. I can only hope that the crowd will not hurt my parents in the process of hurting me. "I know this because…"

Everyone is staring at me expectantly. Halvar's hand moves from gripping the back of my dress to splaying a palm across my lower back, offering a soothing rub. I feel as though he is trying to tell me not to do this. But if they are going to send him to hell, I'll be damned if I let him walk there alone.

I swallow. "I know this because he was with me. All night. In my room."

The crowd once again breaks out into noise. The swarm of voices is overbearing, particularly that of the priests right in my ear, demanding more detail. My mother looks like she is going to faint.

My father's face has gone slack, and this concerns me even more. The village women begin scolding me about my purity, and at this Halvar finally stands, attempting to push me behind him.

"It's not what you think," he says to the crowd, now hungry not just for his flesh but mine. The priests take note of every touch, every inch of contact. He steels himself, taking deep, steadying breaths. "I was there for permission. To ask for her hand."

Heads whip towards my parents at this. Father Levi and Father Patrick do their best to calm the crowd enough so that they can speak to my parents.

Father Dasco's head whips between my parents and me. "Is this true? Is Halvar to marry your daughter?"

An alibi and an anchor, my father holds both in his hands. With one word he could damn us all, or salvage what is left of not just my reputation, but theirs. I can see the wheels turning in his head, I can see him deciding what to do with me. I silently plead to him, not bothering to wipe the tears staining my cheeks.

At last, he straightens and looks at Father Dasco. "Yes, Halvar was in our home last night. He wishes to marry Emelie."

"What of her virtue?" An elder woman says. "It does not bode well for him to be in her bedroom before they are married."

My father remains unmoved. "We had to ascertain what value my daughter holds for a dowry. We are a godly family, we would not allow for any such sin to take place in our home." The bite in his words is for me alone.

"He could have gone out and killed after he left your home!" A voice cries.

"It took," my father speaks through his teeth, "many hours to determine what would be an acceptable arrangement. With the curfew, we found it safer to not send him home. We sent him away at first light."

In other words, he wouldn't have had enough time to kill someone in broad daylight, make it home to clean himself and change, and arrive at the church before the funeral. They all know it, they all saw Halvar seated in this pew well before many of us had arrived.

"So you have given your blessing?"

The crowd has gone fully silent by now. Most of them still glare at me, at Halvar, at the places our skin touches as he tries to shield me. My mother looks at my father; I know she is angry with me, but even more than that, she is obedient to my father's word. What he says, she will abide by. Even if it means giving her only daughter away to the man she had prayed against. The priests look at him too, awaiting an answer. I hold my breath.

"Yes."

The crowd seems somehow angered and sedated by this. I am in turn berated and congratulated by those nearest me. The older generation offers me the former, my former classmates the latter. The elders call over the commotion for everyone to return to their seats. Some are still giving both of us disgusted looks, but the majority start to ease back towards their pews. They have no grounds to find Halvar in the wrong now, though they aren't happy about that.

Everything after that happens quickly. We finish Abel's service in what has to be the tensest moment of my life. Halvar has joined my family in our pew, and all eyes are on us rather than the altar. Neither of my parents will look at me, and I find myself grasping for purchase anywhere I can, digging my fingers into my thighs or the wooden pew in turn. At one point, Halvar puts a hand over my fidgeting one. I think he's trying to calm me, but his touch brings me back to the reality where my entire life is about to change.

After the service, everyone splinters. Father Patrick stays with the congregation, still jittery from all of the morning's happenings. No one is to leave until they deem it safe. Father Levi slinks out of the church to check on the villagers who did not attend the funeral. Father Dasco approaches my family's pew and directs us to follow him. I can feel all eyes on us as we walk back up the aisle and into a hallway that leads out of the church and into a study. It's a small room, and with the door shut it feels even smaller.

Without hesitation, I run into my father's arms, thanking him and crying into his shirt. Though he is stiff, he hugs me back, petting my hair down.

It is then that my mother yanks me out of his arms, slapping and scratching at me. Halvar attempts to shield me from her, taking the brunt of her blows, while my father holds her back.

"What were you thinking, making a scene like that?" She cries. I have never seen her look so unbecoming. Her hair has fallen out of place and tears stream down her angry red cheeks.

Father Dasco looks to my father for an explanation. He clears his throat. "This was...not the way we wanted to announce the news." My mother settles a little in his arms, the reality of the situation finally hitting her. She sinks into his grip.

"Well." Father Dasco starts. "I think it is in everyone's best interest that we get this taken care of as quickly as possible. We will see to it that your daughter is given her due sacrament." He moves to a desk in the middle of the room, drawing up papers. "We have to finish with the funeral proceedings for Abel. After that, we can proceed with your ceremony."

"Today?" I blurt.

Father Dasco looks up at me, unmoved. He nods only once. "Today."

The word slips down my throat and settles in my stomach. I am to be a bride before nightfall. I look up at Halvar, who stares stone-faced at the priest. My insides twist to think that he is already regretting his words. I know it was to save both of us, but guilt pinches me. A life together with my best friend would not be so bad, and yet I fear what he is truly thinking.

"You may wait here while we draw up the proper documents, should you need time to prepare. Either myself or one of my brothers will come to retrieve you when we've finished. Be ready." Then he stalks out, leaving us to discuss amongst ourselves.

My father breaks the silence. "You truly mean to make a wife of my daughter?"

I tense, though I know Halvar cannot back out now.

"I do," he says. "I meant no disrespect on your household

for coming to see Emelie last night. Know that it was only with pure intentions."

"I don't care much for what you've done," Father says. "I care for what you intend to do. You have a home?"

"A modest one, yes." He gestures towards the window, towards the woods. "Just past the tree line. Not much further than you and your men travel for your work."

Mother paces the length of the room. She looks stricken, and it angers me almost as much as the crowd did.

Father carries on like nothing is wrong. "You'll care for her then?"

"It will be a privilege to do so."

Halvar's words set alight something in me, but I am too overcome by the gentle questions my father asks. His willingness to go along with what we've done continues to surprise me, and it moves me to once again throw my arms around him and cry against him, thanking him.

He hugs me with one arm, but his voice is colored with quiet anger. "I would not have you be made a fool in front of the entire village. I'd sooner die than let them eat you alive. But know this, girl. If you work under my nose like that again, I will not respond as kindly."

"Yes, Father," is all I can say.

"So that's that, then?" Mother says from the other side of the room. "You back us into a corner to get what you want?"

"Enough," my father warns.

"At least you'll be married in the church," she snaps, throwing her hands up. "At least I won't have a heretic daughter running around in the woods with some—"

"Mother!"

She scoffs and turns away. My father ignores this and continues interrogating Halvar.

"What reinforcements do you have to protect yourself and your home?"

"The necessary ones." Halvar offers my father the same brief necessities that he is afforded.

I'm surprised by the amount of interest my father has taken in this, though I suppose if anything were to draw him out of his brooding, my marriage would be it. Halvar takes each question in stride, firing back answers worthy of my hand. He shuts down talk of a dowry immediately. My father does not push back very hard to that.

Halvar and I are not given even a moment of privacy to discuss things, our vicinity the only bit of connection for the time being. I want to ask him so many questions, pick his brain for every little thought. I want to know if he thinks he made a mistake. I want to know that he wants this. I debate the risk of talking to him under my breath, weighing what I can say to him that won't give away our ruse. But I am not given the opportunity.

There is a knock at the door.

CHAPTER FOUR

This is not how I pictured myself getting married.

In truth, I didn't picture myself ever getting married, especially after Halvar was exiled. I imagined myself an old maid, begrudgingly taking care of my parents as they aged, taking on Mother's title as village seamstress. I would not be great, but I would be comfortable.

My dreams from my youth swim at the back of my mind; the way I used to dream of this, of a life spent beside him forever. But my childhood crush feels silly now that we stand at an altar side by side by his own doing. I stifle the speck of excitement that threatens to bloom. I have to remind myself that it was to save both of us, to save himself, truly. That he does not feel how I once felt. How I may still feel.

The worst part of all of this is that I am still wearing my cream dress. It makes me look more like a bride than I feel. Halvar, at least, looks like a groom in his dress pants and dark green shirt. What a shame that my favorite dress would have matched it perfectly. I want to laugh at the irony of having experienced a funeral, a death, and a wedding all in one day. We certainly look the part in our mourning clothes, now our matrimonial clothes.

Second to this feeling is the fact that the entirety of Kliransk is witnessing us. Everyone I have ever known fills the pews, watching and waiting for the ceremony to unfold. My parents sit in the front row, eyes wide like crows waiting for the kill. I look away from them before they notice me staring. Instead, I let my eyes wander to the various faces spread across the church. The older villagers still frown, disapproval written all over their faces. But I find kindness where I least expect it. From the middle, Magda gives me a small but encouraging smile. She looks Halvar over, then back to me, her mouth twisting up further. It's not unkind but rather knowing in a way that makes me feel too vulnerable. I lower my eyes once again.

We don't have rings, so instead Father Dasco directs us to join our hands. I hold out my hand, and Halvar so painfully gently takes it in his; I can feel calluses littered across his fingers and the palms of his hand. He said he had taken up a trade, but didn't specify which. Something where he works with his hands, then. Halvar briefly meets my eye, and though his expression is guarded, he seems present in the moment. I don't know if it's real or imagined when his fingers ever so softly stroke mine. I let it comfort me regardless.

All three of the priests take turns praying over us, and we regurgitate the vows they give us. It feels dishonest, not because of the words themselves but because I am being told to say them. Halvar's gaze is intense when he recites them to me, but I can tell by his tone and the way he stumbles over the wording that it feels awkward coming out of his mouth, too.

I almost miss it when Father Dasco finally finishes praying and announces us married. As well as when he tells us to kiss. I stare at Halvar, wide-eyed like a doe. I dreamt of this, too, of kissing him, but not like this. Not in front of everyone. His face reddens and I see his throat work to swallow. Something alights in my gut when I see his eyes flit towards my mouth, the way his pupils widen. I can almost believe he wants this. But my expectations let me down when he simply places a featherlight touch against my lips. It is a ghost of a kiss, one that does not intend to stick around to haunt. I barely have time to close my eyes before the moment passes. He pulls away blushing, and his eyes search for purchase anywhere that isn't my face.

And now we are married. I thought it would feel more colorful, like something inside me set free, but with nearly every seat filled, with the eyes of God bearing down from every wall of the church, I feel more stifled than ever.

I can only assume that Halvar feels the same, and a piece of me already longs to have done this differently, the way our childhood selves would have been happy with. The things I want often feel out of reach and disoriented, but I can say for certain this brings me no clarity. I can only hope that it has bought Halvar security, if nothing else.

Father Dasco stays with the congregation while the remaining elders direct us back into the parish study to sign the paperwork. Halvar's signature is a sloppy, slanted thing and his firm hand sets the ink bleeding around his lettering. In comparison, mine is a waifish, wispy thing. A phantom beside a fiend. The priests sign in quick succession, their signatures not differing much from one another in any way that matters. I wonder if they ever sign documents on the other's behalf.

Once our union is official on paper, the elders turn on us. Father Levi's voice is almost as sour as his expression.

"Best if you leave before sundown."

His harshness does not surprise me. Father Levi has never been one for pleasantries, every word out of him always a sneer or a snarl. He is all bark and no bite. Still, the briskness with which he is dismissing us from the village does send a wave of shock through me.

A tear slips down my mother's cheek. "She is allowed back as she pleases, correct?"

The distinctness of *she* rather than *they* is stark. She is not including Halvar in her plea.

Father Patrick's eyes flit between my mother and his brother in Christ. He rubs a hand across his brow, searching for a way to soften this blow. "Halvar's acceptance is conditional on his behavior. As his wife—"

"For necessities only, I'm afraid." Father Levi interjects with little remorse in his tone.

My mother opens her mouth to speak, to perhaps beg for

intercession, but my father deigns to speak first. "We understand the sanctity of marriage." He wraps an arm around my mother to keep her silent. To keep her complacent.

I knew what I was getting myself into when I made my decision; maybe some wild, untamed part of me pushed me to do this for that very reason.

We follow the elders out of the office. I cling to Halvar's arm as we rejoin the congregation, trying to look the part of a blushing bride. He keeps his arm hooked for me to hold on, but does not reciprocate the touch.

The funeral proceedings have concluded and the people mill about in the aisles, waiting for the elders to deem it safe to return to their homes. The pretense of sanctity has dropped; people are openly gossiping, gawking at Halvar and I. My mother shakes her head and pulls my father into one of the back pews. She does not urge us to follow and so we don't.

I'm not surprised when Magda approaches us on Calder's arm. They smile at us, Calder releasing his hold on Magda to shake Halvar's hand.

"It's about time," he says, clapping a hand to Halvar's arm.

I can feel when he flinches as well as when he tries to brush it off. I blame it on the nerves. Then I latch onto what Calder's said.

I chuckle. "About time for what?"

That only sends him and Magda into a fit of giggles. "Don't play coy," she says. "We all knew."

"It was always clear that you cared for each other," Calder says, "but you made it all the more clear with how you reacted once he left—"

Magda elbows Calder in the side, but she doesn't dispel what he said. She smiles apologetically. "We're just happy that you have each other again."

The idea that my life has been up for speculation while I wasn't aware burns low in my gut, but I stuff the anger back down. Not the time, not when I won't have to see any of their faces for a long, long while. I take her niceties with grace, stuff them with the rest of the rocks in my pockets.

Halvar must notice because he puts a hand over mine that rests on his arm. "Thank you for your well-wishes, I'm glad to know I was missed." If the hint of a smirk at his mouth is at my expense, I allow it if only because he is playing along.

Calder and Halvar fall into conversation, recounting things from when we were all schoolmates. They weren't quite friends, the same way Magda and I were never friends, but they are both clearly trying. I owe them reciprocity if nothing else.

Magda's expression is warm, nothing like the cold analytical glares from the rest of the village. She was always that way and yet I rejected her at every turn, too enveloped in my own bitterness. I can't say I regret that choice; it is one that kept me safe. But having taken my vows, I think I've left safe behind a few steps back.

"He didn't mean anything cruel," she says, tilting her head. "This suits you, you know? Being a wife."

A laugh shocks through me, and my hands fidget across my skirts and my hair, seeking something to do. "I suppose we'll find out."

Father Dasco's voice echoes through the church, declaring Kliransk safe to venture back into. Hordes of people rush out as if there is something to run from.

My parents find us, and while Magda and Calder greet them with the politeness they're expected to give, I don't fail to notice the way Magda's eyes harden, the way Calder grips her arm a little tighter.

My brow furrows. All that I have known, or thought I knew, is unraveling quicker than I can comprehend. Perhaps I was right in at least one thing.

I am not the only outlier.

We follow my parents home for the last time. Father lets us into the house and I study every bit of space as I pass through. It is the only home I have ever known and somehow has never felt like such. The realization that I will not miss it here hits me like a stone, dropping its weight inside me, adding to the pile already there.

I consider the past few days, how tense it has been with my parents, and am further weighed down by the realization that I might not miss them, either. Perhaps that will change once the excitement passes, but I'm beginning to doubt myself more and more.

I hurry to my bedroom to pack, leaving Halvar with my parents in the front room. It makes me uncomfortable that I cannot mitigate whatever they might say to him, but time is not on our side. I stuff a few garments into a sack, leaving behind the ones that are on their very last seams. It leaves me with few options, but I will make do. Hesitating only momentarily, I shed the cream dress and shove it to the bottom of my dresser, favoring instead to change into the green dress. I wrap myself in my only good coat, the only one that will last what is proving to be a brutal winter season.

It is only now that I realize how few clothes I possess, how it has become second nature to put the same ones on every day. I find Halvar's scarf under my pillow and wrap that around myself, too. My books are the real challenge; I shove what I can into the sack and carry the rest. My hands are full and I feel ridiculous, but figure it must be one of Halvar's husbandly duties to help me carry my burdens.

My steps are light as I return down the hallway. I can hear both of my parents' voices as they speak to Halvar in low tones, spouting some nonsense about how he must continue to guide me in the faith. He murmurs something passable as agreement, but I know he is bluffing if only to get them off his back. It wouldn't be the first time he's had to do so. Their voices quiet when I walk in, heads turning towards me. My mother tuts about all the baggage I am carrying and sets off to her bedroom to find something more suitable. She returns with a trunk, which she swiftly helps me pack. Once my life is firmly packed inside, I steel myself to say goodbye.

I expect some show of resistance, a request that I travel to and from at their convenience. But they don't. Instead, they hug me tightly in turn and offer parting words; my father repeats his warning from earlier, to not betray his kindness again. My mother frantically lists off my new wifely duties to attend to. I don't have to tell her I won't be returning tomorrow morning to sew with her—I think she knows.

And when the time comes, they simply stand at the threshold to watch us walk away. I am yet again surprised when we make it only a few meters away before they shut the door on our retreating forms. This feels like an exile in itself. I exhale, feeling a weight I didn't know was on me suddenly lifted. There is no sadness, at least not right now. All I can feel is relief.

The way I love my parents is twisted and gnarled, as is the way they love me, and I feel myself untangling it as our steps take us further and further away.

The temperature plummets as the sun moves across the sky, making me shiver. Halvar swears and removes his coat, wrapping it over the one I am already wearing. He adjusts his scarf that is already around my neck, but still seems displeased. He takes the trunk from me despite my protestations.

"Is this really all you have for the winter?"

"It's all we can afford," I shrug.

"The only seamstress worth a damn in the entire village and she couldn't get her daughter a decent coat," he mutters, shaking his head. "I'm sorry that we'll have to walk."

"My legs work, Halvar." I try to keep my tone light, but my teeth are chattering from both the cold and the anxiety.

He grunts. "Even so, I could have procured a horse."

I raise a brow. "You prefer to travel on foot?"

He chews the inside of his cheek. "I don't mind the distance."

We approach the tree line, tall and foreboding and as inviting as it was when I was a child. I've come close many times, but never dared further than this. I expect to feel different once we pass through it. I expect to feel changed, perhaps like I have taken a risk or broken some rule. But instead, I feel nothing. It's almost disappointing.

In the initial few feet, I can see signs of my father's work; stumps are as plentiful as the trees, and some of the still-standing trees are missing limbs. An ax is stuck to the side of one. But as we get further into the woods, the trees overtake the surroundings and it's clear none of them this far out have been touched by human hands. Their limbs look healthier, covered in a dense amount of leaves. Despite the winter's chill, their foliage remains mostly intact. There are fallen leaves littering the ground, but not enough to thin the covering above. The trees are massive, so tightly packed with leaves at their peak that the ground inside is not as snowy as it is in the village. There is only a thin layer dusting the ground, as the flakes collect on the highest branches of the tallest trees. The wind still whips through, though, and I shiver as it wraps around me. Despite the chill, I am amazed at how lovely it is, how otherworldly, and I almost feel sorry that my village will never see it.

My head is tilted back, mouth open in awe, when Halvar's voice breaks my gaze. "You're not afraid?"

I scoff. "These woods have fascinated me all my life. Far too long to frighten me now."

"Well," he says, "they're your home now."

"It's not as dangerous as they say? I can explore them?"

"I should probably go with you but yes, you can explore them."

I feel satisfied to have been right about something. The presence of danger, at least to the extent the elders claimed, never sat right with me. I can't even bring myself to be mad over having been lied to now that I have escaped it. I am glad to have done this for Halvar's sake alone but if I can find selfish comfort in this arrangement, I will.

Something about living in the woods feels so correct, like a piece of me has finally slipped into place. I was never meant for the sheltered walls of my parents' home. The foliage embraces us, shielding me from what was and welcoming me into what is. Slowly, the anxiety starts to leave me and I feel the color of our surroundings filling up what has emptied inside me.

"Don't you remember," I say, "how many times we were punished for coming too close to the tree line?"

He chuckles, a rueful smile on his face. "You mean when *you* would come too close, and you'd reprimand me for trying to pull you back?"

"That's a selective memory." I nudge my shoulder against his.

"You didn't try to dissuade me until we were going to get caught. That makes you an accomplice."

He rolls his eyes but there's a lightness to it. "I guess I just knew there was nothing to be afraid of."

After a few quiet steps, Halvar clears his throat and drags his feet a bit. I slow, watching him as he struggles to come out with whatever it is he has to say.

"I didn't get a chance to thank you," he says, "for what you've done for me. You didn't—I don't—"

I shake my head, watching my feet as we step over and around fallen branches and roots. "You don't have to thank me."

He comes to a complete stop, then. I stop a few paces ahead of him, craning my neck back at him. In the dimming light, he is haloed by what few rays make it through the leaves. A hand comes up to scratch at his scar, then rubs the back of his neck.

"I do," he murmurs, so low I can barely make it out. "I do have to."

I watch him for another moment, taking in how cowed he looks with his boots toeing the ground and his hands searching for purpose at his sides.

"You're welcome, Halvar."

He shakes off his stupor and picks up his pace once more. "We should hurry if we want to be inside by nightfall."

We've been walking long enough for it to become clear that Halvar lied to my father. His home is far deeper into the woods than he let on. The growing distance between the village and us soothes me. The day has been more than overwhelming, but perhaps this breadth will give me room to step back and reexamine how I feel.

The sun has nearly sunk below the horizon by the time we are in sight of Halvar's home. He called it a cabin, he called it modest. This is something else he seems to have lied about. His home is anything but modest, and much nicer than a cabin. It stands two stories tall, larger than most of the buildings in Kliransk. There are so many windows, I feel my heart might burst. It appears as though I'll have a full view of the surrounding trees from any room in the house.

"Did you build this?" I breathe.

"Over some time, yes."

That, in part, explains why his hands are so rough.

The trees thin out as we get closer until they disperse completely to reveal a clearing around the house. It's a wide expanse, with enough space to run. To play. To do anything I could possibly want to do. When we approach the remaining few trees, Halvar loops an arm around me. The air crackles as we breach the clearing, and it feels like lightning crackling across my skin. I draw in a gasp, which makes Halvar tighten his arm around me.

"What was that?"

His jaw clenches. "The necessary precautions."

It takes a minute to cross the clearing, which thrills me. We climb the few steps up to the house, and Halvar drops his arm to throw open the front door. He sets the trunk down beside it before turning to me.

He shuffles on his feet for a moment without speaking, then says, "Humor me."

"What do you mean?"

Before I can say another word, before I realize what he means, he sweeps me off my feet and carries me over the threshold. He sets me back on my feet just as quickly, then retrieves our things. He makes for the stairs, turning to me once more. His cheeks are furiously red.

"I would have regretted it if I didn't do that," is all he says.

He hurries up the stairs while I stand at the bottom, stunned at both the physical contact and the stairs. I haven't been in a building with stairs besides the church. These are by Halvar's hand, and I marvel at his apparent skill. He never showed any interest in things of this sort as a child, so this must be a talent he came to hone in his adulthood. I follow him up, my hand gliding along the railing.

"Halvar?" I call. There are multiple doors and I do not know which one he means me to follow him into.

"Here," his gruff voice calls. I follow the sound to the end of the hall and find myself in a bedroom, what is now our bedroom I suppose. He has the trunk open on the bed as he unpacks it, taking out my clothes to examine them one at a time. There is a wardrobe along the far wall that is also thrown open, half-full of his own clothes. He looks at one of my frayed dresses, then at me. "This is what you have to wear?"

I shrug. They are all clothes he's seen before; our poverty is nothing for me to be ashamed of. "Funds were tight, and I didn't grow much. It still fits."

He shakes his head. "I can order you new clothes tomorrow. You need a new coat, too. Do you have shoes?" I lift a leg, gesturing to the ones I am wearing. He *tsks* and goes to write down a list. "You would think your mother would have at least made sure you were dressed for the cold."

"I don't need anything new—"

"Emelie." He interrupts. "You were wearing these clothes when we were children. It's high time you had something new. Just, here." He hands me the paper. "Write down your measurements and any colors you like."

"You can afford all of this?" I say, hesitant to write down what I want. It's the first time I've been asked what I want in a very long time.

He nods. "Don't worry about all that. Just finish writing all that by tomorrow so I can take it to a merchant when they pass through."

"Merchants come into the woods?"

"A lot happens in the woods that Kliransk doesn't know about."

This is certainly news to me. I hope that I will find out in time, and so I don't bother to ask him any more questions. I shed both of the coats and his scarf, discarding them on the bed as well. I am working my hair out of its styling when I notice him looking me over.

"What?"

He averts his gaze, eyes snapping back to my face. "Nothing. I just wish you'd worn this dress instead of the other one."

I smile and continue undoing my hair. I had wound a few strands into some braided mess that my fingers struggle to undo. Halvar is still unpacking my things, stopping to look at every book. When he pulls out the *Creatura*, he stiffens.

"You still have this?" He asks. At my proud nod, he shakes his head, stacking all of the books atop one another. "I'm putting these in my study."

We were both wandering the library the day I found the *Creatura*. He didn't stop me from trying to smuggle it, choosing instead to block me from view with his body. I can still see the way he glanced at me over his shoulder, disapproval warring with his smile.

"You shouldn't take that," he whispered.

"And you should move a little to your left," I murmured back.

I come back to the present and catch him watching me again, giving me that same considering stare. Our eyes meet with six years worth of unspoken words. But before I can collect myself to say the right thing, the most pressing, he leaves without another word to the study.

I take the initiative of clearing the bed. When I try to shove the trunk beneath it, I hear something clatter, and I crouch to see what I've hit. My breath catches when I find knives of varying sizes lined up, covering the entire underside of the bed. There are some small enough for wood carvings, for making precise incisions, while some are the length of my forearm. Longer, even. I remove the trunk and try to place them how they were, standing as Halvar reenters the room. He raises a brow.

"I was looking for somewhere to store this," I say, gesturing to the case.

He takes it, and my pile of clothes, to the wardrobe. It stands nearly as tall as him, and much wider. He fits the trunk beneath all of the clothes and folds my things into a neat pile on top of it. He shoves his clothes to one end before shutting the door.

"When we get you new clothes, I'm burning those."

I snort. "They're not that bad."

He levels his gaze to me, unamused. "I can pick out the dress you were wearing when I last saw you, when we were fifteen. It hardly fit you then. You shouldn't have to wear it now."

I'm surprised he remembers that. Our last meeting was nothing special, and yet I've turned it over in my head hundreds of times. What I could have said or done differently had I known it would be the last time, until now.

He was so boyish back then, lanky with a toothy grin. In the same fashion as last night, he had snuck through my window just after sundown for a few bites of dinner. His father wasn't home, he claimed, and he needed to eat. I snuck him bites of meat and bread, and we tossed plans for the following day back and forth. I wanted to read in the meadow. He wanted to go fishing. Ultimately, we agreed on my idea. We didn't bother saying goodbye, not when we expected to say hello again so soon.

I force myself back into the present moment, realizing he is waiting on my response.

"You have excellent memory," I say.

"You just have far too few outfits."

"Are you an expert on the finer things now? Where did you pick up such a taste for fashion?" I expect him to return my smile, but he remains stern.

"There's no reason for you to spend a winter cold."

"Isn't that what winter is about?"

"Emelie."

I expect to find annoyance in his eyes and am once again surprised to see concern. He doesn't have to tell me so, I can see his worry for me crystal clear. I never considered my lack of possessions to be a particularly bad thing, but rather another burden to bear over having been born in Kliransk. Perhaps I considered it too narrowly.

"Thank you," I say quietly. "For the clothes."

"Consider it a wedding present," he says, something near playfulness re-entering his tone.

"Romantic," I say. *Speaking of romance...* "Halvar?"

"Hmm?"

I know what married couples are supposed to do, the church wouldn't let us forget it once I started to come of age. My virtue feels like something I am delicately holding in my hand to offer to him, and I would rather not be caught off guard should he decide to bring it up himself. I have no idea how to proceed should he say yes; I have no idea what his expectations are, if he even has any. With a start, I realize I don't know what *my* expectations are, either. But I imagine that's something we're meant to figure out together.

"Aren't we supposed to….?" I can't bring myself to say it, so instead I gesture towards the bed.

"Fuck?"

"Consummate."

His exhale fills the room, and the tender ease between us once again deflates. I can't decode if he's embarrassed, annoyed, or something else entirely. I realized this would be an awkward conversation, yet I am still surprised when he says, "I can't. I'm sorry."

"But they won't consider us married until we do."

"You want to go by what the church says?"

I don't particularly want to do anything that the church says. Still, his rejection stings. His next words do a little in the way of soothing me, though not by much.

"You are my wife in the eyes of the law, and that is what I follow. Not the church and their rules."

"Oh. Alright, then."

The sun is fully down by now, night having overtaken the day. Neither of us has eaten dinner, but the excitement of the day has squandered any semblance of hunger. I take my nightgown to the washroom and fix myself for bed. I pretend that I'm not putting more effort into my nightly appearance than usual. On an average night, I wouldn't comb my hair and plait it neatly. Nor would I pinch my cheeks to give myself a light flush.

When I reemerge, Halvar is standing stiffly against the edge of the bed.

"This is the only bed," he says. "I can sleep on the floor, or downstairs, if you'd prefer."

I want to burst into laughter, or maybe into flame. "We're married, are we not? We can share a bed." I pull back the covers and climb in to show him it's alright.

He stares at me for a moment longer before stepping to the wardrobe. He discards his shoes next to it and removes his shirt only to chuck that inside as well. He's left in a thin undershirt and his pants, which don't look comfortable to sleep in, but he climbs into bed with them all the same.

He reaches to turn out the lantern set on a table on his side, and only regards me again to say, "You can leave that one on if you'd like. It doesn't bother me," gesturing to the lantern at my bedside. Then he goes silent, and from the sound of his even breathing I have to assume he has fallen asleep.

I lay beside him—my best friend who I thought I might have loved, who is now my husband—in silence as I stare at the ceiling. The events of the day wash over me, and I wish I could discuss them with him, the only person who could possibly understand. And yet he falls asleep with hardly a goodnight to me.

This is not how I pictured myself getting married.

CHAPTER FIVE

It's not quite morning when I wake up. The room is still shrouded in darkness, but Halvar is not lying beside me. The bed is still shaped to him, his absence weighing on the mattress. I run a hand over it to find that the sheets aren't quite cold yet. I sit up, shaking off the lingering grogginess. Moonlight filters in through the windows from between the trees, casting shadows along the floor. I draw myself out of bed, forgoing a candle to let the night guide my way.

My eyes adjust to the hallway as my bare feet pad across the floor. The wall to my left is empty of any decorations or personal touches. On my right is a row of doors with one large window in the middle. The door closest to the bedroom is the washroom, nothing intriguing there. When the door on the far end of the window doesn't give way, I have to presume that it is Halvar's study. I give up and stand by the window, getting a good look down at the earth below me. Snow has buried the clearing, and I watch as more flakes drift breezily down. I feel so very far above the ground, and the thought makes my stomach tingle.

Having given up on sleep, I decide to explore the rest of the house. The stairs creak as I descend them. I test my weight on each step, searching for spots that will keep quiet.

The expanse of the ground floor is vast. I pass through the

expected rooms; a landing, receiving room, dining room. They are all lavish and well-furnished, but don't look particularly lived in. Each room feels rather like a picturesque image of what a home *should* look like. I have to admire the kitchen, though. The one in my parents' home was out of date by many years, not just out of fashion but only passably functional. Halvar's is new and clean and so far out of my skill level. I steel myself for his disappointment once he realizes he has married someone who can barely cook more than the basics.

The kitchen window covers a quarter of one wall and spans from nearly floor to ceiling. I can see the leaves swaying in the gentle breeze. It's as dark out as it is eerie, and yet I feel called to it.

I crack open the back door and the cold doesn't register, not even when my bare feet hit the snow. The clearing expands before me, open and not quite uninviting. The land nearest the house is lined with dormant bushes and shrubs. If I were a gardener perhaps I would want to plant flowers once spring arrives.

Past there is untouched earth open to the sky and everything above. During the day, the sun must shine down on the house and offer slight reprieve from winter's chill. In the summers this would make a comfortable space to sit outside and read. The trees are further out, bordering the house and cutting off what little moonlight has filtered through the clouds. My eyes squint as I try to peer into the dark between the tree trunks. This forest feels alive, like it's breathing in time with me.

I don't realize that I've been walking towards the copse of trees until I am nearly there. I walk as if in a trance, my feet moving even as I think to myself that I should probably turn around. Surely, it wouldn't be so bad to stand amongst the trees for just a minute. The wind whispers to me the same as it did when I was a child, only now the whisper is directly in my ear, daring me to put out my hand.

Yes, this seems right. I flex my fingers, testing the air when a giggle bubbles up out of me. Halvar was right, this isn't dangerous. I could enter the trees and be swallowed whole and it wouldn't hurt. When I reach a hand out to touch the nearest trunk, I feel myself being pulled.

61

I am in the throat of the woods and I am going to be devoured. I want to let it happen—

I nearly scream when hands grasp me until I realize it is Halvar pulling me towards him. He turns me to face him, his hands on either of my shoulders. His face looks frantic and he has no shirt on, though his hair is dusted with snowflakes. He looks me over for injury and, finding none, begins to scold me.

"What are you *doing* out here?"

I shake my head to clear the fog in my mind. "I wanted to look around."

He looks behind me, into the trees I had been walking towards. "We need to get you inside."

Halvar ushers us into the receiving room, brushing flakes from my hair and wrapping me in a blanket that had been draped over the sofa. He looks me over, his brow creasing.

"You're soaked. We need to get you into warmer clothes. How long were you out there?"

"I woke up and you were gone," I say, "so I went looking."

"For me?"

"For anything."

He shakes his head and rubs his hands over my arms, furiously trying to warm me. I hardly even feel the cold, but the way my nightdress clings to my skin tells me I should be freezing. The way he is averting his eyes lets me know I am leaving little to the imagination.

"Let's go upstairs," he says.

"Were you sleeping down here?"

He frowns. "I wasn't sleeping down here. I wasn't sleeping at all." He does not elaborate further.

I try and fail to ignore the fact that he is without a shirt. His skin is tanner than it was, and he is mostly muscle. Still lean, but it's obvious that whatever his trade may be, it is hard work. There are scars peppering his skin that I hate to think are from his father. Angry red slash marks cover the right side of his chest and without thinking, I reach out to brush my fingertips against them.

He's surprised enough to let me, a hiss pulling between his teeth. The scar tissue is rough against my touch, healed but only just. A shiver rolls through him and he closes his eyes, taking a breath.

Then he catches my hand in a heartbreakingly gentle grip, slightly shaking his head. "We should go back to bed."

I let him lead me back upstairs to the bedroom. He sits me at the edge of the bed before rummaging in the wardrobe. Curses slip out when he doesn't find whatever he's looking for.

"Did you only bring one nightgown?"

"I only *have* one nightgown."

He sighs. "You'll catch your death wearing that one. Here, wear this instead." He tosses me one of his shirts before turning his back. "I won't look."

My drowsiness makes it hard to hold my tongue, so it slips out of me to say, "It wouldn't kill you if you did."

His exhale fills the room. "It's for both of our sakes, Emelie."

"That's specific."

"You need to get some rest."

"That's even more specific."

I slip into the shirt. It pools at my hips and falls across my legs, but nowhere near as long as the nightgown. I hear slow footsteps then feel the mattress sink with his weight beside me. He's quiet for another moment, wringing his hands together as he collects his thoughts.

"I ask that you please do not go exploring the woods without me, especially at night. If you want to go for walks, you can ask me. I won't tell you no."

Not about that, at least. That's a start. I nod, too tired to argue. I don't even know if I have an argument to make, he's probably right. In fact, he's definitely right.

"If I asked you why," I say, "would you tell me?"

He considers, then says, "Not tonight."

It's a far cry from the outright refusal of my parents. But it's still not a direct answer, and that gets under my skin just as much. If not tonight, tomorrow then.

He pushes off the bed and makes for the doorway. "Get some sleep, Emelie."

"Where are you going?"

He pauses. "Can't sleep."

"You could try."

"This is me trying." And then he leaves, his figure slowly dissipating into the shadows as he gets further away from me.

If God is real, I feel as though He cursed me with the gift of curiosity and then set me amongst people who hate answering questions.

I sleep well into the morning. Sunlight fights its way through the thin curtains and leaves me with the distinct feeling that the absence of them would leave the room violently bright. Testing my theory, I nudge one aside and allow light to flood the room. The height of the sun leads me to believe that it is far later than I would have ever been allowed to sleep in at home. And yet there is no scolding to be had. It is the first morning in years I haven't been woken up to do some manner of chores, to make breakfast, or at least make the bed. But Halvar's side of the blanket is neatly folded, my side the only disturbance.

I have no measure of his expectations, if he has any at all, so I want to be prepared for anything.

Halvar is nowhere to be found. Not in the sitting room where he brought me last night. Not in the kitchen or the dining room. But something else catches my eye. There is a plate of warm food on the dining table alongside a note that simply reads *Gone to merchant. Stay inside.* The snow is falling more fiercely outside which makes that command easy enough to follow. I turn the note over in my hands; there is no list of chores, nothing he needs me to do before he returns. I want to feel relieved but instead, I feel useless. On the bright side, he made me breakfast.

I sit at the head of the table feeling ladylike in a hollow sort of way, like a child playing pretend. I eat the eggs and smoked meat at my leisure, unhurried by the need to sew or pray or some other activity divorced from me. I experienced several firsts yesterday, but the most surprising of these was Halvar asking me what I want.

Want feels like such a loaded word. I never had to think of such things, or rather never was given an opportunity to. My meals were planned, my career decided once my mother pursued hers, my religion inherited, even my clothes out of the question. Maybe I felt resentful of the fact that we couldn't afford new clothes, but I didn't *need* them. What have I done to earn such an expense? Saved Halvar's skin, maybe, but that was a dual effort.

Beyond discovering what exactly it is that I want, there is also the reigning question of what I *like* to do. I like to read, I know that much. I enjoy making conversation but rarely find someone to return the exchange. I think I like to sing; I'm not very good at it, but my only experience is during mass, so perhaps I am just not suited to singing those songs. Maybe I can dance, or paint. Instead of this nothingness, this lounging around the house, I can try to learn. For now, I think I will read.

Halvar left a few books scattered throughout the ground floor; there is a book on nearly every surface, some with marked pages. I pick up the one nearest me that rests on the bottom step of the stairs. Its cover is plain and unassuming, but from the first page I open to I know I have stumbled across something forbidden.

The text across the top of the page reads *Predators*, which are familiar enough, but the index lists creatures I have never heard of. Even the *Creatura* has not covered many of these beasts. I settle on the couch and dive into the book. I have to stop every few pages to sound out the unfamiliar words; the pages cover creatures from many cultures, things we'd never see in these woods.

I am halfway through the book when the door bangs open and Halvar returns with an armful of bags. I rush to stand and help him, and though he insists he can manage, I take a few from him.

"Please tell me this isn't all for me," I groan.

"Most of it."

"Halvar, this really isn't necessary."

He sighs, kicking the door shut behind him. Then he nods

to the sofa, gesturing for me to sit. He sets the bags on the floor and takes a seat across from me. He looks tired, but rested enough for someone who claimed they couldn't sleep. I don't even want to think about reminding him of last night.

"Why do you say things like that?" He asks.

"Because it's not necessary. I can make do with the clothes I already have, and I don't feel comfortable with you spending this much money on me."

He levels a stare at me with one eyebrow raised. "You've grown since we were fifteen. And back then you had already been wearing these same dresses for several years."

"But it's an expense."

"One I can afford."

"How?"

"I work, and am compensated well. I don't have many expenses beyond running this house. Clothes are hardly what I'd consider lavish."

"What is it you do? For work, I mean."

He hesitates, and his eyes roam over my face. I wonder what he sees there that makes him say with some caution, "I'm a contract hunter."

That explains his hands. It also explains the knives. The thought occurs that I should probably fear for his safety, but since he seems to have made a comfortable living doing this, he must be worth his ware.

His voice breaks through my thoughts. "Does this bother you?"

"Why would it bother me?"

Wordlessly, he shrugs. Before, he would match my thoughts word for word. He was talkative and electric and loud. Surely, people can change as they move from adolescence to adulthood, as I certainly have, but this seems rather radical. Perhaps being alone with his father for however long he had left to live did more damage than I originally thought.

Though I have to admit that I am quieter than I used to be. Or rather, I speak but my words so often go unanswered that I choose to let them hang in the air like crystallized rain. In this case, I choose to leave it be.

I take a few of the bags to bring upstairs, ignoring Halvar's protests that he can do it himself. I make some quip about how I have to make myself useful as the Lady, and he doesn't protest. I think he might even snort.

"You can leave them by the dresser—"

"Halvar." I look at him square on, daring him to meet my gaze. Though it flickers, he does. "Let me organize it. They're my clothes, are they not?"

He swallows, and I watch his Adam's apple bob in his throat. Then he nods, swiftly turning and walking out of the room to leave me to my work. I do just that, getting right to folding and hanging and organizing. The dresser is clearly suited for one person. I end up having to stack many of our clothes on top of each other. His clothes are not varied by much. It's all long-sleeved shirts within the same gloomy color palette, and a few pairs of pants fit for the elements. There is another long knife tucked behind some of his coats, which I shove aside to make room for my *three* new pairs of boots. They are all fine things, far too much in my opinion, but the lady doth protest too much, it seems.

The boots are durable for the cold, but I should be able to make use of them once the snow melts, too. The dresses are unlike anything my mother could have made me, far nicer than anything the local merchants would bring around. There are several greens, my favorite shade among them. I only wrote green on the paper, but his memory seems to be intact.

The coats are the real prize. He bought me enough coats that I can rotate through a new one every day of the week. There are the standard pieces that I can wear with anything, black and gray, nothing spectacular though still better quality than anything I've ever owned. He managed to find a green one, which I hold close for an extra moment. Maybe he's irrevocably changed by what happened to him over the past few years, but he remembers my favorite color.

The last one I hold up has to be my favorite, even more so than the last. This one is a deep green, matching the forest that surrounds us. When held up to the light, threads of blood-red silk weave patterns across the bodice. It is shorter than the rest, perhaps not the best for a storm, but it is clearly of a finer make. It is absolutely the last thing I would have asked for, and yet I am enamored.

By the time I am finished reorganizing our things, it's about time for dinner. I make my way to the kitchen, drawn by the smell of fresh garlic and basil. Halvar is cooking. It's such an unfamiliar sight, the man of the house getting his hands covered in oil and vegetables. If I were a pious woman I would be scandalized. I'd shove him into a chair and urge him to not lift another finger. I would be the caretaker. But I am not pious, and even less a woman, so instead I stand beside him and begin chopping the vegetables he hasn't gotten to yet. He gives me one quizzical look before leaving me to my slicing.

"What are we making?"

"*We*," he says, the word coming out like a foreign language off his tongue, "are making a stew." His hands are working seasoning onto a piece of raw meat—deer, if I am correct—and I have a hard time not watching him out of the corner of my eye. There is a newness to watching this man get his hands dirty, something that will be in service not only to him but to me as well. He is preparing to serve me, and though I am helping, though it is not all that different from when I would help my mother in her kitchen, he did not ask me to help. I offered, and he simply did not refuse me.

I suppose it should feel like we are a team. Like we are partners.

"You're still left-handed, I see." He points with an elbow towards the knife I am using to cut, which is indeed gripped in my left hand.

I hadn't even realized I had slipped back into the old habit. "I suppose I still am," I say.

"Thought they would have worked that out of your system," he says.

A nasty habit my mother had tried to break. I naturally deferred to writing with my left hand from the moment I started my lessons. It only served as fuel for the elders to use against me, something seen as demonic. It was yet another facet of me that was wrong in the eyes of the church. I can still feel the wrist slaps I would receive if I accidentally used my left for anything important. Despite this, I never fully broke the habit, my nature proving too overcoming to curb.

"Without the presence of consequence, it appears that I've descended into sin once again." I start to laugh, but stop once I realize he's glaring at me.

"Consequence," he says slowly. "You shouldn't poke fun at such a thing."

I focus on my cutting. "It was just a few wrist slaps."

"That doesn't make it right," he says through his teeth.

I've struck a nerve. I know Halvar was beaten as a child, we spent so much time together that it would be impossible for me to not notice the bruises and the way he would sometimes limp into lessons. He's right, I shouldn't make light of it.

"I'm sorry, Halvar," I say. Again, a shiver goes through him when I say his name, just like in the town square. And again, I choose to ignore it.

"You have nothing to be sorry for," he says, setting the meat onto a small fire. He takes the vegetables from me and throws them in as well.

I expect him to continue speaking, but he doesn't. Met with his ongoing silence, I move to set the table. The dishes are modest, though nicer than anything in my parents' home. The dining table feels larger with both of us here and I anticipate a quiet night. More lack of speaking, more silence to sit with my thoughts.

To my surprise, Halvar serves the food once it has finished cooking. He urges me to sit and be waited on, which I do with little hesitation. He fixes me a bowl filled to the brim, then sets some bread and wine on either side of it. It's probably the heftiest meal I've had with the exception of holiday feasts. It all seems like too much.

"Halvar, I can't eat all of this."

"You'll catch your death in this cold if you don't," he insists.

He sits not across from me but rather to my right, at the head of the table. I feel disoriented to not be looking at him head-on, but relieved of the pressure of watching him not look at me.

The ritual of eating buffers the awkwardness of having to make conversation. The food is delicious, better than many of the meals I've had in recent memory. I didn't know food *could* taste this good, as opposed to just being something to nourish the body. For a beat, I feel sorry; it's not that my mother is a bad cook, but rather the type to focus on what will keep us alive and not on the verge of starvation. Just several steps away from falling over the edge.

"What did you do today?" I ask, no longer able to stand the lingering silence.

"Saw the merchant, bought your clothes. Contracted some work. I will be away later in the week to see to my business."

"How long does your business keep you away?" The thought of being alone in this house with nothing to do is almost worse than having him here with nothing to do.

"With the way I work, overnight. Maybe a day and a half. If I run into trouble, three days. No more than that."

"That's a long time for me to be alone."

He pauses with the spoon in midair. "Do you not want to be alone? You could sleep in the village—"

"I don't particularly want to see my parents again," I interrupt. "Not yet."

He nods like he understands, and I suppose he does. He witnessed my tenuous relationship with them, he knows how difficult it can be to love the parent who doesn't like you. In fact, he probably knows better than I ever will.

"The house is secure," he says. "You won't be in any danger as long as you stay inside."

"I still need something to do."

"What is it you need to do?"

"Keep busy. Maintain the house, entertain myself, the like."

He cocks an eyebrow. "It's not your job to maintain the house; leave that to me. If it's entertainment you want, tell me what it is you wish to do."

"You don't expect me to...to clean? To do chores?"

He sits back in his chair, his plate empty. He lifts his wine glass, looking to drain that as well. "I did all of that before you came here, I didn't marry you to make you my maid."

No, he married me to save both of us from an angry mob. I must remind myself of that.

His voice centers me in the moment, grounds me away from the insecurity lingering at the back of my mind. "What have you kept yourself busy with all these years? When your mother wasn't holding you hostage as her assistant, that is."

I feel very small when I admit the truth to him. "I don't know. I haven't had time to think about it."

He narrows his eyes. "Your mother worked you that hard?"

"Something like that."

"You know, I remember how much you hated sewing, even back then." He takes a long sip of his wine.

"I still do." I shrug. "Have you no expectations for me as lady of the house?"

He snorts. "There are no such formalities out here. I expect nothing from you. There is no duty for you to fulfill."

I should feel relieved, like a weight lifted. Instead, I feel heavier. Now that I don't know the burden I carry, it feels all the more weighted.

He catches my downturned look, and I can see that he wants to ask me about it, but I speak before he can. "I like to read. You put my books in your study, can I go in there?"

He takes another long sip before answering. "I'll unlock it tomorrow. It's not suitable right now." In other words, it's probably a mess.

It's an effort to completely clear my plate. As I continue eating a dull ache starts to build in my stomach. I give up with more than a few bites left over. I've already eaten more than I am used to, and likely more than I deserve.

I insist on at least clearing the table and washing the dishes. He starts to refuse, but where he is stubborn, I am stronger-willed. We're evenly matched in that sense. If only the rest of the playing field would level itself out.

After the dining room has been cleaned out, I follow Halvar into the receiving room. He smokes a pipe, politely offering me a hit, which I decline. He laughs softly at my refusal, and I give him a look.

He puts a hand up. "No one will punish you if you do."

"Oh, you think that's what I'm worried about?" It's my turn to laugh. "No, I've never smoked, and I think you'll laugh even harder to watch me try." I would look like a child holding such an adult thing, and I'd rather not be made a fool.

"Your loss," he says, taking another hit. The tobacco seems to put him at ease, his shoulders relax as he sinks into the sofa.

"You said something yesterday, when we arrived," I start. "We passed through the clearing and I…I *felt* something. You said it was one of the precautions. What did you mean?"

"I was wondering if you'd caught that." He leans back in his seat and lets out a deep exhale. "If I tell you, you have to know it's the sort of thing you'd have to keep to yourself."

I level a stare at him. "I can keep secrets."

"I don't like asking you to lie," he says. When I am unmoved, he continues. "It's just nothing the church would approve of. Though I know that means little to you. It's nothing of note, truly. Call it a protection barrier. Harnessed from the energy naturally generated by our earth."

"That sounds like…" *Magic.* Though I don't dare utter the word out loud. I don't wish to be laughed at. "That sounds complicated."

He shakes his head. "Simple enough to acquire, for the right price."

"From what such sellers?"

That gives him pause. "Would you trust me if I said it would be safer for you to not know?"

"I do trust you." I pull my legs up underneath me, curiosity pouring out of me. "But the way you say that only makes me want to know more." Hesitation keeps him quiet, and that brings out a boldness in me. I lean forward on the sofa towards him, resting on my hands so our faces are level. "Do you know something?"

He sighs, acquiescing to my questions at last. "I've heard whispers among my circles. Such things are not unheard of."

I spring up onto my knees, looking for my part too eager and intense, but I cannot bring myself to stop. "Explain."

He chuckles, watching me as I loom over him, the way my hair hangs down toward his face. He reaches up like he's going to take a strand between his fingers, but stops himself. "I've seen some with an affinity for it. For magic. Many are healers. I've sought a few out for the injuries I retain while hunting."

"And it worked? It was real magic?" The idea brings a flutter to my stomach.

"I'm no expert. But I haven't had wounds heal as well as when I sought their help. Why do you want to know about it?"

I ponder this and come up short. I can't think of a way to explain it that would make him understand that I just feel *drawn* to the thought of it. Not in the alluring way the forest calls to me, but a gentle thrumming beneath my skin. The same force that compelled me to steal the *Creatura*, to research the monsters the church condemned as sacrilege.

"I think...I think I just want to learn about it."

He considers this. "I can find you some books to read up on it. But know that if you invest yourself in such things, you might as well be putting a target on your back in the eyes of the church."

"It's not like I was wanted there anyway." The words slip out before I realize, and I see the way Halvar glowers at them. "Don't give me that look. You know it's true."

"It being true doesn't make it more pleasant of a reminder," he says, but the bite in his words is weak and fades away just as quickly.

He sets down his pipe.

"You seem content enough with the thought," I say. "What with all of the strange books you leave lying about."

He stiffens. "You read my books?"

I lean across the sofa, my elbow nearly brushing his knee before he moves it away, to grab the book from earlier. "This one. About monsters."

He takes it from me, studies it. "I should have known this would be of interest to you."

"Yes, you should have." I think of the memory of us in the library, and it stings a little to know that he might not remember the same things I do.

He must see the hurt look on my face, but instead of offering a balm with his words he simply says, "I have to wake early if I want to catch the merchant before I start my hunt. We should get some sleep."

I can feel Halvar's hesitation as we get ready for bed. Tension is written in every line of his body. I don't want him to feel forced to lay with me, but I also don't want him to feel distant from me either. My wants and his needs feel delicately balanced, swaying this way and that.

He lies next to me with no protest, though his back is still facing me. I turn out my lantern and sink into the blankets. I am uncertain as to what he feels for me; his constant swinging between hot and cold throws off any understanding I grow to have. He is not the boy he was, but that doesn't mean I can't grow to love the man he is. I stuff away the thought that I never stopped—the thought is far too much to unpack, and I don't have the capacity for it. Not with all of these stones in my pockets.

I suppose as I have been given the space to get to know myself, I can get to know my husband, too. I hold onto the hope that I will have regained my best friend in turn.

CHAPTER SIX

I surprise myself by waking before Halvar. There is a modest amount of sunlight creeping its way into the room, and I watch as it moves across the exposed expanse of Halvar's skin. It dances across his forearms and lights one side of his face. He almost looks peaceful, if not for the tension still written into every line of his body.

I want to touch him. I want to run careless fingers across the planes of his face, trace the indents of his scar, feel the stubble of the beard that is growing in. I want to know how changed the feel of his skin is from six years ago. I want to, and I almost do, but stop myself when he rolls towards me and rouses.

For a brief, wonderful moment, we just watch each other. His brown eyes turn golden in the growing light, and there is a softness to them as he comes to. Wonder shows openly on his face as he studies me, like he's surprised to see me laying beside him. A hand comes up to scrub his face, brushing off the remnants of sleep. One blink, then two. Still, neither one of us dares to look away.

The moment ends as abruptly as it starts as he lurches out of bed with no more than a murmured, "Good morning." He hurries to the wardrobe and makes a show of drawing out clothes for the day. Though he is doing his best to appear preoccupied, I know he can feel my eyes boring into him.

He doesn't look at me when he says, "You're up early."

"I'm awake at a perfectly normal time."

"You weren't yesterday."

"I didn't mean to sleep in. I won't make a habit of it." I sit up and let the blanket fall across my lap. I am wearing one of my new nightgowns, and it's painfully modest, but I like the way the fabric glides like butter against my skin. The movement draws his eye, bringing heat to his cheeks.

"You could sleep the whole damn day away and I wouldn't mind." He continues shuffling through the wardrobe until he unearths a large knapsack.

"Is that for your work?" I ask, crawling to the edge of the bed.

"Yes," he says gruffly. "After I get your books, I'll need to scope the terrain tonight and tomorrow. Then I'll hunt the following day. Will you be able to fend for yourself for a few days?"

"You won't be coming home tonight or tomorrow?"

"I will, but too late for you to wait up." He kneels to reach for the knives under the bed. It puts us at eye level, and I hold his stare. "Do you mind?"

"Do *you*?"

He shakes his head. "Is every sentence you say always a question?"

I pause, feigning like I am considering it. "Not always. You could answer my questions, though. That might limit them."

"I'll keep that in mind."

"How late will you be? I can wait for you to eat dinner." I stand on my knees at the edge of our bed, beside his bag as he packs it.

He keeps his eyes on his work. "If you want to eat dinner in the middle of the night, that's your choice."

"I want to eat dinner with you."

His head snaps up, though he still has to crane his neck down to look me in the eye. There's a strange look on his face. If I didn't know better, I would call it hope. In all likelihood, it's probably some manner of awe at my stubbornness.

"I mean it," I say, "I can prepare something so you don't have to."

He studies me for another moment, then nods. "Alright. I should be home well after the sun goes down. Evening, likely."

"That's fine," I say, following him as he heads out of the room. He makes a straight line for the stairs but before he can get down the hall, I stop him. "Halvar. Can I have my books from the study?"

He looks between the door and me before handing me his bag. "I need to get the key. Take this downstairs. Be careful, it's heavy."

It *is* heavy, and it takes all of my concentration to not tumble down the stairs. I leave the bag on the landing before going to the kitchen to wait. I can hear his footsteps pacing above me in the study, then down the stairs.

"Is this enough for three days?" He asks, coming in with a tall stack.

It's enough for a week. I nod enthusiastically, and he sets them on the dining table in front of me.

"Breakfast?" He offers.

He prepares a serving of eggs and splits it between two plates. I eat with a ferocity that surprises both of us. He watches me for a few moments, then says, "It's not going to run away from you, Emelie."

I don't respond, focusing instead on getting the food down.

His voice is low when he speaks next. "How often were you hungry?"

At my continued silence, my mouth too full to bother, he shakes his head and places his half-eaten plate in front of me. I stare at it, then at him, then back at the plate. I want to feign protest and tell him I can't possibly eat his breakfast, but the indelible truth is that I *am* still hungry. I take the plate, nodding my thanks to Halvar.

He broods, his gaze hard-set as it bores into the table. Part of me wishes he would ask me more about it, the years I spent hungry, but a larger part is too embarrassed to even think about that. He may have witnessed the first fifteen years of it, but it puts into perspective just what a failure I am to have spent several more years in my parents' home, hungry and alone.

That wasn't quite right, though. I wasn't hungry.

I was *famished*.

My mother kept me fed but not quite full. Some of it was due to funds, having to ration what we could afford to get us through the years. But did other mothers ask their children if they felt satisfied? I have to wonder if I were a better daughter, if I kept my head down and prayed loud enough for her to hear, would I have received more than my fair share?

Even worse, was I *ever* given my fair share?

Halvar stands abruptly, pushing his chair back as he does. He goes into the kitchen and packs himself a small bundle of food before coming back to stand at the head of the table. He isn't quite looking at me so much as through me.

"The kitchen is yours whenever you want lunch. You should eat something before I come back."

I nod, getting up to see him off. As he walks into the trees, he turns around only once to wave. And then I am alone again.

Though Halvar doesn't expect me to, I clean as much of the house as is available to me. It's not like I have anything better to do. The windows take the most time but I can't be bothered by how difficult they are to scrub when the view is so breathtaking.

In the daylight, I can more easily see the network of leaves and branches webbing through each other, though the upper floor is still not high enough to see above them. The sun creeps in between gaps to cast a modest amount of sunlight, reflecting off of the snow-covered ground. It's unlike any view in Kliransk, and although we are technically just outside of their bounds, it feels like a completely different world.

The thought of returning sets off anxiety in me. Halvar's house may be large and a lonely kind of crowded, but I could see it becoming a home. That sense of possibility is something I lost far too early with my parents. The fact that I can already distance myself from it—from *them*—feels like a revelation.

I can't see a near future where I would willingly go back. I think I would rather be dragged.

Halvar seems to have done well for himself without help from the village. I wonder how many years he's spent alone out here. If he'd found peace, and if my arrival has disrupted that peace.

The thought creeps in that I've forced myself further into Halvar's life than he ever intended to have me. I wouldn't blame him if he resented me. I bring so little to this marriage besides my burdens. For me, this arrangement has brought escape and an opportunity to perhaps make something of myself. It has bought me back lost time with my best friend. Though to Halvar, he now has to be a provider while dodging my questions and my stares, pretending he doesn't see the way I want him.

He claims to have missed me, but perhaps our versions of longing don't match up. Maybe I am not even his best friend, not the way he is mine.

Hunger pangs low in my stomach once the afternoon sun begins to sink. It is a dull ache, the familiar kind that never truly goes away. Despite this, I can't bring myself to prepare something that is just for me. Yet the thought of making a meal for two is even more nauseating. I may have overestimated myself with my promise to prepare dinner for Halvar to come home to. I don't know what ingredients we have, I don't even know what he prefers to eat. After a quick rummage through the cabinets and the icebox, I settle on roasted chicken and vegetables. That seems like something a man would want at the end of a long work day.

Halvar arrives home as the food finishes cooking. I hear the front door, and footsteps approach as he lets out a tired groan. He dumps his bag on the floor next to the dining table and just stands, watching me.

"This is a sight," he says.

"A welcome one, I hope," I say, forcing an airiness into my voice. If he insists on being the moon, dark and brooding, I can be the stars that light his sky.

He is covered in dirt, leaving tracks on the floors I cleaned not even a few hours ago. It wasn't in jest when he said he doesn't need a maid. His face looks as though he's been unconsciously rubbing it, there are streaks of muck across his cheeks, tangling in his beard. He looks, for lack of a better word, a mess.

"You need a bath," I say.

"And you need to eat," he says, taking plates and silverware out. He sets the table. I bark out a protest—I was *just* about to do that before he walked in—which he ignores.

We are once again sitting at odds, him at the head of the table and me to the left of him. I tell myself it doesn't bother me. We both dig into our food, the lack of conversation not an obligation as long as our mouths are full.

Yet my cursed tongue forces me to speak. "How was your tracking?"

He takes his time answering, chewing on the answer as he does his food. His voice is soft when he says, "It's been a long while since I've been able to talk about my day with someone."

"You don't have to."

He shakes his head. "It's just strange." He takes a drink of wine, letting our words hang in the air for a moment. "To answer your question, it was fine. My work is difficult, not for everyone, but it's what I'm good at. And I make good money. I can't complain."

"You're really not afraid?"

"It's hard to scare me these days."

I think of the panic-stricken look on his face last night when he found me at the tree line's edge, the heaving breaths he had to take to steel himself. My carelessness did that to him.

The mental image is too much, so I push it deep into the recesses of myself where I can't picture the fear in his eyes. Instead, I force myself to be present, here at his table.

"What is it that you hunt?"

"Whatever I'm paid to."

"Such as?"

He ticks off creatures on his fingers. "Bears, foxes, wolves—"

"What kind of wolves?" I ask, leaning over the table. "Are there shifter wolves out here?"

He fixes me with a look. "For having read so much on them, one would think you would know the answer to that."

"I like asking questions."

"I've noticed." He looks down at my plate, gesturing to it. "Not hungry?"

I follow his eye. I've eaten what I would consider enough. There is still a healthy amount left on the plate but my gut turns over at the thought of having any more. Defeated, I shake my head. He takes our plates and goes to wash them. I don't get up to help, draining my wine glass instead. This at least, I still have room for.

I watch Halvar's back as he washes. There is this weird push and pull between us as we play at domesticity. I cook, he cleans. I wonder if this is how our lives are setting up to be, if this is too soon to make assumptions.

He dries his hands with a washcloth as he re-enters the dining room. It is discarded on the table as he bends towards his bag, pulling several books from inside.

"As requested," he says, presenting them to me. They are all clothbound and look to be older than us both. The mere sight of them is scandalous.

I open one and flip through the pages, my eyes glossing over the illustrations and scratchy writing. "This looks like something the church would absolutely denounce."

"Does that make it less appealing to you?"

I grin up at him. "It makes it *exactly* what I was looking for."

A smile ghosts over his mouth, but quickly fades. "I need a bath, as you said."

I pull myself away from my new books long enough to say, "I'll be here."

He leaves me to my reading, every step up the stairs creaking with his weight. The house feels somehow fuller with him here. I didn't like being alone.

Much of the language in the books is familiar yet foreign. I recognize some words as things the elders have indeed denounced in their sermons: *occult, blasphemy, witch*. But the narrative in these books is different. It tells of people young and old, those who answer the call of Mother Nature and use their innate skills to help people. The magic itself seems varied; some are born with gifts beyond average measure, some have an affinity for the scholarly aspect of it and teach themselves spells and rituals. Some simply purchase potions and crystals and make do with what others have made. I linger on this page, turning over the different types of witches. I have to force down the rush this brings me. I am determined to learn as much as I can before exciting myself over something that may not even be possible.

I don't read for long, tired from playing homemaker all day. Our bed welcomes me in. I can hear Halvar washing in the next room, and the sound of it, the normalcy of it all, lulls me towards sleep. I think my half-conscious self feels him get into bed some minutes later, I think he mutters a goodnight.

He's gone before I wake up, his side of the bed cold and made. The sun is not high yet and although it's still early, I feel so out of sorts to not be forced out of bed. Halvar said I could sleep all day if I wanted and the idea is more than tempting. But then the thoughts push in, and I need to move.

There is a note on the kitchen table letting me know I should expect him home earlier than last night. He's left me breakfast—some bites of smoked meat and eggs. There is even a scoop of oatmeal, which I toss out on sight.

The day passes slower than yesterday without the urge to clean the entire house from top to bottom. Instead, I burn through the pile of books set out for me. Without the pressure of sewing or praying or making dinner, I find myself reading slower, finding pleasure in the pages. I try to burn through one of the books on magic, but its text is complex and leaves my head spinning. I set it aside in favor of a novel to get my head on straight. There is no need to rush through half of a book before dinner, and so I don't. If no one else will keep me company, I have these characters to confide in. I let it comfort me.

I prepare a similar dinner to yesterday, crossing my fingers that Halvar won't mind the lack of variety. I suppose that since he's prepared the same breakfast every morning, he won't mind. He doesn't arrive home until after I've set the table and started on my own plate. He is once again covered in dirt, looking exhausted. I hold in my questions, not wanting to pester him while he is clearly on the fringes of sleep. I can't imagine how he does this for a living when he looks so drained after two days.

I don't complain when he goes straight to bed after washing up. I follow but stay awake to read some more, trying my luck again with the magic text. I don't know if it is the lamplight that causes him to stir, or the stress of his work, but he continues to toss and turn as I read. At one point, his foot nudges my leg, and I might've been happy for the point of contact had he not flinched away immediately. I read only one more chapter before shutting the light off. He doesn't settle right away, and I fall under before he fully does.

I don't bother getting up the next morning. I sleep until I physically can't keep my eyes closed anymore, and then I finish the book from the night before with my head nestled in the pillows. Talk of spells and potions and protection mingle in my head. It is utterly fascinating the way all things forbidden to me always have been. Something deep in my gut tingles. Excitement, the sort one feels when met with the familiar after time spent apart.

I only get up to feed myself, or rather grab the breakfast I know Halvar has left out for me. Eating breakfast in bed with a book in my hand feels like it should be a sin rather than a safe haven. It feels too good to not.

Since I am not expecting Halvar until God knows when, I don't bother with a fancy dinner. I prepare a serving of stew for myself, some thrown-together mix of vegetables and broth, and tear up a loaf of bread to go with it. This too, I eat in bed with another book. It proves more difficult than the eggs were, but I manage to not make a mess of myself.

I don't even realize I've fallen asleep while reading until the front door bangs open, drawing me awake. I lurch up to my elbows and wait, listening. Halvar's slow footsteps approach, and once he makes it up the stairs I gasp softly. If he was dirty before, he's filthy now. The pervading night makes it hard for me to see him, but I can tell he's covered in dirt and...I hope that's not blood. He stops outside the washroom, turning to me when he hears my little noise of surprise.

"Why are you awake?"

"You woke me," I say, turning on the lantern. I was right, he is covered in blood. I scramble out of bed, hoping it's not his. For the first time in a long time, I *pray* it's not his. "What happened to you?" I grip his arm, looking him over for a wound.

His eyes are downturned with exhaustion, he's too tired to pull away from my touch. His voice is gravel when he says, "I earned my coin."

He doesn't fight me when I pull him into the bathroom and sit him on the edge of the bathtub. I grab a washcloth and run the hot water as I begin the work of cleaning him off. He'll have to do the grunt of the bathing himself, but I hate to see him covered in blood and not know whose it is. I wipe his face, his neck, his hands. Most of the blood is fresh and wipes away at the touch of the water, but some of it has crusted, leaving me to scrub and hope I'm not irritating his skin. He doesn't say anything, just watches me work.

He lets me touch him and move him and maneuver him until, at last, I realize none of the blood is coming from an open wound. He has fresh scratches and marks that look like they will bruise, but nothing life-threatening. I leave him to finish washing himself, getting back into bed.

I am already half asleep when he comes to bed, and as I drift off the last thing I hear is his muttered, "Thank you."

The morning light draws me awake before him once again. Today he sleeps like the dead, his chest rising and falling in a slow and even rhythm. Even the brightening daylight isn't enough to rouse him. He looks to be at peace. The burdens of hunting, of killer shifter wolves on the loose, and an unwanted wife have all fallen away. He gets to sleep in. And I let him.

He finally rises when the sun is reaching its peak. I hadn't bothered to get up, too preoccupied with watching over him. When he fixes his eyes on me, though, I pretend like I've been reading. If he can tell I'm lying, he doesn't call my bluff.

"It's late," he says by way of good morning.

"It was a late night, too."

He shakes himself fully awake and dresses for the day. He's dressed more relaxed than in the past two days which gives me the small hope that he is going to stay at home today. I don't know why I want that to happen, since that's just more time for us to be forced together. Another reminder of the marriage he doesn't want.

He starts tidying up the room, making his side of the bed and unpacking his knapsack. He fiddles with the wardrobe and replaces his knives in their hiding spot beneath the bed. Then he comes around and picks up the books I have littered at my bedside.

"Are you finished with these?"

"Yes," I say, sitting up on my knees. "Can I get more?"

He looks towards his study door, considers for a moment, then nods. "Follow me."

He pulls a key from his pocket and unlocks the study door, and my eyes are immediately drawn to the far wall. It is covered wall to wall with books. They are stacked haphazardly atop one another, shoved into any available space. I can feel myself gaping and cannot bring myself to feel ashamed.

"You really do like to read," I breathe out.

"Did you think me illiterate?"

I walk to the shelf, running my hands along the spines. "I didn't think you liked it *this* much. I seem to remember you forsaking the books during our lessons, if you bothered to show up at all." A teasing grin is on my face, but it falls when I see the serious look on Halvar's face.

"My father would pull me out of school whenever he felt I…" He considers his words. "…misbehaved."

I cringe, regretting having opened my mouth. I remember how frequently he skipped lessons, how often the beatings must have been.

It chills me to my core and the only thing I can think to do is hold him, but I suppress the urge. He won't even look at me, let alone touch me.

"I'm so sorry, Halvar," I whisper. "I wish you would have told me."

It's a pitiful excuse. I knew enough to draw my own conclusions. My suspicions should have been enough so he wouldn't have had to bare this truth to me at first light.

"It wasn't your burden to bear," is all he says. He clears his throat. "You can read any book you like. If you don't find anything to your satisfaction, I can see about buying more."

My face heats. "This should do, thank you."

Halvar looms over a desk topped with a messy stack of papers and quills. There are a few drawers that I assume are locked due to the keyhole on each one. Behind the desk are a pair of French doors that look out onto a ledge. Along the far wall is a fireplace with two armchairs sitting in front of it. A rug underscores them, drawing the space closer in. It looks comfortable, the only room in the house besides the bedroom that appears lived in.

"Am I allowed in here?" I ask. "Besides now, I mean. When you're not here."

He continues to shuffle papers on the desk. His mouth is a straight line. I think he is about to refuse me before he says, "You should check with me first. But the house is yours as much as it is mine."

"I don't know about that," I mutter.

A pause. "Why's that?"

Despite how awkward it has been between us, honesty feels better for the moment. "I feel like a guest."

He surprises me with the concern that takes over his face. "This is your home now. I'm doing what I can to make you comfortable here. As my wife." He tacks the last bit on like a forgotten detail. As though it's not the important part.

"What about as your friend? You do remember when we were friends, don't you? Those times feel very far away now. I felt closer to you when you moved away, when all I had were the memories."

At last, he puts the papers down. He watches me for one long, eternal moment, his eyes going dark. He takes slow, purposeful steps towards me, his footsteps loud as the wood boards creak beneath him. His gaze never leaves mine. I am backed into the wall, into the shelf behind me. He doesn't stop until he is directly in front of me. I wouldn't have to reach very far to graze his arm. I am reminded of how much taller he is by how far I have to crane my neck back to hold his stare.

"Is this closer?"

My breath catches. "You never touch me. Even in bed, we sleep beside each other and never touch." I watch the muscles in his jaw clench, I watch his shoulders tense with frustration. I can see the irritation building in him. Just like I do with everyone else, I've pushed him too far—

"I know I'm not worthy of you."

Well, then. That was the last thing I expected him to say.

He continues, "I feel guilty for having shackled you to me; I know it was likely not the life you had envisioned for yourself. I don't want you to feel forced to do anything you don't want to do."

There is a heartbreaking honesty on his face. And yet, the admission, what he said...I cannot help it when the laughter bubbles out of me. I would double over in laughter were he not directly in front of me. He watches me for a moment, befuddled.

I manage to collect myself and stand straight, forcing myself to look into his eyes. "You're not very good at reading people, are you?"

His face gives everything away; the confusion furthers, he looks as though I've told him I can sprout wings and take flight.

"You really couldn't tell that I've wanted you ever since we were children?" I blurt out.

His eyes widen only a fraction, and a blush spreads across his cheeks. He sputters for a moment before speaking again. "You don't mean that."

"I do. All I've ever wanted was to be around you. I was

heartbroken when you left. That's why...that's why I was so overcome when I saw you in the town square that day. If one of us should feel guilty, it is I who's shackled us together." I blush at the admission, at my blunt honesty. But he deserves that much from me.

I prepare for a number of responses, but he once again surprises me with, "How do you want me to touch you?"

I swallow. I watch him notice. "As a husband would."

The weight of his stare bores down on me, but rather than making me feel small, I feel seen. And I see him, too. I see the wheels turning in his head, see him deciding how to proceed. He was never this cautious when we were young, and it pains me to think his father turned him into what he is now. But despite the hesitation, the high walls of protection he keeps around himself, I still want him. It takes everything in me to not draw his mouth to mine. I want him to touch me first. We have not kissed since our wedding day; I know he knows this.

He does not make me wait long. His hand finds my hip, roughly pulling me close. His other hand trails down my arm before grasping my hand. His touch is not gentle, but then again I am not fragile.

When his lips find mine, it is not the same featherlight touch that proclaimed us married. No, instead his mouth crashes against mine, and his beard scratches against my skin in a way that is not at all unpleasant. His teeth take my bottom lip, tongue tracing across it. I let out a breathy groan, which only makes him kiss me harder. Then, as suddenly as he started, he pulls away. He stares at me once again.

"Is that how you meant, is that husbandly enough for you?"

My body already feels his absence, the lack of his weight against me. It is heavier than not bearing it. "More. I want more."

His fingers grip my chin, and he leans in so that he is speaking directly against my mouth. His breath tickles my skin. "I liked you too, you know."

"I didn't know," I exhale. "You hid it well."

"Then know it now." And then he kisses me again and I forget I was ever upset to begin with.

CHAPTER SEVEN

My back is pressed against the bookshelf. Halvar takes one arm and snakes it behind me to cushion me. His other hand moves from grasping mine to catching my knee so he can hook my legs around his waist. He brings me face to face with him, easier to kiss. I wind one hand into his hair, the other cradles his head. Kissing him is nothing like how I imagined. I imagined it the way a schoolgirl with a crush would imagine their first kiss. I imagined butterflies and stolen smiles and laughter. This is nothing like that.

I am the forbidden woods outside set aflame.

He maneuvers us over to his desk, discarding the papers scattered atop it so he can sit with me straddling his legs. The position hikes up my nightgown to my hips so that his pants are the only layer between us. This alone feels salacious. Sex has always been a taboo, something to be discussed only in hushed tones behind closed doors. It was reserved for a specific group of people, an exclusive club that I was not a member of. Until now.

I move on instinct, rocking my hips against his. I have no idea what I'm doing, but it can't be wrong judging by the low, throaty moan he lets out. Excitement and nervousness rush through me in equal measure. I drink in his cedar and sage scent like the finest wine I was never allowed to have. I just want him closer. He puts one hand on my lower back, using light pressure to urge me to continue moving against him. His other hand crawls up my thigh, and I feel sparks where his calloused hands touch my bare skin.

"Wait," he says, pulling away after a moment. His breaths come in heavy pants and he has a lust-glazed look in his eyes. "We should slow down," he says.

"Why," I say, trying to pull him in again. "Isn't this what married couples do?"

"It is," he says, peppering me with kisses in between words. "And I want to. But we should probably talk first."

I frown, shifting so we are at eye level. "I've wanted to talk to you, I've *tried* to talk to you."

"I know," he says, his face shadowed. "These things aren't easy for me."

"They used to be."

"That was before."

I bite my lip, insecurity forcing its way to the surface. I don't want to ask, but I do. "Is it me? Is it my fault?"

His brow furrows. "Why the hell would you think that?"

To my absolute embarrassment, my throat thickens and I feel myself tearing up. His face melts in a way I haven't seen in years. He almost looks like his childhood self. It's heartbreaking.

"Please don't cry," he says, cupping my face. All rational thought leaves my head as his thumb strokes my cheekbone. "I don't know what to do when people cry."

A hiccup slips out and my humiliation furthers. But now that I've started being honest I can't seem to stop. "I thought you didn't want me."

"Don't ever think that." He looks angry, but I'm coming to realize that he slips into such a mood not *at* me, but *for* me.

I watch as he carefully weighs what he wants to say, so as to not upset me. I feel ridiculous for exposing so much of my insecurity to him, but I was beginning to drive myself crazy by keeping it all to myself. I am so full of holding everyone else's emotions that I can't carry my own anymore.

"Life got exponentially harder once we left Kliransk. My father moved us out to another village on the other side of the woods. He took us through the most complicated route, doubling back so I wouldn't be able to find my way back to Kliransk on my own. I cried the entire way there."

My heart clenches at that. I put a hand on his arm and am relieved when he doesn't pull away. If anything he leans into the touch.

"You saw what he was like back then. But once we were settled in a new village, away from anyone who already knew us, he could be as cruel as he pleased without repercussion. My father had a specific vision for my future, and it was one that I had to earn in his eyes. I learned to keep my mouth shut when I didn't need to speak, learned to keep to myself. I was wrong to think it would keep him from striking me." He clears his throat, and I see it bob as he tries to continue. This must be hard for him. I ache to make it better. "Touching is hard. I flinch. I don't know if you've noticed that."

Horrified, I look down at how much of us is touching. I start to pull myself off of his lap, but he keeps me in place with a hand.

"How is this alright?" I ask.

"I had to try. It's the surprise that gets to me. I thought that if I initiated it, it would make it easier. To know what's coming."

I resist the urge to pull my hands onto my lap, away from him. "And did it?"

He takes a shuddering breath before answering. "A little."

Touch was never something I second-guessed with him when we were younger. Children don't put things into consideration that way. And with him being my best friend, I always assumed it was fine. I see now that I was wrong, I have been wrong this entire time.

"Your father really hurt you," I whisper, not wanting to make it real by voicing it aloud.

He nods. "My burdens are inherited from him alone. Let's leave it at that."

There is no relief in this revelation, but still, I sag against him.

It is a small comfort to know I haven't ruined everything. Gently, he brings my mouth to his again. His kiss is softer, like he's searching for something. I try to put whatever he's looking for into my kiss.

By all accounts, this feels right. Us back by each other's side after so many years forced apart feels right. Being open with each other feels right. The way he's touching me, hands exploring like I am brand new and not ruined, feels absolutely right. He's got a hand tangled in my hair, fingers twining through my waves softened from sleep, the other roving over my body. I still have the nightgown on, but I might as well be wearing nothing for all he can get his hands on.

I've never been touched like this. I didn't think I would ever be *allowed* to be touched like this. I push down the small voice that whispers that we are doing something wrong, that I am wrong for wanting him this way.

He palms my breast through the nightgown and I groan into his mouth. I can feel his calluses scraping, and I'm jealous of the fabric for feeling it rather than my bare skin. I can't reach as much of him given my position, but I run my hands across his broad shoulders, down his chest, lower. My fingers make it just below the waistline of his pants before he gives pause again.

He pulls away just enough to speak. "I can't," he starts. "I can't in good conscience do this. Not until I talk to you."

"We've been talking," I say, running fingers into his hair.

He shivers, but continues. "I have to tell you something."

That makes me pause as well. "You can."

He bites the inside of his cheek, avoiding my gaze once more. "My father, in his eyes, had reason to beat me. It's not an excuse, and it never made it okay. But he believed it to be."

I nod slowly. "Alright."

This time, he levels a look at me. "It wasn't okay what your parents did, either. Your parents, our teachers, the elders...none of that was okay."

Some buried instinct in me wants to defend my parents. I forgot I had that part of me caged, and now I tug on its leash to make it behave. In truth, I don't want to disagree with him.

"I know my father had a reputation for challenging the elders. He didn't agree with most of their teachings, and everyone knows he let them have a piece of his mind." His hands tighten on my hips. "But in his mind, he thought he was doing right by them. He thought he was protecting Kliransk."

"Protecting them from what?"

He's looking anywhere that isn't my face. "It doesn't go back very far. But—" He takes a steadying breath, and I feel his entire body tensing beneath me. "Shifter blood runs in my veins."

Well.

I don't react. I wait for him to continue to add at least a little bit of context.

"My father was a shifter," he says.

Oh. My body jolts at the news and I think he expects me to scramble away from him because he completely lets me go. But I don't. I stay sitting on his lap, the information processing at a glacial pace.

"Are you a—"

"No," he says quickly, sitting up taller. "Please don't think that of me."

This is the most afraid I have seen him, perhaps ever. I try to school my face to something neutral and inoffensive, but I can't fight off the hurt I feel. There being secrets between us widens the already existing distance. I feel as if I've been standing on the opposite side of a cavern from him, screaming his name where he couldn't even hear me.

"You're angry," he says, not a question.

I shake my head. "Not angry. Hurt."

I don't know if I have a right to be upset with him at all. What good would it do to demand to know why he never told me? I am smarter than that. In fact, I *know* why he never told me. And if his father would have given him hell for doing so, then I'm glad he kept his secret.

All of the pieces start to fall into place. I no longer feel silly for asking about magic last night. That explains why he didn't look surprised, why he didn't look at me like I was being ridiculous. Given his lineage, he's definitely seen stranger things. Is the existence of shifters not magic in itself? Halvar's very birth is magical, in its own way.

One truth rings in my head, clearer than anything else. I am not afraid of him. I wouldn't be even if he was one. I feel it all the way down to my bones that despite his bloodline, there is still no chance it was him who murdered Abel. I know him too well to believe the worst of him.

"How are you not one?" I ask. Slowly, I put my arms around him again, attempting to convey that it's okay. That I am not afraid.

He stiffens again, and places one hand over mine. Slowly, he says, "That's where the beatings come in."

Oh. *Oh.*

"His blood runs in me, therefore shifter blood runs in me. It doesn't make itself known until puberty, and so when I started to show signs, he quite literally...beat the instinct out of me."

Nausea rocks through me. "God, Halvar, I'm so sorry."

He shakes his head. "Don't pity me. It makes it easier if you don't."

"Is that—" I say slowly. "Is that why you left?"

He shakes his head. "No. We might have had to leave anyway. Maybe not then, maybe not ever, but it was the elders who pushed us out when they did."

It both comforts and infuriates me that this could have been avoided had the elders not gotten involved. A different kind of rage ignites in me, devoid of the anger that roiled every time I got angry with my parents. This feeling is colder, less forgiving. They took everything from Halvar, and in doing so left me with no choice but to rot in my parents' home. I am not the victim here, but that does nothing to lessen the sting.

To make matters worse, there is Halvar's pain to reckon with now. I want to protect him from someone who is no longer living.

Having received context for his scars is a balm to my ire the same way salt is a balm to a blister. It only relieves the not knowing. I don't know what to do with all this anger.

The past few days feel so incredibly different now. The villagers' severe reactions to Halvar's return don't make any more sense than they did before, but they don't make any *less* sense, either.

"Did they know?" I ask. "Did the villagers know about your father?"

"No. At least, not with any certainty. Even in his human form, you could tell there was something off about him. They thought he was strange. Maybe possessed. But they couldn't have known."

"Did—"

"Is this an interrogation?" His voice is gentle, and there is the ghost of a smile on his face.

"I shouldn't pester you, I'm sorry." I hook my hands behind his neck, grounding myself in this moment with him.

He touches his forehead to mine and sighs. "I love it when you pester me," he says.

I can't help it when I break out in a smile. All of those times I thought I was frustrating him and pushing him to a breaking point... I have never been more glad to be wrong.

He runs a thumb across my wrist. "I was afraid to tell you. About all of this. I thought you would run back to Kliransk."

"I'm not going anywhere," I say. "I just got you back."

He tips his head down, and damn if he isn't *smiling*. "You don't know what it does to me to hear you say that."

"You could show me."

That sparks something in his eyes, and then we're lost in each other again. We are no longer two tired children of Kliransk, separated by time and circumstance and an uncrossable expanse of trees. Instead, we are chest to chest, hip to hip. His mouth is on mine and his hands are clutching me like I'll slip away from him if he's not careful. I press against him, trying to convey that I meant what I said; I'm not going anywhere.

We don't go much further than kissing and running our hands over what exposed skin we can reach. I don't push him, and he doesn't pull me.

From where his lips are against my neck, he says, "I need time. To get used to this, I mean. I need some time."

"We have all the time," I exhale. "Take what you need."

I can't imagine it any other way. If anything, it is a privilege to wait for him. To be ready, or to maybe never be ready. Either would be fine with me.

"I also," he says, lips trailing my collarbone, "don't want to rush this. I've had a long time to think about how I want you, Emelie. I have no intention of taking you like a thief in the night."

Delicious warmth runs through me, the forest fire not yet quenched. He has to know what this is doing to me. He has to feel the way the goosebumps rise across my skin.

His face settles in the crook of my neck, and then we're just hugging. His arms are a sturdy force around my middle, and I wrap myself around him in turn. We stay like that for a long time, longer than I've ever hugged someone. Our breathing syncs up after a few moments, and I feel the tension leaving him as he deflates against me.

"I missed you," he says after a long silence.

The words break me and put me back together. "I missed you so much. You took part of me with you when you went away."

"Which piece was it," he whispers. "I need to know what to give back."

"As long as I have you, I don't want it back."

He presses a final affirming kiss to my lips before standing, taking me with him, and carrying me down the hallway.

"Don't think I've forgotten that you haven't eaten today." He hefts me more sturdily into his arms. "Breakfast first."

I am nothing short of delighted to be carried down the stairs. I cling to Halvar like he's the only buoy in open water. He brings us to the kitchen and deposits me at the dining table. I reluctantly remove myself from him, propping in a chair as directed. He sets about making us breakfast. It was already late morning when we awoke, and by now the early afternoon sunlight has made its way through the windows. He pays no mind to this and goes about cooking as he would at the break of dawn.

When he sets a full plate in front of me, I eye him with caution. "You prepare more food than I would conceive to eat."

"And yet you try your best to clear your plate at every meal," he counters.

"Because it's there."

He raises a brow as if to say, *Yes, exactly.* I don't want to give him the satisfaction of being right more than once in one day, so instead I dig in wordlessly.

"You're welcome," he quips, taking his usual seat at the head of the table. He takes a bite of his eggs. "Do you like the clothes?"

It's only been a few days, and I haven't had much opportunity to wear them, but the gesture alone would be enough for me to fall at his feet in gratitude. It helps tremendously that the clothes are beautiful and to my taste. "You remembered my favorite color."

"I remember more than I let on," he says, eyes on his plate.

"Such as?"

He thinks back for a moment, then says, "When you healed that shrike we found along the river. It fought you every step of the way, pecking at your fingers until they were bloody. I would've taken a rock to end the poor thing's pain. But not you. You kept at it until it could walk, and then until it could fly again. It's a miracle the thing was able to make it off the ground at all. I don't know of anyone else who would clean the blood off the very thing that was cutting them." A pause, one single held breath. "I always felt your goodness. But I got to witness it that day."

I sit back, stunned. I had nearly forgotten that moment. My fingers were bandaged for weeks; I couldn't hold a pencil without wincing. Still, I never complained. It only mattered to me that the bird lived. My pain was nothing when measured against the shrike's.

"I thought nothing of it," I say, my voice unsteady.

"It meant everything to me," he says. And it's then that I know he is not talking about the bird.

Slowly, I set my utensils down on the table, careful to not let them clatter. I yearn to comfort him, this beautiful man who was raised to hate what he is—what he could have become. But I don't know what the boundary is, what I should or shouldn't do to ease these worries he holds inside of him. All I've gathered from the way he averts his eyes is that he doesn't want to linger on the subject. Silence feels like a blade; I need noise to make things feel all right.

"Will you tell me more about those years we were apart?"

He looks relieved to have something else to talk about. "I left the new village after my father died three years ago. I hardly felt welcome there when he was alive, and even less so once he was gone. There was no chance I could find my way back to Kliransk on my own, and so the woods became my only option. I followed a merchant who had been passing through. He led me to his commune and he and his people took pity on me and supplied me with materials. I built my first home, then. A modest shack on the outskirts of their commune. I didn't want to get involved with anyone, but I didn't want to be alone. It was them that introduced me to life in the woods.

I already knew how to defend myself, and I had a few daggers to my name, but among their people were a few hunters. They were the protectors, of sorts. If this were a more formal situation, I suppose you could say I became an apprentice of theirs. It was hard to feign shock when they told me of the existence of shifters and other monsters, but I knew better than to be honest with anyone. That commune was generous with me, even kind at times. I could have asked them to bring me to Kliransk. But even then, I knew I didn't want to return until I had built a life worth leaving it for again."

"Why are you out here on your own, then?" Having that sort of community surrounding him sounds like a dream.

He shakes his head. "As much as I craved the company, I don't belong in large groups. I stayed with them until I turned twenty. Then I bought out their stock of supplies and found this unclaimed land. I had only been settled in here for a few months when I heard the alarm.

I followed it with no expectations—I didn't even realize it was coming from Kliransk until I arrived. And you know the rest."

By his word, he would have been eighteen when he was orphaned. Freshly adult, barely a man at that. My heart aches for the younger Halvar who had no one, not even his worthless father. Even in our youth, he was never small by any measure, but he lacked the muscle that covers him now. I wonder if the other village helped him to bulk up, or if that is a result of his bloodline. The thought of the scrawny boy I remember being left alone to fend for himself chills me. He should never have had to endure that.

Then again, I was never alone during those years, and yet I endured much of the same. The loneliness, the anger, the guilt.

"I often thought about what would happen to me if I had been exiled like you," I say. "I wouldn't have been able to build a life for myself the way you have. I'm empty of useful skills one needs to make their way in the world."

Halvar hums thoughtfully. "I think you may be mistaking my ruthlessness for usefulness. I've had to make choices I don't agree with to make it to this point."

"And yet you were able to be decisive." I raise a shoulder defeatedly. "I lack that."

"It's not a virtue," he says, his tone edging towards defensive. "There is cruelty to looking into another creature's eyes as you slay them and having to wonder if they are just like you. If they can think and feel the way you do. I've lost sleep over far less."

I swallow, feeling utterly selfish for thinking my presence had anything to do with his inability to sleep some nights. Like that first night he brought me here, how I felt called into the trees. It truly felt like I was being pulled, and I might have gone along with it had Halvar not found me in time. Fear fills my blood with what could have been. A chill goes through me. I know he knows what I'm thinking about; I can tell by the way quiet fury clouds his eyes.

"I meant it when I told you to stay inside. For the most part, the creatures roam about on their own terms. They won't bother you so long as you don't bother them. We are relatively safe out here, as long as we respect their space. But there are some…" His gaze darkens. "Some of them like to play games. But they also like to win."

"So that wasn't a dream," I whisper.

He shakes his head. "I promise to find you faster if it happens again." His eyes don't leave mine this time, and it feels more intimate than the moment we swore vows to each other. My heart catches in my throat.

I think he feels the moment, too, because the fury leaves him and his gaze softens to something akin to tenderness.

"Finish your breakfast," he urges, clearing his plate once more.

After we eat it is a battle to decide who cleans the table and washes the dishes. I insist that I should since he cooked, he insists that he should since he made the mess. In the end, we settle for me washing, him drying.

Wrist deep in water, I ask him, "When will you have to hunt again?"

"When someone contracts me. I make enough to get by so that I can turn down jobs."

"This last one," I say slowly, thinking of the cuts from when he stumbled in that night. I think of the blood. "How much did that earn you?"

He eyes me. "Enough for a new wardrobe for a new wife."

I flick water at him. He bumps me with his hip in return, nearly knocking me over. I want to throttle him for that, secretly hoping this play fighting could turn into something more. My hopes are only slightly dashed when he dries his hands and backs away from the sink.

"I have some work to do," he says. When my face falls, he holds up a hand. "Here, in the study. You can sit with me if you'd like. Though I can promise you it's far from interesting."

I accept the invitation and follow him upstairs. He goes straight to his desk and the mere sight of it—what we did together—makes my face heat. I busy myself with reorganizing his very messy shelves. I like the look of them that way, but I won't be able to sort between his medical textbooks and my novels in this clutter.

My mouth gets the better of me. "Why so many textbooks?"

He doesn't look up from his book when he says, "I function differently than you do. I need to understand how that is."

A hunter and a scholar. I start stacking his books on the top shelf, stretching on my toes in order to reach. I hear him laugh at my struggle.

"It's not my fault you were born freakishly large," I say. "These shelves are too tall, like you."

My *Creatura* is within reach, though, and so I take it and slump into one of the armchairs. It's comfortable enough, the cushion only worn down a little.

At the desk, Halvar leans back in his seat and I feel his gaze drift over to me. "Just so you know, that's not gospel. Some of it is pure fiction."

I look up at him, brow furrowed. "Such as?"

He pushes himself up and walks over to stand behind my chair. His eyes scan the pages for a moment, before pointing to a line.

"This here is wrong. See? Shifters *do* differ in appearance from common wolves. They're much larger. They do retain a faster speed and stronger set of muscles. And they're only as smart as any human is compared to one another. You can nurture intelligence."

I scoff, but he shakes his head.

"You know, I was worried you'd catch on to what I was if you read this," he says softly.

"I stole this years ago," I say. "I've read it so many times the passages might as well be as familiar as prayers. Nothing clued me in as to your inner nature."

That seems to satiate him enough for him to return to his work. When asked, he explains that he's noting what he saw on his hunt over the past few days. Comparing it to things he's read and seen on previous hunts. His devotion to his studies compels me to return to my own, and I am drawn back into the books on magic. We don't speak much as we are invested in our individual worlds, but the silence no longer makes me nervous. Rather, it is the comfortable silence we shared as often as we shared our words when we were children. It feels more intimate now, something to relish in and cherish.

I grow restless the longer I sit, however, and my eyes are drawn towards the French doors. Now that I am paying attention, I notice it is not just a ledge it opens onto, but a full balcony. One large enough for a chair.

"Can I sit out there?" I ask.

Halvar turns his head and raises a brow. "It's freezing out."

"Remind me how many coats you've bought me?"

He rolls his eyes, but there's no genuine annoyance in them. "Not even a week married and I've already spoiled you rotten."

I hop to my feet, already heading to the wardrobe. "I'm taking that as a yes."

I'm able to turn the balcony into something of a haven. Halvar's armchair fits perfectly in the space, leaving me room to swing my legs and prop my elbows on the banister overlooking the land. There is a slight breeze but only a light snowfall. With a coat and a blanket layered around me, the early winter's chill doesn't cut me to the bone. For the first time, the unforgiving cold is beautiful.

With this little bit of peace afforded to me, the day passes us by quicker than days previous. Hours fly with barely a notice. I light candles once the nighttime darkness starts creeping across the sky, resting them on the banister and on the threshold. My books have kept me enraptured, the information sticking to me like a second skin. The past few days of reading have done me well—things are starting to make sense.

After chapters upon chapters, I come across the information I was initially looking for. The reason I asked for these books in the first place.

On instinct, I whistle at Halvar to get his attention and he whips toward me immediately; a familiar call and response from our childhood. His eyes widen when they meet mine, surprised that he remembers or maybe surprised that I do. We smile at each other, the gesture furthering my feeling that things are back to a beautiful normal between us.

"I have a question."

"Of course you do."

I ignore his sarcasm. "What are the wards around this property?" I point to a passage on the page in front of me and he scoots his chair to sit beside mine, mindful of the candles.

He mutters to himself as he reads where I've designated, then he takes my finger and moves it several sentences downward. "Those. I paid for one spell and instructions on how to maintain it myself."

"So you can do magic?"

He shakes his head. "I make sure the existing magic stays alive. If the wards were to fail, I have backup supplies to try and salvage it, but it would take a real practitioner to fully get them up and working as they should."

Warding is a complicated, ancient process. There are conflicting sources as to where the practice came from, but most of the books call for salt, earth, and an initiating spell by a witch. The spell differs by region but is, in essence, a layer of protection against unwanted visitors. I was able to pass through Halvar's wards as his companion.

I am utterly fascinated, and my fingers itch to try it. I have to take a breath and remind myself that just because I *want* to do magic doesn't mean I *can* do magic.

Halvar prepares a simple dinner and sets a plate in front of me, which I eat without abandoning my reading. He eats in contented silence beside me on the balcony, occasionally answering what questions he can. His research is far more sterile and rooted in things more easily proven, but he treats my research with the same dignity. When I empty my plate and then another, he takes the dishes to wash without comment.

When the candles start to burn out and the moonlight grows fainter behind storm clouds, Halvar lightly urges me to bed. I bring the stack of books with me and set them beside the bed, my nose still buried in one of them. I fall asleep between sheets of paper. I think I stir when he removes the book from my chest, or I could be dreaming.

In the following days, I read with a vengeance whenever Halvar is away looking for work. I haven't asked to accompany him. I haven't wanted to do anything besides reading. That familiar feeling creeps back in, that hunger—no, that feeling of being famished.

The wrongness in me feels soothed by the way this too feels wrong. The church simultaneously proclaims magic to be false while also condemning those who practice it. It has never failed to confuse me as to how they can be against something they also claim doesn't exist.

If nothing else, I understand it in this way.

My research is a slow process to undertake, much like the progress between Halvar and I. I find that after so many years, though, I can continue to be patient. With him, with myself, with whatever is to come from this.

CHAPTER EIGHT

The dead of winter came for us, brutal and beautiful in equal measure. Weeks continued to pass, turning into a month and then some, and before we knew it the final month of the year was upon us. The sun began to set earlier, encasing nearly half the day in inescapable moonlight. We lived by candlelight more than anything else.

As we drew nearer to the end of the year, the snow fell heavier and so the netting of leaves above us was unable to maintain our small bubble beneath. It layered so thick that my boots sank in with every step.

We started going for walks, Halvar keeping me tucked tightly to his side as he showed me the paths that would be safest to explore unaccompanied. In due time, I began to recognize the woods as my home just as much as his. If the need were to arise, I could likely navigate the immediate surrounding area on my own. After sundown remained off-limits, though. It didn't help that I had lapsed into the habit of sleeping into the late morning.

When I wasn't expanding my small world into the forest, I was tearing through books; all of the books I had brought and then the ones he owned and even some bought since. I bettered my cooking and cleaning with varying degrees of success. Anything to busy myself whenever Halvar went on a hunt. More than once I woke to him stumbling in after dark covered in his or something else's blood. Usually the latter. I've developed something of a talent for bandaging wounds.

Our bodies drifted closer the longer we spent around one another. Halvar's guard continued to lower, becoming more comfortable with the occasional unguarded touch. I've done my best to not make him flinch, offering him plenty of space to deny me. But that hasn't stopped his kisses from becoming deeper, his roving more exploratory, the need pulsating under both our skins drawing us together in our own gravitational pull. Now, when we lay beside each other in bed, he doesn't fight the tossing and turning that brings him to my side, and I pretend to not be thrilled every time my returned touch calms him into a gentle sleep.

Then there are days like today, with Halvar pouring over his books and the growing pile of notes he keeps. I've tried skimming through them, though they make little sense to me. The balcony has become my domain, the deepening chill not enough to deter me from coming out here. Halvar's desk has been rotated away from the French doors to give me room to move about on my own, giving me a perfect view of him as he works.

I watch him through half-shut eyes, the overcast day casting long shadows through the window, thinking that I wouldn't be opposed to a nap.

"You're doing it again," he says without looking up.

"What?"

"Staring."

"I am doing no such thing." I twist in my chair so that I am leaning haphazardly on the armrest. "You aren't even looking at me, so how would you know?"

He flips forward a few pages in his book, jotting down notes with a ferocious hand. "It's the wolf vision," he says drily.

I cluck my tongue, feigning that I am unamused by his remarks. The truth is that he makes me laugh more than anyone I've ever known.

I don't hide it well, and he can read me just as well as the

106

medical text he's currently occupied by. His eyes speedily drift down the pages—eyes that I looked into every day and then lost, and then found once more idling at the back of a crowd. They are the same brown as the bark outside, and when he turns them to me I see the hunger and pain and grief and determination in them. There are other emotions swimming in them, too. Emotions I have yet to give a name to for fear of my own ego.

I feel it when he holds me, after the tension has faded from his body and he melts against me. I taste it when he kisses me like I am the last bit of oxygen on a dying planet. I think if I were as bold as he believes me to be, I could have given that look a name by now. It is cowardice that causes me to hold my tongue. I won't tell him I love him until I know how it will be received.

"Did you hear me, Emelie?"

I snap my head to him, not realizing that I've been fixated on a spot on the floor for the past few minutes. "I'm sorry, what did you say?"

He chuckles. "I asked if you wanted to go to a festival. The winter solstice is approaching fast."

"I've never been to a festival," I say distantly. I don't think church holidays count with their longer masses full of incense-scented songs and prayers. "What are they like?"

He considers, then shakes his head. "It's better you just see for yourself. I think you'll enjoy it."

"Then yes," I say, standing and giving myself a good stretch. "I'd like to go."

"Good," he says, watching me as I leave the study. "Wear the green dress."

A fortnight later I stand poised in the washroom mirror, feeling some sense of pressure to fix myself into an acceptable portrait of a wife. This is our first outing as a married couple, after all. Halvar isn't one for *friends*, per se, but he mentioned the possibility of seeing fellow hunters at the festival, as well as merchants he does business with and has become friendly with over the years. Despite his insistence that it's not important, I want to make a good impression.

The green dress fits me differently now. Where it used to hang off of me and hide the body I had barely grown into, now it clings to something akin to curves. I knew I had gained weight in the weeks passed; a month and change of eating not just for the sake of survival made sure of that. The mirror was something I had been avoiding up until now, too insecure to face how change looked on me. But now, wearing something familiar in this new body, I can see just how much I have filled in. My waist, once just a cage of bone and skin, has softened into a nice hourglass shape. The skirt falls tightly over my hips, accentuating the roundness that has slowly appeared.

I hadn't noticed until now just how sallow my skin had looked before arriving here. My cheeks have some color to them again; I'd even go as far as to call it a glow. The bags beneath my eyes have shrunk some, though a shadow still lingers there due to nights of irregular sleep. My hair, once dull and brittle, has thickened and regained its wavy texture. I appear to have finally grown into the so-called "woman's body" my mother had fussed about. The thought of my mother makes my heart twinge, just a bit. So I push thoughts of her away.

Much like a woman's vocation, I never wanted a woman's body, either. I never understood why I couldn't just be as I was, why I couldn't simply be *Emelie* before I was *woman*. But the feeling has always been too difficult to vocalize, and doesn't bother me enough to fight against. Even if I could put it into words, it's the exact sort of thing no one wanted to hear from me. Not the elders or my parents. Before, that's all there was. Maybe someday I can put it into words for Halvar, who I know would listen. For the time being, I can carry on as I always have—free-floating between expectations and my truth. It is enough right now, even if it might not always be.

Halvar pokes his head inside the washroom and when his eyes land on me, a look I can only describe as *wanting* washes over his face. I see the predator that his kill sees when he is on the hunt. I see the creature he could have become, all hungry mouth and scraping teeth and licking tongue. I want all of it.

"You listened," he says.

"As commanded," I quip. The look in his eyes makes me want to suggest arriving late to the festival—or even forsaking it altogether—but I know this matters to him. Even if he won't come out and say it in so many words, I know he wants to go, and he wants to bring me with him.

He comes to stand behind me in the mirror, and I note the slight hesitation before he places his hands on my hips and pulls my back against his chest. If anything, it warms my heart that he wants to touch me even as it roils against his instincts. When he manages to surpass his anxieties, it's like he can't get close enough.

"Are you ready for tonight?" He murmurs against my ear. I will never get over the low gravel in his voice. The soft purr against my skin.

"As ready as I'll ever be," I say.

I wear cream leggings beneath the dress and one of the nicer green coats bundled around me. Halvar insists on the scarf, which I don't fight against because it still smells like him. I do protest when he tries to insist on a second pair of socks within my boots. That feels too frivolous. He is dressed far more simply: a black shirt and pants beneath a black coat. His hair is tucked behind his ears, with strands curling over them. I adore having something to tangle my fingers in, and if it weren't for that he likely would have chopped it off by now. By all accounts, we clean up nicely.

This is to be my first night out in the woods.

Our walks have prepared me for this—I am to stay by his side, and if he happens to stray from me I am to wait near the fire until he comes to find me. In the event of some mishap, I know the safest route back to the house. I know to not look between the trees, to ignore any whispers or calls that I may hear. This, specifically, is what we are trying to avoid, thanks to my little *incident* on my first night here.

He must notice the look on my face because he says, "It's not going to happen again."

The part that scares me the most is that I almost want it to.

We are out the door shortly after, forsaking dinner on his assurance that there will be food at this festival. The last rays of sunset are forcing their way through, and it is only by this fleeting light that Halvar feels confident enough to not crush me against him the whole walk there. He does keep one of my hands held tightly in his, as much for his comfort as my own.

Our boots crunch loudly against the snow and I am grateful for Halvar's grip to keep me from hitting the ground. I slip a few times but he, ever my rock, catches me time and again. My free hand is shoved far into my coat pocket, fingertips already stinging from the cold. I don't want to give him the satisfaction of an *I told you so* moment because I refused to wear gloves.

"How do the people of Kliransk not know about these festivals?" From what he's told me, it doesn't seem like the sort of thing the church would approve of.

He snorts. "We're too far in for them to notice anything. But even so, they only see what they want to see."

As we near another clearing, I begin to hear music. It is a violent drumming sound, unlike anything I've ever heard. The sound reverberates against the trees, sinking beneath my skin. There is a fire in the distance and I can see people surrounding it. A *lot* of people.

"Where did all these people come from? Other villages?"

"These woods are a village, in their own way. People live scattered among the trees just as we do." He winks at me. "No Kliransk folk."

The fire is clearly the main attraction, which makes sense due to the still-dropping temperature. But the surrounding clearing is what catches my eye. There are vendors, more than I've ever seen in one place. They peddle wares like swathes of gorgeous fabrics I haven't even dreamed could be worn. There are food stands that smell like absolute heaven, drawing a grumble from my stomach. Another cart catches my eye as something glints, reflecting the firelight. Jewelry.

"I've never owned any jewelry," I murmur absently. I don't know if Halvar hears me or not. His eyes are fixed on the food, searching for something to eat.

As the sun sets, someone tosses more wood onto the fire, making it taller and brighter against the darkening sky. Once the moonlight takes over, the music rises to a frenzied beat, and dancers begin to prance around the fire. Some look trained, some look as if they're just called by the music. I watch them, jealousy roiling in my gut in competition with the hunger.

"What first?" Halvar asks right in my ear, startling me.

"You weren't lying when you said a lot happens out here that they don't know about." I look up at him and am entranced by the way the firelight dances against his skin. "I want to try everything."

He nods, eyes flitting briefly to my mouth. "Food is a good start."

Everything looks and smells amazing. There are spices I've yet to try and dishes that look better than anything we could prepare ourselves. Halvar exchanges pieces of silver for small plates from each stall and we end up with so much that our arms are lined with them. We take up residence on a log that's been overturned near the fire, but still some paces back from the rest of the crowd.

I get caught up watching the dancers once more, in awe of their beauty, before he nudges me to eat. The moment the first bite hits my tongue, I am unable to focus on anything besides the taste. The meat is tender and marinated in spices that warm me to my core, paired with rice stirred with vegetables and garnish. It's *delicious*. I dig in shamelessly, probably looking more feral than anything that lurks out in the woods.

Halvar's low laugh rumbles against me. "I take it it's good."

I don't have the capacity to respond in kind. I am too occupied with getting as much food in me as quickly as possible. I only pay partial attention to strangers greeting Halvar as they pass by. He responds with a simple nod and occasionally a grunted greeting in return. A few heads dip in my direction, some even curtsy. They all seem to revere Halvar, and, by extension, *me*. It's strange and a little uncomfortable considering I am half-buried in my dinner. I am a lady only in costume, not attitude.

The music slows then, going from something fierce and sharp-edged to something watery and flowing. I don't notice I'm swaying in my seat until my shoulder bumps his, my nearly empty plates all but forgotten.

"You should go dance," he says.

I want to laugh until I realize he's being serious. I shake my head vigorously. "I can't. Not like that."

"Why not?"

I gnaw on my bottom lip. "I've never done that before."

"Who's to stop you now?"

I gesture to the crowd of people as if the answer is obvious. He shrugs, unmoved by my excuses.

He picks at the sleeve of my coat. "I think you should go."

I wordlessly watch the dancers for a few more minutes. The moonlight has faded behind the clouds and the fire casts a warm orange glow across the two of us. All of the dancers look to be having the time of their lives. The size of the fire has melted the snow in its immediate vicinity and some people have taken their shoes off to stomp in the wet grass. Coats lay in a pile just aside from the revelry. Some are of fine make, nicer even than the ones I had been gifted; the others look to be handmade and worn down to the threading. Despite the variation, they all lie together in one big, faceless lump in the snow.

I decide to stand. I shake out my arms, my fingers still a little sore from the cold. After one more brief hesitation, I shuck off my coat as well and drop it in Halvar's lap. Then, upon further reflection, I pick it up and march over to the pile of coats and add mine to it. I want to be a part of this world as much as the rest of them. The boots, however, remain on.

I join the circle of dancers, shuffling a bit at first as I try to mimic what everyone else is doing. They're moving in unison, and the movements are slow enough that I can catch on quickly enough. The music is booming and gut-deep, but light in its own way. I feel heavy and clunky as I prance around, but soon I'm giggling too much to care. Everyone I make eye contact with smiles at me and beckons me to move closer into the circle. I'm still stumbling over the steps, but I am far from the only inexperienced one here. There is an older woman on the other side of the circle calling out directions. Her voice is jovial yet commanding. She sounds nurturing, she sounds kind. She sounds like a mother.

"Turn!" She calls out, demonstrating first before we all follow. She laughs, a full-bellied one that reaches through the fire to envelop me in a bone-deep warmth, warmer than even the flames.

As I turn, my eyes latch onto the log where we had been sitting. Halvar is watching me. He's leaning forward, one elbow propped to hold up his chin. He has this intensity on his face that I am becoming all too familiar with.

He is *pleased*.

This makes me want to keep dancing, and I let my arms raise above my head. This feels nothing like church and yet I am filled with a sense of worship. I even let a *whoop* slip out as the circle keeps moving. I lose sight of Halvar but I know he is watching and so I continue, letting a little bit of wildness out.

Following some musical cue I missed, everyone starts to link hands. I grasp the hands of those on either side of me. Beautiful, smiling girls with kind eyes and open faces. We begin a faster dance and I am thankful for the hands holding me, keeping me from tripping. We trot around and around the fire, our steps working a path into the grass. Part of me wishes I had taken off my shoes to feel the earth beneath my feet. I don't think even winter's cold could touch me right now.

The music ends and we all stop to applaud. Bubbling laughter spills out of me but when I look to where Halvar was sitting, I find the log empty. My eyes scan the crowd but the distance from the fire muddles everyone's face. I don't have time to keep looking. A girl rushes up to me and places a floral wreath on my head. She grasps my hands and babbles about how wonderful this all is.

I tear my eyes away from the dark to look at her, then touch a hand to my head. "How are these flowers alive?" I have to yell over the rush of voices, but she doesn't seem to mind.

"Magic!" She laughs and pulls me back into the revel, ignoring my questioning look.

I push down the urge to look for Halvar and throw myself into dancing. The song is much harder to keep up with this time and if it weren't for the encouragement of those around me, I might have sat down in embarrassment.

During a lull when we're not skipping, I quickly step aside and shuck off my boots and socks. When I reenter the circle, the music has reached a chaotic peak and it takes all of my focus to keep up. The sounds fill me up and break in waves against my bones. I am made of the music.

The same woman calls out more commands one after another, her words almost overlapping with how quickly she calls out steps. I have never jumped so high and made such wide arcs with my arms. I have never spun so fast that it felt like flying.

We all break into a run going around the fire, tossing debris in as we go to keep it burning. I squeal with delight as I toss loose twigs and dying leaves into the blaze. My skirt is getting weighed down with mud and my feet are absolutely coated, but I don't care.

As I arc around, I spot Halvar once again sitting on the log. His hands are shoved in his coat pockets and the same look of desire is still in his eyes. I smile at him so wide it feels like my face will split open. He offers a crooked one in return, one corner of his lip turned up. His gaze speaks of suggestion and promise, and I ache to hear it out.

All too soon or perhaps not soon enough, the song ends and I run out of the revel to Halvar. I skid to a stop just in front of him but his open arms grant permission for me to fling myself into them right away. His hands cage me in at once, stroking up and down my arms.

"Get your coat," he says, vigorously trying to warm me. He looks down at my bare feet and damp skirts and clicks his tongue. "You're going to get sick."

Sweat coats the back of my neck and runs down my back. I am still warm from the fire but I know it won't last long, so I go to retrieve my things. I don't do much to clean off the mud, telling myself I can wash it off once we're back home. When I get back to our spot, Halvar is standing expectantly, hands back in his pockets. His stance reveals something I hadn't noticed while he was sitting: a large length of rope is strapped to his side, rolled into a circle that spans nearly his entire thigh.

"What is that?"

He looks down at it casually, as if he forgot it was there. "It's a whip." He says this like it should be obvious, and maybe to him, it is. At my confusion, he continues, "One of the merchants. I thought it would be helpful for my work."

"It's got to be the length of you, at least."

"Good for me to not get close to my prey," he says simply. I suppose these things are normal for him, strategizing death to his advantage.

"Were you watching me?" I ask. I know he was but I want to hear it from him.

He nods, something playful entering his eyes. "Come," he says, nodding towards the trees. "I want to show you something."

I furrow my brow, remembering his warnings from earlier. But if he feels comfortable, I trust his instincts. We walk just out of sight of the festival, past all of the vendors and drunken crowds. We only just pass the clearing to enter the trees, barely a breath inside the untamed wilderness. He pulls me behind a tree and presses me to it, kissing me firmly as his hands come up to hold my arms.

"You were amazing," he says between kisses. "I couldn't take my eyes off of you."

My hands slide up his chest, both exploring him as well as stealing his warmth. The sweat has started to cool and the winter air is seeping in again. I can feel the desperation in his kiss and I wonder how long he's been waiting to do this. I kiss him without shame and without any pretense. There is no need for any of that between us, there never has been.

"Maybe I should dance around bonfires more often," I joke, biting his bottom lip.

He groans into my mouth, a smile forming. "You jest, but I love watching you fall back in love with your life."

Love. He used the word love. I want to point it out, but I don't. Instead, I offer myself to him to see if he takes it. He does.

His kisses grow needier, and his lips travel down my cheek and across my collarbone until he reaches my neck. There he stays, letting his teeth come out a bit as he nibbles at my skin. If it bruises, I will wear it as a badge of honor. One of his hands presses fingertips lightly to my pulse point. I gasp as his fingers meet bare skin. His hands are so *cold*.

"Sorry," he murmurs against my neck.

"Don't be," I respond.

He is disheveling me, ravishing me against this tree. We have yet to go much further than exploratory touches and kisses, and I wonder if tonight will be the night. If we will become one among the forest.

His mouth lands over the hollow of my throat, and his beard tickles me. I try to fight the laugh that bubbles up, not wanting to give him the satisfaction, but it's too late. He holds me there and I collapse against him in a fit of giggles, powerless to his much stronger grip.

I open my mouth to call for peace when he stiffens. I stop immediately, thinking that we've crossed some unspoken boundary. But when he stands and looks deeper into the woods, something in my blood chills.

"What was that?"

"I didn't hear anything," I say, thinking that if I don't voice my fear it might not make it real.

"Get back to the fire," he says, pushing me towards the clearing.

"What?" I right my coat and smooth down my hair, still a little dazed.

"I said get back to the fire—" But his voice is swallowed by a

116

much deeper one, a roaring that fills the open air around us.

And then I see it.

It's not quite an animal. It is far too large to be anything that I have seen on the fringes of the tree line. It stands on all fours, and its legs are taller than Halvar at his full height. It's covered in black fur and has a tail whipping about its back. I think I can see a set of eyes, but if my own aren't deceiving me there might be two sets. It is long and robust, and I want to compare it to a cow...if a cow had person-sized legs and too many eyes. It moves in turns silkily and clunkily, like it can't decide if it knows how to walk. I have never seen anything like it, even in my creature books.

I don't scream. I just stare at it wide-eyed and open-mouthed. Halvar has already unsheathed two knives from beneath his coat. He looks back at me only once, and I see the agony on his face. We both know it's too late for me to run back to the festival, I'll draw the creature to everyone else there. Sure, there may be other hunters out there, but it is not a guarantee that they arrived armed, or that they even stayed this late into the night. We could scream for help, but the music and sounds of revel will likely cover it. Or worse, our screams could attract more predators.

We are, for all intents and purposes, on our own.

Halvar launches himself at the thing. He expertly wields the knives as if they are an extension of his arms. He looks complete with them in hand. He slashes at the creature's legs, attempting to take it down from the bottom. It's so large and so heavy that it doesn't react quickly enough to Halvar's first cut, and when his knife makes impact, the thing screeches an unearthly sound. It's ready for the next hit, though, and manages to dodge it.

Watching Halvar fight is similar to watching the dancers around the fire; he seems practiced and sure of himself as if this is not his first time fighting a giant monstrous creature.

"I thought you said you hunted animals! Bears, foxes, deer," I cry.

"I *do*," he calls back, maintaining focus on his prey. "When I'm paid to."

117

It settles in me that this must be the thing Kliransk doesn't know about, one of the monsters that roams the woods. I feel angry that he didn't tell me, understanding as to why he wouldn't, fear for his life, and—strangely enough—a rush of admiration at how well he knows his way around a knife.

Spoken too soon.

Halvar moves in to slash at the creature but it raises a clawed... foot? Paw? And swipes at him. It makes contact and he goes flying into a snowbank several yards away. The creature stumbles towards him, slowed by the frozen ground. The snow is only so much of a deterrent though, and soon enough it will be upon him.

Blind rage fills me and I stumble through the small path they've made, looking for something, *anything*, to distract it with. My eyes land on something in the snow.

Halvar's whip. He must have dropped it in the fight.

I heave it into my hands—*it is so heavy*. But the creature is nearing Halvar and I don't have any other options. I unravel the whip and let the majority of it hang down to the ground. I have no idea what I'm doing, but it's better than nothing. I lift it, tossing the weight of it over my shoulder, and then I run at it and hurl the whip at its back legs.

The creature screeches again as the whip makes contact. Its hind legs give out and it collapses onto its rear. I caused little damage besides startling it, but it's all the distraction Halvar needs to collect himself and get a hold of one of the remaining knives in his holster. He mounts the creature and jams his knife between the creature's eyes—its front-facing eyes at least. It roils against him but no longer has the advantage to fight back. Halvar retracts his knife and shoves his way off, making his way to its collapsed legs. He slashes all four ankle tendons and then shoves at the torso until it rolls onto its side, and then he plunges the knife a final damning time into the creature's heart.

He turns to me, blood sprayed across his face and chest. Where I expected to find fury, I only see a numb, neutral stare.

"Thank you," he says. Then he makes a simple show of

collecting his weapons and comes toward me to find me still clutching his whip. He takes it from me, and once it leaves my hands I realize the rope cut open my palms. I don't even feel the sting, perhaps thanks to the cold or the pure unadulterated fear still running through my veins.

When I fail to respond, he bundles me in his arms and hoists me up, and after a moment I realize we are running. The surrounding woods pass us by in a blur, we are running far faster than I expected him to be capable of. Faster than anyone should be able to run. I think little of it. After what we've just seen, I suppose superior speed is not something to concern myself over.

We arrive back at the house in record time, maybe just a handful of minutes. He doesn't stop in the foyer, or at the stair landing. Instead, he carries me all the way up the stairs and into the washroom. I don't protest when he strips off my dress, muddied and now stained with the creature's blood. He takes off the wreath and sets it gently on the basin. Then he strips off his own bloodied clothes and maneuvers both of us into the tub. Distantly, I note that this is the first time we are completely bare to one another.

Halvar fills the tub with blistering hot water and dumps a few oils in. He sits against the back of the tub with me sitting against him. He waits for the water to fill before dumping more scented oils into his hands as he begins to scrub the blood and dirt off of us both.

My silence must be disconcerting him because, for once, he speaks without my having to ask.

"I find no pleasure in killing monsters." His hands are rubbing across my sternum, and under normal circumstances, I would find it romantic, perhaps even suggestive. But the fear and shock have yet to wear off, and I simply want to hear him continue to talk if only to assure me that he is okay. "It feels personal every time, since I am the one in their territory. It affords me a comfortable lifestyle, but had I been optioned with other paths, I might have chosen something else instead."

He begins washing my hair, and this finally allows me to relax. I sink against him, a groan slipping out. This is a luxury I have never been afforded, and I almost feel sorry for him because now I intend to ask for this *all the time*. He senses my mood shift and places one soft kiss to my shoulder.

"Part of me fears the life I would have had if I had undergone the transformation. Being hunted by the people I now call my peers." His voice trails off, but I can tell he's not finished, and so I wait. "I still have to fight it sometimes. The change. When I have a surge of energy, I feel it rushing under my skin. The want to shift. The work that I do has become routine for me, but having to fight while knowing that you were nearby filled me with a wrath I haven't been familiar with in a long time. I wouldn't have stayed prone out in the snow while it charged at me were it not for the sheer will it takes to fight that instinct. If you hadn't come in when you did, I might have given in to it."

I wonder how I might have reacted had he shifted into the thing he fears most. Maybe I would worry *for* him, but not for my own sake. He could shift into something horrible and ugly, feral and fearsome, and I would welcome it the same way I have now.

"Does it hurt?" I ask, my voice raw.

His hands pause in my hair, then resume their washing once he begins speaking. "It's not quite to that point anymore. It did, when I was younger and couldn't control myself as well. Now it's more like remembering an old hurt."

"You said the monsters wouldn't hurt us as long as we left them alone," I say. "What did we do to aggravate this one?"

He hums, considering his answer. "It was probably startled by the music and the cheering and the fire. Though the fact that I rushed to attack it likely aggravated it further."

"Do you regret doing so?"

"No," he says swiftly, instinctually. "I will never regret decisions made in service of defending you."

I let his words sink in as I settle against him. Halvar doesn't hurry to get us out of the bath; instead, we lounge with our bodies pressed together and let the night wash down the drain.

Our vows were clunky, awkward statements that we regurgitated out of the mouths of people that did not care to know us in any way that mattered. But if nothing else, I meant it when I said I would stay with him. For better or for worse. The challenge now is to figure out what *worse* means to each of us.

CHAPTER NINE

A sense of calm has passed over the both of us now that we sit in his study. I still can't stand to be even a few paces from Halvar so I sit perched on the corner of his desk, mindful of my still dripping hair and the bathrobe draped around me. My hands wrap around the steaming mug of tea he made for me. Tendrils of heat curl above it and slowly ground me back in reality. He is vigorously taking notes and from what I can make out of his handwriting, he is recounting the events from tonight, cross-referencing them with his previous hunts.

Now that the shock has started to wear off, the anger has crept back in. I don't want a fight, because I do understand why he wouldn't tell me such a thing. I just wish he had.

"So not just bears," I say, trying to soften the sharpness edging my voice.

His hand stills on the page. "No, not just bears."

"That's why you come home bloodied and barely able to walk some nights." I have begged for clarity and now it feels like a slap in the face. "How long have you hunted monsters?"

He puts his head in his hand. "For pay, only for the past three years. But I've known how to track and defend myself against certain breeds for years. It's second nature by now."

"Why didn't you tell me when you told me about the shifter

blood?"

"It's a shameful thing."

"You were ashamed of your bloodline, too, and yet you told me about that."

"I wouldn't lie to you about something like that," he insists.

I cross my arms. "But you *would* lie to me."

He completely sets down his work then, turning in his seat to face me. "What would you have said if I told you?" The sharpness I had been working to fight off has edged its way into his tone, and the sound grates me and makes me want to fight back.

"I would have accepted it," I snap, setting down the tea. "Like I have everything else."

He throws up his hands. "I need you to work with me."

"I need you to give me something to work with," I fire back. A sharp exhale falls out of me, and I see the hardness grow over his face, watch him recede into his shell. "We are supposed to be *partners*, Halvar. I need you to let me in. I am not your father."

"And I am not yours," he says, gritted teeth holding in carefully curated anger. "Nor am I your mother. You don't have to be suspicious of my intentions with you."

"It's difficult when I don't know your intentions at all! You can hunt monsters, or you can become one. It's not going to make a difference in how I feel for you." I play the coward once more, not giving a name to the things I feel. "You say that these things are hard for you, I understand that. But at some point, you must consider whether or not you are doing anything to make it easier for you. You could start by trusting me."

He takes several deep breaths, in through the nose, out through the mouth. "You are. My best friend. My truest one. You are the only and the every. I do trust you, more than anyone. But I don't want to scare you. As I told you before, this isn't exactly something I'm proud of."

Even though his words work their way into my heart, I cannot help the tempering anger that still lingers. I huff out a frustrated laugh.

"And you think I'm proud of every decision I've made? That's what the trust is for, trusting that you won't judge me for the things I've done."

"I'm killing my own kind," he says through gritted teeth. "That is a step removed from you losing your faith."

I flinch as if struck, and I know he sees the hurt that is plainly written across my features. "I am not some child to be coddled, I am your *wife*. You would do well to treat me as such."

Feeling backed into a corner, I use the only weapon left in my arsenal: I acquiesce. More than most, I know how to make silence sting sharper than any harsh words. I stand, ready to storm out of the room until my anger cools. But he catches my wrist as I move away, a gentle, pleading touch.

"Please," he says, and the openness on his face makes me want to hear him out.

I don't have the energy to be humiliated when the tears begin to fall. "I *told* you how frustrating it was to never be told anything of value by my parents. You once told me that you aren't afraid of the dark, yet you leave me in it when it's convenient for you."

He nods like he understands, and I truly hope he does. "Forgive me for making an ass of myself. You are not to be coddled, and I apologize for not seeing you for what you are."

I swipe the back of my hand across my face. "I'm not asking you to bare your soul to me. Your truths are yours to keep. But when it's something life or death, then yes, I *would* like to know. That includes the fact that you hunt monsters for money."

He flinches hard, not the subtle twitch when he is startled, but fully shrinks into himself. His skin blanches and I can hear him taking ragged breaths. I pause, thinking over what I could have said to make him react this way, when I notice his shoulders are shaking.

"You said my truths are mine to keep, but as much as I'd like to, it feels wrong to not tell you what my life was like without you in it." He looks at me, his features downturned and tired. Not the tiredness that calls one to sleep, but the soul-deep kind that can't be eased with rest. "You won't like what I have to say."

I stand up straighter. "I don't have to like it. I accept whatever it is you have to tell me."

He laughs, a rueful sound already full of regret. "You say that now."

"Tell me what it is," I say, reaching a hand towards him. My heart breaks a little when he pulls away from the touch. Still, I wait for him to come out and say it. There is no room for my assumptions here.

He takes a breath to steady himself. "The blood that stains my hands does not just belong to beasts. My father was never sick. Not with anything that would have killed him. His only sickness was his cruelty."

There are unspoken words between what he's said. If he expects me to read between the lines, I refuse. I won't shed his secrets for him. This is his truth to tell. He sits in my silence for a few moments, letting it wash over him as if it can protect him. I want to tell him there's nothing he needs to shield himself from. I decided long before this to take him as he is.

I made my decision the moment I rose from my pew to shield him from that crowd. Perhaps this was put into motion years before that, when I chose him time and again over friends and family in Kliransk. Either way, I have not strayed from this path before, and I will stand firm in it now.

At last, he takes a breath, and it rattles out of him like he's fighting to keep going. I recognize this fear as the same that overtook him when he revealed his bloodline to me. The truth dawns on me before he says it because there is only one thing that can draw this reaction out of him.

"His death was by my hand."

It takes a moment to sink in. "On purpose?"

He winces, but nods.

I no longer feel the ground beneath my feet. I so firmly believed that Halvar could not be a killer. I reminded myself of that for days on end. I proclaimed it to the whole of Kliransk. There was nothing I believed more solidly. Only now for Halvar to admit that not only does he kill beasts of prey, he's killed another man.

Not a good man. A brutal, cruel man who most definitely deserved to die. Yet even with his hulking frame and the darkness that lingers behind his eyes, I cannot picture Halvar taking life in such a way.

"Why?" I breathe.

"Why do you think?" He says, his voice small. A broken sound comes from the back of his throat. God forbid he starts to cry, because that will be my undoing.

I stand stiffly before him, my arms hanging uselessly at my sides. For once, I am at a complete loss for words. Halvar pushes back from the desk and stands, pacing to the other end of the study.

"I knew this would happen if I told you," he says, one hand threading in his hair. He pulls, like he's trying to rip the memory out of his head. "I knew I would scare you away. After just getting you back I'm going to lose you again."

"Hold on," I say, striding towards him.

He flinches, like he's anticipating a fiery reaction from me. He is likely used to the backs of hands meeting his cheeks. Knuckles kissing his lips in retaliation. Violence is all he has known, and that in itself ignites my anger anew. Anger at the world, anger at his father for doing this to him.

But my anger has no place here.

What Halvar needs now is nothing of the sort. Instead, I do my best to soften my features. I raise a hand, bracing it a breath away from his scarred cheek. When he nods his permission, I cup his face. I hold him the way he has always deserved. With a lover's touch.

"I'm not afraid of you," I say, keeping my voice gentle as if the slightest show of temper could scare him away. And I find that I mean it. I was startled, taken aback. But more than anything, more than anyone else, I *understand*.

He melts against me, relief flooding through his body.

"May I speak freely?" I say, rife with hesitation. When he nods,

I unburden myself of that darker-natured part of me. "I'm glad your father is dead. I'm not sorry to say that."

Grief and regret are still palpable on him, written in every tense line of his body. But he allows me to hold him and let it be known that though shocked, I am not put off by his demons. I hold true to my vows not despite them but with them at the forefront of my mind.

The fact that we are here, holding each other, makes all of these bouts of darkness worth it. I once thought I might be content being his, but contentment feels long gone now. This is something deeper, something more worthy of working through hardship for.

"I don't want you to carry my burdens," he says against my skin. "But it makes it easier on me as long as you know they're there."

I don't respond. I just twine a hand through his hair and draw him closer. We stay like that, tangled and touching. It is a near-perfect moment, and I wish I could pocket it to replace those heavy stones that have been weighing me down.

Halvar pulls me towards the desk, sinking into his chair while drawing me to stand between his legs. Thanks to his being seated it is much easier to maintain eye contact. He places his hands on my waist, looking for his part apologetic and remorseful. "I didn't want to worry you. I realize what you saw tonight was frightening, but I am usually better prepared and have the upper hand."

"That's not what concerns me," I say, shaking my head. "And I have to admit that you're right. You carry much heavier secrets than I do. I shouldn't compare them."

"They are not to be compared," he says. "It's not going to make your burden any lighter to acknowledge that mine is heavier. They can both be heavy."

I knot my hands together, needing to touch something that isn't him so I can have a moment to collect myself. "Maybe we have different definitions of what counts as heavy. I can be strong enough for us both."

He sighs, leaning into me. When he speaks, it's almost as if he's talking to himself, like I am interrupting his inner thoughts.

"Sometimes I wish things could be different. This life has allowed me to make something of myself, and for that I am grateful. But I'm not sorry for the things I've done."

"I don't need you to be sorry," I say, brushing a strand of hair back from where it's fallen in his face. "I need you here with me. Not just your body, I want the rest as much."

He takes both of my hands and places them over his heart, over the scars beneath his shirt. "It was yours before you asked."

I lean in. "Will you let me in, then? Will you tell me the important things?"

He nods. "I won't leave you in the dark."

Our foreheads press together and for a moment I just breathe in his scent. His hair smells of the oils from the bath, the sweat and stains from the night long gone.

"We arrived home considerably fast," I murmur against his hair.

"We did," he says, voice wary.

"So you kept that much of your gift."

He winces. "I'd hesitate to call it a gift. But yes, I do possess a faster gait and stronger grip than the average man."

I pull away so I can study his face. "I suppose that makes you the perfect hunter, given your advantages."

"Not just that," he says. He considers for a moment. True to his word, I can almost see the moment he decides to trust me. "I have an innate understanding of them. Monsters, I mean. Their patterns and habits often make more sense to me than human nature. They think the way I would, if put in their position. It makes them much easier to hunt."

"Do you ever regret that you are unable to shift?"

He blinks at me, taken aback by the question. This is clearly something he's never thought about and likely never been asked. He slouches back in his chair and props himself on an elbow. He looks at me with new eyes, roving across my face.

"I don't think I make a very good man," he says. "I doubt I

would be a better monster."

"I think you are good." I reach out to touch his cheek, hesitating a hair's breadth away before he permits me. "I think you are more than good."

He turns his head to kiss my palm. "You're generous to think that. I've dirtied my hands beyond redemption. I've had to compromise my beliefs just to stay alive. I left you—" he takes a deep breath, "—when you were vulnerable and shouldn't have been alone with people who cared little for you. I should have fought harder to stay. I'm not a good man. Most days, I don't feel like a man at all. I'd rather not be one, truth be told. But I'm trying to be better than I was. For you, Emelie."

My breath catches on his words. His feelings so closely mirror my own, and I wonder if now would be a good time to tell him that. But we aren't talking about me right now, and so I wait with the knowledge that once I am ready, I can tell him with confidence.

"I would have you," I say, my voice low and smooth as silk, "man or monster or anything else you want to be."

He leans in and kisses me deeply. It is a claiming kiss, a reminder that I am his and he is mine. My hand is still on his cheek, and I stroke my fingers across his scar. Then he pulls away and gazes at me with a softness that makes me want to draw him back in.

He gestures towards my armchair just past the balcony doors. "Stay," he says, his voice a gentle plea.

It is an easy request to fulfill. A few of my books are stacked at the desk's corner, and seeing nothing better to do, I pick up the *Creatura* before flopping into my seat.

I flip to a random page and am met with a new sight. I've read this book cover to cover so many times that the spine is worn down, but the monsters have always just been drawings on a page. Now, the image jumps out at me with a vengeance. It's not exactly the creature we saw tonight, but it's similar in size and color. The angles are much smoother in the drawing, a more perfect rendition of the jarring thing we encountered. The writing at the top is in a language I can't read, the word made up of too many jumbled consonants for me to try and pronounce. The text below claims that its name translates roughly to

Woodland Walker.

"Halvar," I say, my voice pinched with fear.

He stands immediately, coming to check on what I've found. When he sees the page I have open, he stiffens. "Let me see that."

I hand him the book and wait for him to come up with an explanation. "How many of these have you hunted before?"

His jaw is pulled tight, confusion and frustration fighting their way out of him. "I avoid it when I can. There's no reason for the walkers to be roaming our vicinity unless they had a reason to crawl out of whatever corner they came from. Other predators, or maybe a group of humans scared it off. But to then come so close to more people?"

"It reeks of wrongness," I say, my voice coming out small.

He nods. "It does."

In our lessons as children, we were taught that there were many things to fear in the woods. There were the typical predators, and then there were shifter wolves. They hammered in fear towards the wolves in particular. Back then I thought they were as numerous as the trees. I thought the woods were crawling with them, that you wouldn't be able to go ten paces without encountering one.

Certainly, by now we should have seen something besides the creature tonight. Or at least, more of that very same creature. Given Halvar's experience, we should not have been caught so unaware. The only other encounter I can think of is the one I had on my first night here. I haven't felt that same pull towards the trees as I did then, but now I have to wonder what whispers would call to me if I were caught unaware again.

I hadn't asked Halvar what it was that wanted me to go play. He hadn't offered to explain.

Halvar takes my book back to his desk and opens one of his many notebooks. He flips through its pages, searching for something among the notes that make sense to him. After another minute, he tuts and closes both books.

He puts them back on the shelf, shoulders drooping in defeat.

"We can look into it more tomorrow. Right now, we should rest."

I am all too eager to agree. Exhaustion coats my bones and I can only imagine how Halvar feels. Despite this, the exhilaration of the festival combined with the sheer terror of the forest encounter has ensured that though we are tired, we won't be sleeping any time soon.

I follow him back to our bedroom. I've grown accustomed to calling it *our* room. It no longer feels like a concept to dance around, our marriage. Not something to be avoided and muttered between sentences.

As we're settling in for the evening, Halvar's eyes brighten with fresh remembrance.

"I have something for you."

He leans over the edge of the bed to rustle through the pockets of his discarded pants. He rights himself with a tiny box in hand, palm up in offering. A gift. I can't remember the last time I received a gift. Even my birthday has not been something of note since childhood.

Removing the lid reveals a golden charm on a chain. The charm is round with some flora embedded into the metal. It's a necklace. I look at him. He's bashful, but clearly very proud of his gift. I want to cry, I want to kiss him, I want to do *shameful things* to him.

He shrugs, trying to pass it off for modesty. "You said you'd never owned any jewelry." He helps me latch the clasp, his fingers fumbling as he works to get it on. The charm falls against my sternum. The cold metal is a shock to my nerves but it quickly warms to my skin. I never want to take it off.

"It's not a wedding ring," he continues, "but it's something for now."

"I love it," I say. "Thank you."

At least we end the night on a sweeter note. A softer one, after all of the prickliness of the evening past. Despite this, sleep does not come easily to either of us, and it feels as though the morning arrives all too soon.

Halvar rises well before I do, urging me to get some more sleep as he does. I don't disobey. The rush of last night has finally faded and I finally feel able to *rest*. I linger in the place between sleeping and waking, lulled by the sounds of the house coming to life but not able to slip away from them completely. I can hear him making breakfast, pacing the floors downstairs. The creaking boards help me visualize what he's doing. It goes quiet when he settles down to eat.

An hour or so later, Halvar returns to our bedroom, puzzlement on his face. He sits on my side of the bed, stroking one calloused hand up and down my arm.

"Have you been planting flowers in the clearing?"

I burrow into my pillow, shrugging him off. "No. When would I have had time for that?"

"There's a thicket of daffodils blooming outside, on top of the snow. I can't make heads or tails of it."

Now that. That makes me sit up, sleep long forgotten. "What did you say?"

"Daffodils," he repeats. "I've never seen so many in one cluster. Not to mention the snow."

I think of my old bedroom window and the perpetual bloom that littered the ground beneath it. My mother used to accuse me of stealing seeds from the market. But even stolen seeds can't grow out of frozen ground.

Then something nags at me, something from the festival.

"What is it?" Halvar pushes. "What's wrong?"

I shake my head. "One of the girls at the revel—one of the dancers—said something strange to me. I asked her how the floral wreaths were able to stay alive in the cold. I've read enough books on wildlife to know that flowers shouldn't be growing in this weather. Even the best of gardeners shouldn't be able to outwit it."

"So what did she say?"

I hesitate, suddenly feeling silly for even considering such a thing. But since we have decided to pull each other out of the dark, I suppose it is only fair. "She said it was magic. You must think I'm crazy for thinking that I can—"

"It's not crazy," he assures me. "I am the last person to doubt such things."

Quickly, I explain what has been holding firm at the back of my mind. I tell him about my bedroom window, about how many winters have been accompanied by a bloom. How it never made sense before, and it almost does now.

I bite my lip, insecurity almost making me hold my tongue. But not quite. "What if I have an affinity for it?"

"What's that?" He murmurs.

"Magic. An affinity for magic."

He stills. "Do you think you do?"

I shrug. "I don't know. I want to figure that out."

"It seems like the sort of thing that would be hard to not know."

I huff. "I feel things, Halvar. Call it excitement, recognition, whatever you please. Everything I've researched has called to me. But I can't say for certain it's not just my fascinations taking over."

"I believe you," he says. "I can bring you supplies from the market—"

"I want to go with you." I hadn't dared voice this request aloud yet, but it would pain me to hold my tongue. We've been on enough walks that I know my way around the area surrounding our home, but the vast expanse beyond here is still unknown to me. There are so many things I want to learn.

I see the hesitation in his eyes even as he nods. "You remember our plan, if things go wrong? You remember how to get home?"

I nod long enough to watch the hesitation fade away. "I remember."

"There's likely a snowstorm coming," he says, looking out the window. "We'll have to wait for it to pass. But I can give you something to prepare." He reaches beneath the bed once more, and from there he draws a dagger of medium length, its blade curving slightly at the end. "I figure this will be easier to handle than a whip."

I take it from him, and my wrist nearly collapses beneath its weight. Despite its sleek look, the handle is heavy. "I don't know how to use this."

"You didn't know how to wield a whip either. This, I can teach you in a matter of days."

I weigh it in my hands. "You expect me to become a dagger-wielding warrior?"

"I expect you to be able to handle yourself alone in the woods." He levels a stare at me. "That's what you want, isn't it?"

It didn't occur to me that I'd have to adopt Halvar's tactics in order to survive. I've read plenty of stories about princesses handy with a sword, fierce women who could set the entire world on fire. I never pictured myself as one of them. Then again, I never pictured myself as a witch, either. I might be both or none at all, but I will be something. I think of the meek, quiet girl who sewed other people's torn clothes while her own barely fit. The pretend pious girl who couldn't make herself voice her own opinions.

I had wished her well; now I want her dead. If I can't set the world on fire, I can surely set myself ablaze. Whatever rises from the ashes will be what is meant to be.

I look up at Halvar. "Yes, it is."

CHAPTER TEN

The snowstorm does not let up for days. We spend the time curled around one another in bed with tea and warm plates of roasted meats and vegetables circulating in and out of rotation. When I manage to tear myself away from Halvar, I bury myself in my books, devouring page after page as I let the information seep in. It is, at the same time, so much and still not enough.

A passage on the phases of the moon and its effects on power has captivated me when he stirs from sleep beside me, pressing his cheek against my arm. His beard scratches me and his eyes slowly blink awake. We watch each other for a minute, clarity coming to him as he fully realizes how much of us is touching. Instead of pulling away, as he does some days, he drapes an arm around me and pulls in closer.

It has become difficult to tell the time with the storm and our ongoing residence in bed, but it should be midday given the faint light fighting its way through the clouds. We should get up and make supper. We should prepare supplies to seek out a merchant. We should get back to our research. But I cannot make myself get up. And I don't have to.

He reaches up and tucks a stray lock of hair behind my ear. Voice still heavy with sleep, he says, "I never thought I'd get to have this."

"I did," I admit, my heart fluttering. "I could picture us here so clearly. I've always felt like…like it was meant to be this way."

"I should have told you back then," he says. "I should have told you how I felt."

"Do you think it would have changed anything?" I don't mean for the question to sound harsh, but I do have to wonder.

His face hardens a fraction. "My father still would have been a brute, and the elders still would have hated him. But if I didn't leave with him, I could have left with you."

"And gone where? To that other village? We wouldn't have survived."

"I would have made it work."

"You can't always *make* things work," I say, soothing a hand across his face. The harshness fades beneath my touch. "Sometimes you just have to let things happen."

"You say that, and yet you helped to make this happen." He gestures between us. "I am a coward in that sense; I needed you to set things in motion. I didn't have the strength back then to come and claim you as mine. But from the moment you stood between me and that crowd, I knew I would do anything for you. I knew it long before, honestly, but that moment gave me the strength to act."

"You think me brave where others call me foolish."

"It is never foolish to act on your heart's command."

"Perhaps," I muse. "It did work out in my favor."

This breaks the fragile moment between us, or rather reaffirms it. He pulls me on top of him to kiss me. One hand holds firm at the back of my neck, the other roving down my body. Damn the nightgown, I need him closer. But when I try to slip out of it, he stops me with a hand on my wrist.

"Patience," he growls. His hands resume their roving, and it's all I can do to hold myself together.

We kiss for long, uninterrupted moments. I can't keep my hands still—they twine in his hair, settle at his waist, slip between our bodies to rub him. It feels gluttonous to feel this content, to want so much of him and to keep receiving it.

I am damned. I welcome it.

A sudden clap of thunder scares the life out of me, and I nearly fall off the bed in my fright. Halvar bursts out laughing before attempting to calm me by rubbing soothing strokes up and down my arms.

"Not a fan of the storm?" He teases.

"I wasn't expecting *that!*" Despite my racing heart, I settle back down atop him, the mood sufficiently fizzled for the time being. "Mock me all you like, but you'll be sorry when I pass away from the shock."

He stifles his laughter, clearly unmoved by my threat. "Apologies, wife."

"You should be, *husband*," I spit out. I climb off of him, straightening my nightgown. As I get out of bed, my foot nudges against one of the knife hilts hidden beneath. I retrieve it and point at him with it. "When is my next lesson?"

He sits up. "If you're ready, now."

I opt for a simple shirt and pants, he dons only a loose pair of pants. I quickly plait my hair and pin back the loose strands, not wanting a single distraction. When the snow storm first hit, Halvar pushed aside all of the furniture in the sitting room to give me space for destruction. I have only managed a few basic maneuvers with the dagger so far, but it's better than nothing.

"Get in position," he says, squaring his feet. In this way, I am the hunter and he is the predator refusing to be prey.

"I love it when you say that," I say, lunging at him with the dagger.

He blocks it easily, laughing. "You have a filthy mind."

This distracts him enough that he leaves his left side open. A habit I've noticed during our lessons. I lunge towards him, stopping inches away from his flesh. It easily could have been a fatal hit were I actually trying to hurt him.

He raises his hands in acquiescence. "You've been paying attention."

"I always do."

He chuckles, taking the dagger from me. "Now *that* is a lie. You slip into your own head whenever you're not getting attention. Sometimes even then. Now, elbows up."

He positions himself with the dagger. It's my turn to attack, yet I keep ending up on the defensive due to his far superior skill. I am practically useless without a weapon in hand and he quickly overpowers me.

He frowns. "You need to be able to defend yourself if disarmed."

"It's difficult when you throw yourself at me with a dagger in hand."

"Fine," he says, tossing it aside. He raises his fists. "We'll try the old-fashioned way."

We meet each other blow to blow. He punches, I parry it off. I try to catch his guard down, he raises it. He's holding back, I can tell, but less than he was before.

In a bout of overconfidence, I spin to launch an elbow, which he catches in his palm. We stay like that for a moment, heaving breaths as I glare at him.

"I would have made that."

"You think too impulsively. Try that in a real fight and they'll take out your knees while your back is turned."

"Fine," I say, pushing away from him. "You win."

"It's not a matter of win or lose, Emelie. The forest doesn't keep score." He picks up the dagger and hands it back to me. "You're getting better, your skills just need polishing."

I don't shy away from brushing my fingers against his when I take the dagger. "Then let's get back to it."

We run drills over and over again. I am overpowered more often than I am successful, but he assures me this is only due to his intense amount of training. If I were to encounter a less experienced hunter or an off-guard beast, I might be able to hold my own. I still fumble with the dagger, but it's better than nothing.

After thoroughly tiring me out, Halvar kneels beside the tub where I'm seated, bandaging my calloused hands. My mother was wrong. Built for women's work, these hands are not.

"The storm should ease up by tomorrow," he says as he finishes up one hand. "We'll find a market at first light."

"How many are out there?"

"The people live scattered, though some group into communes. Merchants travel through the woods looking for people to sell to, or people travel to the merchants' houses. There is some semblance of a schedule, so we're able to find each other."

"How do you not get lost?"

"Wards." He says simply. "Though some of the more old-fashioned types tie fabric to trees to direct others. Do you know what you want?"

"Somewhat. It depends what wares the merchant has."

He stands, dusting off his pants. "I'll take enough silver for you to buy a few weeks' worth of supplies." He offers a hand to help me up. I take it, wincing when the pressure hits my raw ones.

I follow him out of the washroom and towards the kitchen. Vegetables are laid out on the counter and I get to chopping them while Halvar thaws out meat he rationed right before the storm hit its peak. Where a Kliransk winter limited our meal options, Halvar pushes through the frost and ferns to find the best kills.

"If I hadn't seen proof with my own eyes, I might not have believed you when you told me there were others out here."

"I don't blame you," he says from the stove. "We do our best to stay hidden. I picked this spot for that very reason."

Thinking of his life before me wounds me, though I know it shouldn't. I should feel proud of him for rising above his circumstances. I should take my pain and put it somewhere he can't see. But I've done that for so long, and I am so tired.

"You lived such a life before me." I wipe my hands and start setting the table, too shy to meet his eyes as I speak. "I think I was starting to lose my mind before you returned. I couldn't take the mundane routine. The utter nothingness of my every day. The alarm didn't even frighten me." I set down the plates harsher than I mean to, and the glass rattles against the wood. "It was at least *something* different. It woke me up from a long, unending sleep."

I brace my arms against the table, hunched in on myself. Wordlessly, he walks over and gently takes the plates from me, bringing them back to the stove to serve. Returning with full dishes, he sets one in front of me and gestures for me to sit. He follows suit but waits for me to start eating before he speaks again.

Quietly, he asks, "Do you want to talk about it?"

The hand lifting a fork to my mouth stills. I hear the unasked question. We have talked about it in some detail—I've spent entire days telling him and telling him about what went on in those six empty years. He's not asking to hear what happened. He's not asking how I feel.

He's asking about the pieces of that old life that still linger in me now; my hesitations and insecurities, the way I assume the worst when he goes quiet for too long, how my eyes brim with tears if he pulls away from me too quickly.

He knows about the earthquake, he wants to know about the aftershocks.

I put down my fork. "More than anything, I'm angry that it went on for so long. I was bored...so bored and so lonely. In many ways, I'm envious of you. In six years you learned a trade, made a living for yourself, built a home. You accomplished so much, and I still can't stitch in a straight line. I have no passions, no talents, no prospects. Had you not already known me, I would've been considered completely ineligible."

"You forgo your kindness, your compassion, your wittiness, your intelligence—"

"I'm not useful."

He shakes his head. "Your worth is not measured in coins, Emelie. Damn what your mother told you. It's not a moral failing that you can't sew."

"It's not about the sewing!" I cry, flattening my hands on the table. "It's the fact that I realized it from an early age, and I never bothered to figure out what I *am* good at. I don't even know what I like. How is this a life?"

I can feel the tears stream down my cheeks but I don't try to wipe them away. They're just going to keep falling, anyway. Halvar watches me and I brace myself for pity, but I see nothing but firm resolve in his eyes. He takes my hand in his, ever so softly stroking his fingers against mine.

"Tomorrow," he affirms. "We'll look for your things tomorrow."

We finish our dinner in companionable silence. Halvar clears the table and washes the dishes before retiring to the sitting room for a smoke. As always, he offers the pipe to me and as always, I decline it, sinking into the sofa cushions instead.

I wave a hand in front of my face. "It's a wonder all of your clothes don't reek of tobacco."

He chuckles. "I would love to introduce you to this new phenomenon of washing clothes."

I kick the toe of my boot against his. "That tone won't earn you any favors."

"Maybe not," he muses, taking a long drag. "But escorting you to the merchant will."

I raise an eyebrow. "So now it's transactional?"

"I can only give you so many wedding presents," he says with a wink.

I shake my head, trying and failing to hide my smile. The weight of our discussion hasn't fully abandoned me, and I can't help it when my mind drifts back to the old village once more.

There hasn't been an alarm in weeks.

It unnerves me how, after decades of silence, the air rang with that death knell only to return to silence.

I am no expert, but even to my inexperienced mind this makes no sense. Despite all I have seen, I still doubt the existence of a shifter preying on the people of Kliransk. But the bodies...the funerals...

Either the creatures are getting smarter, or the elders and villagers are more foolish than previously believed. Perhaps they've been ringing the wrong alarm.

"There you go again," Halvar says, his tone affectionate. "Into your own head."

He sets down his pipe and opens his arm for me, and I curl into his side on instinct. I let my breathing sync with his, trying to let it calm me.

"There is so much wrong out there. In Kliransk, too." My voice feels very small in this very large house next to this very large man.

"I know. It bothers me, too." He sighs, and my body shifts with his breath. "This doesn't follow any pattern I recognize."

"Does it need to follow one?"

He hums, considering. "Not necessarily, but by nature, creatures do fall into habits. This is sporadic, and predators cannot survive on such a rhythm."

"I am nagged with wanting to know what's going on. For my own peace of mind, and for my parents." I heave a sigh. "My parents are another problem all their own. One I am less inclined to deal with."

He presses a kiss to my forehead. "One problem at a time, my love."

"One problem at a time," I repeat.

The following morning, Halvar wakes me with a gentle nudge and a plate shoved in front of my half-conscious face. The smell of toasted bread and eggs brings me fully out of my dreams. Sunlight hasn't quite made its way through the curtains yet.

"It's dawn," he says. "The worst of it has passed. There's heavy snow outside, though. You'll need to bundle up more than usual."

I sit up and make quick work of my breakfast. Through a mouthful, I ask, "When do we leave?"

"As soon as you've eaten. I want to make use of any sunlight to melt the snow. The clouds are still thick in the sky, but they're starting to thin in parts."

The excitement pushes me to eat quickly. I heed Halvar's advice and don two pairs of lined leggings beneath my thickest dress and top it with one of the green overcoats. I have learned from my mistakes and layer two pairs of socks in my boots, and also wrap Halvar's scarf around my neck. Beneath the coat, he attaches a harness around my waist and places my dagger inside. It spans nearly the length of my torso and rests against my stomach. I am becoming familiar with its weight.

Halvar harnesses himself with daggers of differing lengths as well as fastens the whip to his side, and I have to wonder at the sheer amount of steel on him. Were it not for his coat, he would appear a walking butcher. When I question if he'll be alright with just one coat over his shirt, he waves away my concerns.

Even the layers of warmth aren't enough to completely shield me. When we step into the open air, I curl into myself and groan at the bite of the breeze. I remind myself it will be worth it. Halvar curls me into his side and I think I hear his breath hitch when we step into the trees. Gradually, he relaxes enough to let me drift away from him, but still close enough to grip my gloved hand in his bare one.

Some of the path looks familiar, and when we pass a clearing, I remember the fire and how it felt to dance around it. When I look up, I see kerchiefs of various shades tied to branches.

Despite the storm, the woods have retained their beauty. If anything, the thick snowfall has only added to it. It's gloomy out, and what little sunlight there is manages to break through and light our way. Clouds cover the sky, threatening to break open at any given moment. An ever-present reminder of the power the sky holds over the earth. I want to offer reverence to it, to thank it for letting up enough to allow us to pass through.

"There," Halvar says, pointing into a thicker copse of trees, "if you walk some miles in that direction, you'll find the commune I used to stay with."

I follow his line of sight, but can only make out bark and branches. I turn to him, his face decorated with shadow and frost sticking to his beard. "I'd like to see it someday."

He nods, pulling me back onto the path. "Someday."

A few paces off the path brings us to another clearing full of carts and stalls and people. The merchants.

Halvar detaches a pouch from his waist belt and pours a few pieces of silver into a smaller bag. "This should be enough. If it's not, give the merchant my name and they'll give you whatever you like. Meet me back at this spot once you've got everything you want."

"And you?"

He nods towards a cart that is visibly overflowing with weapons. "Going to see how lethal I can get."

We part ways with full pockets and empty hands. I wander to a stall advertising elixirs and brews, and the merchant immediately starts rattling on about all of the healing properties he can sell me. Some of the effects sound a little embellished, but I am fascinated nonetheless. I trade a few coins for a blue bottle of rainwater that was charged beneath a full moon.

At another stall, I spend a small fortune on crystals: rose quartz, clear quartz, amethyst, selenite. I even snag a chain with a protection crystal hanging from it for Halvar. I am unsure whether or not he'll wear it, but I hope he'll appreciate the gesture.

I go from stall to stall, picking up candles and sticks of chalk and wax and a vial of oils. My arms are full to the brim by the time I've spent all of the silver. I spy Halvar across the way and whistle. He turns immediately, paying the merchant before jogging back to me. He swears when he sees how much I've bought and starts stuffing everything into his knapsack. I see a new knife strapped to his thigh, as well as what looks to be a fishnet hung across his shoulders.

When he notices my stare he says, "For hunting."

"I should hope so," I say, "I was beginning to fear that it was meant for me."

He scoffs, leaning down to kiss my cheek. "I've ensnared you in matrimony, I require no net." He pulls me to his side as we step back onto the path towards home. "Did you have a good time spending my hard-earned fortune?"

"I could have done worse given more coin." I hold up the chain

I picked out for him. "This is for you. You don't have to wear it—"

Before the sentence is fully out of my mouth he's already taken it and fastened it around his neck. He tucks it into the collar of his shirt and pats it like it's a secret treasure for only us two.

"I love it."

"You don't want to know what it's for?"

"It's for me. That's all I need to know." When I elbow his side, he bursts out laughing. "Tell me."

"It's for protection," I say. "For when you're out hunting."

He presses a kiss to the top of my head. "I feel safer already."

As we begin to wind our way back towards the house, Halvar's expression grows troubled. He chews on his bottom lip, worrying away the skin.

"I spoke with a few of the merchants. They passed through Kliransk before here. Or tried to. They said it didn't look right, something about the people acting off."

"In what way?"

He lets out a breath. "The exact words he used were, 'so sick with fear that they cannot tell up from down.'"

My parents, I think, coming to a rough halt. I nearly skid in the snow, but Halvar rights me with one arm. For a moment I stand there, warring with the concern that threatens to drown out everything else. But another feeling is fighting against it, much louder and fiercer.

Why should I worry, when they've never spent more than a day being considerate of my feelings?

I shake out of my stupor, eyes meeting Halvar's. "If that's the life they want to live, then that's the decision they've made."

He eyes me warily, not all that convinced of my bravado. But I simply take his hand and lead him back onto the frosted path.

Back at the house, I sit on the floor of Halvar's study, transformed into a workspace of my own. I have my supplies scattered around me, and a book balanced open on my knee. Following the instructions is not dissimilar to following a recipe, but where I am careful to not veer off the detailed measurements of something edible, the book urges me to follow my intuition.

Halvar half-watches me from his desk while he cleans and sharpens his knives, a rite of passage every time he brings home a new one. They're stacked in a noisy huddle next to him, shifting whenever the floorboards creak under their combined weight.

I light one of the candles and set it aside, taking a breath. The space takes on a sacred feel, much like the high I was always chasing in church. The one I failed to catch.

I am unsure what exactly to do with the crystals, so I leave them in a pile at my feet. Then I close my eyes and try to focus.

This focus is interrupted by a gruff voice. "What exactly are you doing?"

"Manifesting," I say, not opening my eyes.

"Is it difficult?"

I crack one eye open to find him watching me, his hands stilled on a dagger. "It would be easier if I had silence."

He smiles, not even pretending to look sheepish, but he says no more. He leaves me to my own devices, and I slip back into the corner of my mind where those selfish wants and desires reside. Selfish sounds like a dirty word, but given how little I've had to work with, I am trying not to fault myself for wanting so much.

I try to tell myself that I am worthy. That I am not at fault for my parents' disappointment. I tell myself it's alright for me to want things that are different from what was planned for me. I try to validate my anger, my frustration, my suspicion. It doesn't quite settle in me the way I hoped it would, but I tell it to myself in repetitions until I at least partially believe it.

I smell smoke and open my eyes to see the candle has snuffed itself out. I curse myself for perhaps not catching the flame properly, but when I try to relight it the wick won't catch. Damn the merchant if he sold me a fluke. I set the doused candle aside and return to the book, searching for whatever it is I've done wrong.

I get caught up reading a passage about crystals again, and I don't resurface until Halvar tells me it's time for dinner. I leave the crystals on the banister, hoping they'll soak up the moonlight. The rest, I leave spread out on the floor.

While we're eating, Halvar asks, "How did the *manifesting* go?"

I shrug. "It's not as easy as it sounds. I have to believe in the things I'm asking for."

"And what did you ask for?"

Embarrassed by my insecurities, I shake my head. "Things I'm lacking."

In truth, it was too hard to get my parents out of my head. With my eyes closed all I can see is my mother's disdain and my father's passiveness. It's hard to not feel engulfed in that loneliness I lived in for so many years. What was done is hard to undo, even so many miles removed from them.

I prop myself up, not wanting to continue wallowing. "Can you show me how to check the wards?"

He frowns, puzzled. "You want to learn?"

"I do," I say. "I think it would be a good beginner step for me."

"It's not a simple spell."

"And yet you, with no magic, can do it."

He hesitates only another moment before standing. "Wait here," he says, before rushing upstairs. I track his footsteps to the study before they stop, then return. He returns to the dining table with a dagger in hand. "Come, before it gets too dark."

It's already dark outside, but the clouds have thinned to let a substantial amount of moonlight through. We walk to the edge of our property, and it's then that I notice it: a faint humming noise. Up until now, I had thought it was the sound of bugs or the trickling woodsy air. Halvar walks to a tree bordering the clearing. I've never been over this way, and so that's why I never saw the symbol carved into the trunk. It's dark, the etches of the carving filled with what looks to be mixed earth. Halvar turns and points in every other direction, north, south, and west.

"There are letters carved at each corner of this property. It creates a circle of protection. They've lasted as long as I've been here, with only minor touch-ups now and again."

"Will you show me how?"

He shifts, and it's then I notice he's brought his knapsack. He sets it on the ground, the snow already melting where the marked tree stands. He pulls out a vial of salt and hands it to me.

"Make a semicircle around the inner part of the trunk, just the part that touches the clearing—stop there—yes, like that."

I do as he says and am surprised at the delight that fills me. I can't help it when a smile breaks across my face.

Halvar chuckles. "You look more cheerful than I ever do. I consider this a chore."

"I'd gladly do this every day," I reply.

"Well," he says, "it doesn't require maintenance every day. This is just a precaution."

I straighten when another sound catches my attention. My heart, so full just a moment ago, now clenches in my chest. The sound is all too familiar. It's the same one from both my dreams and my nightmares.

The whispers.

"Halvar."

He grips my shoulders. "I hear it too." He tries to take the salt from me. "Get back in the house."

I stand my ground, clutching the salt even harder. "No. I'm not going to follow it."

"But—"

I glare at him, putting all of the fire of my fury into my eyes. "Tell me what's out there."

His eyes widen a fraction at my sudden anger, though I don't miss the spark of pride in them as well. "It's some forest spirit. I haven't quite figured out if it's a friend or foe yet."

I turn to peer into the darkness between the trees. "You haven't tried hunting them?"

"No point. Not until they tried calling to you."

"They've never tried talking to you, then?"

"They *talk* to you?"

I turn fully towards the trees now. "Not in so many words. It's more like a feeling. It's... I could hear it when we were children, too. I just want to know what it is." I look back at him to find his face twisted in panic, but also note the deep breaths he's taking to calm himself. The hand he has on me is his only anchor to remind him I'm alright. "You haven't even tried to figure out what they really are."

I take one step to test him, and when he follows, I walk us to a gap in between the trees at the border of the clearing. To the limit of the wards. I kneel in the snow, dragging Halvar down with me. He keeps one hand on his dagger, and I *tsk* at him.

"You're going to scare them off."

"That's the point."

I roll my eyes, then turn back to the darkness. His other hand is still protectively gripping my shoulder. I want to lean into it, but also shake it off if it means getting some of my questions answered.

We see it at the same time. I know this because of our collective gasps. It's not large, just a tiny glittering speck of light. My mortal eyes might mistake it for a firefly if I wasn't actively seeking it out. Halvar was right, it's a spirit. As it flutters closer, I feel him pull back while I lean in.

"It's okay," I say to it. "He's not going to hurt you."

The whispering becomes a full symphony in my ears, and I don't know if he can hear it too, but it's a glorious sound to me. The spirit seems curious, like a small child. I hold up a hand, not passing the wards. The spirit flutters closer and closer until it reaches the wards. It can't pass, but maybe I can—

"Don't." Halvar urges. "Please."

Instead, I hold up my hand and wave at it. The spirit follows my hand, swaying back and forth in front of my palm. We're separated by a window-thin amount of space, and I can feel the heat radiating off of it.

Halvar watches in fascinated confusion. We keep up this little dance for a few moments before more lights flicker in the distance.

More spirits. The whispering rises to a near-deafening drone in my ears, and I almost miss it when Halvar tries to urge me back inside.

There are so many lights now, so many spirits. I hold up both hands, guiding the spirits back and forth in some game I don't think either of us understands. When I put my hands down, the spirits flutter in a circle, creating long lines of glowing light.

"They're beautiful," I whisper. Even Halvar seems to be admiring them.

Until their soft warm glow turns an angry red. The lights burn bright as flame, and the whispering changes from a gentle trilling to a high-pitched screech. Noise fills my head and I cry out as the frequency scrapes against my nerves. I cover my ears and drop my head onto my knees, the sound of it nearly unbearable.

Halvar helps me to my feet and attempts to lead me back inside. I stumble more than once, all at once called to and repelled by the sounds still overriding my sense. He all but slams the door shut and ushers me into a seat. My ears are still ringing but the pressure has lightened up.

"Do you think we made them mad?" I ask, rubbing my temples.

He shakes his head, his face ashen. "You didn't see what I saw. After you dropped down, they all rushed back into the forest. Towards something. I think—" He swallows past the lump in his throat. "I think something else was out there."

He brings me a glass of water and a warm washcloth, which he presses to the back of my neck. I thank him and chug down the water. It does little to relieve the aching that has settled in me.

I let out a heavy breath, dropping the washcloth onto the table. "Strange happenings here, strange happenings there. We know something is wrong, and I think the woods know it, too."

He considers for a moment. "It doesn't make any less sense than what we've already seen. But we can't know for certain."

"No, but we can try." I rush up the stairs towards the study. Perhaps the *Creatura* will have some insight into what we saw. I am fully prepared to study for the rest of the evening, dinner all but forgotten, when I stop in the doorway.

The candle is alight once more.

A rush of pride flows through me, and I feel Halvar catch up behind me. I turn to him with an open mouth, ready to explain what has happened here. I want this moment to feel real.

But, as with so many opportunities, I don't get a chance to do so.

We hear it at the same time, nearly out of earshot but not quite so far that we can't *just* make out the sound.

The alarm.

CHAPTER ELEVEN

"Get to the bedroom," Halvar says.

The urgency in his voice sends me out of my stupor enough to rush to our room. His footsteps follow close behind, and then he lurches for the knives beneath the bed. He rummages in the wardrobe for something—a holster—and fixes it to his waist and thighs before strapping several knives into the slots. Throwing a coat atop all of this, he rushes towards the door.

He turns for a quick moment. "*Please* stay inside."

And then he's gone.

I rush to the window and can barely see him as he runs into the trees. I am suddenly all too aware of how alone I am out here. In my parents' home, under their watchful eyes, I at least knew that they were okay. Here, I cannot know who the alarm rings for. I can only wonder which elder found the body, if they are already thinking of ways to blame Halvar for this.

I pace the length of our bedroom enough times that I'm surprised I haven't worn a trench into the floors. The urge to stand watch at the window is strong, but after what I learned at dinner, the glass separating me from the trees feels much thinner. I want him to come back. I want to know he's safe. I want to know my parents are safe. I want so many things out of my control.

It could be minutes or hours that I've been pacing when I hear the front door open and Halvar's heavy footsteps run up the stairs. I rush to the landing to meet him and nearly collapse in relief to see him unharmed. There's not a scratch on him, no new ones at least.

He grips my shoulders when he meets me. "There's nothing out there. The perimeter of the village is secure."

"You went all the way to Kliransk?"

He nods grimly. "Just outside of the trees they'll venture into. I didn't see anything out of sorts. But the animals are acting strange. Something is wrong."

"What do we do?"

"We wait," he says. "If something was stalking the village, it would have passed through our neck of the woods by now. But the terrain is mostly undisturbed."

Whatever is out there must be very smart if it's outwitting a hunter as experienced as Halvar. My hands shake with the thought. I hate not knowing things.

"How long do we wait? Something could have happened to my parents, or the neighbors." Panic rises in me, swift and volatile. I pick up my pacing again, feeling out of control of my own body.

"We go to Kliransk." Halvar's voice is firm, decisive. "Tomorrow. We won't do ourselves any favors traveling there tonight, and frankly, I don't want to if something is out there. But we can make our way there at first light and hear what they have to say at their meeting."

My shoulders sag in relief. It will be something of a balm to see my parents and know they're alive. But to be back in Kliransk for a village's worth of paranoid parishioners to cast suspicion on us…

"We have each other," he says quietly, as if reading my thoughts. "We are our own alibi."

"I just hope that's enough," I mutter.

I consider the day finished after that. With the coming trouble ahead, I fall into bed and let sleep claim me.

Halvar wakes me earlier than I would've liked, gently stirring me from a dream. Once we are dressed and fed, we ready ourselves to leave. I bundle myself in his scarf and one of the thicker coats. Beneath the finery is a plain black dress, perfectly fine to mourn in. He takes an extra chunk of bread as we head out the door, giving me a knowing look.

"The walk is going to make you hungry."

The clearing outside of our home is still awash in darkness, the snow barely disturbing the forest floor. I can't tell if it's just the clouds blocking out the sun or the fact that it's still practically night, but I can barely see ten paces in front of me. It is a comfort to feel hidden within the trees.

I breathe in this moment of fleeting peace. It's not enough, and I don't know if that makes me selfish.

The snow starts falling heavier as we get closer to the village and the trees start to thin. All too soon, I see an ax embedded in a trunk and the edge of the tree line is in sight. Once we pass through, our little secluded haven will burst. I put on the face of the Emelie that my parents tolerate.

Halvar notices the change and squeezes my hand once in comfort. I can see the houses, the run-down excuse for a market.

I want to go home. Not the one I was born in, but the one Halvar and I have started to build together.

Halvar stops me with a hand. "Wait."

He doesn't need to explain why. I hear the voices too.

"Where do you think—"

"Emelie!"

My heart stops when I hear someone call my name, then settles again once I see it's only Magda. Her eyes are bloodshot like she's been crying, but no tears stain her cheeks. She doesn't look sad. If anything, she looks angry.

Behind her are several of our old classmates and peers. They stand clustered just inside the tree line, narrowly hiding between trunks that haven't been butchered. Their eyes flit over to us, not bothering to hide the suspicion in them, but no one voices any protest.

Magda runs up to us and throws her arms around me. I freeze momentarily before returning the embrace. I don't know that I've ever hugged anyone my age besides Halvar.

"You don't understand what it's been like since you left," she says against my shoulder. "It's gotten so much worse."

I bark out a laugh, pushing away from her. "You're going to tell me I don't understand? Why do you think I left?"

She steps back, looking struck. "You underestimate how well some of us can play pretend, Emelie."

When she storms off towards her group of friends, Halvar and I follow, unsure what else we can do. They mutter to each other in low tones. Everyone looks exhausted, dark circles rimming eyes and barely-suppressed yawns hidden behind hands.

"What's going on?" I ask, unable to take their shifting eyes.

Magda won't look at me when she says, "We can't find Calder."

"Can't find him?" I look between all of the faces spread about. The majority of our class is here. Most, except for Calder. "What do you mean?"

"After the last alarm, after the funeral…" Her eyes flick to mine before looking away again. "We all decided to check in with each other if it rang again. So when it went off last night, Eiden went from house to house."

Eiden, a boy from our lessons, crosses his arms. "He wouldn't come to his window. I waited for nearly an hour."

Magda's head is bowed, her feet kicking in the snow. "He knows to meet us here. Curfew's about to lift."

Eiden scoffs. "Screw the curfew. They're just going to add more rules today. That's probably why they set off the damn alarm."

I look between each of them, then over to our classmates standing ramrod straight with disdain clear on their faces. This is not the Kliransk I thought I had left.

"There could still be a wolf," another girl from our class interjects.

"If there really was a wolf, don't you think we'd know by now?"

Eiden snaps.

"She's right," Halvar says, ignoring the way heads snap toward him. "I've come across some strange tracks in the woods. I wouldn't rule anything out."

A shudder rolls through me when I think of the Walker. I can't decide which is worse, the truth we're being fed, or the truth we cannot see.

"What do you think you're doing out here?"

Our heads whip towards the sound. Some of the village mothers have clustered at the opening of the tree line. They don't dare to pass through, but they gawk at us like we are something to be feared. Maybe we are.

We failed to notice the masses of villagers making their way toward the church. People must have left their homes the moment curfew was lifted. I wonder what excuses my peers thought they could make. If they truly thought they wouldn't be expected at the town meeting.

"Christ," Magda mutters under her breath. "Here we go."

They all file towards the village, shoulders cowed in shame. Whether it's for show or not, even I am fooled. Halvar and I follow, but pause once we are out in the open. Faces turn towards us. Some of their eyes light up with brief recognition, some with curiosity, some with flat-out vitriol. For a minute we just watch people go; I know every single face almost as well as I know my own. And yet the only thing I can recall is the way they look at Halvar and I with fear and reproach.

I am not sorry to have left.

Magda and the others split up as they walk towards the church, keeping a distance from one another that won't matter once the village mothers alert the elders to their having broken curfew. She turns back to me only once, dipping her chin low in some unspoken command. The message is clear enough: stay safe and stay quiet.

We are some of the last to arrive, which is perfectly fine by me. Once inside the church, we linger at the back of the crowd. I pick my parents out with ease, perched in the front pew and waiting with expectant ears for what the priests have to say.

Had I not made my choices, that would be me sitting beside them with my head bowed and hands grasped. The picture of the perfect pious daughter. I was never good to that version of myself, never good enough to be her. Now that she's gone, I hope she can be happy. I hope I can, too.

Halvar's light squeeze on my arm grounds me back in reality.

"Are you alright?"

I nod curtly, which should tell him well enough that I am not, but I am trying to be.

Father Levi steps forward and clears his throat. The mass of villagers perk up, hungry for information. Perhaps for justice as well. With Halvar's secret truth hidden in my throat, I feel I am a liability. I want to protect him from their paranoia, but fear my protectiveness will cue their suspicion even more. I suppose that makes me paranoid, too.

"It has been brought to our attention that a few members of the congregation breached the curfew this morning. Seeing as the curfew exists solely for your protection, my brothers and I can only assume that breaking it means that you do not want our protection."

Right to the point, then. Will they continue to exile people until they are only left with the most obedient?

"Or," Father Levi continues, "it means that you have been corrupted by outside forces."

My entire body tenses, and from my periphery I can see Halvar does, too. Heads turn towards us, glaring now with unfettered hatred. When my mother's eyes find mine, I cannot decide if the fear in them is for my sake or her own.

Halvar instinctively takes a step in front of me, putting an arm up to shield me. It feels horribly familiar. We have lived this nightmare once before. I can only imagine what they want to take from us this time.

"We mean no harm." Halvar's voice booms through the church, a commanding sound even as his words are subordinate.

"We've only come to see what the alarm is about."

Father Levi opens his mouth, perhaps to argue or to condemn, but Father Patrick silences him with a hand. "Let us not be rash, brother. They, too, were our children once."

And to my amazement, Father Levi acquiesces. Heads turn away to face the front of the church again, no longer interested in crucifying us as long as the elders have had their say. If a single one of them can change their minds, I wonder what might have been different if they had better things to say.

Father Dasco takes advantage of the silence. "A single loss of life is a tragedy. Three in the span of a few weeks is a sign from God that we are not living by His teachings. As your spiritual guides, we have failed you in that sense. And for that, we apologize."

Halvar scoffs. I dig my fingers into my skirts to avoid digging into my skin.

"Every single one of us must do all that we can to live in the faith, to walk in the faith. We are made in the image of God and we must be a proper reflection. We are at the mercy of His plan, and if we are to learn anything from these losses of life, it's that this is all a part of His plan."

I recoil at that. To claim that any of these deaths was for a greater purpose is a disgusting exaggeration of the truth. The grief of the village is so heavy and overbearing; how can this be for the greater good?

"It's not right," Halvar mutters. "None of this is."

"In an effort to further ourselves in God's image, we are instating daily masses, effective immediately. We will have two services a day, performed by either myself or one of my brothers. There will be a morning and afternoon mass, after which the curfew will be enforced. By sunset, all work and social interaction is to cease and doors are to be barred."

None of this sounds too extreme by Kliransk standards. By my own, it sounds like hell on earth.

"And," Father Dasco continues, his glare finding Halvar and

I. "We will be closing the border. Effective immediately."

A jolt rolls through me as discussions erupt all at once. Most of the older villagers look pleased, as if they were waiting for this all along. Scattered throughout the church, my peers look downcast. Disappointment mixed with frustration. But there is also a jittering current flowing through the room.

The elders are unable to get the crowd to completely quiet down. Similar to last time, the people start to throw out questions to the elders. They field them with non-answers and Bible verses. Though there is one pressing question they cannot ignore.

Who is dead?

Dread sinks low in my gut. I want to run to Magda and throw my arms around her before the elders can say it, as if that could shield her from the news. Because I know. We all know.

It is Father Levi who delivers the blow, with his mouth drawn into a hard line. "Calder was caught by the shifter."

Outrage passes over the villagers; another son taken from the collective mothers and fathers of this cursed village. I lower my head, not to hide tears but to hide the sneer that has curled my lip. Something is rotten in Kliransk.

"I want to leave," I mutter to Halvar.

"And go where?"

"Anywhere. Somewhere. Just not here."

"Patience," he whispers. "We can't afford to look suspicious."

Father Patrick manages to soothe the crowd with his soft-edged voice. "Calder's death will not be in vain. Nor will Abel's. We will do our best to move forward as a community. Together. Allow us to guide you towards a better future for Kliransk."

I might imagine the way the elders' eyes float towards Halvar and I with the unspoken addendum: *Without you.*

We are the outsiders now. It doesn't matter that I was among them two short months ago. I chose my side, and they have remained firm in theirs.

Each of the elders take a turn saying their piece, and then

dismiss the people to attend to their tasks before the curfew shuts everyone back inside. It was a brief and brutal meeting, almost worse than the droning lecture I was expecting.

In the courtyard out front, Magda and the rest commune in a tight circle. I can see each of their families waiting some paces away, attempting to urge them home, but none of them are to be swayed. I pull Halvar alongside me as I join them.

Magda's hand tightens on my arm when we approach. "I know you can't stay. But will you write?"

I nod, unsure I could tell her no even if I wanted to. Behind her, Eiden and the others are sharing the same concern I've been holding inside. What is to become of the village. What could become of them if they voice disagreement too loudly and with too bold a tongue. They, too, remember the exodus from our childhood. We lost so many townspeople to poverty and lack of resources. Far away as they are, neighboring villages seemed the better option. I wonder if we will see familiar faces pass through the trees seeking shelter.

Magda shifts on her feet, still visibly uncomfortable. "You know we're not so different, really."

"In what way?"

"You know exactly what I'm talking about."

"Do I?"

I am not being completely fair to her. It might be nice to have a friend.

She makes a feeble attempt at wiping her tears before crossing her arms over her chest. "Fine, let me be frank then. Nothing about this feels right, and my suspicions are beginning to be cast in places besides the woods. Everyone is acting so strange."

So, she can feel it too. That something is wrong here and it is spreading. She has to have felt it before now. The wrongness, the suffocation. My eyes flick to Halvar, who is keeping his gaze firmly interested in the open air around us.

I turn back to Magda. "I feel it too. And I'm sorry that it's affected you this way."

160

She scoffs, rolling her eyes. "Apologies do nothing for me now. What I want are solutions."

I gesture between myself and Halvar. "So do we."

"Do you have anything yet?"

I shake my head. "Nothing useful."

Magda bites her lip, forcing back more tears. "They're all convinced this is some act of God sent to punish us. But perhaps Eiden was right. Have you ever seen a wolf, Emelie?"

I resist the urge to look at Halvar.

Stuffing my hands in my pockets, I settle for a resolution. "I'll send word once we have something of note. Start anticipating the postmen before your father does."

Magda nods. She's about to turn and walk away, back to her grieving, when my cursed curiosity gets the better of me as it always does. When I call her name again, she looks over her shoulder, waiting.

"Did you love him?"

Her face remains unmoved. "You don't have to love someone for it to hurt when you lose them."

With that, she follows Eiden and the others towards their families up the road. Her words repeat in my head, and I can't help but conjure the moment my parents shut the door on Halvar and I's retreating forms. How surprised I was by that, how conflicted I feel about it now.

I shove the image away; my grief is no good here.

People are still milling in and about the church, waiting to speak with the elders or afraid to come outside for fear of an invisible wolf. I turn this way and that, looking for faces that look too much like mine.

Halvar leans in. "Do you want to see your parents?"

"I want the option to." It's the truth. Despite our friction, despite their treatment of me, I don't hate them. I have only had a taste of freedom, and while I want to devour it whole, I can't picture a life where I never see my mother and father. "I want to know that they're okay."

He starts to nod, then stops himself. "May I ask you

161

something?"

"You don't need to ask if you can ask me something," I say.

"I'm not like you," he says. "I'm not bold enough to just say whatever I'm thinking."

I blush at the implication that I am bold. I would never describe myself as such. Not when I've spent my entire life struggling under Kliransk's collective thumb.

He continues, "Your relationship with your parents as it is, why do you care what happens to them?"

This feels like a conversation we've been dancing around for weeks now. He was privy to all of my arguments with them growing up. He is intimately familiar with all of the ways they made me feel: not good enough, not woman enough, not devout enough. He knows that I have always been a burning pyre to their dry kindling. And yet I am defending them, like my instincts demand of me even now.

"They're still my parents," is all I can think to say.

His mouth is a hard line. "Yes, your parents who left you hungry and improperly clothed for all the time you were in their charge. Your parents who chose God over their own daughter time and time again. Who could have brought you to a better life when they had the chance, and they denied it."

I don't know why this ignites my temper. He's not wrong, and I have no reason to argue with him. But my traitorous mouth works before I can stop myself.

"Like your father was any better."

It is a low blow, and I regret it immediately. I know my words have struck somewhere deep because I can see a flash of hurt in his eyes.

He swallows, then leans forward so he's only a breath away. I don't know if I want to pull away or close the distance between us. He manages to maintain eye contact, but I can see him struggling to do so.

"The fact that my father was no better," he says slowly, "is how I know that yours were just as bad. They might not have beat you the way mine did, but don't think I don't notice the way you shrink in their presence. I hate to watch it happen, Emelie. You are worth more than you know. Far more."

I exhale and feel hot tears pushing their way up my throat. But I can't cry, not here. Not in front of so many watching eyes. I don't want to think about the fact that he understands even better than I do why I resent my parents so strongly.

In this moment, I can't stand the fact that he sees me. That he fundamentally understands the pieces of me that I have yet to work through. It is too vulnerable, and I push down the part of me that is thrilled by this, the part that has longed to feel seen and went hidden for so long.

He scratches at his scar, his unconscious nervous habit. It is three long gashes with a fourth short one bottoming it out, covering nearly the entirety of his left cheek. The gashes branch out near his temple before curving in to meet at a single point between his nose and upper lip. They cave into his skin in such a way that even if I were blind, I could make them out. They still burn an angry pinkish red and look painful, though I know they've long since healed.

I want to ask how he got them, but I know better.

Instead, I swallow my pride. "I'm sorry. I shouldn't lash out at you."

He waves off my apology. It's not an acceptance or even a dismissal, really. I swallow the frustration that still lingers and push on.

"No, really, I shouldn't have said what I did. You're right, and that's why I got angry. That doesn't give me a right to direct it at you. I don't need to defend my parents to you. But that doesn't change the fact that I want to see them—on my own terms, at least."

He won't look at me even as he speaks. "It was very hard for me to come back and see the way they were treating you. If I were a better man I would have said something, and if I were a worse one I would have done something. Like fighting your father. I can't understand how you can stand to speak to them at all. But if it's what you want, I'll help you. I don't need to understand."

His kindness stuns me, and for a moment I forget that we are technically arguing and that I have already acquiesced. At his submission, I want to fall to my knees and beg his forgiveness.

"It's been very difficult for me, too," I say. "I don't know why I love them the way I do. We've been at odds for most of my life, and I wish I were someone who could leave without looking back."

"It's because you are good," he says quietly. "Even against your better judgment."

I melt a little, and the tears threaten to work their way back up. I push them down once more. "Do you mean that?"

"I've always known it. You've shown it to me time and time again. Like when you defended a sorry son of a bitch who was being attacked by an angry mob and got yourself married to him." The half-smile on his face crinkles his eyes. I want to kiss the places where his face twists with signs of happiness. I want it to never go away.

"I'm not sorry I did that," I whisper, my boldness once again doing me a favor.

"Neither am I," he says, holding my gaze at last.

I can't tell who leans in first, but we meet in the middle and press our lips together. He kisses me softly, putting the forgiveness for my apology in it. I take it, drinking it in greedily.

But the small bubble we've created bursts when a shadow falls over us.

My parents look the same as I last saw them, which shouldn't be surprising as it hasn't been so long. But I feel so different, so changed, while they seem to have stayed in place. My mother is still all harsh angles and fierce expectations. She still has an air of preemptive disappointment surrounding her. Coupled with that now is fear. Raw and unashamed. My father's face is a blank slate as it always is, if a little more tired.

"Calder's parents must be in shambles," I say, breaking the silence.

"I'm surprised that you care," my mother says, all bite. She isn't holding back now, perhaps because I have a husband to protect me. Now that I don't have to live under her roof, she doesn't have to bother with pretense.

"Of course I care," I snap.

She scoffs. "Yet you run away at the first opportunity. Abandoning your only home for a man you barely knew as a *child*—"

The voice that comes out next is not my own. "Don't speak about my husband as if he weren't here."

I can feel the shock radiating off everyone, Halvar especially. It is a minuscule change, but the toe of his boot moves to touch mine. It is as much affection either of us are willing to show in front of my parents. As for my mother, her face goes slack, but she collects herself quickly. I think she might respect me for defending my husband. I suppose it's something a godly woman would do.

My father clears his throat. "This was not how we wanted to do this."

He opens his arms, and it takes me a moment to realize he is waiting for me to embrace him. I fall into his arms easily enough; it's not him who's done anything to hurt me. Though I suppose the lack of anything is what hurts all the same.

"We've missed you," he murmurs into my hair.

"I would come back," I say, "if they would let me."

This makes him drop his arms. I return to Halvar's side and don't fight it when he tucks me into his side.

My father frowns, a familiar expression. It's chilling to see it directed at me. "This is what the elders have decreed. Who am I to question them?"

"And who are they to speak for you?"

"Emelie," my mother warns.

"They are who we look to for guidance." Father's words are curt and to the point. "We are nothing if we do not follow God, and the elders are the closest we have to a mouthpiece. We are doing our best, daughter. You must see that."

My voice shakes but my words are firm. "I fail to see the world as you do. Yours is not a life I would have chosen, if given options."

"We've made do," my mother says, raising a brow. "I should hope you can come to say the same."

It's probably the kindest thing she's capable of saying. And so I take it.

"We should go," I say, my tone echoing my mother's bite. "As the elders have commanded."

I don't give them room to respond. I nudge Halvar, wordlessly begging him to follow me before I fall apart. He reads my unspoken request and hurries us towards the border. A small part of me hopes one of them will call us back. But just as before, they don't.

As we reach the tree line, I turn my head, hoping to get one more look at them. Instead, I see a small cluster of villagers watching us. I think they expect something to happen once we pass through the trees, something like I once anticipated. I look forward to disappointing them.

I see Magda in the crowd, watching us go. I lift one hand in farewell. She doesn't reciprocate but inclines her chin to show that she knows it was for her. I am just about to turn back when I spot Father Dasco watching us through narrowed eyes. He stands a ways away from the rest of the onlookers and it's an eerie sight, him in his black robes that flow in the breeze. I am glad for it when we pick up our pace.

Once we are safely out of sight, the mask drops. Rejection mixes with grief and confusion. I feel like I am losing so much that I didn't even know I had. A heaving sob bursts out of me and I sag against the nearest tree trunk. It hurts to stand, to breathe, to be alive.

Without question, Halvar hefts me into his arms and rushes us home at that inhuman pace. I cry the entire way there and don't stop once he brings me inside and up to our room.

The pain refuses to stop all day. I refuse meals, as well as Halvar's invitation to sit with him in his study. I don't want to leave our bed. My legs feel too heavy. He comes and goes depending on how heavy my tears fall. At times I pull him onto the bed with me, needing an anchor to still me in my storm. Other times I send him away, too ashamed to have him see me this way.

166

Once night falls, Halvar forgoes the lanterns in favor of setting candles out to bathe the room in a soft glow. It is such a gentle gesture, so soft and unlike any I've ever received, that it cracks something inside of me. It washes the sadness away until only the uglier emotions are left.

Without the blanket of sorrow, all I can feel is anger. I let it seep out of me, too tired to keep it pent up. Every word out of my mother's mouth is just shy of a curse. It is so painful to never be enough for her, and her remarks do nothing but *aggravate me*—

A burst of energy pulses out of my skin. That pent-up anger feels physical, like it's leaving my body in a rush.

Every candle in the room flickers out at once.

Halvar stills, momentarily stunned. Then he lets out a breathy laugh. "Good one."

"That was me?"

"You were right," he says, standing. "You certainly are called to it."

I sit frozen, disbelief coursing through me. "I can't believe I did that."

"I can." He sounds affirmed, like this was something he already knew. "You're more powerful than you believe."

My hand swipes across my eyes, clearing them of tears. "Maybe I can use this to fix things. I don't want to fail Magda. I don't want Calder to have died for nothing."

Halvar sits beside me on the bed, reaching for me tentatively. I let him take my hand. "It's not your responsibility to fix everything that's wrong in the world."

"Not the whole world," I agree. "But my world. Will you help me with at least that much?"

He picks up my hand and brings it to his lips, pressing them against my skin with featherlight pressure. "I made a vow to do just that."

The room is nearly pitch-black, but he must see the blush that warms my face. "Together, then?"

He nods. "Together."

CHAPTER TWELVE

I had expected the cold—and the ongoing faceless threat of death—to shrink my world. I had expected a set of rules and expectations that would keep me locked inside to wait for spring. But to my surprise, the door has remained open to me whenever I want to go for walks. Halvar's never given me permission to do whatever I want; he's given me room to realize that I did not *need* permission. That I've never needed it from anyone.

I've started going for walks on my own, determined to know these paths as well as he does. I've retained more of a hunger for it, wanting to know more and see it for myself. I cannot get enough of the woods. I have perfected the routes that Halvar laid out for me and have started to map out paths of my own. After a few weeks of paying careful attention, I've become familiar with miles in every direction. My world has suddenly grown so much larger.

Today the air is unsparingly cold. I have to count the weeks on my fingers; it's been nearly three months since Halvar and I married, three months since he walked out of these woods and back into my life. Three months since I walked back in with him. The new year is in good form, full of possibility.

I walk with one arm looped through a woven basket, the other pulling up any surviving flora that has sprouted through the thick snowfall. There is nothing in particular I'm looking for, but my intuition has pushed me to explore. I am still learning how to listen to myself. How to trust myself.

The trees thin out ahead of me to make way for a clearing, the very same one where we found the merchants weeks ago. They haven't come through this clearing since, though Halvar says they should return in the coming days if they stick to the unspoken rhythm set by the surrounding communes. I've passed a few of them on my walks, spotted houses in the distance, or encountered passersby down the paths. Some faces I recognize from the Solstice festival, some are as unfamiliar to me as the ever-expanding trees I come across.

My steps slow once I reach the border of the clearing. This is further than I meant to go. I peer down into my basket, and, upon finding it full enough to make some manner of elixirs, I turn back towards home. The sun is far from sinking below the horizon, but I prefer to make it back with plenty of time. I retrace my steps, relying on the sights surrounding me to guide me back.

A twig snaps to my left, coming from the clearing. I flinch but force my eyes forward. If I ignore it, then it will ignore me, whatever it is. This wouldn't be the first animal I've encountered on my walks, but I double-check the dagger holstered to my side just in case. It rests against my hip, heavy and hostile.

Another *snap*, closer now. This time I do freeze, turning only my head towards the sound. At first, I don't see anything, low-hanging branches webbing together to block my line of vision. I tighten my hand around the dagger's hilt, pulling it out of its sheath with practiced calm.

I see legs first, muscular with thick, flexing tendons and taller than me standing at my full height. The limbs end in large hooves that somehow rest just atop the layer of snow rather than sink into it. It stalks further out of the trees, not looking at me though it's definitely aware of me. It looks like a deer but taller. *Much* taller. For an extra second, I wonder if it *is* a deer, but it emits some kind of alien wildness that removes it from any average animal.

Though they should have shed with the winter's cold, antlers sit

170

high on its head. They twist around each other in a way that should look grotesque, but the pattern is so intricate that it's almost reminiscent of a crown. Even on all fours, it stands easily above eight feet. I shudder to think of this *thing* standing next to Halvar and still towering over him.

We lock eyes, and the look of them sends another shiver through me. One eye is glassy and round, retaining warmth as a living thing should, but the *other*... Its right eye is completely white, the pupil washed of any pigment. It makes the dark brown of its regular eye look like the unforgiving pitch black of the night sky. I would mistake it to be blind in that eye if I didn't feel it staring at me. Witnessing me. Still, the deer retains its serene air. As if I haven't intruded on its afternoon walk, and it on mine. Just like Halvar claimed of the shifters, it looks smarter than it should be. I can see the understanding in its eyes, the consciousness. It is far from human, but just as far from animal as well. Purely creature. I stick to my side of the path, my hand weaponized but still. I won't draw before it does.

After a few extra-long heartbeats, the creature shakes out of its casual stupor and continues walking deeper into the woods. As if we never met one another. Only after it is out of sight do I allow myself to exhale. I keep Halvar's earlier reminder in mind like a prayer: *they won't bother you if you don't bother them.* Each creature has a varying definition of *bother*, and it might be simple dumb luck that has kept me safe up to this point. Sometimes I like to pretend that the animals and creatures know my face; they know I belong here as much as they do, and that is why they leave me be. It is a game of pretend I don't mind playing.

I don't linger out in the woods any longer. I debate whether or not I should tell Halvar about my encounter, but ultimately I have to believe that he will trust my judgment.

In the study, he sits buried between piles of books and pads of paper covered in his scribbling. The nature of the deaths over the past few weeks has kept him here, trying to use words to figure out what his eyes can't see when he ventures out to track. He is still unable to find a pattern, unable to make sense of everything that's happened. My own research has done even less to further our theories. Whether or not magic plays a part in this has yet to be seen.

We have heard little from Kliransk besides the alarms.

With the border closed, we can't attend the funerals or the town halls. Though I'm sure that we'd only find prejudice and rules we're not inclined to follow. It leaves me worried for my parents, but I can only do so much from this side of the border. I have my magic and my studies, but the deaths are a wide and tangled tapestry I can only see sections of. Without the full picture, I can only make educated guesses while I wait to see what unfolds next. I should have listened to my own advice sooner; I can't always make things happen.

The death knoll has rung thrice more since our last visit. If there is a body for every pang, that brings the death toll to six. Six bodies who used to be souls walking around and breathing as I do now. Who had dreams that will never be brought to full potential.

It's not your responsibility to fix everything that's wrong in the world. True, but I have so much unused potential where the dead now have none. I can't let it be for nothing. And another selfish corner of my heart whispers that should I fall to the same fate, I don't want to die like them. With so much I could have done, but didn't.

Halvar looks up from his desk when I enter the study. A smile graces his face, and he taps his pen against his notes. "Find anything useful?" He gestures to my basket.

I hold it up for him to see. "We'll find out. I saw something while I was out there, though."

He tenses, the smile dropping. "Something?"

"A creature," I clarify. "It didn't come close to me, we left each other alone. But it did see me."

He looks at me from beneath his brows, chews on the inside of his cheek as he processes what I've said. "You had your knife?"

I nod, patting where it sits in my holster. He nods along with me, putting down his pen. He leans back in his seat and crosses his arms. I can see him wrestling with his instinct to protect, which is incompatible with the inherent freedom owed to me. He respects the wildness I am slowly learning to unleash. I know he wants this for me

172

as much as I do. But I also know that it is a challenge for him to not want to come with me, to fight off every creature that comes near me.

I am finding that not every battle needs fighting. Some can be set aside in favor of laying down our weapons and sticking to our own paths. It is a method akin to peacemaking. Peace is something I have never known, and in truth, I still don't. But I do know that it's easier to respect the creatures than to fear them. And as long as I am still alive among them, I can imagine that they are coming to respect me, too.

That being said, knowing how to wield the dagger comes with its own variety of peace.

"I could use another lesson," I say, unsheathing it from the holster. "It'd make me feel a little better."

He looks relieved to have an excuse to set down his work. "Gladly."

The receiving room has been transformed into a training ring with a rug laid out to soften our falls and the rest of the furniture shoved against the wall. We're never in here unless it's to train, so the nice sofas and end tables feel superfluous.

I've taken a liking to wearing pants and shirts as opposed to dresses. This allows me to move more, to feel bigger than my body. I can lunge at Halvar with my dagger and easily fall back when he parries my blow. He curses when I catch him on his open left side once again, giving me the upper hand. I disarm him with only moderate resistance and grin up at him, holding his own dagger.

"I win."

He ruffles my hair, taking his dagger back. "I'll give it to you, I was trying that time. You could take on someone my size if you had to."

I've had several lessons with the dagger since our first one, and through the soreness and pain, I've *improved*. I have not failed to notice how different my reflection looks; now, my arms are lined with muscle that wasn't there before. Not only that, I *feel* stronger too. It's a pleasant surprise, one I intend to nourish.

I insist on running more drills, urging him to not hold out on me. I want to know what I could be up against out there. Not just the creatures but the people who could be just as dangerous, if not more.

Despite my insistence, I can tell Halvar is still holding back. He doesn't want to hurt me. But what he doesn't understand is that I need to hurt now so I can heal later. So I use his hesitancies to my advantage. When he lunges toward me, I drop to a knee and take out his ankles as he tries to adjust his footing. He loses it, thanks to me, and tumbles onto his back. I kneel over him and press the dagger a breath away from his neck, a self-satisfied smile cracking open on my face.

"I win again."

He stays statue-still, unable to move due to the knife's edge. His eyes stay locked on me, pride glinting in them. "Hunter, meet prey."

We break for dinner before returning to our respective research. He and I compare notes where we can, trying to make sense of the strange behavior of the creatures, trying to find where Kliransk fits into all of this. Why now, after all this time?

I've written to Magda a few times with no response. It was difficult to get words on the page without admitting to any damning details, should our letters be compromised. I write in veiled language, hoping she catches my meaning. The lack of reply tells me either she has not quite understood, or she simply hasn't been able to. Given the state of the village, I am not surprised by her silence.

Halvar gives up before I do, retiring to our room rather than further confusing himself. I sit on the study floor, surrounded by my books. The creature books do little in the way of guiding me so I instead return to one of the occult books. Finding the section detailing various kinds of wards, I take up the chalk and copy the symbols onto the floorboards. My lines are imperfect but I repeat the process until I have the patterns memorized. Since Halvar can't do it himself, I want to be able to rework the wards should they ever fail. I don't want to end up like the spirits, running in screeching fear from some unseen foe.

"Coming to bed?" A shirtless Halvar stands braced in the doorway, rubbing a hand over his face.

"Soon," I say, focusing on the chalk.

"I'm glad you're making use of my floors," he says, sarcasm dripping with every word.

"Go brood elsewhere." I wave him away, listening as his laughter trails down the hall and back to our bedroom.

At my side, the candle burns strong and sure. Despite how long it's been lit, the wax looks undisturbed. I smile, hoping I am right to think that it is a reflection of my confidence.

I want to try manifesting again.

I close my eyes, and this time, I don't try to convince myself of things. I just *believe* them. I *am* worthy. I'm *not* at fault for my parents' disappointment. My anger, my frustrations, my suspicions, all of that *is* valid.

When I open my eyes, the room is bathed in the soft glow of the candle. I feel a sense of what I can only assume is peace. The emptiness that had been lingering in me is still there, but I place a hand on my sternum and feel a renewed sense of purpose there, too. For once, it feels like it's coming from within me. My own sense of power.

Warmth runs through me. For the first time in months, I feel the darkness in me slipping back as it's bathed in light. I feel like a person again. I feel alive. It feels wrong for me to experience this alone.

I need Halvar.

My bare feet pad down the hallway, making hardly a sound. From the threshold of our bedroom, I watch him lounge in our bed. Only one lantern is lit, the light low and alluring. It shines against his tanned skin, the beautiful scars there tangling with the shadows.

He turns his head to look at me, and maybe he sees the need in my eyes because he sits up slowly, pulling the covers back.

"Come here," he murmurs.

Our bodies reach for one another as if compelled. He pulls me onto him and cradles my face. His other arm snakes around my waist and keeps me flush to him. His eyes soften as he looks at me, and I can't tell if it's the lantern light or tears making his eyes shine. Those familiar eyes; it is such a gift that I am able to look into them once more. I took those years with him for granted, and then I lost him. I won't make that same mistake again. My pride is not worth the price of not telling him how I feel.

"I love you," I say, willing the shakiness out of my voice. I place a hand against his chest, against the scarred skin and the heart beating beneath. "I have loved you my entire life."

There is such a look on his face and I realize, even as my heart breaks, that it's hope mixed in with relief. As if he feared I would say anything different. I want to kiss that look away if it means bringing joy back to his face.

"I love you," he says softly. "If I had to do it all again, I'd do it gladly knowing it would lead me back to you." His hand moves to tangle in my hair at the nape of my neck. It's like he can't touch enough of me at once. "You are good, and you are worthy, Emelie. Damn anyone who makes you feel otherwise."

I let out a laugh, tears freely falling out with it. "You make it easy for me to believe that."

"That's not good enough," he says, his hands tightening on me. "Let me show you. Please."

With practiced ease, he strips me bare. Clothes are abandoned off the edge of the bed, forgotten and unnecessary. When I try to cup him in my hand, he stops me.

"You first," he says, gently laying me on my back. He kneels between my legs, the look on his face reverent. He's looking at me like I'm something to be worshiped. This is something purer than even love.

This is adoration.

He positions my legs over his shoulders so his face is flush with my sex. Inches away, I can feel his breath. This is wholly new to both of us, and I shake with anticipation. He looks at me for permission once more, and in this moment I know I can make him beg. I can tell him I want to stop and he would redress me and lay beside me and go to bed with no issue.

He is the wanting worshiper, and I am the benevolent god.

I don't say anything. I just open my legs wider.

That is all the permission he needs to put his mouth on me. It starts slow; he presses a modest kiss to the soft flesh waiting there. My breath hitches at the touch, and it's either that or the taste of me that unleashes him. His kisses shift from reserved to fully ravishing. All of it feels good, but some of it feels even *better*. I tangle a hand in his hair and use light force to direct him where his touch feels the best. We're learning together, learning *me* together.

I can't help but roll my hips as the pleasure starts to build. I don't have to hide the moans that fall out at his prompting. More than once, our eyes meet from across the length of my body and the pure lust in his eyes is enough to push me towards that edge.

Right when it starts feeling too good, right when I think I'm done for, right before I fall over the edge, he suddenly pulls away. I collapse back onto the bed, panting. He sits back on his knees and wipes his mouth, not breaking eye contact.

"Not yet," he says, his voice laced with promise of the *yet* that is to come. He shifts so he can lean back on his elbows, his own legs spread now. He looks so languid, and there's something so assured about the smirk that takes over his face. He looks down at his own bared sex, already hard, then back to me. "My turn."

Ever obedient, I crawl towards him on my stomach, the expanse of our bed feeling like an ocean I have to swim across. I look up at him once to be sure, since this is also new for us. He sees the question in my eyes and nods, leaning down to brush one kiss against my lips. I can taste *me* on his mouth.

He sits back again and I press closed lips against the tip of him. He hisses at the tease, a quiet urging for *more more more*. I remind myself to be the benevolent god as I take him in my mouth. Like him, I start slow, listening for sounds of what feels good for him. I speed up and slow down, enjoying the way he lets out moans like he can't possibly contain himself.

I pull back some to flick my tongue around his head, and a small cry escapes him. A small pleasured giggle falls out of me, enamored by his noises. At this, a hand comes to rest on my head, using the lightest bit of pressure to push me back down. I meet his request, taking even more of him into my mouth. Then, just as forcefully, he pulls me away.

"I need you," he groans. "*Now.*"

It is far from a seamless process. He positions himself between my legs, but when he tries to push into me, I let out a small whimper. Concern flashes in his eyes, but the lust is still there.

"It might hurt some," he says. "Tell me if you want me to stop."

I shake my head. "Please don't."

Perhaps it's the begging in my tone that urges him on, or the frantic *want* that's overtaken us both, but he doesn't. He pushes his hard length into me, slowly, so I can get used to the feel of him. Once he's filled me, he waits with patience for me to let him continue. I rock my hips a little, and he meets my movement, pulling out some and then pushing back in. Both of us let out throaty groans.

It's a different kind of intimacy to be as one. I felt assured as his wife already, but to have our bodies united makes me well up with emotion, so much so that I can't contain it.

"No tears," he says, kissing away what falls down my cheeks, but I hear the change in his voice. And that's when I see that his own eyes are brimming. Droplets fall onto my face, and he laughs at the irony.

His thrusts become more confident as we become acquainted with the feeling. Maybe it's the embarrassment of crying or the raw passion of how good this feels that makes him bury his face in my neck. I hold him there, crying out with every push of him into my most vulnerable place. He whispers sweet nothings against my skin, kissing my neck before digging his teeth into the same spot. The feeling only makes my voice pitch higher, overwhelmed with how *much* I am feeling.

"I love you," I moan. "I missed you."

One of his arms snakes underneath me to hug me to him. "You'll never have to miss me again," he says. "I promise." He pulls back to watch my face. "I have so many promises I want to make to you."

Between moans I get out, "I hated our vows, you know. I wanted them to be ours."

"Damn them. Forget all that you've heard. These are my vows to you." His hips meet mine in an unending wave, filling me with pleasure, filling me with *him*. "I will protect you." He presses a kiss to my collarbone. "I will honor you." Another kiss to the fresh bruise on my neck. "I will uplift you." A kiss to my breast. "My partner, my best friend." He grabs the back of one of my knees and wraps my leg around his waist. I groan at the better fit. "I will fucking *love* you in this life and every one after this."

I rock my hips faster, too eager to have him in me. I can't get enough of him; I don't *want* to have enough. I want to want him like this for the rest of my days. I meet him thrust for thrust, fucking him back. My arms wrap around his neck, cradling me to him. I repeat the vows back to him, choking up when I get to the *best friend* line. I mean everything I say, but I mean that part the most.

The next time we approach that edge, we fall over together. I finish first with his name on my lips, and he follows shortly after in the same manner. He collapses on top of me with apologies, but when he tries to move off of me I hold him with a sure hand. I still need him close. We lie like that for a few minutes, panting and sweaty and absolutely covered in each other.

I expected to feel different, changed somehow. But the shame and fear surrounding this in my youth are nowhere to be seen. Instead, all I feel is loved. I acknowledge what a step this is for the two of us, and I feel so grateful that Halvar took that step with me, that we did it together.

He rolls onto his side, keeping his face in the crook of my neck. He has an arm draped across my stomach. I think he needs to feel close to me, too. I stroke soothing touches up and down his arm, his side, his back. We exchange soft words in the dark, the lantern long since burnt out.

"Did you like that?" He asks, his voice stirring out of the darkness.

"No," I say, turning to face him so our chests are flush together.

179

"I loved it."

He kisses my nose. "You're not hurt?"

There's a pleasant soreness between my legs, but our tender explorations of each other over the past few weeks leading up to this have gotten me acquainted with the feeling. It is not so much pain as a harsher sibling to pleasure.

By now we are sufficiently exhausted and I welcome the darkness that envelops us. Halvar draws the blanket over both of us and nestles into his pillow. So much of us is touching and none of it feels wrong. I offer to give him his space, to pull away should he need it, but he only shakes his head and tightens his arm around me.

"I need you so much closer."

It doesn't take long for either of us to drift off to sleep. For once, I am not awoken by his tossing and turning throughout the night. We sleep peacefully, wrapped up in each other and sharing breath. At first light, I feel him untangle himself from me as he gets up for the day. When he notices me peeking up at him, he leans down to press a kiss to my forehead, smoothing my hair back.

"Go back to sleep," he whispers.

I listen to him dress and head downstairs. Part of me thinks I should get up and join him, but the rest of me is too exhausted. Even the smell of breakfast isn't enough to lure me downstairs.

When I blink awake fully, there is a note on the pillow next to me.

Out hunting. Be back by dawn. Please stay inside.

I rise for the day with a quick stretch. I've taken to staying in my nightgowns on the slower days. With Halvar gone, I have little to do besides clean or read and right now I care to do neither. It's already late morning, and with how long I slept it should be no problem to wait up for him should he need any bandaging. It almost feels silly to admit that I want him home already. I respect his practice and the comfort it affords the both of us, but I can't ignore the pit in my stomach that shows up every time he leaves. Perhaps it's an after effect of last night's intimacy, but the pit is more like a gaping hole in me, an inner plea for him to come home already.

Or, more likely, it's hunger.

In the kitchen, he's left me breakfast. Simpler today, toasted bread with jam as well as a mug of tea, still warm. I take my breakfast on the balcony with my crystals surrounding me, trying to get a feel for the energy of each. After that, I practice drawing the ward symbols. Then I offer up a manifestation. I try mixing materials into an empty vial to make a healing elixir. It smells earthy, and that must mean it's correct.

I have worked through all of my materials by the time the afternoon sun is glowing golden, reflecting brightly off the melting snow. It's still striking to me that outside of this cocoon of trees, the snow falls harder and stays longer. With the exception of the storm that's passed, it tends to feel like late fall out here. That canopy does make it difficult to tell time though, what with all of the shade it offers.

I burn through a novel before dinner, needing distraction from the pit that is ever expanding in me. By the time I've finished, I feel worse. So I make dinner. I eat alone, feeling more hollow than before. So I start another book.

By midnight I can't keep still.

I clean the house top to bottom in a frenzy. It is absolutely spotless by the time I'm finished, as if we were never here at all. I take a bath to wash off the day, put on a fresh nightgown. I braid my hair, undo it. Rebraid it.

I pace the entirety of the house, counting how many floorboards creak. I map out paths up and down the stairs that would leave me unheard, as well as the noisiest path. I reorganize the books on the shelf. I think about preparing a second dinner. Nothing is helping.

At dawn, I know something is wrong.

Halvar's note said he'd be back *by* dawn. That means he could have come home sooner but didn't. I try laying down for a mere minute before I can't take the anxiety that is racketing my body. Instead, I pace in front of the bedroom window, watching and waiting for any sign of him.

The early morning sunlight is battling its way through the trees, and the darkness is still winning. It is thanks to that alone that I am able to see the lights flickering at the edge of the tree line.

Not lights. Spirits.

They glow an angry red as they did the last time I saw them, only this time instead of fluttering away, they spin in tiny circles amongst themselves. They look to be throwing themselves against the wards. Some of them fly high up towards my line of sight, then back down. I watch them for a moment, befuddled. If they are running from something, it's coming this way. But if they *were* running, they would know they can't get past the wards.

Unless they are trying to get my attention.

I run onto the balcony, nearly tripping over my chair's legs. I listen hard for those familiar whispers or even the cursed screeching. The sound I'm met with is somewhere in between. A high-pitched buzzing that is still frantic, but clearly trying to communicate. When I lean over the banister to try and get a better look, they glow impossibly brighter, flying faster until they are nearly blurred.

I don't know what instinct pushes me to go down there, but I listen to it. I throw on pants loose enough to run in as well as one of Halvar's shirts atop one of my own. I toss clothes out of the wardrobe until I find one of his harnesses.

There are so many belt loops. I latch it around me as tight as I can get and stuff several of his knives in. I don't know how to use most of them with their different shapes and weights, but I'll be damned if I leave this house empty-handed. My own dagger sits at my hip where I can reach it with ease. I throw on the first coat I reach for—the rich green one embroidered with red. It's not the most suited for this weather or this task, but I can only hope that its shorter length will allow me the easiest access to the holster. Then I stuff my feet into boots, hoping it's good enough to keep me warm.

I rush into the study and stuff whatever I can see into a sack: salt, the elixir I mixed this morning, bandages, chalk. I don't know why but that same instinct is screaming at me to just *do it*.

Then I run to the wards. I barely feel the cold as I do. As I near the tree line, the spirits suddenly break into the woods, some of them flying far ahead and some of them hanging back as a guide for me. They're making a trail, carving out a path for me. Out of habit, I want to follow one of the paths Halvar and I marked as safe, but I have no options besides following these frantic bundles of light.

And so I run.

CHAPTER THIRTEEN

I run for what must be miles. I don't think I've run this much in my life. My lungs should be burning. My legs should be well on their way to giving out. And yet the rush of pure fear pushes me forward.

There are vein-like paths in every direction, worn flat beneath years of footsteps over the grass that once grew there. Trading routes, perhaps. We pass a clearing that must be the market. I keep my eyes above, towards the ward symbols and banners, trying to keep track of where I am and where we're going. Wherever Halvar's gone to, it can't be far from here.

Ahead of me is a giant black tree with overgrown roots. It commands space like it owns the forest. Some of its roots overlap and create a small alcove at its base. It's hollow and it stares out at me, dark and hungry. The spirits fly upwards into its branches, and then I lose sight of them. Here, he must be here.

I flinch when I think I hear a growl, and my mind jumps to the shifters I have been telling myself aren't a problem. But then I hear it again, only this time stretched out. Like a groan. My heart drops to my feet and I start silently begging anyone who will listen to please let it not be him, not like this. And then I spot a boot sticking out of the alcove. And from there, a leg. The rest is coated in darkness.

I let out a sob because I immediately know it's him.

I run to him, cursing as the roots catch my boots and cause me to trip every other step. He's on his back, the dirt beneath him disrupted like he crawled with what little strength he had. He is covered in blood, and from the pallid look of his skin, it's his own. I skid to my knees and pull his head into my lap. He groans, and damn it if it isn't the most glorious sound because it means he's *alive.*

His eyes shoot open and a stream of curses flows out of him, which sets off a coughing fit. "What the fuck are you doing here, Emelie?" He tries to sit up but his arms shake too furiously to support him and he collapses back onto me.

Through my sobs, I explain how I waited for him. How I sensed something was wrong, how the spirits tried to warn me, how they led me here. He reaches up with an unstable hand and notes the weaponry covering my torso. He lets out what might be a laugh at first, but it quickly devolves into a cough.

"You have to leave," he heaves. "It's going to come back."

I shake my head so hard I make myself dizzy. "*I am not leaving you here.*" I know I sound hysterical. I barely sound human at all.

"You have to go," he repeats.

The knapsack. I shuck it off and rifle through it until I find the elixir. I ignore his protests as I lift the vial to his mouth and force it open. He tries to cough it up at first. Confusion muddles his face but I force him to drink. I don't know if it will work, but I followed the instructions too closely for it not to.

The stakes are too high for it not to.

He takes several slow breaths, and I start sobbing again when the color returns to his face. He's still in no condition to move, though. We are essentially trapped here.

"We're going to be okay," I say, shrugging out of my coat and blanketing him in it. "The sun is already rising. We just need to make it until then."

There is a roaring in the distance. I feel him stiffen, and when he tries to rise this time, he makes it to his elbows. He sways slightly but stays. His eyes search until they land on the whip, discarded at the opening of the alcove. I drag it to him. He doesn't look any more confident with it in his hand, but it's better than without, I suppose.

When the roaring picks up again, I dive back into the knapsack for salt. I unsheathe one of the smaller daggers, good for carving, and then push to my feet. Halvar tries to protest, but he can do little to stop me. Without this, we won't last until sunrise. There's no guarantee the light will be any protection, either.

I step out of the protection of the alcove and climb onto the roots to reach the base of the tree trunk. Dagger in hand, I start to carve the first ward symbol. My hand is shaking so hard that I fear it will be completely wrong, but muscle memory kicks in and does the work for me.

I climb back down and run to the next tree, much smaller than the last one, and do the same. I repeat this process two more times, pausing in between each to listen for roaring or for footsteps. Once the carvings are complete, I quickly salt the earth. The low buzz that picks up tells me I've done it. I've warded us in. And whatever is roaring, out.

I crawl back into the alcove and toss the dagger aside. Halvar watches me in awe as I pull out bandages and an ointment. I make quick work of what wounds I can see, starting with his face and arms, though there are not enough bandages to completely cover him. But when I lift his shirt to see what damage is there I pull back with a hiss. His ribcage is completely purple and sits at an angle that is just *wrong*.

I swallow the fresh tears that threaten to work their way up. "What happened?"

He shakes his head. "Let down my guard." His voice sounds rougher than usual and every breath seems like a struggle for him. From the look of his midsection, he is in even more pain than he's letting on.

I think of his bad habit, the way he leaves his damned left side open. Indeed, his ribs are caving in on his left.

I try wrapping what I can in bandages, but he's in too much pain for me to do even that. Instead, I gently try to right his clothes. Tucked beneath his collar is his crystal. The one I gave him for protection. I clutch it in my fist, my mind a constant stream of *thank you thank you thank you thank you*—

"I tried to shift," he finally says. "I had no other choice."

His breathing gets shallow again, and he sounds like he can't get enough air in. There is still a bit of the elixir left, and I make him drink. This time, once he swallows, he's able to bear his weight enough to sit up, albeit slumped against a root. He adjusts a few of his bandages and heaves a sigh.

"I just had to survive." His voice gets a little clearer as he's able to take deeper breaths. Still nowhere near enough, but at least he's talking. "I did what I had to. I couldn't leave you alone."

I bite my cheek, focusing on that pain instead of the misery wracking my body.

"I couldn't do it," he heaves. "I couldn't shift in time."

Groaning, I drop my face into my hands. For a moment I just breathe, focusing on the rhythm of that. He faced his greatest fear, his most dangerously kept secret, all to stay alive for me. My inner voice tells me I am not worth such a sacrifice, but I ignore it because to him, I am worth it. And so I must believe it, too. I cannot let it be for nothing.

He doesn't speak for so long that it startles me when he breaks the silence once more. "We aren't far from Kliransk."

"We can't go there like this," I insist, gesturing wildly between us. "They'll chase us out on sight."

"Do you have," he breathes, "any better ideas?"

I don't.

In a matter of moments, I've repacked the knapsack and stocked my harness with Halvar's supplies. I feel heavier than I have ever felt in my life. And there is still him to consider. I attach his whip to both of our sides to tether us together, but also because I physically cannot handle any more weight on my own.

I am crouched beside him, still getting my bearings, when I hear footsteps draw close. My head snaps up and I lock eyes with it at once. Beyond the wards stalks the same manner of creature that attacked us the night of the solstice festival. Only this time, it moves much smoother, its walk less crass and more refined. It's considerably smaller, but bulkier. It must be younger, and therefore stronger.

I don't think. My hand moves of its own accord to the knives strapped to my chest. I grab for a light one, easily thrown, and fling it through the air towards the creature. Because of the wards, it hasn't noticed us yet, and so surprise is my only advantage.

I am not a practiced knife thrower. My only real experience is tossing them around between tree trunks, curious to see how much force would be required to stick a landing. Beyond that, it is just something I had read about in books, something that seemed like it would work. And to my utter shock, it does.

The blade nicks the sensitive skin of the creature's neck before bouncing onto the snow beneath it. Though the creature remains uninjured, I've done enough to spook it. It rears back on its hind legs and screeches before sprinting deeper into the trees. I silently beg the forest to direct it towards another hunter, one more equipped and willing to take down such a beast.

"I think I'm hallucinating," Halvar says. I just roll my eyes and help him up.

Thanks to downing the entire elixir, he is able to stand. With a little assistance on my end, we are able to walk. I hear every pained breath, each one a sword through my heart.

He raises one weak arm. "South. Go south."

Daylight builds as we walk. We walk slowly to ease Halvar's discomfort as well as to avoid toppling into one painful pile. I have the worst feeling that if we fall, we won't be getting back up.

The walk could be shorter or longer than all of our other trips to and from Kliransk, but I wouldn't be able to tell given our pace. This part of the woods is unfamiliar to me, no clear path marked as safe. It's just as beautiful as the rest of the woods, and to an untrained eye would look the same as any other area. But I do not know these trees; the air here doesn't know me. I feel like a guest once again. Despite this, I take in as much as I can, memorizing what landmarks I see so if I have to, I can find my way again.

"Just a bit further," Halvar says weakly. I can't tell if he's comforting me or himself. He's started dragging his feet and leaning most of his weight on me. If we have as little left to go as he claims, it's all he can make on his own two feet.

A death-field greets us.

The tree line ends abruptly, and where there used to be full-grown trees there are now just stumps, and even those are few in number. This carnage goes on for at least a mile in either direction, like someone took a bite out of the woods.

Kliransk glares at us from the other side. A skeleton of what it was the last time we saw it.

The sun has risen enough that some of the early risers have started their days. I see figures walking to and from the market, some to the church. I start waving my free hand, needing someone—anyone—to see us and help us.

I don't fail to see the irony when my mother greets us at the border of what used to be the tree line. As we near her, Halvar collapses to his knees in the snow, thicker now that there are no branches to collect the flakes. She looks between us, bewildered, like I am a feral animal. I cling to her skirts as I fall with him, sobs wracking my body as reality hits me.

"Please," I beg her. "Help us."

A healer does what she can for Halvar, then leaves my mother and I with instructions for his care. Should we need her again, her home is only down the road. He is fast asleep in my bed, his body more bandage than skin. I watch his chest rise and fall for several long moments, needing to see it for myself to believe that he is okay.

From the doorway, my mother says in a voice gentler than I am used to, "What happened?"

I don't turn around, don't want to let her watch as I come up with a lie. Crossing my arms, I say, "We were attacked by a bear."

189

Whether or not she believes me, her tone reveals nothing. "The healer is a fine woman. She knows what she's doing."

I scoff. I know this already, because I lived here for twenty-one years seeing the same faces every day. And the faces continue to dwindle. On the other side of the alarms are bodies. Everyone in the village wears mourning black, offering constant vigil.

I turn to my mother, wiping my tears as I do. I can't quite meet her gaze. "Can I have something to eat, please?"

She gestures for me to follow her into the kitchen. For once, I am thankful for the boarded windows; our arrival caused something of a scene, drawing a small crowd. It didn't help that I was in hysterics and covered in steel.

She tells me to sit while she makes me a cup of tea. It doesn't have two drops of honey in it—the way I like it. How Halvar makes it for me. I almost burst into laughter when she places a bowl of oatmeal in front of me. I take up the spoon and eat it without complaint, my body too drained to deny any bit of food. It tastes so bland compared to the rich flavors Halvar presents me with every morning. If he were awake, everything would be okay. If he were well, we would be lounging in our home, eating good food and debating how to spend his latest earnings. Maybe we would argue, or reminisce. I would take him being angry with me right now over this.

Mother sits across from me with her own mug of tea in hand. She looks exhausted. "You're not hurt?"

I shake my head. "I'm fine."

Her eyes gloss over me, lingering on the knives still harnessed to me. "This is new."

"His," I explain. I want this conversation to be over.

She takes a long sip, swallowing slowly. "Your father just left for work. He's gone for most of the daylight hours now, few as they are."

The sight of the destroyed tree line was enough to make my stomach drop. "What has he done?"

"What needs to be done," she says baldly. "This is his job, to reinforce the barricades and make sure the houses can sustain what is to come. What's already here."

I cannot think of a winter prior to this one where he had to take this much of the woods down in order to keep Kliransk standing. It does not bode well for whatever future they have left. At this rate, the surrounding land will be bald for miles in every direction.

"You know I'm risking my neck for you." My mother's voice is curt. It is not a question.

I continue to eat, giving myself time to think of a response. I can feel her eyes on me but I don't give her the satisfaction of hurrying me into a response.

At last, I raise my eyes to hers. I keep my voice level, my face neutral. "Do you want me to thank you?"

"I want you to acknowledge it."

"Acknowledge what? That you're helping your daughter who came to you in crisis? That is the bare minimum I should expect from you, yet here you are asking for me to fall at your feet."

She slams down her mug, making the tea slosh at its rim. "You left, Emelie. The borders are supposed to remain shut to you. Yet, even so, I let you in not only to the village but into my home. Can you imagine what the elders will say? What they'll think?"

I glare at her, schooling my face until I can swallow the hot threat of tears. "I was naked and you clothed me, I was sick and you visited me, I was in prison and you came to me."

I may be a nonbeliever, but I was never a poor student. I know just as well as her how scripture says to treat outsiders. Damn what the elders will say or think.

Mother looks as though I've slapped her from the way her face has gone slack. She shouldn't be shocked. She may have never bothered to get to know me, but I am still her daughter. I wear half of her face. I am the reflection she chooses to overlook.

Rather than confront me, she shakes herself from her stupor and chooses to fill me in on the things I have missed while away. She tells me the names of those who have died. I recognize all of them,

I can call each face to mind. But I find no connection between them beyond the fact that they are all gone now.

To combat the carnage, the village has taken to a stricter curfew. Everyone must remain inside from one hour before sunset until one hour after sunrise. I let out a sigh of relief—it was nothing short of a miracle that we arrived right as the curfew was lifted. My father and his men are the only exceptions to this rule; they require the maximum amount of daylight in order to have enough wood chopped in a day. Distantly, I note that this means my mother is alone most of the day with her sewing. I wonder if that bothers her, or if she prefers the quiet.

I make non-committal comments here and there, nodding when I am supposed to and forcing my face into surprise and sadness when appropriate. In the back of my mind, I want to laugh at the fact that gossiping is a sin. But that doesn't matter to her. This is not a sin that carries any *real* weight.

In return for her stories I give her tidbits of my life, carefully curated and sanitized to fit the version of me that she knows and probably loves. I have learned to cook more meals beyond the basics. I clean my house until it is spotless. I obey my husband and am agreeable and docile and don't start arguments and certainly don't practice witchcraft in my spare time.

There is a cough from the next room and I don't bother to excuse myself before rushing to check on Halvar. He's awake, blinking back to consciousness. He looks confused, like he's forgotten where we are. What happened to us. To him. I settle on the edge of the mattress, careful to not shift its weight and possibly make him uncomfortable. When his eyes fully open and he notices me sitting and waiting for him, he visibly relaxes.

He looks down at himself, then quietly says, "You should see the other guy."

The laughter this forces out of me mixes with my sobs. "You're okay."

"I'm okay." He tilts his head on the pillows to look up at me, eyes bloodshot with exhaustion but still so soft as he beholds me.

"How long have I been asleep?"

"A few hours," I say. The open door feels like a liability, so I shut it silently and place the knapsack in front of it as a warning. I take his hand as I sit, mindful of his bandages. "I told the healer you were attacked by a bear. She thinks you're very lucky to not have sustained any major injuries."

He frowns as he settles his free hand against his ribs. Bruises flower around the bandages, and he doesn't look quite put back together, but he already looks much better than when I found him.

"I thought I had broken my ribs," he says slowly.

I nod. "You did."

I watch as he works through what I am not saying. When he looks up at me, his eyes are full of wary awe. "The drink you gave me…"

"I made it," I say. "I found the recipe in one of my books. I just wanted to see if it would work."

"You weren't sure if it would work when you gave it to me." Not a question.

I brush some of his loose hair back. "We were running out of options. And time."

"And it worked."

"It worked."

He licks his lips, and I pass him a glass of water from the nightstand. He can't quite hold it himself yet, so I bring the rim of the glass to his lips and try not to drown him. He nods his thanks. As with most things he thanks me for, it feels like the minimum expected of me as his partner.

"So the healer thinks I've escaped a run-in with a bear with only a few bruises and scratches."

"Something like that," I say. "Your ribs are definitely bruised and will need time to heal, but the rest of the injuries look superficial. When I found you—" I swallow the lump in my throat. "You looked like you were falling apart from the inside out."

He sighs, an ancient and heavy sound. "I was losing the fight.

My instinct to shift kicked in, and I just didn't fight it. It wasn't pretty. It was like my body knew what to do, but my mind stopped the process before it could begin. It felt like every bone in my body was breaking at the same time. I felt my father's hands on me, I heard him telling me how worthless I would be if I did it. It's too late for me to undo what's done."

I push down the shiver that wants to crawl across my skin. I'm grateful for his honesty even as his words wound me deeper.

Both of us flinch when there is a knock on my bedroom door. I rush to answer before my mother can barge in. Kicking the sack aside, I block the threshold with my body and poke my head out to see what she wants. She looks a little affronted that I don't throw open the door to her, but frankly I don't want her anywhere near my injured husband, despite her help this morning.

She clears her throat, straightening as she recovers. "I'm going to morning mass."

"Alright," I say slowly.

She raises a brow. "Would you like to come?"

I don't want to attend mass. I don't want to be inside the church. But the events of last night, of the past few weeks and months, linger at the back of my mind. I won't receive any clarity sitting at home and twiddling my thumbs.

I tell her to wait as I shut the door. To Halvar, I say, "Will you be alright on your own for an hour?"

He nods but gives me a quizzical look. "You want to go?"

"No," I say, unfastening the many buckles on the harness. It drops to the floor with a clatter. "I want out of the dark."

I shuck out of my layers and throw open my old wardrobe. Few dresses still hang there, and I cringe at how obvious the restitching is to my fresh eyes. The one that looks like it will fit best is the one I dread most: what was my best dress. My wedding dress. I'm momentarily stunned when I put it on; it used to hang off of me like a sack, shapeless and unflattering. Now my figure is definitive beneath the cream fabric. Woman's body, indeed.

194

I fuss over Halvar before leaving, placing the glass of water within his reach and making sure he has enough blankets and pillows. He urges me to go on; I know he is also hungry for information. Tired of being left in the dark. My theory that the wood spirits know what is wrong here in Kliransk is not solid, but I am willing to bet on myself.

I meet my mother in the sitting room. She eyes my dress, and me beneath it. She looks displeased.

"You know, if you still lived here I would've been able to take out that dress again, what with how much weight you've put on."

I throw on my coat and open the door. "Well, then it's a good thing I don't live here anymore."

The roads look like a mourning procession. Every other person we encounter is draped in black, my mother included. She has a high-necked dress on with white trim. It strikes me to realize that this is a new dress, I don't recognize it at all. I hold in my scoff at how she finds no issue in spending money when it's not on her daughter. I might have been better off trying to blend in with the crowd; I would've been even better off having never come. But that is not the way of things.

There are fewer people out than expected for a weekday morning. I see so many familiar faces, albeit fewer than before. No one looks at each other as we walk towards the church; heads are bowed, whether in prayer or fear is unknown to me. These masses, unlike Sundays, are optional. They are held to offer up penance for whatever sins the elders are convinced are causing a train of death across Kliransk. The thought disgusts me, and I have to force myself to not curl my lip.

It looks as though no one has bothered to clear the walkways in days, maybe even longer. We trudge through inches of snow where there used to be cobblestone paths. In front of each house is an even deeper pile of snow, disturbed only by the clear marking of footprints at the front door. Were it not for the people out and about, I would think it looked deserted.

The church, of course, is in perfect condition. If anything, it looks better than when I left. The windows are shiny and clean. The walls look reinforced, unaffected by the weather. As we pass through the threshold, I lower my eyes to avoid Father Levi's burning gaze. Instead, I keep my eyes on the floors, freshly swept. Then to the pews, polished and primed for an audience.

As usual, we sit near the front. It feels familiar, and I wonder if this is the same pew we sat in that fateful morning. Sentiment aside, I am uncomfortable being so close to the elders' line of sight.

I kept my eyes down on our way in, but now that the service has begun and they've taken their spots on the altar, I can see them in full light. They look *terrible*.

Father Patrick looks like he hasn't slept in days. Dark circles line his under eyes, and his skin looks wan and paper-thin.

Father Levi simply looks angry. That is a soft way of putting it—his face is drawn in a way that accentuates every line, deepened by the cold expression he wears.

Then there is Father Dasco, looking for all the world calm and collected. The assured look on his face is somehow more unsettling than the others. There is at least something human in Father Levi and Father Patrick's faces, the raw emotion that comes when one is surrounded by death. Father Dasco's face lacks this humanness, and the practiced mask he has on re-opens the pit in my stomach in full force.

Given the lack of people, mass moves quickly. Efficiently. Predictably. When communion is offered, I know I am not eligible but I get in line anyway, not wanting to field questions about my potential sins with my mother.

I can see the surprise in Father Dasco's eyes when I step in front of him, hands open and waiting. I see the moment of hesitation—he doesn't want to give it to me. Of course, I am an outsider now. It would make sense to deprive me of salvation when I am not one of his flock.

Perhaps to avoid gossip, or fearing that I'll make a scene, he hands it to me with a hollow sounding, "The body of Christ."

I make sure to put a little sin into my voice when I say, "Amen."

Years of memories drudge up when the wafer touches my tongue. I taste my failures and shortcomings as a daughter, the version of myself I was never meant to be. As I walk back to my seat, I can feel the eyes of all three of the elders boring into the back of my head.

I expect to head home immediately so my mother may start her workday, but Father Dasco stops her at the door and pulls her into the study. She doesn't tell me to wait, but I know better by now. I shuffle my feet awkwardly as I wait at the front of the church. With the quickly emptying church, I wonder if I have time to look around, see if anything out of place makes itself known to me. But I don't have time. Because someone approaches me.

"Hi, Emelie," Magda chirps, her voice soft and tinny. "Can I talk to you?"

I nod slowly, surprise giving me pause, but the assertion emboldens her. She grips my arm with a surprisingly tight hand. I start to ask her what she's doing, but she just drags me behind one of the pillars and shushes me.

"What are you doing here?" She demands in a low whisper.

"What am *I* doing here? What's the matter with *you*? You didn't answer any of my letters—"

"We don't have time for this." She looks around like a scared animal. "Just tell me, what are you doing back here?"

"My husband was injured out in the woods. We came to seek a healer."

She looks over her shoulder once more before continuing. And when she does, she does not mince words. "They haven't let the merchants cross the border. We're coasting with what rations they've stocked, but we are running out of food *fast*. I go to the masses just so I can have the communion wafer. They won't allow us to ask questions anymore. It's like my entire day is run on their word. I can't work enough hours to set aside a wage for myself. They won't even tell us what happens when they ring the alarms, we are just expected to show

197

up for the funeral the following Sunday. If it weren't for the caskets I would doubt that there were deaths at all."

Well, Mother certainly didn't let me in on those details.

Her grip on my arm tightens. I wince and try to pull away, which only makes her hold tighter. "You have to get out of Kliransk while they'll let you. They haven't let the messengers pass through. I couldn't get a letter out if I tried."

I frown. That explains the lack of response.

She opens her mouth to say more, but we hear Father Dasco and my mother approaching from the study. She pulls me into a fierce hug that steals the breath from me, and in my ear, she whispers, "I can't take this. Find a way out for us."

She steps away from me and puts a blank look on her face. In a forced, higher-pitched voice, a voice for the elders, she tells me how wonderful it was to see me and she'd love to have dinner together before I leave Kliransk. Then she's gone and left my head spinning.

My mother steps forward. "Magda is a lovely girl. I didn't know the two of you were close."

"She…" I have to think on my feet. "She had some questions about running a household. Not that I'm an expert."

Mother nods but quickly moves on. Never listening, always waiting for her turn to talk. She brings Father Dasco forward with a tight smile on her face. "Father Dasco has a lot to discuss with us. He's going to join us for dinner this evening."

My stomach sinks impossibly further, but I plaster a fake smile on. "Lovely. I'll help prepare the main course."

He bows slightly. The formality feels inappropriate. That should be reserved for someone more deserving. I feel so small in comparison to them, my mother in particular.

"I look forward to the honor," Father Dasco says, his tone saying otherwise.

As we walk away, my mother none the wiser, I feel the pit in my stomach grow with every step. The very atmosphere of the church makes me sick, and the presence of the elders only makes it worse. As little at home I feel with my parents, Father Dasco's visit is only going to taint it further. I don't want him anywhere near Halvar.

But Magda's words, her sheer terror and insistence of wrongness, stick with me. I have to know what is going on, and the answer to my questions has invited itself into my parents' home.

I have to bear it, awful as it may feel.

CHAPTER FOURTEEN

I haven't baked bread in years.

I nearly forgot how, but once my hands are covered in flour the memories rush back in. My hands are already starting to ache as I knead the dough, but it gives me something to do. Once it's panned and baking I set to work seasoning the meat. I can see my mother stealing glances from the sitting room, judging my cooking. I try to stay focused. It's all that is keeping me from sinking into the pit in my stomach.

My head won't keep quiet; visions of all that is going on and potentially could be going on run through my head in an unending hymn when all I want is silence. The impending threat of the elder invading my space sets my skin crawling. And as much as I try not to, I can't help but see Halvar's collapsed rib cage, the way his skin purpled—

"My love," he says softly from his seat. The words are for me alone, too low for my parents' listening ears. "Come back."

I look at him, my hunter husband who walked into the woods without fear and left in pieces. He's wearing my father's clothes now. The top two buttons of his shirt are undone, exposing the bandages crossing his chest and the crystal hanging over it. He looks smaller, like a child.

He looks vulnerable, and I hate it.

His eyes soften as if he can read my thoughts. He offers a slight tip of the chin to show me he's here, he's okay, he's alive.

Food. I have to make the food.

Dinner is smoked and seasoned deer with a vegetable and beef stew on the side. The bread finishes last. I rummage through the cabinets for our better sets of plates, the ones we rarely use. I can't remember the last time I had to set five place settings, and we don't have enough silverware. I have to make do with the more common pieces, which I set out for myself.

I don't even want to be here. I don't need the nicest things.

There is a knock right as the food finishes. I hurry to get everything on the table while Father Dasco is let in, not wanting to look more inept than I already feel.

Father welcomes him in like his presence in our home is the most natural thing in the world. I stand back, brushing my hands on my skirts as they come into the kitchen. Mother comes to stand beside me, her hands crossed in front of her like the good wife she is. I copy her stance, feeling like a fraud. Father Dasco greets all of us, and I don't miss how he looks down his nose at Halvar.

He prays over the food, a lengthy process that makes me tap my foot. Halvar gives me a cautioning look before my mother notices. Once the prayers are finished and Father Dasco has taken his seat, my mother and I plate everything and serve. She hands Father Dasco the first plate, then my father, then Halvar. We serve ourselves last.

It's difficult to navigate the table with so many hands and plates and candles covering its surface. There are, in my opinion, far too many candles. True, it's dark without the lingering sunlight, but I nearly knock one or two over while reaching for the carafe of water on the opposite edge. I ignore the glares this earns me.

I am the first to clear my plate, and so I am the first to reach to refill it. Between my father and Father Dasco's words, I hear my mother mutter something about how I've had enough.

Her words send my temper flaring. The past few months have

taught me so much, but one of the hardest lessons I've had to learn is that she never gave me enough. I was never supposed to be skin and bone, shivering at the slightest breeze. She made me hate food, hate *myself* for wanting more. I have grown too much to be comfortable beneath her criticism. I don't have any space left to hold her hate, I feel like it's going to burst out of me—

The candle closest to me sputters out.

I freeze with my hand on a serving spoon. The table quiets and all eyes shoot to the candle. My mother gets up, muttering about the draft. She strikes a match and holds it to the wick, but it takes several tries for the flame to take. Father Dasco's brow furrows and his eyes dance around the room, looking for something to blame. I put my hands in my lap and clutch the fabric of my dress, holding it so fiercely I'm surprised it doesn't tear. *Not here.*

After relighting the candle, she takes her seat again and bypasses the silence by asking Father Dasco about his homily today. This recaptures his attention enough for a quick speech but to my dismay, he turns his attention to Halvar once he's finished.

"You survived quite the attack today, I hear. A bear, was it?" He takes a bite of the deer, chewing thoughtfully.

Halvar tries to clear his throat, then suppresses a cough. He's barely touched his food. "I was caught off my guard. A mistake I won't make again."

Father Dasco hums, then says, "God was watching over you, for you to have survived with nary a scratch."

"You should see beneath these bandages." Halvar's tone is edging somewhere between conversational and hostile. To the untrained ear, he is pleasant enough, but not one to question.

And yet Father Dasco pushes.

"Strange, that you were attacked by an animal that is typically in hibernation this time of year." He takes a sip of water, letting the veiled accusation hang in the air. If he knows we're lying, then he's setting a trap.

Halvar takes a breath and I hear it rattle in his chest. "That was how it caught me off-guard. I don't watch out for bears this time of year."

Father Dasco turns his eye on me, and out of the corner of my eye, I see Halvar stiffen. "You were the one to find him?"

I nod, still fidgeting with my skirt. "I heard the commotion from our house, and I just followed the sounds. He was already taking care of it by the time I arrived."

"And you carried him all the way back to Kliransk." Not a question, not quite an accusation.

I nod again. "He was able to support himself for most of the walk. I was more of a crutch, if anything." My stomach is in knots, and I cannot tell if it is imagined or real the way the flame dances on a nonexistent breeze.

"Injuries like his are typically hard to travel with. God must have been with you, indeed."

I know exactly what words will get him off our backs. I put the traitorous words on my tongue, though they taste like poison. "We are thankful to God for being beside us through all of this. To Him be the glory."

My mother and father echo the sentiment. My father won't think twice about it, and for once I am grateful to be on the lacking end of his attention span. Mother, though suspicious, won't look too closely. Not after I accompanied her to church and prepared a feast for the village priest. I am the good, godly daughter she raised. The one she always wanted.

The flame stops dancing. If possible, it starts to burn brighter, stronger. I watch it for a moment, entranced, then remember myself. I pretend like I am engrossed in my food once more.

But I catch Father Dasco's eye as I do, and realize he's been watching me. It's too late, he's seen where my attention lies. And there, too, his attention goes. For the rest of dinner, we take turns watching the flame, and as the anxiety builds in me once more it gets dimmer. And dimmer.

But it stays lit.

"You are aware," Father Dasco starts, setting down his water glass. "That under our conditions, you are technically breaking your exile."

Everyone in the room holds their breath. Halvar fists his silverware, arms shaking with the effort.

I clear my throat, ready to defend ourselves, but my father beats me to it.

"They were in trouble, Father."

"Yes," he muses, "but they could also be bringing trouble."

"I know my daughter," my father says, a quiet rage brimming beneath his words. It is the closest I've seen him come to disobedience. He doesn't know me as he believes he does, but his effort is appreciated all the same.

In the back of my mind, I remind myself that he is only defending me because I promised to not lie to him again. I have lied again, and that makes his defiance all the more agonizing to watch. But the elders cannot punish him too severely as long as they rely on him.

Undeterred, Father Dasco turns his eye on me. "Were we your last resort?"

More like our only resort. But how can I explain that the woods are a maze without making them sound more dangerous than he already thinks them to be?

I can only nod. It's not enough for him, but he acquiesces.

"See to it that you return home once your husband is well enough," he says. Command runs smoothly off his tongue like a river. He doesn't even acknowledge Halvar as he dismisses us.

It is nearing curfew. As Father Dasco leaves, he blesses each of us in turn, Halvar receiving a lengthier one for his injuries and overall health. With one foot out the door he speaks to us all, though I feel his gaze linger on me as he says:

"Best fix that nasty draft."

And then he's gone with the fleeting sunlight, his figure a dwindling shadow on its way back to the church.

Father shuts the door and exhales, settling back into his favored chair. He kicks off his boots, and I remember this is the first opportunity he's had to relax since returning from work. Even as the thought of his work sinks my stomach, I can't help but feel sorry for the burden he now carries. In the eyes of the villagers, their safety lies in his hands just as much as the elders. Being revered seems more of a curse than a blessing, expectation more of a strike than a soft touch.

I know that bit well.

I busy myself with washing dishes as I absorb all of the information I've gathered this afternoon. Father Dasco told me more than he realized, and I now have pieces of truth, scattered and displaced as they may be.

The nagging feeling of wrongness is more prevalent; Kliransk itself feels wrong. The graveyard of forest outside is a problem all its own. The surrounding ground already looks worse for the wear, though the snow likely covers the worst of it. In their minds, they must think that the lack of trees will prevent predators from coming close, having no cover for their stalking.

I cannot see an endgame beyond stopping death. The alarm hasn't rung in a week or so, and while the paranoia is valid in a sense, what if it never rings again? What if there were a few hungry animals struggling to survive the oncoming winter and a few villagers wandered too close to their territory? What if it all stops once spring comes?

It could have been a fluke, a freak accident, not some folktale come to life. And if shifter wolves truly are at fault, why haven't Halvar and I come across any in the woods? Would Halvar know if he came across someone who shared his gifts? If wolves can walk among men, speaking their language and sharing their space, it must be impossible to tell the difference. It doesn't make sense to me.

But the woods know. The spirits have been trying to tell us—to tell *me*—this since I arrived at Halvar's home.

I feel a headache coming on and all I want is to talk this through with Halvar. Our research has to be worth something. I return to the sitting room to find him fielding questions from my father, who is practically interrogating him about coming out of a bear attack alive.

I step between them and start to lift Halvar, making excuses about bedrest and bandages. Together, we get him settled back into my bed and I block the door for privacy.

"Tell me what you're thinking," he says, catching the eager look on my face.

"I think regardless of any wolves or death, the elders don't care much whether it stops."

He nods, motioning for me to help him get his shirt off. "That much is clear. Their motives lie somewhere beyond protecting the people."

"Yes, but *why*?"

He shrugs. "Why does any tyrant oppress its people?"

The question plays in my head, mixing in with everything else I've learned tonight. I don't get very far before Halvar groans, clutching his midsection. Sleep has helped, but even his superior healing abilities are too slow to keep up with the damage the creature caused. He needs help.

He needs more of the elixir.

I shuffle through the knapsack, but the bottle is empty. I have some supplies to make more, but not enough. Without thinking too hard, I strip out of the dress and put my clothes from this morning back on. I haven't had a chance to wash them; they're covered in dirt and Halvar's blood, which means no one will notice if they get a little dirtier.

"Those don't look like comfortable bedclothes," Halvar observes.

I make quick work of the harnesses and then get my boots on. "That's because I'm not going to bed."

"Do I want to know what you're planning?"

I rebraid my hair and pin it to the nape of my neck. "You need my healing elixir, and I am out of ingredients. So I'm going to get more."

He eyes the harness. "And you need half of my armory?"

"Necessary precaution."

206

He pushes up to his elbows, though I see how it pains him to do so. "I know by now I can't stop you from seeing out your will, so I won't even try. But I can urge you to be careful. Stick to the shadows, stay out of sight."

"It's curfew," I say, like it should be obvious. "Everyone will be indoors by now."

"Even so," he says, laying back down.

I lean over him, bringing my face close to his. Strands of loose hair fall towards him, curtaining us to one another. My eyes rove across his face, across his tired eyes and his scar, then flicker to his lips.

"Can I kiss you?" I ask.

"Please," he murmurs.

My lips are feathers against his, afraid to put any more pressure. It is a fleeting kiss, and then I am at the window repositioning the boards so I can sneak out of the same opening he once snuck in through. I put one foot through and then look back at him, smirking.

"What?"

"I feel very much like you right now," I say.

He looks me over, affection coloring his cheeks. "You look very much like yourself. Moreso, even."

With a smile I let those be our parting words. Beneath my window, the daffodils that once thrived there have now withered and succumbed to the winter's chill. The sight of it wilts something inside me, too.

I round the house towards our small garden before I can linger on it. I had hoped I wouldn't need to go further than our yard, but my mother has let the plants die out in the cold. She has a skilled enough hand to keep most things alive through winter, but perhaps fear or business kept her from doing so. The only thing I am able to salvage is a few pieces of thyme.

As I make my way down our row of houses, I salvage what I can from neighboring gardens. It's easy to sneak along corners and underneath windows with no one out to witness me. The quickening dark covers any clumsiness on my part, and a not-small piece of me is thrilled by this. The rest of me just wants to get back home to Halvar.

A bushel of sage is all I have yet to find when I start to hear voices. I freeze, pressing into the back wall of the nearest house. I beg the shadows to cling to me, to hide me from whoever is out past curfew.

I am the least surprised to hear the mingling voices of the elders talking amongst themselves. Their voices are not so distinct that I can tell which of them is speaking, but I know all three of them are there. Their voices are low, hurried. Like they are in a rush. I creep towards the sound, only a few steps.

They knock on the door and a male voice answers. The elders mutter something and after a pause, I hear a tinny voice come to the door. My stomach drops when I recognize it as Magda's. I look up and realize this is indeed her home. I can't make out exactly what they're saying, but I'm afraid to get any closer to hear better. They're inviting her somewhere soon, likely tomorrow, something to do with the church. She pauses before agreeing. Even without seeing her, I can hear the dread in her voice, though she tries to cover it up with cheerfulness. They offer some parting blessing before their voices fade along with their footsteps.

Dread sinks in me. Whatever it is they want her for at the church, she absolutely should not go. Rounding towards the back of the house, I try to find her bedroom. Peeking through windows informs me which is most likely hers. I wait there, and my knees start to ache from kneeling, but I can't risk getting caught by anyone besides her. In the meantime, I use twine to knot my collected herbs together and shove them into my pockets.

Candlelight starts to fill her room, leaking out of her window and I just barely fit into the shadows below it. With one careful eye, I look inside and am met with the sight of Magda, still lighting candles. I tap on the window once, twice, three times before she notices. She jumps and a small yelp escapes her before she covers her mouth. She looks to her bedroom door, placing a chair beneath the handle. Then she cracks the window.

"What are you doing here?" She hisses. "The elders just left, they could have spotted you—"

"I heard them," I interrupt. No time for back and forth. "Whatever they want you for tomorrow, don't go."

"I can't just defy them."

"Feign sickness. Blame your monthly bleeding. Just say *something* that will get you out of it. I don't trust whatever they have planned."

She pauses. "What do you know?"

"Not enough," I admit. "Father Dasco had dinner with my parents this afternoon. He knows far more than he lets on."

"What does that have to do with anything?" Her brow furrows.

"That, I also don't know. But I've seen things out there in the woods. The animals can sense a change, even if we can't feel it yet. And they don't like it."

"The animals... Emelie, animals don't think like we do."

"They're smarter than you think. I've witnessed it."

She leans against the windowpane, confusion and bewilderment mingling across her face. "I'll do as you say. But you should be careful about who you go around spreading such rumors to. Knowledgeable animals out in the forbidden woods aren't exactly in line with their ideas."

"Stranger things have happened," I say.

"I believe it," she nods. "But I'm few and far between. Discourse is rampant among our friends."

I'm hesitant to call our former classmates *friends*, but I don't argue it. "How do you mean?"

"Some of them act as if they don't remember what it was like when we were young. How hard it was around the first exodus. I fear another one is to come at this rate."

I remember the hardship all too well. How tensions rose to a boiling point before our population fractioned. If Kliransk gets any smaller, it will burn itself out faster than a summertime candle.

I dust my pants off before walking away, offering Magda one final warning. "Keep your wits about you. I think they're counting on the hope that we won't."

She gives one firm nod before shutting her window. I make my way to the edge of the road before running to the tree line to see what herbs I can find out there. Past the fallen stumps and scattered axes, I find the sage I was lacking as well as a few bundles of rosemary. I stuff them in my pocket with the rest of the herbs and keep to the shadows as I make my way home. I don't encounter anyone else, curfew firmly in session now.

Most of the lights are off at my parents' house except for my bedroom. I pry the window open and stumble back in, greeted by my husband. If it weren't for the fact that he is being held together by bandages, I'd say he looks relaxed.

I forgo telling him what I heard until after I make the elixir. My desk will have to do as a workstation. I grind everything together with water from the carafe I snuck in, then refill the bottle I had used originally. The color is darker than it was the first time, though I used all the same ingredients.

I don't like the look of it. Even the herbs in Kliransk have a darkness to them. But I have no other options. I make him drink it, and then he chases it with the remaining water from the carafe. He groans again, though this time it is more out of relief than pain.

"I don't know what it is you do, but it helps." He grips the crystal around his neck, holding it up for me to see. "This too. I never thanked you for it, but I credit it with keeping me alive."

I sniffle. I never thought I would be worth anything beyond mediocre sewing, but I continue to prove myself wrong. It's a nice feeling, to be wrong.

I undress again, not bothering with any nightclothes. I get the rest of Halvar's clothes off so we're both in our underthings. I clean his bandages and rebandage whatever needs fixing. He no longer flinches from my touch; we are too familiar to each other now. Whatever discomfort he feels is from his wounds alone, and I wish I could take that from him, soak the pain into my body so he would never have to feel it again. I would do that for him without thanks, without reciprocation, if it meant he'd only ever feel alright.

He takes up most of the bed and I don't complain when my

body teeters on the edge all night. Once or twice he tries to pull me into his side but winces at the pain, and so I keep my distance. It's a fitful night for us both, him waking up to adjust, his adjustments waking me in turn. I make him drink whenever he wakes us both, which seems to stave off the pain enough for him to fall back asleep for some time.

Morning arrives without pretense, sunlight streaming in through the gap between boards. I feel more tired than I did when I got in bed, which just feels like a sad joke. I tend to Halvar in whatever way he requires before helping him dress for the day. With his rebuilding strength and my elixir, he should be well enough to go home in a few days.

Father is already out the door by the time I make it to the kitchen. Mother has two bowls of oatmeal laid out, which I reluctantly take back to Halvar. He scoffs when I set it in front of him, picking at it with his spoon.

"She made better breakfast when we were kids."

"Those days feel long gone," I say. "I've been eating this for years."

At that, he stills. I see the familiar quiet rage cross his face. "Every day?"

"Every day," I nod. When his eyes flash, I say, "What?"

He shakes his head. "How did you survive this many winters on so little?"

I shrug, suddenly self-conscious. "It wasn't that bad."

"*That bad* is still bad, Emelie."

I don't respond, and we eat our breakfast in silence. I wait until my mother leaves for morning mass to take our dishes back to the kitchen. In the silence of the empty house I clean, then I keep cleaning. I clean the rest of the kitchen, the sitting room, the halls, even my room. I don't dare venture into my parents' room, but I can't think about all that's happened without doing *something*. Halvar watches me as I pass back and forth. He entertains my theories and asks the occasional question.

Things *almost* make sense. In Halvar's words, the elders want power. The deaths by wolves give them an excuse to take more for themselves. He's still missing the spirits, as well as the strange behavior of the creatures out in the woods. It's like we've laid out a map with the compass all skewed.

When my mother comes home, I help her with her sewing with little complaint. Time passes slower while Halvar recovers, and there's little else to do but wait around. And as much as I think, as much as I toil over everything, it doesn't make any more sense just because I want it to. Magda is at the back of my mind; I hope she came up with an excuse to get out of meeting with the elders.

By lunch I'm restless, and my better judgment isn't strong enough to warn me otherwise, so I put on my good dress again and layer on my coat. Halvar cautions me briefly and then I'm out the door, giving some excuse about errands to my mother. The streets are sparse, and the people I do pass either glare at me or keep their heads down, stealing glances when they think I'm not looking.

Magda doesn't look completely surprised when she opens her window to me. She lets me inside and begins recounting her morning to me. How the elders visited again after she sent word that she wouldn't be able to make it to the church tonight. How she made her father send them away with excuses of sickness. How she couldn't sleep last night, shaking with fear.

"They tried to convince me to come anyway. They were very persistent."

"What did you tell them?"

She shrugs. "I said I was contagious and didn't want to risk infecting them, and the congregation in turn. That finally dissuaded them." A shiver runs through her. "I hate the church. It gives me such a bad feeling to be in there."

I nod. "I never liked it in there either."

"I wish you knew what it's been like here." She shakes her head, then looks at me. "But at the same time, I'm glad you made it out. If anyone could, it would have been you."

I take the compliment, strange as it might be. I didn't think anyone paid that sort of attention to me. I always felt strange among my peers. Not the way that I fit in in the woods. It's a sick sort of comfort to know she felt strange growing up here, too. That she was the same out of sorts as me.

I tell her carefully curated bits of information to see what she makes of it. We compare what we know, and I still feel that something is missing.

Once I've had enough, I make my way back to the house. As I pass the threshold I freeze, noticing immediately how unnaturally quiet the house is. Mother should be at afternoon mass by now, Father still at work. I rush to the bedroom, needing to see that Halvar is okay—

Father Dasco stands above my bed, speaking in a low voice to Halvar. Their heads turn in unison as I storm in. I nearly bump into the threshold as I come to a sudden stop. Halvar stares at me with wide eyes, trying to wordlessly convey something I cannot understand with my panic-stricken brain. What is he *doing* here?

"Emelie," the elder says, his voice cold. "I came to pray over your husband. Your mother let me in on her way to mass."

I straighten, brushing hair out of my face. "I thought you'd also be at mass, Father."

"Father Levi and Father Patrick perform the mass. I tend to my villagers at this time."

I think of the elders claiming Halvar was no longer one of them after he moved away. I think of the fact that, by their own logic, I am no longer one of them either.

"I came by to pray," he says, taking slow steps around my room. He stops in front of my desk, and my blood chills. He's looking at the leftover herbs, the empty elixir bottle. "I came just for that, when I saw these. Whatever are these for? Are you cooking in your bedroom?"

I stammer. "It's…it's to make a salve. I wanted to ease Halvar's pain."

"Noble," he says. "Had prayer not crossed your mind? If it's God's will for Halvar to suffer—" He walks to the bed and places a firm hand on Halvar's ankle, making him wince. "Who are we to question that?"

I flinch, reaching out a hand, but stop myself short. "I just, I—"

"Do you know anything about sacrilege, Emelie?"

"I... It means to go against what is sacred."

Halvar watches me bug-eyed from the bed. The veins in his neck are pulsing, like he's barely keeping himself contained. I silently urge him to.

Father Dasco picks up a loose bit of thyme. "And do you know what we hold sacred here in Kliransk?"

A lot of superstition and fear. I feel small when I settle for saying, "God's word."

He chuckles. "You retained that, at least. Your ability to please. You always knew how to tell people just what they wanted to hear." He turns to Halvar, raising an eyebrow. "A fine skill for a wife, I would assume. She can tell you that you're not worthless, just like your father, and it won't matter if it's true."

Halvar looks like he's going to burst out of his skin. His breathing is ragged. There is far too much energy building up in him. Possibly enough to upset his instincts.

To make him shift.

I have to get Father Dasco away from him. I scramble for a plan, looking for the right words, looking for anything that won't land us ankle-deep in trouble.

But Father Dasco already has something in mind. "I think we should continue this conversation in private. Why don't you come with me back to the church?"

Halvar is shaking furiously. His eyes are devoid of anything besides violence. I cannot let him lose control in front of Father Dasco. They'll kill him if he does.

I have to go. I have to follow Father Dasco.

"Let me get my coat," I say, then remember I am already wearing one. Father Dasco just chuckles again and goes to wait by the door.

I waste no time rushing to my bundle of clothes from the night before, shuffling through them until I find my dagger. I shove it into my boot and then take a few practice steps with it. Satisfied, I go to Halvar's side, putting my hands on his shoulders. Fury is written all over his face. I can see the temper he's barely keeping leashed.

"I'll be okay, it'll all be okay," I whisper. "I can't have you shifting in front of him. I'll hear him out, tell him whatever it is he wants to hear from me. I'll lie however I have to. Just try to calm down. Can you do that for me?"

He takes a few deep breaths, but the anger is still palpable. "If he hurts you—"

"He won't." I force my voice to sound more confident than I feel. "He can scold me all he likes. I'm not afraid."

Halvar hesitates a moment, then reaches around his neck, tugging the crystal off. He hands it to me, pressing it into my palm. He ignores my refusal, forcing it against my skin.

"Take it," he urges. "Please."

Though I am certain he needs it more than I do, I put the crystal around my neck. "There. I'm protected."

In turn, I remove my necklace—the one he gave me—and place it around his neck. He doesn't say anything while I fumble with the clasp, just watches me with those furious eyes. He takes the charm between his fingers once it's latched. It looks out of place, so delicate, against his damaged skin.

"Now you're protected, too," I say, my voice so thin.

I leave him then. Walking away from him hurts, but I remind myself that I am doing this for him. He needs the distance that I am putting between him and the elder. I tighten my coat around me.

Then, I follow Father Dasco outside and towards the church, feeling very much like a lamb to the slaughter.

215

CHAPTER FIFTEEN

The walk to the church is not a lengthy one; no walk in this village is. We arrive at the double doors within minutes. As we pass over the threshold, I take a look over my shoulder to see if there is anyone to witness me going inside. There isn't.

Father Dasco doesn't say anything as he leads me through the church, now void of people. Afternoon mass has been over for a bit from the looks of it. My mother and I must have missed each other by minutes at most. I wonder what she'll think when she finds me not at home. I wonder what Halvar will tell her—if he will tell her the truth or come up with a lie to save both our skins.

I follow the priest back into the study where Father Patrick and Father Levi are already waiting. They look expectant. Like they knew Father Dasco would bring me back.

I wring my hands together and don't bother to remove my coat. I want this over as quickly as possible so I can get back to caring for Halvar. When they gesture for me to sit, I hesitate before taking a seat on the opposite side of the desk Father Levi sits at. Father Dasco busies himself with organizing papers that litter the top of it, and Father Patrick paces by the window. They all seem tense, in their black cassocks with their hands held in front of them.

I think of the way I've always viewed them, as some mockery

of the Holy Trinity. Father Dasco is the Father, his self-inflated ego and air of righteousness unable to allow him to lower himself to any other status. Father Levi is the Son, carrying as much of a godly attitude, but with the striking flaws that render him human. That leaves Father Patrick, with his wan skin and skittish nature, the role of the Holy Ghost.

They take their time before speaking to me. Father Dasco organizes, Father Levi notes something down on the remaining papers in front of him, Father Patrick continues to pace. This seems a grand way to waste my time.

After a pause, Father Levi says, "You know, we were supposed to meet with Magda this afternoon. You're friends, are you not?"

I shrug. "Acquaintances. I wouldn't call us close."

Father Levi hums, eyes on the desk. He doesn't look at me when he speaks. "Not close enough to say so, but close enough to sneak out to her window after curfew?"

I freeze, my nails scratching through the wood of the armrest. I sputter for a moment, coming up with absolutely nothing to say. I have no excuses.

"Did you think yourself a spy?" His voice is cold. Callous. "If so, you would do better not to sneak around right as doors are being shut. Better to wait until the dark has fully fallen before creeping beneath people's windows. And to cover your tracks in the snow, at that."

I'm too dumbfounded at having been caught to even bother denying it. Damn my carelessness. Damn it all. I can't truly be angry with myself when this should have been clear to me from the start; I am in way over my head. I start spinning together lies in my head, reasons that I could have snuck out to see Magda that won't incriminate either of us or let the elders in on what I know. Or rather, what I only *think* I know.

"It's only right that we should tell you," Father Levi says, shuffling through the papers on the desk, "that we received your letters to her. They contained some very interesting information."

217

I am an animal caught in a trap, too stupid to outwit these more experienced hunters.

"We are in the business of forgiveness," Father Levi continues, though his face is still lined with nothing of the sort. "You can confess to us now, and we'll offer you repentance."

Father Dasco and Father Levi's stares bear down on me, heavy with the weight of the judgment they're already casting. At the window, Father Patrick paces with his hands white-knuckled in his robes.

I silently thank myself for not putting anything incriminating in the letters. "What sin is there in writing to a neighbor? Or…or visiting her while in town? I left my house too close to curfew and did not want to risk getting Magda in trouble along with myself." I bypass the meat of their questions, hoping avoidance will grant me space to think of some ruse that won't put a bounty of blasphemy on my head.

"And what business do you have with her?"

I furrow my brow, doing my best to appear confused. "As I told Father Dasco yesterday, she had a few questions for me. I was happy to answer them for her. But in my rush to do so, I forgot how quickly the sun goes down on these winter nights." I giggle like this is something typical of a young, flighty woman like myself. "I figured it best to get my errand over with while I was still in town."

"Did you intend to leave soon?" Father Dasco raises an eyebrow, having seen the state of my husband. Surely, he knows that we aren't going anywhere.

I swallow. "Once my husband is well enough, yes."

Their eyes all flicker to one another, holding some unspoken conversation. They seem to decide something, then, and Father Dasco gestures towards the door.

"You remember where the confessional is, yes?"

I nod. Of course I do; you don't live your entire life in one place without memorizing every inch of it. I follow his direction and slip into the hallway. He lingers back with the other elders, speaking in hushed tones.

The halls of the church are dark, undisturbed by the still-risen

218

sun outside. The windows aren't barred—they are too tall to do so. But the stained glass prevents the majority of sunlight from seeping in in any substantial way. I walk on memory alone towards the confessional booth and am greeted by its dark wood doors staring back at me like an open mouth. I push it further open and feed myself to it. I slide into the confessor's side and fidget with the screen that will separate me from whichever elder comes to hear my confession. There is a panel that slides open and closed for a semblance of privacy. It feels pointless to do so now, but I slide it shut all the same.

I think that if I were to be buried alive it would feel less suffocating than this.

No light gets into the booth, and my eyes take a few moments to adjust to the dark. The bench has some soft covering over the old wood, and the back paneling juts out in some spots with elegant detailing. I trace my fingers over its ridges and bumps; I've become familiar with the pattern over the years, so even without light I recognize it.

I can hear the other door open and some shuffling as one of the elders steps inside. From the sound of his sigh alone, I can tell it's Father Dasco. There is a prolonged silence; I think he's praying to himself. Perhaps bracing himself to hear whatever sins he's already assumed I have committed.

"We begin in the name of the Father, the Son, and the Holy Spirit," he starts.

"Amen." These words feel both familiar and foreign rolling off my tongue. "Bless me, Father, for I have sinned. It's been…many months since my last confession." I can't count how much time has passed, it had to have been a few weeks prior to Halvar's return. I can't even remember what I confessed. Likely something benign, like having an attitude or too many worldly desires.

"Now," he says, clearing his throat, "why don't you tell me why you've returned to Kliransk."

I frown. This is not how confession is supposed to work. I am supposed to tell him what sins I've committed, what dirty laundry I have stuffed away where no one else can see. He is not supposed to ask me to fess up.

"I told you, Father, my husband was attacked by a bear."

He chuckles, a humorless sound that seeps through the panel separating us. "No, the real reason."

"I have told you the real reason—"

"Lying is an additional sin, Emelie." The way he says my name makes my skin crawl. I want the sound to never come out of his mouth again.

I start picking at the fabric atop the bench. It feels like a woolen blanket, offering a tiny reprieve from the hardness of the seat. There is another pause while he waits for me to give him the real reason for our being here. He won't get it, not willingly at least.

The half-truths come easily enough. "He was attacked, and I was unable to navigate us to a healer with enough time. But I knew the way back to Kliransk. I promise you, Father, it was a last resort."

"Things have changed a great amount since you left. We rise and set with the sun. We say our prayers at least twice a day. We make sure to listen."

"To whom?" I cannot stop myself from asking. His condescending tone is pulling on my already frayed nerves. "To God? Or to his mouthpieces?"

Father Dasco is stunned into momentary silence, then he clears his throat and says, "You should have learned in your education what this position means in the eyes of the church. Where God cannot reach, we lend a hand."

I continue to pick at the covering. Only now it is peeling away from the bench, like it isn't being held down by anything. My fingertips graze the wood beneath. "Is there compensation expected for lending a hand?" The undying loyalty of the villagers? Their blind devotion beyond a weekly service?

"Every one of us, myself and my brothers included, are only indebted to our Lord." He taps on the panel separating us, causing me to jump. "But we are not in this booth to talk about me, and I trust that you know that. Now, why don't you tell me more about your conversations with Magda."

"I'm not sure what more there is to tell."

"Start from the beginning. Start with the letters."

I bite back a curse. I can only try to build off of what they already know. Wracking my brain, I try to remember what I wrote. What secrets I spilled. "I wanted to talk about all of the deaths. To process my grief. You have to understand Father, it was frightening to know of the alarms as mere drills as a child, only to hear them again as the real thing."

These are not complete lies, though not whole truths either. I *was* frightened by the number of alarms. The fear has faded some as I've gone deeper in my research, but he doesn't need to know that part.

Father Dasco doesn't push anymore on the letters, but he doesn't relent on Magda. "What did she have to ask you after mass yesterday?"

This, I have already comprised an excuse for. "She wanted to know about running a household. Cooking, cleaning, the like." I force out a breathy laugh, making myself sound casual despite my rising panic. I probably sound half-hysterical. "I suppose I can confess to gossiping, if only about my own life."

"And these questions were pressing enough to be out post-curfew?"

"I thought I would have enough sunlight. I was mistaken."

A pause. "It takes strength to own up to our failures."

I exhale, relief flooding through me. I feel like I have passed some test, and now perhaps he will let me go and I can return to Halvar's side—

"It takes even greater cowardice to lie."

And all of the air leaves my body in one fell swoop. I clutch the soft covering in my fists, tearing it away from the bench. This draws my attention away from Father Dasco's accusations. He continues speaking, lecturing words about my failure as a child of God. How far I have drifted from the path I am meant to be on. I only half-listen, rising to my feet so I may turn and see what is beneath me.

The covering comes away completely with a little yanking. I discard it into a small bundle on the floor. The bench beneath is mostly smooth, comfortable enough if one has only a quick confession to make. The blanket seems unnecessary somehow, a kindness too great for the elders to extend to their flock. In fact, I can't remember it *having* a covering in years prior.

All of me doubts that they suddenly took pity on the comfort of their confessors. That ever-present feeling of wrongness seeps deeper under my skin, the walls of the confessional feeling even tighter and devoid of space than before. I kneel in front of the seat, feeling these familiar walls with new intention.

"You've always gone looking for things not meant for you," Father Dasco says. I freeze, momentarily thinking I've been caught. But then he says, "Stealing books from the library, such a childish thing to do. Father Levi was correct in saying you don't make a very good spy. Our librarian informed us of your antics. She didn't want to get you in trouble, not until you stole one of their restricted texts. Did you ever end up reading the *Creatura*? We so dearly missed that book in our collection."

I clench and unclench my fists. I am neither a warrior nor a witch. I am an even bigger fool than I thought. He's telling me what he knows without having to actually *say* it. What such pious child would steal books on forbidden creatures and get too close to the dangerous border? What sort of God-fearing woman questions the men in charge?

I spout the only thing I can think to say, a lame excuse. "Children get into things they're told not to. It's human nature."

"Human nature," he muses. "That's what we're trying to curb."

I run my hands along the floor, looking for something to find. I will myself to not be shaken by what he is saying, but my entire body feels like it's going to sink into the floor.

On the other side, Father Dasco continues, "Tell me about the herbs, Emelie." The sickly sweet smell of thyme and sage mixes in the air, and I know he's pulled my findings out from somewhere in his robes.

"A—a healer," I stammer. "A healer near our home showed me how to make a salve to relieve muscle aches. I was only trying to recreate that."

"Healer…" he repeats. "You've spoken with our local healer a few times over the years, have you not? She makes the same salves as you describe, yet you seem to be missing a few ingredients. Poor instruction, perhaps?"

"I would have to agree," I choke out. My fingers slip between where the bench meets the back paneling, disappearing into a crevice.

It's a false backing.

It rattles a bit as I touch it and so I pull away, afraid any noise will tip Father Dasco off to what I have discovered. I am not sure where the false backing will lead to. And worse, I am not certain that if I try to remove it, Father Dasco's side won't come free as well.

"I know that you are aware that if you made anything besides a salve," he says, "it would be considered blasphemy."

I hold my breath. "Yes." My hands find the loose panel again, finding that it stops on my side of the booth. Maybe if I am quiet, he won't notice.

"And you are aware that that is grounds for punishment."

My muscles tighten. "Yes." The backing is held fast against the bench, each piece holding the other in place. There has to be a latch somewhere.

"You set quite the precedent for the other young people of Kliransk when you left." He *tsks*. "That makes my job—as well as my brothers'—very difficult. Our only goals as leaders have been for your benefit—not just yours, but the entire community's. In an ever-changing world, with so many avenues of sin and temptation, we have to be a constant. Change is too much for the people of this village; the order of things exists to protect you all."

His words make my blood boil. I have heard variations of much of the same sentiment over the years, but now, after everything that has happened, it just sounds *wrong*.

"You speak of consistency, yet decree new rules at the slightest change in temperature. How does that make sense?"

He exhales deeply. "You remind me of Abel. So young, so spirited. So full of questions."

My body goes deathly still. Father Dasco's words reopen the pit in my stomach with a vengeance. *Wrong wrong wrong wrong wrong wrong...*

I clench my hands, trying to calm myself. Trying to formulate a way to get free of this awful feeling, this awful place—

Where my hands tighten, I hear a *click*. And the backing slides out of place. The back wall of the confessional dips towards me, and I frantically catch it before it completely collapses. I set it against the door and stare ahead of me. The booth is set up against the far wall of the church, where there are no pews, and no study on the other side. Parishioners are not allowed past this wall of the church, and in my young naive brain, I always assumed the elders lived on the other side of this wall. But there are no bedrooms, no living spaces. Instead, I stare into the gaping mouth of a tunnel.

"Emelie?"

My head snaps to the panel between us. It feels so much thinner now. Father Dasco sounds merely annoyed at my lack of response. He hadn't heard, then. How thick are these confessional walls? How loudly must people confess their sins in order to be heard?

"I—" I look between the booth and the tunnel. It's dark, unnaturally so inside. I have no idea where it leads. It could roundabout back into the town square, or deeper through Kliransk for all I know. It could be a dead end.

It could be my chance to escape.

"You would do well to renounce any wrongdoing on your part. I would hate for you to be accused of something you haven't done. You haven't partaken in witchcraft, have you, Emelie?"

"No," I whisper, my voice coming out mousy and not at all convincing.

"Good." His voice oozes disdain. It is the voice of a beast with its teeth already around my throat. "Now try again, this time like you believe it."

I look back at the tunnel, willing my eyes to adjust to the darkness. Maybe if I could see where I was going, I wouldn't be so afraid. The foolish side of me wonders if I could burst out of the confessional and run straight home before they caught me. But I am not that fast. I am not that brave.

I am not that foolish, either.

"No," I say again, this time more forceful. "I haven't."

"Better." He exhales deeply, like he's considering something. "A few repetitions of the Lord's prayer isn't quite the right penance for you, I don't think. What would you have yourself do to make up for the things you've done? Sew a few hundred dresses for your mother? Pray a few dozen rosaries? What would make you feel *sorry*, Emelie?"

I can't breathe. He knows too much. *Far* too much. He knows exactly which scar to push at to inflict as much pain as when the wound was made. I feel like he can see through the wooden wall that separates us; the panel might as well not even be there for all the privacy it offers. I don't have to confess anything to him—*he already knows*.

If I am damned already, I might as well go honestly. "Being here. Being here makes me sorry."

"It's a shame you feel that way," he says. "Because now that you're back, I can't let you leave."

There is a stunning silence on both ends of the confessional. I think in his mind, Father Dasco expects his revelation to keep me rooted in place. To beg his forgiveness, perhaps, or God's. To fall back into the role laid out for me from the moment I was born in this cursed town. To forsake what I have come to know since escaping, to leave that all behind in exchange for his good favor. To be seen as righteous. To be right, in his mind.

I have surprised myself plenty of times over the past few months. I think I surprise Father Dasco, too, when I run into the tunnel instead.

If I am thankful for nothing else Halvar has done for me—if I had to reject everything—the one thing I can say I *am* thankful for is

225

the fact that he bought me new boots. The floor of the tunnel is damp and it's difficult to stay on my feet, but my boots are of fine make, keeping me upright through this sprint.

I hear Father Dasco shout my name once, twice, three times before it goes quiet behind me. I can only assume that he's gone to get the others, giving me some much-needed time to get ahead before they pursue me. Unless they know where this tunnel lets out, which they likely do, and are on their way to wait for me there.

I can't go back now. I have to keep running. Wherever this tunnel leads, I will have to make my way from there and hope that they don't get there first.

I don't slip so much as slide along the rocky path. It's on a slight decline, and gravity keeps pulling me further forward, like it's swallowing me whole. I realize with a sinking feeling that I am headed beneath the church. The mouth of the tunnel is wide enough that I can stretch both arms out and still not touch either side, so I keep to one side and drag my hand along the wall. The jagged rocky texture cuts into my hands, and I feel something warm and wet along my skin— likely my own blood. I don't let go, too afraid that if I do, I won't find my way at all. Getting lost down here would be like digging my own grave and planting my tombstone atop it.

I refuse to die down here.

I am not the naive girl I once was. I know Father Dasco brought up Abel to me for a reason, and it confirms the lingering suspicions that I haven't wanted to confront. The things I've known bone-deep for most of my life. What has festered over this godforsaken winter. My gut has been screaming to me just how *wrong* it feels here.

In so few words, he damned himself, and our roles in that confessional switched. He confessed to me what I didn't want to be right about.

They're killing them.

If they're going to kill me too, if I am going to die in Kliransk, let it be near the trees so they can bury my body in the same grass that I have lived and loved atop. I want to rot beneath the same trees that I once played under with Halvar. Not in this church, not in this dank tunnel that seems to go on forever. No, if I am going to die, then let me pick the burial ground.

The path veers right suddenly, and I don't move with it quickly enough. My left shoulder slams into the wall in front of me and I hear a sickening crunch. I whimper and try to shake it out, finding that my arm can still move. It's not broken, if anything just popped out of place. I have no time to nurse myself, I have to keep going. I don't know if it's my fear and paranoia crafting the footsteps I hear rushing behind me, and I don't want to find out.

I pick up my pace, my good arm clutching the throbbing one. I wince every time I move it, a searing pain rushing through the entire shoulder. If I had time to stop, I could use my coat to make a sling, but I cannot afford the minutes I'd spend. I will have to chance being useless without my dominant arm.

I try to picture the church above me. It's larger than any other building in Kliransk, but not by *this* much. The tunnel has to be moving beneath the market by now, if not further. How far do these roots reach? I have to wonder if the elders use these passages to get around, and if so, how much access these tunnels give them. The thought chills me that while any of us could be working or eating dinner, the elders could be beneath, listening for anyone who slips out of line.

The tunnel diverges again, and by now my eyes have adjusted enough to make out three paths in front of me. I can continue moving straight ahead, I can go right, or I can go left. I curse my piss-poor sense of direction and bank right. If I am correct, this one *should* move me back in the direction of my parents' home. Back to Halvar.

I skid to a stop then, nearly crashing into the pillar separating the tunnels. I can't lead the elders to Halvar, broken and defenseless. My parents will likely do nothing to protect him. But I also can't waste time; for all I know, they could be headed to him now.

The image of Father Dasco standing above my bed and staring down at my husband fills me with a protective rage, something new that is quickly becoming familiar to me. I have to trust that this is the way to go. I have to trust myself. I shake off everything Father Dasco said to me and keep running.

I barely make it several yards before I realize this route was a mistake.

When one of the elders tackles me, the lanky, bony body crashing into me reveals him as Father Levi. We go fumbling to the ground, the muck and moisture of it coating my skirts. He holds my arms to my side, and I let out a cry as he displaces my bad shoulder.

The remaining elders follow shortly after. In the blurry darkness, I can see that they each have something in hand. I think Father Patrick has a cross, Father Dasco a small pitcher.

"Witch!" Father Dasco cries. "We command you to release your demons!"

The three of them start praying, and something wet hits my face. I can see Father Dasco whipping his arm and I realize he's sprinkling me with holy water. They chant the Lord's prayer like their lives depend on it, and I think they genuinely believe it does.

Father Levi squeezes me, aggravating my shoulder even further out of place, and I can't help it when I let out a scream. This seems to encourage them, their prayers growing louder. Maybe they think their prayers are working. But they're only hurting me. I don't know how to make them stop.

I read about exorcisms in my research. I knew they existed, but this is twisted far beyond what I thought it would be. What it should be. How can I tell them that there are no demons in me when my mere existence is a blight in their eyes?

I curl my legs beneath me, wrenching against Father Levi in agony. He still has my arms pinned to my sides. My boot meets my hand, and that's when I remember the knife. I look between the three elders, all of their eyes closed firmly in prayer. I am still being sprinkled with holy water, still having a cross thrust in my face. Still being exorcised of my supposed demons.

I go lax in Father Levi's arms, stop my thrashing and fighting. This makes his grip loosen a bit, as if he thinks their attempt is working. My fingers scramble into my boot, and I can't...quite...reach the dagger...

My fingers lodge around the hilt, and I yank it from its sheath. Then, blindly, I sink it into Father Levi's arm. He screams and releases me completely. I stumble to my feet and take off running again, this time through the center tunnel with the horrified cries of the elders echoing off the walls. I think I can see a light ahead, and I hope against hope that this is the way out.

I reach the light, and it is an exit. Another gaping mouth covered by a barred gate. I shove, and immediately hear its hinges groan against my weight. It slides against the snow, now more like slush in this area, and it gives enough for me to throw it open the rest of the way.

Once outside, I take a moment to get my bearings. I don't know where I am, nor do I have a clue as to how this entrance hasn't been found by another child of Kliransk. It's not exactly hidden with its high metal bars. Around me, I can't pick out anything that I recognize, which is unusual for me. I thought I knew this village better but I have once again been proven wrong.

Behind me, I can see a sloping expanse that leads back up to the village. I'm below Kliransk, then. Down a back alleyway that the elders must have blocked off or proclaimed forbidden long before it became known to me. I can hike up the hill to the village and take the chance that someone will be out and receptive to what I have just been through, but given the iron knuckle grip the elders have, that seems unlikely.

On the other side of me is the woods.

I can take my chances with the people, or with the creatures. For a brief, horrible moment, I cannot decide which is more monstrous. I battle with my options, but the echoing shouts behind me tell me I am out of time. I can't will my way into a better solution. I cannot afford to be indecisive, clarity now feeling like a luxury far beyond my means. With one final glance up the hill, I make my choice.

I run into the woods.

CHAPTER SIXTEEN

It's getting dark, and being out in the dark in the woods has never worked out well for me.

The trees are less disturbed on this side of Kliransk. I run far enough past the tree line that I can't be seen by anyone passing by, but not so far that I can't see them. I follow a rough path towards my side of town, using any landmarks I see to mark where I am.

There are few people out with curfew rapidly approaching. Raw human instinct urges me to run into the town square screaming for help. But I cannot know with enough certainty that the elders haven't twisted their minds in their favor enough so that I wouldn't be dragged right back to the church. I realize with dread that washes over me like a bucket of ice water that I don't trust the villagers enough to ask for help. I don't know who they would believe.

I don't know if I trust my mother to believe me.

I stick to the trees instead.

My heart lurches when I see a light peek out from my parents' home, and a figure steps onto the front entrance. My mother pokes her body out of the front door and looks in the direction of the church, her arms crossed. I'm too far to see her face, but her posture is tense. She takes one long look up and down the road, then goes back inside, shutting the door behind her.

Maybe I've misjudged her. But that maybe isn't strong enough to send me running into her arms. I nestle against a tree trunk and distantly consider the prospect, trying to catch my breath. My shoulder burns and the thought of making a sling comes back to me, but given the growing dark and the snow that is falling heavier than it was during the day, I can't chance removing my coat. My skirts are damp from the mucky floor of the tunnel, and frost is crawling its way up towards my bodice, clinging to the fabric. If I survive this night, I'll probably face the worst sickness of my life, but even that seems like a gift right now.

I can't stay still. My house is in perfect line of sight, but I still don't want to chance simply walking inside. My mother's confusion at the threshold informs me that the elders have not made their way to my childhood home yet. That means Halvar is safe, for now. Although he's likely uncomfortable and wondering where I am, he is safe nonetheless. I cannot ask for more at this moment.

I walk a few yards deeper, keeping the house in my line of vision. The snow crunches beneath my boots and I'm growing colder by the minute. My coat is thick enough to shield me from the worst of it, but it's still not enough. If I could run inside, I would. But what then? Drag my injured husband all the way to our home in the middle of the woods, with an agitated creature possibly still on the loose? We'd sooner be caught dead.

I think of the knife I launched at the creature that attacked Halvar. It was instinct to defend, and blind foolishness on my part to throw away a weapon, and I'm still shocked that it worked.

Knife. I left my knife in Father Levi's arm.

If I am damned, it is my own fault. I have nothing but my wits to defend myself with, and half of the time I don't trust myself enough to believe that I am doing what is best. If I had, I would have caught onto the elders' ploy months ago.

It makes sense in hindsight, their superstitions disguising their strict rules meant to will us into obedience. But still, why? Power for the sake of power doesn't seem to abide by scripture. If anything, it feels antithetical to their very cause.

Stepping over roots and larger piles of snow, I try to put the pieces together. It still feels lacking. I thought I would get a moment of gratification but all I feel is the nagging emptiness of knowing I was right about something I desperately wanted to be wrong about.

Distant footsteps and the crunching of snow underfoot jar me enough that I start running again. The footfalls are slow, cautious. They don't know where I am yet. But they're going in the right direction. Seeing no other option, I bank left. This takes me deeper into the woods, circling back towards the church. Every step away from my parents' house, from Halvar, stirs the rising panic in me, but what else can I do? If I can just make it back to the church, I can hold watch while I wait for them to go inside for curfew—

I'm not paying attention when something rams into me face-first and we both collapse into the snow. I start scrambling back, ignoring the pain that shoots through my shoulder and the way the debris scratches at my still-bloody hands. The figure groans, sitting back on their knees. A head tilts back towards the moonlight filtering through the trees, and it sheds light on Father Patrick's face. I've gifted him a nosebleed.

He looks frantically in all directions, then holds a hand to his face as he pushes himself to his feet. His other hand is outstretched towards me. "Hurry, we must make haste."

I clamber further back, conscious of the trail of blood my cut hands leave in the snow. I try to push myself to my feet, but my goddamned shoulder keeps giving out and I can't quite get my bearings. I feel disoriented and vulnerable and useless as I try and fail to stand.

I have to do a double take at Father Patrick because it is only then that I realize he's crying. He wipes his face with the same hand holding his nose, smearing blood across his cheeks. I don't think he notices, he's crying so hard.

"I never wanted this," he sobs. "I never wanted this…"

He staggers back a few steps, looking between the trees and through the thickening snowfall. His cries are unabashed, open-mouthed and mournful. If I didn't know better, I would think he was mourning all that has been lost.

I flinch when he screams into the open air, "*You hear me? I never wanted this!"* He turns back to me for one brief moment, whispers, "I'm sorry."

Then the other elders are upon us, bursting out from between the trees and tackling Father Patrick to stifle his yelling. I hadn't heard them coming. I hadn't had time to listen. I don't have time for anything anymore.

"You fool!" Father Levi snarls. "Do you want the entire village to hear us?"

Father Patrick doesn't fight them, just collapses into Father Levi's arms. To his credit, Father Levi holds him up even as his face twists in pain from his wound. Then he looks at me, and the disgust morphs into pure loathing. He nods to Father Dasco, who rushes to my side and pins my good arm behind my back.

"So spirited," Father Levi practically spits, "just like the others."

"What others?" I choke out, though I already know who he means.

"Abel, Calder, those other blasphemous prats we had to take care of."

Take care. What a disgusting euphemism for the things they've done. The wording itself frames their crimes as something to be seen as a virtue. Care, what care is there in ending their lives?

The realization hits me that they believe themselves to be doing the right thing. They truly think they are carrying out God's will.

"There was never a wolf, was there?"

Father Dasco twists my arm and I yelp. If he dislocates my good shoulder, I'll be even more useless than I already feel. I try to move with him, but his other hand pushes down on my bad shoulder, and that's when I start to cry.

"There are worse things in this world than wolves, Emelie." His sneer is the promise of violence and retribution for any perceived wrongdoing in his eyes. I am the offender, and I will be punished. "Sin manifests in many forms, and we tried for years to turn Kliransk into something worthy. But you all refuse to listen. You refuse to heed God's word. We offer you salvation, and you spit in our faces."

Father Levi pitches in, "What do you think it says to every other young person in Kliransk when you walk in and out of the woods as you please? It tells them that they can do whatever they want, regardless of consequence, and come back when convenient to them."

Despite the pain, I twist in Father Dasco's grasp. "Convenient? You think any of this has been *convenient* for me? I'm only here because my husband would die without a healer!"

"You and your husband sleep in your mother's home, the same mother you scorn despite her efforts to raise you in a godly manner," Father Dasco says. "I hear her confessions. She knows exactly what a failure she's been as a parent to you."

Grief rises in me. My mother did fail at raising me, but not for any of the reasons they're thinking. She was cold and distant and didn't care to know who I was outside of a church. She didn't feed my passions or my curiosity or even my body most days. She left me hungry and wanting. But none of that matters to them, because I still lost my faith. And that is the worst crime of all.

"I tried for so many years," I sob, years of insecurity reaching their boiling point. "I tried to do right by God and it was never enough. I was never enough. And I thought I was the only one."

Father Dasco scoffs. "They all said the same thing."

His words chill me, but he doesn't stop, even as the snow falls harder around us. Father Patrick is crying into Father Levi's shoulder, while Father Levi stares stone-faced.

"I thought we could fix Abel," Father Dasco says. "We brought him to several interventions in the church, trying to fix his irreverent ways. Even going as far as finding him while hard at work amongst these very trees. He was one of your father's better men, always staying later than the others. He denied us up until the very end. When he stormed off into the deep woods, we expected him to simply cool off, then come back and listen to reason."

Father Levi picks up where Father Dasco leaves off. "But it seemed our...disagreement disturbed the natural life, and when the creature came to lay claim to its territory and Abel was called home to God, we knew we had to return to Kliransk to protect the people."

Halvar's words from so many weeks ago float back into my memory. Father Levi is right about one thing, they disturbed the creature and so it retaliated. The creature has no way of knowing that it didn't get to the root of the problem. It simply saw a body and lunged, hungry for peace. How cruel that all it would breed was more violence.

"We always told you that the woods were dangerous. If you all would have just listened," Father Levi scoffs. Father Patrick shakes beside him, looking like a shell of the leader I thought he was.

"Some good came out of it," Father Dasco says. "After that first alarm, something changed within the people of Kliransk. You started to come to heel. You start to listen. We thought we were finally making progress after so many years of trying. But it didn't last. More of you started asking questions, not just about us. You started questioning God. And we could not let that blasphemy go unchecked."

Father Levi says, "We tried the same intervention with each of them, and were left with the same results every time. They chose to flee. They chose sin. They chose the woods."

"You all want what you cannot have," Father Dasco shakes his head, "no matter how many times we try to tell you it's not good for you."

I have to wonder if this intervention they speak of is the same one they just tried with me. What demons are there but curiosity?

"This village has never known true authority," Father Dasco cuts in. "If you can't handle our demands, simple as they are, what makes you think you're worthy enough to serve the Lord?"

Through my tears, I say, "And people deserve to die because of that?"

"They chose their deaths," Father Levi says. "We simply brought them out here to pray over them, to show them what their other option was. We did not expect each of them to choose wrong."

Horror washes over me. They brought all of those people out here to pray, and faced them with a lifetime in Kliransk or the unknown out in the woods... And they all chose to run.

My breathing starts to come too fast, like I can't get enough air in.

Unless they saw it with their own eyes, how can they know that these people are dead? Whose bodies were in those closed caskets? They could be out there, hungry and alone, wandering the woods to this day. Is this what the spirits were trying to warn me of?

Father Dasco must see the confusion mingling with fear on my face, because he says, "Abel was a mistake. We never intended for him to die. He didn't get to choose, but if that was God's will for his life, then we have come to accept that."

A roar sounds in the distance, and we all turn towards it, fear collectively gripping us. Then, all three of them turn back to me.

"And now you get to choose."

Father Levi lets go of Father Patrick and comes to grab my bad arm with his good one. He and Father Dasco start dragging me toward the sound, Father Patrick straggling behind us. I thrash, further pulling my shoulder out of place. This can't be happening, not after all I've learned.

It cannot end like this.

In a frenzy, I throw my full weight against Father Levi, who groans and reaches for his wounded arm. His robes cling to his skin thanks to the blood pouring from it. I use my leverage to wrench away from Father Dasco, who is too shocked to tighten his grip. I break away from them, and for a moment I think Father Patrick will try and stop me. But he simply stares at me with panic in his wide eyes, and I take his hesitation and run in the direction of my parents' house.

My entire body feels like it's bound to fall apart. I've run more in the past few days—the past few hours—than I have in my entire life. The house is in sight within moments. I can see it sitting quietly, its windows dark with its suit of armor protecting it.

The elders are right behind me. I trip over roots and loose branches. I am not fast enough. I know they're going to catch me again, so I do the only thing I can think of. It likely won't do anything for me, but maybe it will be a sign that I tried. That I was alive up until now.

I put two fingers in my mouth and let out a furious, high-pitched whistle.

Then hands surround me, covering my mouth so I can't even cry out when they yank my arms back as they drag me back into the tree line. The lights across the village are low. There is no one to witness this death procession.

Another roar from somewhere deep within the woods. We move towards it instead of away, my feet dragging the entire way. The struggle has cost me my coat. The green fabric could almost pass for shrubbery, but the embroidery sticks out blood red against the white snow. I shiver as the cold meets me, quickly sinking into my bones. I can hear Father Patrick muffling his cries behind us, muttering something about *not another one* and *there has to be some other way…*

I recognize so many of the trees we pass. If nothing else, they will be witness to my demise. I will not go unknown into the darkness but instead surrounded by brush and canopies of trees that have become familiar with my footsteps. I cannot stop the flow of events, so I will ride the rocky current. I can only hope that wherever I go next is similar to here. I want to feel how I felt among the trees with Halvar. Not just over the past few months, but the way we were as children. Carefree and happy to just be near one another. If I can have that in death, perhaps it won't be so bad.

The roaring grows louder and more frequent as we near it. I can hear its footsteps stalking through the trees. I have already made my choice, my body too broken to run and my spirit too firm to bend to the elders.

We make it to a clearing nearly a mile in. There, they force me to my knees and sprinkle me with holy water. It mixes with the snowflakes as it dusts my cheeks and my hair, dampening it so that it sticks to my face. Their voices mingle furiously as they pray. I cannot tell who is speaking and who is simply repeating. It doesn't matter now.

I think I can see one of the creatures edging the other side of the clearing. Its steps are slow, unsure. It seems to be as afraid of us as they are of it. I am not afraid. This creature knows me. I tried to stick my knife in its neck.

The elders back away then, their prayers growing louder the further they walk away from me. I stay on my knees with my hands slack at my sides; if I tried to lift them I don't think I could anymore. A little smile crosses my face as I realize Halvar will at least have an alibi for my death, his broken body resting in my parents' home. I offered him security once with my life, and now again with my death.

The Walker appears motionless, yet I still hear footsteps. Furious, running footsteps. I laugh softly, thinking perhaps I am already dead and simply haven't caught up with my body yet. The laugh builds until I am hysterical, both laughing and crying. That old familiar roar builds within me, bubbling over, filling every inch of air around us.

But just as I did that night of the first alarm, I realize it's not me. There is a roaring coming from somewhere else. Something else. The sound is one that runs all the way under my skin and into my bones, between my ribs to pierce my heart. I know this sound.

The creature opposite the clearing rushes back into the covering of trees. Like it's running from the sound. Like it's afraid. What frightens a monster?

A bigger, badder one.

A flurry of fur and limbs and teeth bursts through the trees behind us, and I whirl around in time to see it lunge for the elders. Father Levi and Father Dasco jump out of the way in time, but not Father Patrick. If I wasn't paying attention, if I had looked any later, I might not have seen how he opened his arms to it. How his shoulders sagged in relief. But for once, I am paying attention. Just as I see this creature sink its teeth into Father Patrick's neck and tear away flesh from bone. He sinks to his knees in the snow, welcoming death.

I fall, and as I hit the ground, the cold numbs the shooting pain that goes through my shoulder. The wolf rears back, spitting out Father Patrick's hunk of flesh. Next to its panting form lies my coat, now frayed where its teeth met the fabric. It shakes its head, and its eyes land on me.

I know those eyes. I know that stance.

A new fire lights within me and I rise to my feet, intending

238

to run to him, but Father Dasco tackles me instead. He braces me in front of him like a shield, and it's all I can do to not succumb to my laughter again.

I am not going to die here.

The elders look upon their fallen brother's body, panicked breaths heaving out of their chests. Father Levi doubles over and vomits onto the forest floor. I think I see tears brimming in Father Dasco's eyes. But then they look up at the wolf and do their best to collect themselves.

Father Levi approaches me, my very own dagger in hand. The one I cut him with. He holds it up to my neck for the wolf to see. "Stay back!" His voice is full of violent command, and I feel the blade nick my skin ever so slightly. Some of the fear comes flooding back in, but it doesn't overtake me the way it did before.

Father Dasco bares his teeth, appearing so painfully human in comparison. He snarls, "Just like his father."

My brows furrow, putting together what he's said. He catches my confused look and barks out a laugh. He's laughing so hard that he doubles over, bracing himself on his knees.

"Did you really think we didn't know what he was? How his bloodline tainted the very soul of Kliransk?"

On my other side, Father Levi pitches in. "Why do you think we sent him away? We couldn't have a shifter living amongst our flock."

My brain is spinning too much to keep this all in. "How did you—"

"We tried converting his father," Father Dasco says. "Attempted the same tactics we used on you. Imagine our surprise when his struggling turned to shifting."

"We weren't foolish enough to try and kill him," Father Levi says. "Not when we could easily be killed in return. But he understood, even in his devil-form, that he was not to return."

"Enough of this chatter." Father Dasco shoves Father Levi, who winces at the touch.

Together, the two of them half-carry me across the clearing. I am not so much walking as I am being dragged, every rough moment pushing me against the flat of the blade Father Levi holds. The wolf keeps pace just a few steps behind, growling whenever I wince or trip.

Once we reach the far end of the clearing, the elders lean me against a tree trunk. Father Dasco searches his robes for the holy water. I brace myself for the chill, cringing against the blade still held fast to my skin. As they pray, Father Levi lowers the threat from my neck, allowing me to breathe freely. My relief is short-lived, though, when I recognize which verse they are proclaiming over me.

"'…it is better for you to lose one part of your body than for your whole body to go into hell.'"

I don't feel the sting immediately when Father Levi drives the blade home in my left arm, piercing the soft flesh of my bicep.

Horrified, I realize he's stabbed completely through my flesh so I am stuck to the tree behind me. It happened so fast I didn't have time to scream, but now I do. A sharp, piercing sound that ricochets through my entire body. It burns as hot as the hell I imagine they think they're sending me to.

The wolf snarls furiously but holds back on its haunches. What could it possibly do to help? If he attacks one, the other will strike me. Possibly killing me, if this is any indication. We are essentially at their mercy.

My chest heaves as I try to breathe, the pain too much to hold in. I can't struggle so as to not exacerbate the wound. I have to watch what happens and hold onto the fact that if they're going to kill me, they are going to die soon after.

How they manage to continue praying while I stand impaled before them, I have no idea. Perhaps they stock themselves so full of holy words they don't have any space left for compassion or kindness.

I think I might be starting to pass out, perhaps from that very same fear and exhaustion, because I start to see a light. Several, blinking lights. Tiny glittering specks of lights.

I hold in a sob of relief. Not lights at all, as I always mistake them. But the spirits once again. The wolf whines from where it paces

240

between the trees. It knows, too.

A few of the spirits blink in quick succession and then disappear into the eastbound section of trees, before circling back and repeating this pattern. I wrack my brain, trying to place where we are. Trying to remember what lies in that direction. At my hesitation, a cluster of spirits hovers high in the trees, circling one spot.

Their collective light illuminates what was barely visible before: a kerchief, dyed so that its fabric sticks out against the dark brown of the bark. I gasp, drawing Father Dasco's eye to me. I force out a few coughs, but once I've started I cannot stop. The cold is getting through to me, thanks to my damned skirts. He stops glaring at me and instead leans away in repulsion. I keep my eyes above, searching in the dark for more kerchiefs.

They are sparsely placed, but on the trees that lack one, I search their trunks at eye level and find wards carved. Together, they map out exactly where we are. I know the way from here.

I know how to get home.

The wolf pants as it paws at the ground. Frustration etches at its body even in this form. If I were capable of smiling right now, I would at the familiarity even in the change. I feel for it, however. Impatience gnaws at me. I can't stay like this. I won't. I refuse to.

When the elders lower their eyes to their prayer books, I will the wolf to meet my gaze. I look between the knife sticking out of my arm and the elders. Understanding blinks into the wolf's eyes.

I don't have time to think beyond what I am about to do, so I just do it. I take one deep breath in, force my less-injured arm up to the hilt, and yank it out. I don't scream so much as roar, blood pouring down my arm. I lunge for the elder closest to me—Father Levi—and slash at whatever I can reach. Meanwhile, the wolf goes for Father Dasco, teeth snapping as he forces him further into the trees. I use up what little leverage I have. Then my feet are moving and I am running like I am being chased by Death itself. I suppose in some way, I am.

The wolf snarls behind me and I turn only long enough to see it blocking the elders from following me. It snaps and lunges at them, keeping them leashed. As I turn back around, I see it run after me, so much faster than them or I. It catches up with me quickly, lowering itself enough for me to climb on its back.

"To the house," I urge, and we set off faster than I have ever moved in my life.

Unfortunately, our movement draws the Walker out from its hiding place. It can't quite keep pace with the wolf, but it's closer than the elders. From its low roaring, I can't tell if it's running after us or with us. I hope for the latter and hang on.

I don't have much of a grip left in my useless arms, so my knees squeeze the sides of the wolf for all they're worth. Everything aches and if I could just let my body go limp and fall into the foliage, I would. But I can't leave the wolf alone.

We reach home faster than I would have been able to alone. A rueful smile plays on my lips, remembering the first night we ran through the woods. I feel the sting as we pass through the wards. The wolf skids to a stop in the clearing and I slide off, running for the marked trees that bracket our land. The elders crash into the wards, collapsing into a heap at the border. Behind them, the creature veers off into the trees, slinking back into the shadows as if it were never there.

I check the wards at each corner and find them intact. They're as strong as they were the night I replenished them, which is a good sign. The elders watch from the other side, their eyes alight with malice.

"Witchcraft," Father Levi sneers.

I spit in his direction. "It's old magic, no more sacrilege than the prayers you stuff down our throats. At least this, I believe in."

"Witch," Father Dasco echoes. "You should be burned at the stake."

"And you should have your tongues cut out for all the false words you preach to the people, but that is not my judgment to cast." I start across the clearing, passing them as I do. I can hear them muttering prayers and crossing themselves. As if that will do anything.

But the air starts to hiss, not at all how the wards sound. And I see them sprinkling snow around the warded trunks. I can feel it when the protection starts to waver. The wolf growls, crawling towards them to perhaps attack, but behind them, the creature stalks out from the shadows.

I scream, "The wards! They're dropping the wards!"

The Walker moves slowly, calculated. The elders scatter sanctified snow, frozen holy water, around another warded tree and I feel a great whoosh as I am exposed to them. And to the creature.

For a moment, everyone is still. Then, everything moves in one great surge of chaos. The creature starts to lunge, and I cannot tell which of us it means to attack. The wolf doesn't hesitate, crashing into the Walker with its full body weight. The two of them wrestle into the trees, all teeth and fury and primal anger.

The elders are on their feet and running toward me. Faced with the unending woods—and perhaps more creatures—I risk the house. It's pitch black inside as I throw the door open and shut behind me. I race up the stairs, tripping up the last few steps. Bedroom. I have to get to the bedroom.

I hear the front door bang open and footsteps clamber across the floorboards. I take my chances and stuff myself into the wardrobe. My dangling fingers find the hilt of a dagger, stashed absentmindedly atop a pile of clothes. I close my fist around it, ignoring how the hilt presses against my fresh wounds.

I can hear them fumbling from room to room, the dark house unfamiliar as a brand new territory. I hear the shattering of glass, the groaning of furniture being overturned. They sound relentless. It chills me; I will be found out soon enough.

The floors groan with every step they take. I can track their rampage across the house from the sounds alone. They move from the kitchen to the sitting room and back. To the dining table and then the foyer. Up the stairs to the study. The washroom. Down the hall to the threshold of the bedroom and then back. The floors practically sing, mapping out a path. They don't know that not all of the floorboards creak.

But I do.

I picture the paths I laid out during that long night I spent alone. I don't just know the way out, I created it. Once the creaking fades down the stairs, I track their movements into the dining room, and there they stay. Likely formulating a plan. But they are not the hunters anymore. A good hunter knows how to track, how to plan out the best course of action. I am not a good hunter. But I was trained by the best.

Like a phantom, I slowly etch open the wardrobe door and slip one toe out, testing the floorboard below. It holds, and I put my full weight on it and tiptoe into the room. I make it to the doorway when I start to hear their voices again. They speak in low, angry whispers and I can't quite make out the words. I don't care much for words anymore, though. What I require is action.

So, so carefully, I make my way down the hall. Every step is a gamble, but one I have the upper hand in. The stairs are the real challenge. Each step is a test, and I hesitate to put my full weight on each one, which slows me down. By the time I make it to the bottom of the stairs, I can hear the elders rustling through the cabinets, looking for something I can't see.

The front door is a few paces away, left ajar. The elders are fools. Old, aggrandized fools. I slip outside in the same ghostly way, but I am not in the clear yet.

My uninjured arm is not my favored one for writing. But after years of wrist-slaps, I can make it carve out the ward symbols with the dagger. I am lacking the vial of salt I usually use, but I will have to make do. My mouth is dry from all of the running and screaming and sobbing, leaving behind a bitter taste. Sweat pours down my temples despite the chill wracking my body. I am covered in salt, made of it.

Dragging my palms across my forehead and cheeks, I soak up the salty sweat there before hacking a wad of salty spit into my hands. Then, I step up to the left side of the door and smear the wet concoction along the wall.

I repeat this on the other side of the door, splinters attacking my palms as I do. I have to run to the other side of the house to repeat the process, and I hope against hope that I have done it right. The loss of fluids is making me feel lightheaded, but there is work to be done yet.

"Over here," I call out, my voice gravel in my throat.

The elders rush to the open door with violence undisguised on their faces. But, as I anticipated, they crash against the wards. I hear their skin sizzle as it stings them.

I stand before them, blood gushing from so many wounds, with my shoulders sitting crooked in their sockets. Snow and muck cover me, and my hair sits flat against my scalp. I probably look about as powerful as I feel, but all I need to appear as is the monster they already believe me to be: the witch of the wood.

"You cannot hurt me," I say, my voice feeling like it belongs to a stranger. "Not unless I will it. You can twist the minds of every single villager until you have a flock that can't shit out their dinner before you say so, but I will not be one of them. You cannot hurt me any more than I have already been hurt." I grit my teeth, my body starting to feel the effects of this nightmare. I rest my hands against my knees, not trusting myself to stand anymore. Just a little longer. "I will not be your sheep."

The elders look upon me like I am everything they taught us to fear. I feel bigger than my body. With ears so large. *The better to hear the creature's stalking footsteps.* With eyes wide open. *The better to see it creeping up towards the wards.* Where I can see its big teeth. *The better to eat them with.*

I look back at the woods and let out one more whistle, strong enough to blow the goddamn house down. The wolf sprints toward the house, the creature following close behind. I lock eyes with the wolf, the same golden brown eyes I have looked into for so many years. I see the twinkle in them, and I know he knows what to do.

The wolf veers away from the house at the last possible moment, leaving a rush of air that tosses my hair. The Walker, however, is not as smart. Before the elders have time to react, I reach forward and slash through the delicate lines that make up the carved symbol there. I hear the fizzle as the ward drops, and the creature uses that opportunity to launch itself inside.

The elders try to run, and I can see them scrambling over each other in desperate hopes of escaping. But I've already redrawn the ward, already smeared fresh saliva, trapping them inside.

I hear their screams. I hear crashing and the sounds of destruction. This won't be a home much longer, but that's alright. We have the entire woods open to us.

I think I start to smile as I collapse into the snow. I think I hear the pattering of soft footsteps beside me, feel a wet nose nuzzle me as my consciousness starts to slip. I can't be sure, though, because everything goes dark.

CHAPTER SEVENTEEN

I think I feel myself being dragged, and panic starts to build as I come to and see the ground moving beneath me. I realize my legs aren't touching the ground—in fact, I am *far* above the snow that lies beneath. Blindly, I try to thrash with what little strength I have but pause when I hear a whine from behind.

It takes a few more moments for me to realize I am being carried by the wolf, the back of my dress caught firmly in its maw. The world shifts again as we skid to a stop so the wolf can gently set me down on the frozen ground. It lowers itself onto its haunches and I haul myself up with whatever worthless strength I have left. My arms scream with the effort, but it is either this or continue being dragged. Once I am mostly secure, we take off running once more, and then the darkness pulls me under.

I wake with a start, my entire body in chills. I've been laid in the snow, a soft muzzle attempting to nudge me back to consciousness. I groan and push myself up to sitting, taking in the woods around me. The trees are thinned out here, and I can see a wide expanse of barren ground a few yards away. I test each of my muscles to little success.

My shoulders feel as though I'd be better off removing my arms, and the gash on my bicep burns. My hands are worse for the wear, looking like they've never seen a day of *women's work* in their life. Had I woken up in hell, I'd likely be in less pain than I am right now.

Groaning cuts through the air and I gasp as I turn to meet it. My heart lurches. "*Halvar.*"

I have never seen such horror.

I would know him in any form, but this one seems far removed from any other. He is caught in between shifting, his body both beast and human. His limbs are too long and angled in all the wrong ways. Elbows lurch forward and back as they find the sockets, knees are bent backward as he sits back on his haunches.

His joints pop like crackling firewood, muscles twitching beneath his stretching skin as it tries to right itself. His jaw stretched far beyond where it should be, neck wrenching from side to side as the vertebra shrink back to size. The spine below is crooked and oblong. He is so much taller than he was before.

Slowly, painfully so, he shrinks back into himself. Claws retract into knuckles, and bones crack as they reset into place. I wince at every sound of his bones breaking back into the shape of a person. He collapses onto his front and unearths a groan that seems to reset him. For a moment he lays there, writhing against the frosted ground. He is nude but doesn't seem bothered by the cold. The snow beneath him melts away to reveal the dirt beneath, and light tendrils of smoke emit from all of his joints.

Carefully, like he's worried he'll shatter if he moves too much, he pushes up on his hands and looks at me, exhaustion dredging across his features. He says only two words, but they're enough to force me back to my feet and running again.

"*Get help.*"

I am so dizzy from the blood loss, and if I have to run much further I think I will break completely. But I can't leave both of us here in this state. I'd be signing our death away. He got us this far. I can take us the rest of the way.

The trees thin out not towards a clearing as I'd first thought, but a road. I follow it for a few paces until I can see buildings in the distance. Groups of them huddled together the same way bodies huddle for warmth. Some are houses, some overhead stalls for a marketplace—I think I even see a library. It takes my muddled brain a few moments to realize what I'm looking at.

A village.

It's small, no competition to Kliransk in size. The trees pick up again behind the row of buildings and the woods continue from there. It's not so much a clearing as a clever overtaking of the sparseness where the trees have thinned out. It has to house only a few dozen people, if that. I don't care to figure out where their healer resides among them. Instead, I drag my useless body towards the door closest to me and throw my full weight against it, calling out for help as a sob wrecks me. I collapse against the door, my throat too raw to even scream.

An older woman opens the door, looking like she's just seen a ghost. I suppose I can't blame her—it is the middle of the night and a sobbing, bloody mess of a person she's never seen before has dropped onto her doorstep. If I were her, I'd be just as frightened.

I hear her call out for someone in the home before heaping me into her arms. I babble some excuses and beg her to find my husband. I must give her enough to work with because she sends a man—her husband, I presume—off running to the neighbors. He starts knocking on doors, waking house after house. As I am escorted into a neighboring cottage, I turn back to see a group of men running into the trees. Then I am ushered into a washroom and fussed over by multiple women. Someone asks what happened to me, but another tells her to hush, scolding them to focus on helping me first.

I am stripped of my soaked dress and I don't have enough dignity to be embarrassed about it. I only protest when they try to remove the crystal from around my neck. They don't ask questions, but they do as I say. One woman keeps her hands at my waist to keep me from struggling; I don't have any energy left to tell her I won't fight them. Another takes a washcloth to my cuts, soaking my shredded skin

249

in something that burns. When I flinch away from her as she nears my shoulders, she lightens her touch.

"You'll have to relocate the arm," she mutters to a woman who must be the healer.

Yet another woman dumps water and hair oils over my head. It is a luxurious treatment, reminiscent of stories of lost princesses brought back to their kingdoms. I sink into myself, allowing my mind to leave what is true so I can pretend instead.

It works as they wash me and dress my wounds. It works as they braid my hair and wrap me in a nightgown and robe. It works as they lead me to a room with a row of cots and lay me down. It works as I lay there, trembling from something deeper than the winter's chill.

It stops working when I hear the front door burst open and a cacophony of men's voices shouting for help. A few of the women rush towards the threshold to heed their call. It's Halvar, it must be. I try to leap out of the cot, but the remaining women hold me down. I lurch forward and back like a wild animal, needing to get free, out of the safety of their arms and into the safety of his, but their grip doesn't waver. They brush my hair back, cooing to me like I am a child or perhaps a baby bird unable to take flight.

"He is in our most capable hands," one says. "We must let her work."

I allow them to lay me down, but despite the pain wringing all over my body, I crane my neck to listen through the open door. The men are all speaking over one another, and to the healer. Asking questions and demanding answers. I hear Halvar's name a few times and confusion mixes in with the rest of the emotions torturing my mind. Where are we?

The village women leave me to rest once they are satisfied that I am no longer on Death's doorstep, banging and crying as I did to one of their own. I'm left with a warning to not overextend my arms for a few weeks: no heavy lifting, no chores, no exertion.

From the next room, I can hear the healer working on Halvar. She takes longer with him—his injuries far surpass mine. There is the sharp crack of bone and he lets out a deep cry. I lay in my cot, silent sobs wracking my body. I cannot intervene at the risk of making things worse.

I don't think his abilities can do much to hurry along the healing process at this point. All of the progress he had made over the past few days is likely undone. We are essentially grounded here until he gets better.

The house goes quiet after some time. Low lantern light glows from the hall, tempting and taunting me. I count ten breaths before I force myself out of bed. I listen for resistance and, finding none, tiptoe out of the room to find Halvar.

It is not a large house, so I don't have to look far. I find him next door, in a room lined with cots similar to the one I was put in. For being such a small village, they are certainly equipped for disaster.

He lies in a cot along the back wall, eyes closed though I can tell he's not asleep just yet. My steps make the floorboards creak and he peeks one eye open. When he sees it's me, he lifts a limp hand in a sad attempt at a wave. I try to smile, try to laugh even, because I am so happy he's awake and in one piece and just *okay*, but instead I feel hot tears stream out of my eyes. It hurts too much to heave a sob, so I just let the tears fall in an endless river.

"I'm okay," he breathes, his voice rattling in his chest.

"At what cost?" I whisper.

"You are worth any price," he says, sleep crawling across his voice.

I drag another cot alongside his and collapse into it. I want to touch him. I want to feel his skin beneath mine and know that he is alright. I want to, and I almost do, but my shoulder barks out in protest.

Instead of agonizing, I ask him, "Where are we?"

"The commune I used to stay with."

Well, that explains why the men knew his name. The immediate kindness they showed us can't be just because of that, though, as I showed up on their doorstep alone. The innate goodness of these people becomes clear to me at once, and I am glad that Halvar had something akin to a support system here.

251

By the time I work up the strength to ask more questions, the sound of his steady breathing reaches me. He's fallen asleep. I know he's tired, and I am, too. But my mind is racing far too quickly for me to even consider letting everything go quiet. Instead, I stare at the ceiling, considering all of the paths that pushed us in this direction. I lay there for however long, maybe minutes, maybe hours.

I want to be glad that the elders are dead. I want to gloat that they have floated into whatever version of punishment they've scared the masses into fearing. But I can't. I cannot escape the dread that fills me as I realize that although we have escaped one problem, we now have to deal with the consequences that will likely leave me in pieces in a completely different manner.

A cold sweat breaks out across my body and all I can think of are my parents. I cannot escape the feeling that my mother will be furious with me. That even in their death, she will choose the elders over me. Maybe things would be easier that way; if she renounced me, I could stop loving her without feeling sorry for myself.

We cannot leave things as they are—*I* cannot leave things as they are. I don't think I'll ever sleep again knowing what a state Kliransk has been left in. We have to go back and pick up the pieces we've left scattered to the winds. I can't tell the villagers the truth; I doubt they would believe me even if I did. But what lie can I tell that won't sound like it's ripped from fiction? The people won't fall for friendly shifter wolves and power-hungry priests. They're more likely to believe that a demonic presence upended everything they've known in a matter of hours. The thought of feeding into their paranoia sickens me, but they are so far removed from truth I think that honesty would feel like a lie to them.

This is not a decision I can make on my own. I need Halvar's input. All I can do for now is let my body rest, even if my mind won't. I close my eyes, try to get comfortable. But that is the moment that the door opens and one of the village women decides to come speak with me.

The healer—Sedris—enters. She takes a few cautious steps inside, then, at my approval, takes up a seat next to my cot. "I thought

I might find you here. Are you feeling better?"

"I am," I reply, nodding.

She gestures towards Halvar, now fast asleep. "He's grown much since we saw him last. A fine husband he makes, I'm sure."

"He is. The best, actually. I don't know what I would do without him. I am...very thankful that you helped us."

She bobs her head, taking a deep breath. "Did he lead you to us?"

It wouldn't be the whole truth to say yes, seeing as I was unconscious for most of the walk here. But I can't exactly explain his *condition* without risking his safety once more. So I just nod, the lie easier to tell since she spelled it out for me.

"Would you like to tell me what happened?"

Her voice is gentle, not prying. I could very well say *no, I don't want to talk about it,* and she would leave it to rest. I don't want to lie to her again, seeing as she helped us even when she didn't have to. But Halvar did not feel safe enough to tell them the truth, and it is not my truth to tell.

She sees the hesitation on my face and starts to back off before I urge her to wait. She settles back in her seat and the open expression on her face tells me she is willing to listen at my discretion.

I take a breath. "We were attacked by men from Kliransk." A half-truth, she doesn't need to know the details. At least for now. "I don't know if you know of it—"

"We are familiar with Kliransk." The look on her face alone tells me more than words ever could. She knows of it and decidedly does not take kindly to it. We are among friends here, it seems. "I'm not surprised that you made it all the way out here. You wouldn't be the first."

Her words shoot ice through my veins, and she likely doesn't even realize it. But instead of elaborating, she stands and goes to a table along the far wall to retrieve an ointment. I look down at my hands—I've been clenching my fists so hard that my nails have cut open my palms again. When she returns with the ointment and starts re-bandaging my hands, my eyes shoot daggers at her as I wait for her to explain.

She catches my look and shakes her head. "They've chased a few of you out now. Just a few weeks ago we took in one of their younglings. He was so shaken, the poor thing."

I hold my breath. "Is he here now?"

She finishes one hand and gestures for the other. It takes a good stretch for me to even offer her that much. "I've lost track by now, so many pass through here without staying. There may be a few of the others. I can check for you in the morning."

I give a shallow nod of agreement, remembering that it is still the dead of night. We've brought all of these people out of their beds and used their resources. Halvar won't be pleased with that; I imagine he'll offer whatever service he can provide once he's healed.

"We won't inconvenience you for long," I say, already feeling the imposition. "We just need to recover our strength enough to make it back home…"

My voice trails off as I remember that we most likely won't have a home to come back to. Even the little bit I witnessed in my last moments of consciousness was its own contained echo of chaos. I remember the smashing of furniture, the shattering of windows. The bodies of the elders should still be in there, unless the creature managed to drag them away. My stomach twists at the thought of it feasting in our home, leaving us the nasty bits even it doesn't want. The wards should have dropped by now, a temporary alternative to the ones that had protected the perimeter.

She pats my arm, mindful of my various wounds. "Stay as long as you need. This was once his home. The door is still open to him. To both of you." With that, she excuses herself and leaves the room. Likely back to the bed I startled her out of.

The moment the door shuts and her footsteps fade down the hall, Halvar mutters from his bed, "Is she gone?"

I jump, surprised to hear his voice come out of the stillness. "She is."

"Good."

He reaches across our cots and takes my hand in his, careful to leave my arm where it lies. The tender feel of his fingers stroking over my skin lulls me into a neutral state where I can be persuaded to rest. Sleep claims both of us shortly thereafter, and we do not wake, not fully at least, until the sun forces its way through the windows.

Breakfast has been left on the side table, though it aches too much to even accomplish that basic task by myself. I feel inept when Halvar insists on feeding bites of biscuit and jam into my mouth. Even torn apart from the inside out he fusses over me. I don't think I'll ever get used to how much he cares.

He tries to push past my questions as to how he's feeling, but of course, I push back. Quietly, almost as if he's ashamed, he admits to feeling like death. As I suspected, his natural abilities aren't enough to surpass the damage last night caused. He's healing at the rate a human would heal from a non-life threatening injury—slowly but surely. It will be weeks before he's back to his old self. And even then, we cannot yet know how the shift will affect his body in the long run. Having suppressed his instincts for so long, he is hesitant to let nature take its course.

I ask perhaps a thousand questions about the shift. He takes my questions in stride, conversation pausing when he needs an extra minute to let his lungs take in air. His breath still rattles in his chest, though it sounds nowhere near as bad as it did that night in the woods.

I ask how he did it—he says his instincts simply took over. I ask if anyone saw him—he says no. Did it hurt? Yes. Does he regret it? No.

"I'd rather become a monster, if it meant saving you, than go on living without you." There is nothing short of cold resolve in his eyes.

I roll my cheek against my pillow, exhaustion having not fully left me. "You're not a monster." When he starts to refuse, I press on. "Halvar, I'm only alive because of you. What kind of monster does that make you?"

He watches my face for a moment, then sighs. "It's easier for me to hate myself than to admit it felt good. To shift. I'm not resentful of it like I thought I'd be. I can't say I'm eager to do it again anytime soon, but maybe… Maybe someday."

I want to relish in his revelation, but I can't. Not while knowing a truth that could change so much for him. I have to tell him the real reason he was exiled. He can see the hesitancy on my face, which doesn't make it any easier for me.

"The elders knew," I start. "They knew about your father. They saw him shift and were too afraid of him to kill him. So they sent you both away instead."

He practically deflates into the mattress. His gaze is fixed on the ceiling, lost in something unseen to me. A few moments pass before he breathes out in one gentle *whoosh*, and I know the sound well. It is a sigh of relief, of a weight being lifted.

"Well," he says. "Isn't that something?"

After a small eternity, he turns to me and I can see how downturned his eyes have become, how sad he looks. "Do you know what my father always said when I asked one too many questions? He said that my inner nature was becoming too strong, that the elders were starting to notice. He told me it was my fault. He made me *believe* that it was my fault."

Even as my stomach sinks, I am glad to have told him. I refuse to keep him in the dark as his father and the elders did for so long.

It makes sense why the elders would not have told the villagers the truth; to admit that they let go of a shifter for fear of their own lives would be to admit defeat in the face of a foe, and their collective pride would never allow such a thing. Alternatively, the villagers would be less inclined to trust leaders who would make such a decision. But Halvar's father was a callous man who kept his truths laid bare. Most of them. It would have made sense for him to tell Halvar why they were exiled. The sad truth is that it also makes sense for him to have kept it to himself, to use it as a weapon against his son.

I want to find the right thing to say, pick out the best words to comfort him, but I can't. Because Sedris chooses that moment to return. It's easy to want privacy when you're in someone else's home.

In someone else's bed.

"How are we feeling today?" She asks, standing above Halvar. She presses her fingers over a few spots on his body, making note of his every wince and groan.

"Fine."

She hums. "Honesty will help you heal faster."

"I feel like shit."

She nods, opening a bottle of some brownish liquid. She pours a small amount into the lid and hands it to Halvar to drink. When he hesitates, she pulls back. "What's wrong? Do you need assistance with drinking?"

He shakes his head, eyeing the container warily. "If this is some sort of test, I'm not participating."

Her brow furrows, and she looks between us, then back to the liquid. "I'm not sure what you mean. This is going to help you, I promise."

As if to prove her point, Halvar starts to cough again, groaning at every bout of pressure against his ribs. She edges the lip of the lid towards his mouth, urging him to drink. Hesitation slows his hand but the pain pushes him to accept it and take it from her. He downs it in one shot, wiping the back of his hand across his mouth.

"There, not so bad," she says. She leaves his bedside and comes around to look at my bandages. Sedris unbinds my arm and begins cleaning my wound. The stinging has mostly faded. Now it just aches. "Let me guess. You were told that using herbs and mixtures in healing is some form of blasphemy, right?"

I tense beneath her working hands. Like Halvar, I have to wonder if this is some kind of test, if failure will mean consequence. Weighing my options, I have to agree with her—honesty will help us heal. Slowly, I start to bob my chin.

She nods. "That seems standard with you Kliransk folk. What did they teach you in your lessons?"

I clear my throat. "It's not so much our schooling as...everything else. The church runs the village, it's they who decide what is and isn't."

She discards my dirty bandages and starts wrapping my arm in clean ones. "You would think, given their occupation, they would leave decisions of those sorts to their maker."

The way she says it, so flippantly and without judgment, makes me immediately decide to trust her. I shoot Halvar a look, trying to wordlessly convey my decision. He blinks back at me, confusion and then clarity crossing his face. His nod is all the encouragement I need to open up to this stranger, to tell her a fraction of what has happened to us. I can't tell her everything without exposing our darkest corners, but what I do tell her clouds her face with anger. She adds comments and questions where necessary, but for the most part, allows me to tell my tale.

By the time I get to telling her about my time in the confessional, I'm choked up. Halvar's expression is nothing short of murderous. It is painful to have to bare my experiences in front of him without having briefed him first, and I make a mental note to give him the rest of the details once we are alone.

Sedris leaves us to make lunch once I've said my piece. I use the brief time we have to give Halvar the details I couldn't bear to tell a stranger, even one who saved our lives. I tell him of the exorcism, even as the terror causes my shoulders to shake and forces me to pause to catch my breath. I tell him of Father Patrick's sacrifice, the spells I was able to cast, the map of the house I had laid out. How it felt to carve into the walls of our home and use my own power to seal it shut. The power I felt even at my weakest.

"I want to undo having killed them last night," he says, "so now that I know what they've done to you, I can do it again. Slower, with more intent."

"Technically," I say, "the creature killed two of them."

"Thanks to your plan," he points out. "You took what they were doing and turned it against them. That takes more than power. It takes cunning, and intelligence, and a great deal of strength. I never doubted you. As for the elders, that was nothing but cowardice and cruelty on their part. It makes sense that they would antagonize the creatures into killing the villagers. Keep the rest on a short leash."

Clarity washes over his face, and I watch the frustration and confusion fade away as he processes everything I've told him. We were so close to putting the pieces together ourselves, even with so much missing. And with that in mind, how can either of us regard this as a failure?

"I had an inkling," he continues, taking in breath where he can, "after you returned home from your encounter with the deer. Because it made sense to me that you would be unharmed."

"I left it alone," I say.

"You left it alone," he echoes, "and so it left you alone."

All things considered, our research has brought both of us a deeper understanding of the woods. Maybe it will bring Halvar greater clarity regarding his work. Maybe I will be able to go for walks again without fear. None of that matters right now, though. It won't matter until we finish pulling ourselves out of the dark.

Sedris returns with bowls of broth and finely cut slices of bread. We thank her, and then we are left alone once again. Being left alone is something of a comfort, as it can only mean they trust us to not drop dead from our injuries. It tells me we're going to survive this.

"So," Halvar says between mouthfuls. "What do we do next?"

I sigh. "I don't want to, but we have to go back to Kliransk."

"What for? Let the rats scatter away from the light. It's not our responsibility to lead them out of the dark."

"We can't leave them like this, with no direction or leadership. The village will die out sooner than they were set to."

"So you think we should be the ones to lead them?"

"I think we should direct them to someone who can."

"And who is that?" He hands me the rest of his bread, but I shove it back onto his plate. He needs his strength just as much as I do, if not more.

I swallow another spoonful of broth, only lifting the spoon just above the lip of the bowl. "I don't know. But we won't find it in Kliransk."

The exodus was startling to witness as a child. I saw droves of people walk into the woods, never to return. Never to be heard from again. If anyone ever sent word via traveling messengers, or word of mouth passing between merchants, their words never reached us. The silence only furthered what the elders made us fear most: they were killed somewhere out in the woods, and the same would happen to anyone else who dared risk the journey. Somehow, we have to push past that fear. It is deep-seated, but I won't be able to live with myself if we don't at least *try*.

When Sedris comes to collect our dishes, I clear my throat. "Yesterday, you said that you would look for someone for me. I wanted to know if you got around to it."

Sedris's brow furrows, and then raises in understanding. "Ah, the other Kliransk folk. The one you're looking for has left. Gone on to find his peace in some other village."

I suck in a breath. "Do you remember his name?"

She pauses for a moment, thinking. "I believe he said his name was Calder. I don't know if that means anything to you."

I can feel my throat swelling with tears, so I just thank her and wait for her to leave. Once she shuts the door, I cover my face with my hands and let out it all out in hiccuping sobs. Halvar doesn't say any more, he only reaches out a hand to stroke my hair while I cry.

Nothing hurts now, knowing that at least one of them is alive. That the elders' grip on the collective throat of Kliransk did not suffocate all of us.

That night, I return the favor when Halvar's feelings over his father finally overwhelm him. I hate watching him cry but I silently hope that with each tear that spills, the sorrow will start to leave his body and that someday these things won't hurt him anymore. I hope the same for myself, too.

We're able to leave our beds at will after a few days, but Halvar continues to pretend like his injuries still incapacitate him. Given that the entire village had seen the state he arrived in, they would be baffled by his progress in such a short amount of time. Even after all their help, he can't bear to expose his secret to anyone else, and so he lies. A necessary evil, he claims.

I make friends with the village women, showing my thanks to them however I can without straining myself. They are all so warm, so kind even though I am little more than a stranger to them. I could have been dangerous, a liability, but they took me in as one of their own and for that I am grateful. Whether that is due to their innate kindness or their fondness for Halvar, I don't need to know.

We wear out our welcome after two weeks. Everyone in the commune insists that we can stay longer if we wish, but with the road ahead of us, it's best to keep moving. I am sorry to leave, and that is something I never thought I would have to say. I can see it pains Halvar too, to leave these people who took him in not once but twice. He is not one for friends, but maybe this is something deeper than that.

They send us off with knapsacks stuffed to the brim with spare clothes, food, and medicine. Halvar tries to offer to send money once we settle in, which they vehemently deny. In the end, we walk away at peace, the last we are likely to see for some time.

He takes my hand in his, and we gaze at each other before setting off deeper into the trees. He squeezes my hand and his eyes soften at the corners. They catch the sunlight that's made its way to us, and for once he looks rested. I wish he could always be like this. But we won't have peace until we clean up the mess we've made, and so we step onto the path without knowing exactly where it will end.

CHAPTER EIGHTEEN

Despite everything we have been through, despite the creatures that still stalk through the trees and snarl when we get too close, I feel safer in the woods than I do when we reach the border of Kliransk.

To say that the village is in shambles would be a generous description. Even though the sun is high in the sky, no one walks about. Doors are barred with planks of wood, and above a few mantles, I notice crosses drawn in a shaky hand. That looks to be the extent of work done over the weeks passed.

We cannot go to the church to speak with the leaders, because there are none left. Killed by either my hand or my husband's. We have to go further down the line of succession. To whom would the villagers turn in their time of crisis? Many of the head tradesmen are too old and set in their vocations to take on the role of village leader. The younger men have too little experience and already have the burden of learning their trade. I doubt they'd look to the women, not as a first or second or even third resort. Wives and daughters, who are supposed to be obedient with heads kept low and prayers reserved for their husbands' and fathers' intentions. Not them, either.

I think of the way Father Dasco revered my father, how the rest of the village seemed to follow suit. It would make sense for him to take on the mantle. I wonder if that is something he would even take pride in. Heavy is the head, as they say. Seeing no other options, we set off in the direction of my parents' house. I doubt they'll even deign to speak to us, but all I can do is knock.

At first, all I hear is silence from the other side of the door. Then, crashing, as if someone is stumbling about. I hear a thump against the door, but it doesn't open. Likely due to the wood nailed across the threshold. I hear my mother's voice come through, fiery as it always is but with a tinge of hysteria to it.

"*Emelie?* What is the meaning of this?"

I clear my throat, pre-prepared words ready to slide off my tongue. "I'm sorry I left, Mother. I never meant to worry you."

"Worry me?" She laughs, a crazed, angry sound. "You left me reeling, thinking you had been killed in the middle of the night by some creature! What happened to you?"

"I can explain," I insist, though it won't be the whole truth. It can't be, not when it comes to her. "Is Father there? Can you open the door?"

There is a pause. "Tell me what happened, Emelie."

She is not going to open the door.

I sigh and lean my forehead against the wood. This would be much easier without the open air of Kliransk pressing down on me, witnessing my false confession. This is not the way I wanted to speak with her.

"Please, Mother. It's a long story."

I can hear her just on the other side, separated from me by only a few inches. "I...I can't open the door. It's not safe."

"I'm right here, Mother. Halvar is right here. We won't let anything happen to you."

"Emelie..."

My gut sinks and I realize something with a sudden certainty. *I* am the thing that she doesn't want happening to her. I am the threat. I am the wolf lingering between the trees, waiting for some poor soul to wander too far out.

I fight down hot tears and push away from the door, gesturing for Halvar to follow. "Fine," I say, stepping away. "You'll find out the truth soon enough."

I storm down the path toward the town square. Halvar is a few paces behind me, holding back any extra energy he may need for later. Hands shoved in his pockets, he follows diligently. We formed some semblance of a plan, and at this point, all he has to do is not let me fall apart. Easier said than done.

The town square has not been cleared of snow in what must be weeks. The cobblestone section of floor that separates the untamed ground from a place to stand is nowhere to be seen. I know we must be atop it, I know this territory too well to mistake where we stand. But I cannot make out the tiles. All I can see is snow. On muscle memory alone I make it up to the platform that is raised just slightly above the rest of the ground, the same one the elders used to stand upon and proclaim their inane rules and superstitions and falsities. I plant my feet firmly, and I can feel Halvar behind me, ready at a moment's notice.

I open my mouth and I scream, louder than I would think myself capable of. *"People of Kliransk!"*

My voice hangs in the empty air, even the snow afraid to fall around it. As expected, no one comes rushing out of their homes, but I see a few faces peek out of their windows. Some are pulled back but return with a stubbornness I have come to learn is common among the children of this village. Where we are told to hold back, we learn to push forward.

"My husband and I came to your border seeking help after we were attacked. The elders sent us back into the woods with nothing more than the clothes on our backs. We are lucky to be alive." My throat already burns from the exertion. I swallow down the pain and try to ignore it.

A few curious faces poke out of front doors now. It seems no one wants to be the first to come forward. No one wants to be the first sinner. It's easier to be the first to cast a stone.

"They followed us into the trees to make sure we left for good, and we haven't seen them since."

I hate lying to all of these people about who the elders truly are, but would they believe me if I told the truth? If I told them the people they looked to for guidance had been exploiting their fear and absolute trust?

"You are not safe here! Kliransk will die out within weeks under these conditions! Look around you, everything is barricaded. No traders have passed through. This is no way to live. Please, you must listen to reason!"

That gets bodies out of doors. People, bolder than I could ever hope to be in the face of this oppression, slowly step out of their homes and make their way toward the square. I can see that they are all young, around my age. These were my classmates, my peers. I thought they were so far removed that they could never understand how I felt. Now I see that I was the one who didn't understand.

One body makes its way over to us quicker than the rest, their walk a determined gait. As they get closer, I see that it is the woman who I have never given enough credit.

Magda.

She comes to stand directly in front of us with an open face and open ears. Perhaps it is because of her lead that several more come to follow. I see the people I have known as long as I've been alive and never bothered to let in. Now they look at me like they're ready to hear what I have to say. They're looking at me like I'm a leader.

I don't want to be that for them. I have no desire for power, for masses of people to take my judgment as law. I can see how it could appeal to people like the elders. But I am not like them. I just want the people to know that there is more out there, and that I at least know how to get them that far.

"Kliransk is not safe with such an unstable border and with no leaders." As I speak, more come out of their homes, some older and less open to what I have to say. But they can hear me, and that's all that matters. "We must take you to safety in other villages, within and around the trees. You cannot stay here if you want to survive."

"Where are the elders?" Someone calls out.

"I told you, they followed us out and we lost them."

Someone sneers, "Are we supposed to believe you did not lead them to their deaths? That you did not have your husband kill them?"

That sets off an uproar, with people arguing amongst themselves. I hear shouts of agreement and those of dissent. Villagers are becoming unruly, wracked by weeks of mourning and unknowing. Halvar comes to stand beside me. Once, he might have tried to shield me behind him. But now we stand on even ground. Emboldened by his presence, I try to plead my cause, insisting that they will be better off if they follow the path laid out during the exodus. I can't just leave them here to die.

A voice rises above the rest, as strained as mine.

Magda yells, "I believe her."

She spins in a circle so that she may face the people. The crowd quiets, some looking at her in disbelief and maybe something akin to pride. I can see her father among their faces, further back with the rest of the older villagers. He does not look pleased to see his daughter speak up.

"We have no reason to doubt her. The elders left us a fortnight ago with no access to the trade routes. With no supplies to continue their legacy. Are we to wait around and simply hope they come back?"

Another familiar voice speaks from the back. My heart drops when I see my mother wrapped in shawls. "We cannot simply abandon the elders' plan for us. They speak for the Lord."

"Their plan means nothing if they have abandoned us!" Magda says.

Some of the older ones protest in the name of God, spouting off the poisoned, pious words that they have been fed for decades. Unlike their children, and their children's children, they have known a life before the elders. They remember the hardships from before. But I know the history, and I can see that it is even worse now. This was all I had ever known until Halvar showed me there was so much more. I reach a hand out, grasping for his. He holds on tight.

"You cannot wait in hopes that they will return," I say. "Kliransk is too unstable as is. You'll starve without access to the merchants. You are too vulnerable without protection from experienced hunters. You *must* follow us to safer villages. You can wait another fortnight, or even longer than that, but without supplies, you *will* die."

My voice cracks on the final words. I don't want my parents to die. I can see them at the back of the crowd, their faces drawn and their bodies wracked with exhaustion. My father holds my mother close to his side, and if nothing else I am thankful they have each other. They are a true match, equally set in their ways.

"We must leave at once," Halvar says, his voice booming above mine, "if we are to have safe passage to a commune."

On the walk here, Halvar listed all of the communes and villages he knew of scattered among the trees. We are nowhere near equipped to accompany this many people to the village on the other side of the great expanse of woods, or any of the ones past there. Together, we decided it best we guide the villagers to a few communes, and from there they can choose where to go. Willing travelers pass through often enough. If the villagers want to make it out of the woods, they are better off finding someone who can take them that way.

"We will wait at the northernmost border. We hope you will follow."

I step off the platform and walk without looking back. It will hurt too much to see what is to happen. I'd rather wait until it's too late.

But as we walk hand in hand, someone stops me. Arms wrap around me from behind, crushing me in an embrace. Halvar lets go of my hand and steps back, his face giving away nothing. I try to turn in the person's arms, and every point of contact informs me, slowly, of who this is.

My mother shakes as she holds me, her grip iron-tight. My father stands behind her, his face solemn if not a little sad. I am terrified to assume what this means.

She whispers against my ear, "What have you done?"

All I can think to say is, "What needs to be done."

267

A sob escapes her and she holds me tighter, and though the gesture should feel loving, it also feels somewhat hostile. She is angry, this I know. Whether *at* me, *for* me, or *because* of me, I do not. My father's reaction, or lack thereof, gives me nothing to go off of.

I look between her and my father. "You're not coming, are you?"

My father shakes his head. "We have to wait it out and see what the elders will do when they return."

"But Father—" I stop myself. How can I make them know that the elders *won't* be returning without revealing how I know this? Either I damn them, or myself.

It's a choice that would have been more difficult for the version of myself who didn't know what she wanted yet. The quiet girl who spent her days with her mother's needle in hand would have given up everything for her parents. That's what she was going to do, before I interrupted her plans.

It's not difficult now. I know what I must do.

"Then I guess this is goodbye." I don't allow my voice to waver. I can't.

They nod like they were expecting this. Like this is the most understandable course of action. I know that once I leave and take a party of Kliransk villagers with me, they will be left with even less than they had before. As Magda informed me, the traders don't pass through as frequently as they used to. They will have less food, less varied goods to peddle. It will be a baseless existence of work for the sake of working, just to get by. It won't last, and they won't realize this until it's too late.

My father crushes me in an embrace, kissing the top of my head. "Be good," are his last words to me. He regards Halvar with something short of respect, maybe a fearful acquiescence of his hold on me. Then, with one last pleading look, he and my mother turn back in the direction of their home.

I don't let the tears fall until they are out of sight. The child inside of me wants to run after them and beg them to follow. For them

268

to hold me and tell me they're proud of me for surviving and trying to do the same for Kliransk. But I cannot fix them. I cannot change their minds. I cannot make them stop believing the things they believe. I have to let them be as they are and hope that someday, they will soften towards the path I have taken.

By now, hordes of people are making their way toward us. With them, they carry bags filled to the brim with their entire lives. It doesn't escape me that it's mainly the younger people who are joining us. I see an aged face here and there, but for the most part, the gaggle is made up of people I took my lessons with. People who grew up with Halvar and I.

Some of the boys—the men, now—go to Halvar for direction. A few of them offer hands for him to shake. Anyone else would miss the moment of hesitation, the old familiar anxiety crawling up his throat before he reaches out and accepts the gesture. But I don't. I take the handshake as a sign he is trying, and I will comfort him for that later.

He gives them a rundown of where we will be taking them, urging them to pair off as we stop along the way. The communes will likely only take a few people at a time, but we should be able to find enough space for everyone.

Magda comes to my side, bumping me with her shoulder. Her bag hangs in the crook of her elbow. It's small and clearly not filled with much. I have to wonder if she brought anything substantial at all.

She follows my gaze and pulls the bag higher on her shoulder. "I wanted to leave what didn't matter behind." I hear the unspoken things that implies. Her father and the career that she, too, was forced into. The rotting center of this place.

After a few more minutes of waiting, people stop coming out of their houses to follow us. It's time to go. Halvar and I look at one another and join our hands, and then we lead the villagers out of Kliransk and into the woods.

This second exodus is more tiresome than I expected. As much as I don't want to feel like a leader, the mass of villagers walk several paces behind, looking to us for guidance. I feel watched in the worst sort of way. If we were to get lost, they would regard it as our fault. I second-guess many of my steps along the way. But every tree is familiar to me. I know this way well enough. The deeper we go, the more settled I feel, like the woodsy air is refilling my emptied soul.

We pass through two communes and drop off nearly half of our group. Everyone is shocked to see how many people have been living this close to Kliransk without their realizing. I let Halvar speak on our behalf, asking for asylum after the village's collapse. He knows some of these people, has kept up a camaraderie with his fellow hunters and the tradesmen he's met throughout his career. This lends more trust in our favor, another reason for me to be grateful for him. I could not have talked our way into this on my own.

We stop for the night at the second commune. Our people make camp, or something akin to it, beneath the stars. It's not ideal, but a few of the men take up the first watch. I manage to convince Halvar to wake me for the second watch, and though I know he trusts me, I do catch him pretending to sleep. He keeps one eye on me. I try to wave his watchfulness off, knowing that without sleep he's going to be a grump for the rest of the walk. He doesn't listen, and maybe part of me is pleased by that.

The following day takes us deeper into the woods, and we slowly lose our people to passing communes and traveling merchants. By the time the sun reaches its peak there are only a handful of us left, Magda included.

Halvar fumbles with his coat button. "There is another commune some miles northwest. We can get you most of the way there before we part ways."

Magda looks between us. "Where will you go?"

I can't tell her about our home, why we can't *truly* go back there. And besides our privacy, I am not certain of what we'll do. I look at Halvar. My equal, my husband, my best friend.

He shrugs. "We're going to float around between some of my connections before settling down again." I don't know how much truth stands to that, but I agree nonetheless.

At the outskirts of the next commune, Magda grips my hands

in hers. Her big eyes are open even wider, and she grips me like she's about to lose me, which I suppose she is.

"Promise to keep in touch?"

I can't look at her and refuse her, so I nod, patting the hand that holds mine. "I'll send word when we travel next. We will meet again, somehow."

She surprises me by pulling me into a fierce hug. Into my ear, she whispers, "I knew you'd find a way out."

I bury my face in her shoulder. The words mean more to me than she knows. Maybe someday I'll tell her.

Halvar negotiates lodging for the remaining members of our party, and he must do a damn good job of convincing them because the village leader almost looks sorry to learn we won't be joining them. They wave goodbye to us from the border and my heart tugs just a tiny bit to see Magda's form get smaller and smaller as we walk away.

I never picture goodbyes as being difficult. It's comforting, in a way, to have something that hurts to walk away from. Not that my friendship with Magda is anything of note, not quite yet. But it could become something.

I am starting to feel the effects of traveling, and Halvar must notice because he lets me lean some of my weight into his side for the rest of the walk. He still can't carry me, and I imagine he's cursing himself for that. I can at least hold myself upright for the remainder of the way home. Or what was our home. It's strange to pass through our border without wards. It feels wrong. Incomplete.

Halvar stops short at the sight of the house. "Did you...did you ward the creature inside? Has it been in there for a *fortnight*?"

I can't help it when I chuckle. "Not all wards are permanent, Halvar. It was a temporary spell. Just like the one I enchanted around the alcove when I found you out in the woods. I may be a witch, but I'm not cruel."

He snorts and pulls me to him, kissing the top of my head. "You're vicious when you want to be."

"Ah, but my bark is worse than my bite."

271

His hand tightens at my waist. "I'm willing to challenge that."

I laugh as I shove away from him and start towards the tomb of our house. "Come on, there's work to be done."

"You mean work for *me* to get done," he grumbles, following me inside.

The destruction is worse than I anticipated. Halvar stops me at the threshold, fearing that the roof will collapse if we step the wrong way. I know he won't say so, but he's worried about more than merely stumbling over broken furniture.

I can already see blood trailing around both sides of the foyer. How far it leads, where it ends, I don't know. Part of me is morbidly curious, the same part that urged me to steal the *Creatura* from the library. I have never been averse to such things.

Carefully, testing each step we take, we make our way through the first floor, clearing broken glass and toppled belongings as we go. He walks in front of me, shielding me from any view we might come across. The blood trail ends at one of the windows, shattered into a makeshift exit for something large and inhuman. Good riddance.

Among the ruins, I find a cross necklace, as well as a book of prayer. If the sight of them is any clue as to the state of the elders' bodies, I decide that I don't want to see what is left of them.

Together we collect whatever remnants of our life we can salvage. The ground floor is a lost cause for the most part, but the majority of furniture and decor was not of sentimental value and can be replaced. When he arrives at one corner of the sitting room, Halvar gasps and uses his body to shield whatever he sees. Human instinct makes me whip my head towards the sound, but self-preservation makes me look away when I catch sight of a bloodied arm.

I decide to take my chances with the stairs. They sound stable, the creaking much noisier if anything. The upper floor, thankfully, has taken far less damage. Furniture is still toppled. The wooden walls are covered in scratch marks and what is most likely blood. The windows I loved so much have been shattered. But the hallway is walkable, and I can see that there are still belongings to be packed.

I take what I can from the wardrobe and shove them into trunks. Some of our clothes are shredded, or splattered with dark substances that I don't care to study. I root through what is still wearable, using my own judgment as a guide.

Halvar follows me upstairs, his face a little more ashen than it was earlier. He harnesses himself with every knife he can carry. And whatever he can't carry goes into a knapsack. It makes him *clink* when he walks, which makes me giggle.

I pack our books, stuffing them into every available crevice. These, I refuse to compromise on. I know we can afford to rebuild our library, but I cannot bear to leave this collection behind.

When our life as a couple is packed into bags, we regroup in the clearing that surrounds what was our home. I look up at the broken walls of windows, up towards the bedroom where we professed our love to one another. Where we became one. So many nights spent beside each other, too afraid to speak what we already knew was true. Even more nights spent making up for time lost. It would be impossible for me to not feel sad about it.

"I can build us a bigger home," Halvar says, putting an arm around me. "With enough room for the two of us, and whatever else may come along. Every inch of it will be a testament to us." I smile at the implied promise of our future, something I never thought I would get to have.

I burrow into his side. "How can I help?"

He looks down at me, affection coloring his gaze. "Are you any good at drawing? I'll need plans."

I purse my lips, considering. "I'm not sure. I guess I'd have to try in order to find out."

"We have time," he says. He presses a kiss to the top of my head before gathering as many of our bags as he can carry. "I know a place for us to stay in the meantime."

I take up what I can and follow him. I'd follow him anywhere, but forward into our future is a good start. The afternoon light covers everything in an orange glow, adding a warmth that has been missing for months now. It's still cold, but it will be spring again soon.

As we walk, the light begins to leave us, but the night isn't something to be feared anymore. Not when we still have the fading sunlight for some yards, and when that dwindles out, small twinkling lights blink awake to guide us on our way.

EPILOGUE

The winter months are much easier to survive when you are surrounded by warmth. Like the sun that shines down on an unassuming cottage at the edge of a familiar commune. A temporary one, while your husband builds you a home in a clearing not too far off. Or the smiles on the faces of the women who take you in and nurture your burgeoning skills mixing elixirs and salting the earth. Even then, nothing feels quite as warm as the way he looks at you every time you walk into a room, like it's the first time he's seeing you. Like he's drinking in every detail. Like he never wants this moment to end.

The moment, as it stands, is nothing earth-shattering. I am in the same chair I have occupied every afternoon over these past weeks, book in hand. It is a story Halvar recommended, not something I would have chosen for myself but I try to give it the same attention I give my favored tales. He is seated at the desk he built for himself, correcting the plans for our new home. He has spent so many days away building. I urge him to not rush the process, and he insists he isn't, but the exhaustion that frames his face speaks otherwise. It is the good kind of tired, though. The bone-deep kind that sets in after a day of hard work on an important project.

"You know," he says, "if you have a book in hand, you should get to reading it."

"I am."

"No, you're not. You're staring again. You do that quite a bit."

I sigh. "You wouldn't notice if you weren't staring at *me*."

"Your eyes bore into my head. I can feel you cursing me from here." He looks up then, grinning like a devil. "If it's my attention you want, all you have to do is ask."

I stand, straightening my skirts. "I believe you included *giving me endless amounts of attention* somewhere in your vows."

He chuckles and turns over the building plans. "Apologies, deprived one. Please forgive my faults as a husband."

I move towards the door, looking back at him once I reach the threshold. "You can make it up to me tonight at the Equinox festival."

Winter has not totally given way to spring, but that doesn't dampen the spirit of the coming holiday. The spring equinox is something of a big deal out here, which is new to me. Aside from the winter solstice festival, so many months past, I have never celebrated a seasonal festival of this magnitude. This commune and the surrounding ones have collaborated to turn the entire woods into a playground for mischief and renewal. I have spent the past month tending to a patch of daffodils, keeping them alive through the early spring chill. A less experienced gardener might have let them die out in the cold, but natural persuasion is in my favor, and so they are alive and well.

Yesterday was spent in a circle of villagers, weaving my daffodils into wreaths for us to wear on our heads when we journey into the woods as a group. I may have put together a more opulent crown for myself, but I don't find it a vice to take pride in the work I have accomplished. I may have also made one for Halvar, though I have not yet convinced him to wear it.

I've laid out a dress for tonight; a brand new green dress. Purchased by Halvar at first sight at a market. I tried insisting that I didn't need such a thing, but I couldn't help but fawn at the look of it. It is less modest than any other dress I would wear out, with sleeves that cap at the shoulders and leave my collarbones on fine display. It's a good few inches shorter than any of my other dresses, exposing the lower half of my legs. It is, without question, my prized possession.

The fabric sits on my body like it was created for this specific occasion alone. Before, I never looked at my body like it was something to be admired. It kept me alive, if only just barely. The shape of me used to be something that held expectation for something I didn't feel. But I have come to realize that I don't need to feel like a woman to appreciate the way I look. I am still getting familiar with the curves and rolls and edges of me. When dressed like this, it's easier to see myself as Halvar does. Like I'm beautiful.

I leave my hair loose except for the front strands, which I braid back into the daffodil crown. I clasp on my necklace, a crystal gifted to me by Halvar. It replaces the golden charm he lost when he shifted, though I can't deny that I much prefer matching the necklace he wears around his own neck. I like having something that marks me as his, a symbol of our commitment even though our fingers remain bare. *In time*, he promises. But I don't want for such things; I have his heart. His soul is entangled with mine. What need do I have for rings?

He walks in the room then, and I hear his footsteps halt at the door. His breath catches, and when I toss my hair over a shoulder to look at him, his eyes are wide. I smile, not needing an explanation to know that I've stunned him. He picked out this dress, he watched me weave this crown. Yet the surprise on his face is the true prize.

"Don't look at me like that," he warns, his voice low.

I bat my lashes, the picture of innocence. "Like how?"

"Like you want to be late for the festival."

I twine a lock of hair around my fingers and shrug. "Would that be such a bad thing?"

He shuts the door behind him, which feels silly since we have this house to ourselves. He takes a few steps closer but doesn't touch me. Not yet. For a moment, we just watch each other, that calculating gaze of his showing just how the wheels turn in his head. It is something to consider; some of the villagers are expecting me to help with last-minute preparations for tonight. We need to leave early enough to travel with the fleeting daylight. Time is a luxury not afforded in this instance.

Halvar, the hunter that he is, loves playing the long game. The chase is what riles him, accompanied by careful planning and strategy. A stroke of my hair as I'm washing dishes. A carefully placed hand on my lower back as he steps around me. Maintaining eye contact as he asks me a question. One kiss as we're getting into bed, the kind that leaves me begging for more. His mind is hard-wired this way, and I've become as well-versed in it as a passage from my favorite book. And right now I can see that he knows we don't have time for games.

He makes his move, pulling me into a kiss that lights a fire in me hot enough to make me forget the long cold season we've just escaped. A few steps and then we're both on the bed, but I tense when he tries to lay me down. He pulls back, confused.

I touch a hand to my head. "Don't want to ruin my hair."

He chuckles, and his solution is to lay back himself, pulling me with him. His pants and shirt are forgotten quickly enough, but instead of shucking off my dress, he toys with the hem that pools around his waist.

"You could leave this on," he says, looking up at me through his dark lashes. "Would make things faster."

At his insistence, I do. Our lovemaking is hurried but retains the softness and ease that we've come to find within one another. I feel powerful astride him, like I'm in control of something in my life.

At times like these, I can let go of the heavy thoughts that linger in me. The ones I still find difficult to move past completely. I know it is the same for him—he allows his tension to deflate and the memories to escape him. It is not that we let the darkness that exists in both of us fade away, rather we allow our darkness to see each other as we truly are. At times like these, it only has to be this: heavy breath and open-mouthed kisses. Bruises that bloom at my neck and chest. Whispers of *I love you* between pants.

We finish as we so often do—together. This time, though, there is no holding each other in the aftermath. Instead, we force ourselves out of bed. He rights my dress, pushes frayed strands of hair back into place. He dresses in some of his finer clothes, the ones he never wears. I don a coat to match him and am about to make for the door when I stop myself.

He watches me take pause, eyes following me as I rush back to the wardrobe. It's much smaller than our old one, and our clothes mix in one tightly packed mishmash. Still, I find what I'm looking for with ease since it sits atop everything else I own. I drape his scarf around my shoulders, and then I feel complete.

"Ready?"

I nod. "Ready."

We *just* make it in time to walk with the rest of the commune. A few of the women eye me suspiciously, smirking at my flushed face and chest. I wave off their looks and hold out the basket of crowns. They each take one and place them atop their hair. A few of them turn to their partners for help. There is so much love surrounding us.

I hold up the one I made for Halvar and he takes it, brow furrowing. He doesn't immediately put it on, toying with it between his hands. I pretend not to notice when, as we make our way deeper into the trees, he places it in his hair.

I know when we are near the festival because I can hear the music. It's different from last time, more light and jovial than the winter solstice. I hear strings and some airy sound that I think is a woodwind. There are still the drums, of course, but the musicians take somewhat of a lighter hand with them. I hope the heavier, more booming songs are reserved for later on.

We are one of the last groups to arrive. Members of neighboring communes and villages are already gathered and enjoying themselves. There are the usual stalls of food and wares, which draw my eye but don't draw me in. I came intending to save our coins, but Halvar follows my gaze and I see him make a mental note of it.

We part with a kiss and I follow a few of the villagers to pass out the wreaths we've made. I don't recognize any of the people who take one, but each and all regard me with the familiarity of a friend, throwing their arms around me and kissing my cheeks.

"You're going to dance, aren't you?" One asks, looking back

towards the fire that is still being kindled.

"Later," I nod, "after the sun goes down."

Said sun is still low in the sky. It's been setting later and later as the season crawls across its change. This part of the festival, still cast in the setting rays of the day, is reserved for food and conversation. I greet everyone I pass on my way back to Halvar, who is negotiating prices with a food vendor. He hands me a plate of roasted meat and rice, as well as a small carafe of wine for us to share.

We find space on a downed log and enjoy our dinner. We've spent many nights eating other people's food recently since it took some time for Halvar to build the cottage we stay in now. I've become a little spoiled in that sense, not having to dirty my hands just to survive. It's been an easy adjustment to make. It helps when the food is as delicious as it is now. I wish I knew where these merchants traveled from so I could research the trends and customs. Perhaps I'll march up to them and ask, after a few sips of that wine.

We don't bother with cups, simply passing the entire carafe back and forth between us. Halvar picks the best bits of meat off his plate and onto mine. I've long since lost the will to pretend to protest since it's a favor I've come to appreciate as much as I do. Besides, I know I'll need the energy.

Moonlight fights its way through the canopy of treetops to shine down on the festival. By now, the fire has grown large enough to draw people to it. The music changes on some unspoken cue, becoming heavier. Darker. The kind I want to dance to.

My face must speak for itself because someone rushes over to pull me to my feet. Magda. Halvar takes my plate and I drop my coat on the seat next to him. I embrace her, fingers digging into her back like she is the only solid force for miles. She looks at the other dancers, invitation in her eyes. This time, I don't hesitate to kick off my boots before I take Magda's extended hand and we run barefoot towards the fire, throaty laughs spilling out of us like wine from the carafe.

We join the circle beside the rest of the dancers and follow their lead. I feel a little more confident this time, so I try to direct a clumsy Magda, who is tripping over her own feet. I laugh a little at the memory of the first time I did this. She's already braver than I am for jumping in headfirst.

"I've never done this before!" She yells, a smile breaking her face open so wide.

"Just follow along!" I yell back.

We mimic the movements of everyone around us, following the rises and falls of the music. The musicians try to cater to all of the dancers, slowing when they can tell we need a breath, speeding up when they can see the energy building within us. I let out a cheer when we all join hands in time with the song, our feet stomping not quite in unison but something close enough to it.

A woman—likely the same as last time—starts calling out directions as the music speeds up. The musicians are less generous with us now, speeding up without remorse. The drums come in heavier, and I can feel the thrumming under my skin. The sound calls to the power in me; the quiet, demanding one that has always advocated for more for me. I listen to it, letting that part of me take control.

I roll my body along with the sound, swinging my hips and shoulders without shame. It is a gift I am able to move them at all, I recognize that now. I lift one arm above my head, my left remaining low at my side, as I toss my hair back and forth. The music is alive and it makes me want to feel the same. And I *do*.

One song fades into the next, and when this one begins we all know it's time to run. It kicks up a breeze that makes the flames dance along with us, and to keep it going a few of us toss debris in to strengthen the fire. Thanks to the warmer weather, my feet don't sink into the mud and drag down my skirts. This time, I run freely and without pause.

I catch Halvar watching me as I pass our spot. I whistle as I pass, not a calling but a brief acknowledgment that I see him. The sound is as familiar to him as my voice, and he tries to echo it but doesn't quite pull it off as well. Were I near him, it would sound like an adorable sputtering.

The song doesn't quite fade away as much as it explodes into silence. The dancers skid to a stop and we clap for the musicians, who stand and take a quick bow. I wrap my arms around Magda, feeding her compliments about how well she did. She pulls away and takes my hands, jumping up and down a little.

"Whatever that was, I want to do it again."

And when the music picks up again, we do. We twirl and shake and hop around the fire for a small eternity until thirst and pure exhaustion command me to stop.

I make it the few remaining steps to Halvar and collapse onto the log next to him. I thank him when he automatically hands me a cup of water. It takes a few tries to catch my breath. My wrist wipes the sweat from my brow, but I don't even bother with my hair. It's not ruined—it's a sign of my movement. It's a badge of honor.

Halvar breaks the silence. "Do you have it in you for another dance?"

I nod, taking another sip out of my cup, but am shocked when he comes to his feet and holds out a hand. I nearly spit out the water. "*You* want to dance?"

"I want to dance with *you*," he says, hand still extended.

It's then that I notice the music has slowed to something soft and sweet. It's a gentle wave that rocks between the tree trunks and low-hanging branches. I take his hand and let him pull me back towards the fire. We are not the only couple there, but we might as well be.

He pulls me against his body, one hand wrapped around my waist and one laced between my fingers. At first we just sway, our bodies drifting together and apart and together again in the current the song makes. There is no need for words, I simply let his body inform mine of how we move. It's easy between us, as it's always been. As I hope it always will be.

"I thought about this for a long time."

"Dancing?"

"Dancing with you," he corrects. Then he shrugs. "And just of you."

"Pure, wholesome thoughts I would hope," I tease.

He chuckles. "Some of those. Some others, too."

I swat his arm which only makes him laugh harder. We settle back into the dance like it's the most natural thing we've ever done. I never pictured him one to dance, and I get the feeling he's doing this mostly for my sake.

When I get old someday, this will be one thing I look back on with the softness that nostalgia brings to memories. The same way I look back on our childhood. We were so small, and we knew so little. But we always knew each other. I know him better now than I knew him then, but it's him all the same. I welcome whatever change the future will bring us. Whatever darkness, whatever light. Whatever, as long as it's with him.

"Tell me what you're thinking," he says softly.

I hum. "I'm thinking about how tired my feet are."

Without word, he wraps both arms around me and lifts me off the ground, swaying with me in his arms.

"Better?"

I kiss him once. Twice. "Best."

The music coasts into something less suited for slow dancing, but we stay like that. Wrapped up in one another. A few delayed snowflakes start to fall, dusting our hair and clothes. The last dregs of the cold are still making themselves known. But I know that soon this perpetual winter will move forward, and so will we. Spring is going to come soon, and it will be another thing I have yet to experience for the first time again in this new phase of my life. It doesn't scare me anymore.

The whispers started with the first snowfall, and they'll linger into spring, but now they answer to me. They call me by name and I answer with a full-bodied voice. Back then, I didn't understand so much. I didn't understand companionship, love, peace.

I think I understand now.

ACKNOWLEDGMENTS

Writing a book was, surprisingly, both easier and more difficult than I expected. I expected blood, sweat, tears—you know, like everyone says. But it was a gentle process to start. I came up with this idea at fourteen or fifteen during freshman biology class, writing paragraphs when the lights were off as we watched instructional videos. The story I wrote then was very different from the one you have in your hands now, but I am certain it happened that way for the better.

I was working on a completely different project when I decided to start writing SACRILEGE. I needed a palette cleanser in between writing chapters on that project, and so this story popped back into my head. I came up with an opening line, then a few hours later I had a first chapter. I hated it at first, I thought it was one of the weakest things I had ever written. I wasn't used to writing first person present tense, so why now? But it just came so naturally. And I just kept writing. And then I started showing it to people. And the crazy part was they liked it. I didn't realize that I wanted this to be a book until it was well on its way to becoming one. Wholeheartedly, this book would not be what it is without the help of so many amazing people. It takes a village (I couldn't resist, I'm sorry) and now I'm turning the spotlight on them. I hope you come to appreciate these people as much as I do.

Cat, a simple paragraph will never be enough to match your contribution to this book. In short, for checking my grammar and forcing me to realize that I do not know when to cut off a paragraph, for always being a ball of sunshine even when it's a cloudy day, for being just as hyped for the story even when life got in the way, for never failing to tell me how excited you were for me and making me believe you, thank you.

B Thomas, for making me believe that this could be something worthwhile, for understanding my Catholic trauma jokes, for honestly and sincerely telling me when it was good and when it needed work, for imagining a future where other people loved this too, thank you for saying, "Yes, I want to read your work."

Leon, for being so unapologetically enthusiastic and willing to hear out my wildest ideas, for being better at plotting than me and coming up with so many crucial details, for receiving and sending five minute voice memos, for being my cheerleader when I couldn't see the forest for the trees, thank you.

Sarah, for working tirelessly to make this exactly what I wanted, for being so creative beyond my wildest dreams, for seeing my vision for what it is, for always being receptive and holding space, you are an absolute rock and I am lucky to know you. Thank you.

Sam, for reading the whole thing in a solid two days, for the unwavering space you hold for me, and generally just being a wonderful friend, thank you.

Sara, for the phone calls we shared when life got in the way, for assuring me that this was still something of value when I dared to forget, for being you, thank you.

To my original team of beta readers, Scar, Amy, Amy, Mel, Lexi, Jakes, thank you for being the first people to be excited about this work, for workshopping the early rough drafts with me, for making the memes and sending songs and loving these characters. Know that it is invaluable to me.

To my friends, Night, Harmony, Nat, and Jem, for making me feel like I was writing with an end goal, for being excited while knowing so little, for being there in ways you didn't realize were so helpful to me. Thank you.

To the bog king himself, Hozier, for writing In the Woods Somewhere and kick-starting this creative process.

Lastly, but never least, for Isaac. My partner, my rock. For telling me how sexy I am for writing late into the night. For healing the parts of me that needed to be okay to write this book. For laughing in the face of my fear and showing me I could too. For letting me use your laptop when mine started to give out on me. For coming up with the climax of this book. For showing me that the love I read about and write about can and does exist in real life. For showing me that I can want more for myself and demanding that I take it. For loving me. Thank you.

T.N. VITUS

ABOUT THE AUTHOR

T.N. Vitus is a lifelong writer who dove back into fiction in early 2020 after an extended love affair with poetry. Their writing typically explores the effects of a Catholic upbringing through horror and fantasy inspired themes, as well as the complicated relationships humans have with one another. They are also heavily inspired by the music they listen to. When not writing, they can be found dancing, reading, or encouraging (peer-pressuring) their friends to get on their manuscripts. They live in California, where they are more often than not the passenger princess in their loving partner's car.

T.N. can be found on Twitter @evenstarsss